Tempted by passion,
he gambled with his heart—
but a wily and beautiful cardsharp
held all the aces

TEMPTATION

With no warning he swung her into his arms and marched into the house with her, Amanda's shrieks piercing his eardrums every step of the way. "Put me down, you overbred brute! Damn you, Grant Gardner! I won't let you do this!"

He strode into her room, slammed the door shut, and tossed her onto the bed. "You can't stop me, Amanda, and in a few minutes, you won't even want to try. You'll be begging for me to make love to you."

She tried to scramble off the other side of the bed, but he caught her skirts and dragged her back. "You arrogant jackass!" she screamed. "I'll kill you for this!"

"You might try," he said imperiously, "for about ten seconds. But in the end you and I will die together, in that heart-stopping moment when we become one with each other, when nothing else in the world matters except touching that elusive piece of heaven only the two of us can grasp together."

He was looming over her, then his lips claimed hers . . .

Other Avon Books by
Catherine Hart

TEMPEST

TEMPTATION

CATHERINE HART

AVON BOOKS  NEW YORK

TEMPTATION is an original publication of Avon Books. This work has never before appeared in book form. This work is a novel. Any similarity to actual persons or events is purely coincidental.

AVON BOOKS
A division of
The Hearst Corporation
1350 Avenue of the Americas
New York, New York 10019

First Avon Books Printing: May 1992

AVON TRADEMARK REG. U.S. PAT. OFF. AND IN OTHER COUNTRIES, MARCA REGISTRADA, HECHO EN U.S.A.

Printed in the U.S.A.

RA 10 9 8 7 6 5 4 3 2 1

I dedicate this book, with all the love in my heart, to my darling husband—the only man in the world who could have put up with me for all these years. Happy twenty-fifth wedding anniversary, sweetheart. We made it to the silver—now let's go for the gold!

Chapter 1

PEOPLE. Noise. Voices raised in the sounds and silences of hope and despair. Shouts of triumph amid pained groans of disappointment. The flat, droning calls and commands from the various tables crowded into the gambling salon.

"Last card."

"Place your final wagers, please."

"Queen high bets."

"The house wins."

"Pair of jacks showing."

The rhythmic click of the ball as the roulette wheel spun around and around, carrying with it the hopes and dreams of would-be winners. The clack of ivory against ivory as dice tumbled over one another. The rasp of numerous decks of cards being shuffled, cut, and dealt. The clink of coins and chips tossed together in growing heaps on green-baize tables.

And the smells—acrid, eye-stinging cigar smoke hugging the ceiling like a billowing gray cloud, never quite dispersed by the overhead fans or the river breezes wafting through the open doors at each end of the salon. The odd blending of dozens of different colognes and perfumes—some cheap, others exquisitely expensive. Liquor. Sweat. The stench of greed. The allure of money and power. Overlaying it all, the fishy, musty odor of the muddy Mississippi as the *Lady Gambler* slowly wended its way northward from New Orleans to Cincinnati.

To Amanda Sites it was all so familiar. The roll and sway of the riverboat. The games. The cards. The sights and sounds of steady gambling. Witnessing fortunes recklessly wagered—won and lost on the turn of a card, a toss of the dice, or a spin of the pitiless roulette wheel.

As she presided over the blackjack table, Amanda let her gaze drift across the room, her motions as she dealt so ingrained by years of practice that she could have done it in her sleep. Despite the heat, a combination of humid southern breezes and the cluster of bodies crammed into the large room, most of the men wore formal evening attire: dark coats and trousers with starched white shirts and stiff collars which had been ever-so-crisp at the beginning of the evening but were now beginning to wilt like blossoms too long picked. Everywhere, the glint of jewels and gold glistened in the lamplight, most especially about the necks of the lady passengers. Silks and satins of every hue shimmered. Altogether, men and women alike, resembled peacocks proudly strutting their brilliant feathers and practically begging to be plucked bare of their bright plumage.

The image brought a smile to Amanda's lips, and she fought to swallow a chuckle at how true it would prove to be. Before the voyage was done, many a treasured necklace would exchange hands, carelessly bet and lost. Many a dollar would find its way into new pockets, much of it into the growing coffers of the owners of the *Lady Gambler,* thanks to Amanda and her fellow employees, all dealers of the various gambling games aboard the riverboat.

Bringing her attention back to the play at hand, Amanda swiftly calculated the cards showing on the table. Noting the pair of sixes in front of an elderly, gray-haired lady, she inquired politely, "Do you want to split those, Mrs. Whittaker?"

Normally suggestions of this sort from the dealer were frowned upon by the management, but on every trip there were one or two players to whom Amanda took a particular liking, and Mrs. Whittaker was the one Amanda had chosen to take beneath her wing this time. There was just something about the pleasant, apple-cheeked lady that appealed to her. She was the perfect picture of somebody's grandmother, rather vague and forgetful, and very naive when it came to gambling.

"Oh, dear!" the woman breathed, her eyes wide and slightly unfocused. "Yes, I suppose that would be a good idea, don't you?"

The gentleman next to her sighed and shook his head. Play at this table was bound to be slow this evening, until Mrs. Whittaker decided to retire from the game. Still, the sight of Amanda's amply displayed bosom was enough to make him keep his seat for a while yet. Not only was she an excellent banker, but she was also much better to look at than some of the other dealers, even if she was also somewhat of a distraction. He had to admire the riverboat owners for having decided to use women dealers at a few choice tables. It was a unique and innovative move on their part, and very good for business.

"Hit me," he said, then groaned in disgust as the ten Amanda dealt him took him over the count of twenty-one.

"Next time, perhaps, Mr. Arnold," Amanda commiserated.

He nodded, wondering how she managed to remember his name, among countless others. Not only was she one of the most beautiful women he'd ever seen, but she seemed to have a head for names and numbers, which probably accounted for her tremendous talent at the gaming tables.

Once more he let his eyes stray to the cleavage exposed by the deep cut of her gown. Lord, but he'd pay a king's ransom to wrap his tongue around those milk-white globes! They jiggled slightly as she dealt a new round of cards, and he nearly felt himself salivating. Swallowing hard, he almost stuttered, "You'll soon be done dealing for the night, won't you, Miss Sites?"

She nodded, the silky black curls gathered to one side of her head bobbing. "Yes. Why do you ask?"

She already knew why. It was the same, night after night, trip after trip. Men wanting her company, trying to lure her into their cabins and their beds. Assuming she would, at some point, if the price was right, agree to spend the night with them. It was one of the hazards of her profession, compounded by the way she was required to dress for her job, she supposed, that made them think she would be free with her charms.

The riverboat owners were paying for her work clothing and had final approval on the finished product, and allure was what they had decided they wanted for their lady card dealers. The gaudy gowns, bedecked with sequins, clung to her like a second skin. Despite Amanda's adamant objections, they were all styled very seductively, with scant bodices and long slits in the slim skirts to display her sleek legs and net stockings. She supposed she should be relieved that, in this spring of 1876, those god-awful bustles were still out of style, at least. It was enough that her high-heeled slippers set her toes and arches screaming for relief after a long evening of work in the gambling salon.

"I was hoping for the pleasure of your company after you'd finished working," Arnold told her, affirming her suspicions.

"I'm sorry, but I'm previously engaged for this evening," she answered smoothly, long used to having to reject offers of this sort.

"I thought you might be," he intoned, though his words carried lingering skepticism.

"Oh, yes! Miss Amanda is quite popular amid the gambling crowd, you know," Mrs. Whittaker piped up cheerfully. "Especially when it comes to high-stakes poker. She's even invited me to come along to watch the game tonight if I want, to see how it's played, though I wouldn't dare sit in on one myself for fear of losing everything I own! But wasn't it nice of her to ask me?''

Arnold was nonplussed, to the point that he was barely aware of the card Amanda had placed before him. ''Poker?'' he asked.

Nodding, her mind tabulating the cards on the table, she replied, ''Draw poker. Jacks or better. Hundred-dollar low limit to ante. I'd ask you to join us, but the table is full, unless one of the other six players fails to show up.''

''Thank you, but the game sounds a little rich for my blood.'' Then he asked the obvious question. ''How is it you can afford to sit in on a game with such high stakes? Will you be playing for the house?''

The smile she sent him was so chilly it should have created icebergs in the river. ''It's a private game, Mr. Arnold. No one stakes me but myself—and Lady Luck.''

''Oh, my dear! You are much too modest!'' Mrs. Whittaker gushed. ''Why, your reputation as a card-sharp is almost legendary on the river! I wasn't aboard two minutes before I heard your name mentioned. And your amazing aptitude with cards. From what I've seen so far, I must agree. You certainly are blessed with a skill for gambling.''

Blessed, or cursed. Amanda had never been sure which. Still, it kept food in her stomach, and a roof over her head, such as it was. And it was the only life she'd ever really known.

Her mother had died when she was born. Rather than turn her over to distant relatives or put her in an orphanage, her father, to his credit, had chosen to raise her himself, despite the multitude of problems that created.

Dan Sites was a riverboat gambler of some repute. It was the only way he knew to make a living. So, with a newborn infant on one hip and a bag full of diapers on the other, he carted her with him up and down the river. When the War Between the States broke out, he and his four-year-old daughter settled in New Orleans for the duration. Dan joined the local militia there for a time, but quietly retired to gambling once the Union forces captured the city a year later.

Meanwhile, Amanda spent her next four years in several of the finest brothels and gambling halls New Orleans could offer, dandled on the knees of generals, high-priced harlots, cardsharps, and madams. In accordance with her father's rising and falling affluency, she spent a spattering of time in exclusive schools learning reading, penmanship, basic arithmetic, and French. More often, when luck had turned against them, she learned of the seedier side of life from the security of her father's lap.

At the age of six, she could curse fluently in three languages, though she could speak properly in only two, and didn't actually know the meanings of the curses she imitated so readily. She could read and write. She knew more about men and women—their differing anatomies, and their bedroom frolicking—than any child should, even while her innocent mind understood little of what she saw and overheard. With a dexterity far beyond her years, she could shuffle and deal four decks of cards at once, mentally keeping count of the cards played and those still in the deck, better than most adults. While some children were considered prodigies in music or mathematics or science, Amanda became a miniature wizardess at gambling.

They were back on the river by the time she was eight, and for the last eleven years a variety of steamboats had been her only home, a gently rolling bunk in a small cabin her only bed. With her father's help, and her inborn curiosity and love of books urging her on, she continued her studies despite the lack of classrooms or qualified tutors.

She'd just turned sixteen, with her own job cleaning the passenger cabins on the *Lady Gambler,* when her father had been killed in a heated argument over a game of cards. For three years now, Amanda had been on her own, with only her wits and her remarkable gambling skills to sustain her. They'd held her in good stead when the owner of the riverboat had offered her a position as a dealer in the gambling salon.

It wasn't a bad life, despite its pitfalls. Among the crew of the *Lady Gambler* she had many good friends, almost like a real family, ready to rush to her defense in those rare moments when she found herself in more difficulty than she could handle on her own. She had free room and board, clothing provided for her work, regular meals and wages. And anything she won in private games outside her usual working hours was hers to keep.

On the whole, however, she'd had to learn to stand on her own at a very vulnerable age, just on the threshold of womanhood. Without benefit of her father's guidance, she'd had to learn to thwart unwanted advances; to outwit those who would have stolen her innocence, her earnings, or both without qualm or conscience; to form her own ideas and ideals; to make her own decisions; and to live with the consequences of her actions.

For the most part, she did fine. Though she detested the gowns she was required to wear, thinking them little better than those of a tart, she tolerated them, and dreamed of someday wearing decent, beautiful gowns like those worn by the finest lady passengers. She had a sizable nest egg squirreled away and hidden beneath a loose floorboard under her bunk, but not nearly enough to fulfill her secret fantasy of one day owning a real house of her own on solid ground, maybe one with a picket fence and roses climbing all around.

But her biggest, most elusive wish was to someday find a man with whom to share her dreams of home and hearth and children running underfoot, a husband to love her and hold her and cherish her. Not merely someone who wanted her body for an evening's pleasure, here today and gone tomorrow. She wanted a man who promised forever, and security, rather than offering to keep her as his mistress for a time, until he tired of her charms. However, as a woman riverboat gambler, she seemed destined to collect far more indecent propositions than legitimate proposals. If there was a knight in shining armor somewhere in her future, he was certainly taking his own sweet time about finding her!

It was after eleven o'clock by the time Amanda turned the blackjack table over to a fellow dealer. With less than an hour to refresh herself before the poker game was scheduled to begin, she headed quickly to the galley, where she raided the large pantry in search of a snack to sustain her through the long hours to come.

Booty in hand, she went to her cabin, where she took a few minutes to freshen her appearance and give her aching feet a short reprieve from their torturous trappings. It was a well-bandied fact on board that Amanda had an incorrigible habit of shucking her shoes wherever and whenever she could get away with it. Left to her own devices, she would have gone eternally barefoot, it was wagered.

Retrieving her small cache of winnings from its hiding place, she tried to realign her thoughts toward the coming confrontation. With a scant twelve hundred dollars to wager, for her it was similar to planning a campaign of war. How much should she limit herself to? How much could she afford to lose and still feel comfortable?

Of course, a lot would depend on how the game went, but Amanda always tried to set limits for herself ahead of time, and usually she stuck to them. Very rarely did she place her entire savings in jeopardy, or allow herself daring risks on uncertain hands. All too often she'd seen other players do just that, and rue the consequences afterward. Even her father, who had taught her most of what she knew, had been prone to chancing everything on one incredible win, many times to her dismay.

Now, contrary to her usual caution, she tucked the drawstring bag, with its entire contents, into her reticule and gave a fatalistic shrug. There was a strange feeling within her this night, something wild and reckless brewing inside, as if Lady Luck rode on her shoulder.

"We'll see," she cautioned herself. "We'll just see how the cards fall."

Amanda had her hand on the door latch when Betsy, her roommate, breezed into the tiny cabin. Petite, blond, with a squeaky little-girl voice, she'd earned the title of "Bitsy Betsy" among the crew of the riverboat. With nary a pause, she headed straight for the bunk she and Amanda shared and flopped onto it. "Whew! If I'd had to shuffle one more deck of cards, my fingers would have fallen off! I thought this night would never end! I swear it seemed to stretch into next week!"

At last she came up for breath and glanced at Amanda, who still stood at the door, grinning. "Land sakes, Mandy! You're not ready for more of the same punishment, are you?"

Amanda nodded. "High-stakes game tonight with Mr. Macy's group."

"Ugh! That marvelously wealthy Midas who's always trying to get his golden clutches into you? Poor Mandy!" Betsy retorted. Her playful grimace became a rueful grin as she added, "Then again, who isn't constantly pantin' and gropin' after you? If you could manage to grow a wart on your chin or something, maybe it would give them pause enough to notice the rest of us workin' girls!"

"You get your fair share of attention," Amanda pointed out on a laugh.

"True. But none of it serious enough. Or should I say, proper enough? If I had a dollar for every crude suggestion thrown my way, I'd be rich! And you, O Reigning Queen of the *Lady Gambler,* would possess your own palace instead of being chained aboard this floating casino."

"Ah, the stuff dreams are made of!" Amanda sighed dramatically, drawing a high-pitched giggle from Betsy that almost made her wince. The blonde had a laugh that sounded like a mouse with its tail caught in a trap. "I suppose we should be grateful. At least here we have the option of declining all those licentious offers, and at least a dozen burly, loyal crewmen to back up our refusals."

Betsy tittered again, the sound grating over Amanda's ears. "God A'mighty, yes! I thought I'd die when Amos caught Crandall with his paws halfway down your bodice last week," she recalled with wide eyes. "You backed into that dark corner under the stairs and screamin' like a shrew, and Crandall huffin' like a steam engine about to blow! It's a bloomin' wonder Amos didn't kill him then and there, instead of just haulin' his carcass overboard for a good coolin' off!"

She paused, a dreamy look coming into her big brown eyes. "Someday, Mandy, if we wish long enough and hard enough, we'll have it all. Homes. Husbands. Decent clothes. Respectability. Won't we? Is that too much to ask out of life?"

When Amanda reached the small, private salon, the other six players were already seated around the table. Money was being exchanged for chips; several sealed decks of cards were set at hand. Spittoons and ashtrays were strategically placed. A variety of liquor and glasses were on a cart near the table.

"Ah, Amanda! There you are!" Art Macy, who was hosting the game this evening, stood to greet her with a welcoming grin. In a polite gesture, he held her chair and seated her. "Gentlemen, may I present Miss Amanda Sites, the final member of tonight's party, and the prettiest of the lot, I might add."

Amanda was already acquainted with three of the men. Macy was a wealthy, middle-aged businessman who frequently traveled the river route between New Orleans and St. Louis, entertaining himself with a bit of gambling on his travels. Fiddler was an old friend of Amanda's father, a veteran gambler both on the river and ashore, and rather like an adopted uncle to her. He welcomed her with a smile and a rather piratical wink. Bronson was another riverboat gambler who often frequented the *Lady Gambler* when his luck was running high. They'd played against each other numerous times. He greeted her with a brusque nod.

The remaining three men were strangers. Their expressions upon meeting Amanda ranged from surprise to ill-concealed skepticism. As introductions were made, Mr. Oslow, a traveling salesman, scowled openly. Ben Widmark and Tad Gardner, young men in their early twenties, exchanged looks of interest, as if making a side bet on which of them could lure the lovely Amanda into his bed first.

Amanda greeted them all with a polite smile and a nod of her head. The newcomers would soon learn what the other three already knew. Amanda Sites was not here to flirt and entertain. She was here to play poker, very seriously and very proficiently.

Fiddler offered to get Amanda a drink, chuckling to himself when she requested warm beer. Years of sipping from his mug or Dan's had made their mark on her, and she'd been drinking the malty beverage since before she'd been weaned from her bottle. Another habit carried over from her childhood was her passion for chewing gum. Whenever she was in a private game, where she could be more herself, she would invariably break out a package of gum, much to Fiddler's delight and the dismay of the other players, as she snapped and popped it throughout the game. If anyone dared to complain, she promptly put him in his place by declaring that if she had to put up with his cigar smoke, he could stand her small noises.

"Shall we begin?" Macy suggested. He restated the agreed-upon terms of the game. "Draw poker, pair of jacks or better to open. Joker wild; dealer's choice of anything else wild. Fresh deck every tenth round, or upon request. White chips go for a hundred dollars, red for five hundred, blue for a thousand. And anyone caught cheating gets tossed overboard minus his baggage or his winnings," he added for the benefit of the three newcomers to their gambling group.

The game commenced, the betting somewhat cautious to start, but by the tenth round the play was picking up a bit. Mrs. Whittaker put in an appearance, but after about an hour she became bored and left. Oslow dropped out early on. After three hours and several losing hands, Bronson did likewise. By the time the remaining five players took a short break to stretch their muscles, Amanda had quadrupled her purse and defiantly removed her shoes. Fiddler decided to cut his losses for the night and find his own bed, wishing Amanda continued luck as he took his leave. By fourthirty, only Amanda, Macy, and Tad Gardner remained in the game. Widmark had reluctantly conceded that the late hour and the liquor he'd consumed were fogging his judgment too much to keep playing, though he stayed to watch the rest of them compete and to lend his friend encouragement.

Sunrise was almost upon them. Amanda had been winning steadily throughout the night and now had a sizable stack of chips before her. Macy was still in fair funds himself. Tad was desperately low on chips, but determined to play it out to the bitter end.

When Nettie, the cook, poked her head in the door, choked on the cigar smoke, and demanded to know who had sliced into her smoked ham during the night, Amanda grinned and confessed to being the guilty culprit. "You know I can't resist your baked ham, Nettie. It's your own fault, you know, for being such a marvelous cook."

"Hmph!" Nettie grumbled, but Amanda could sense the older woman softening. On her off hours, Amanda often exchanged gossip with her in the galley, lending a hand at odd jobs like chopping vegetables. Nettie had even attempted, with some success, to teach Amanda to cook.

"You about ready to quit soon, or should I bring y'all some coffee?" Nettie grumped.

"Coffee, please. I've got to give these gentlemen a chance to recoup their losses before I leave."

"Magnanimous of you, Amanda." Macy chuckled around the cigar snugged into the corner of his mouth.

"When are you going to be just as generous in other areas?"

Her hands flew as she shuffled the cards with expert precision. "Such as?" she asked, one delicate brow arched over a bleary blue eye.

"Such as agreeing to share my bed," he answered bluntly, bringing her eyes wide open and eliciting a startled cough from Gardner's end of the table. Even Widmark, who was more than half asleep in his chair, came wide awake in anticipation of Amanda's answer.

To her credit, Amanda remained unruffled, dealing each of them five cards, swiftly and without mishap. "When cows fly, Art. We've been over this before. I will not sleep with you. I will not become your mistress, no matter how much you offer me."

"Why not?" He picked up his cards and studied them, casting a quick glance at her face in the hope of catching her off guard, but her bland features registered only the weariness of the hour. He matched the ante and raised the bet by another five hundred dollars. Gardner did likewise, with a thoughtful frown marring his brow.

"Because I'm not a loose woman, despite what you obviously think. And because you are a married man." With one look at her hand, she matched the bet and raised another hundred.

"Married or not, I can still afford to keep you in luxury, if that's what's bothering you. And all the chewing gum your busy little jaws can handle." He matched her bet once more.

Tad Gardner was more slow to respond, but decided he might as well see it through.

"Thank you, no. Please stop asking me, or I swear I'll refuse to even speak to you again." Counting out the required amount of chips, she tossed them into the center of the table. "Go home to your wife and children, Mr. Macy, and cease pestering me. If it's any consolation, you are not the first man, and probably won't be the last, to meet with my refusal. I will not be a kept woman, sir, when I can well fend for myself, as you can see." She waved a slim-fingered hand over the stack of chips before her.

"If God were just, you'd fall on hard times and straight into my arms," he said with a shake of his head. He set two cards aside and indicated for her to deal him two more.

"If God were just, I'd be a queen and you'd be a short, bald monk," she answered softly, an amused glint making he eyes sparkle as Macy grimaced at her words. Widmark choked back a laugh. His friend sat glumly contemplating the cards in his hand and his funds.

Half an hour later, Gardner had thrown his final chip into the pot. They were in the middle of a hand, and he'd just drawn three fresh cards, but had nothing left with which to bet on them. As luck would have it, it was his best hand of the entire game. He'd lost every dollar to his name, and some that wasn't his to lose, and he was desperate to win it back. He had to, unless he wanted his brother to flay him alive when he got home.

Perspiration dotted his forehead and streamed down his back as he argued with himself over the wisdom of his next move. But what else could he do? With a sense of fatality, he watched Amanda match the standing bet and raise it by five hundred dollars, all on the original hand she had drawn from Tad's own deal. Macy thought for a moment, then did the same, though his own chips had dwindled in the last few plays. The next move was Tad's.

A wild, feverish look came into his red-rimmed eyes as he glared at his two opponents. "Will you take a personal note?"

Macy, his jaw set, was the first to ask, "On your bank?"

Tad shook his head. "No." His older brother had to approve any funds removed from the account for the farm. "This would be a note for property I own in Kentucky. A horse farm. Ben can verify its worth."

Widmark finally found his tongue and blurted out,

"Jesus, Tad! You can't mean it. Grant will kill you for sure!"

"It's my inheritance," Tad pointed out grimly.

"Precisely. All the more reason for your brother to strangle you."

Tad shook his head. "He's bound to have fits either way. If I can make up my losses now, he'll be none the wiser. If not, my neck is on the chopping block."

"But your land. Your horses. Your home!"

"What is this property worth?" Macy put in, weighing the idea for its merits.

"I'd be signing over the equivalent of twenty thousand dollars or more."

"That's a low estimate," his friend said with a frown.

"Oh, my stars!" Amanda's startled exclamation escaped her as she stared at Tad Gardner in disbelief. "Are you certain you want to do this?"

Gardner sighed heavily. "At this point, I really don't have much choice."

"But we're talking about your home."

"Lock, stock, and stables," Tad agreed miserably. "In the Gardner family for three generations. It took my grandfather six years just to complete construction on the house."

"Then think twice before you risk losing it all," Amanda suggested.

Tad shook his head. "This is the only way I stand to keep it."

Macy, much less sentimental and more practical, made a decision. "I'll accept your marker, and match it in cash." He pulled a wad of bills from his pocket and peeled off several thousand dollars.

"Amanda?"

All eyes now turned her way. She was the clear winner of the night so far, with a mountain of chips surrounding her. A swift calculation told her she had roughly fourteen thousand dollars before her, not counting the amount still in her reticule. A small fortune. More than she'd ever had in her possession at any time in her life. Certainly enough to buy that house she'd always wanted, a closetful of good clothes, and maybe even enough to put down on a small business venture of some sort.

Dared she risk it all now, when she could decline and walk away from the table with her future secure? Even to match the current wager, she would have to come up with several thousand more, which she did not have.

Unless she threw in her diamond necklace and ear-bobs, gifts from her father from one of his biggest winnings. Precious momentos she'd vowed never to part with, no matter what. Treasures to be handed down to her own daughter someday, if she were ever blessed with one.

"Are you in or not?" Macy prodded impatiently.

There was no need for a second glance at her cards, the promising hand she knew she'd held at the end of the last deal. Like a sleepwalker totally unaware of and not responsible for his own actions, Amanda's fingers went to the clasp of her necklace, slowly releasing the catch. The earbobs followed, the glittering jewels landing in a jumbled heap in the center of the table. Then her chips, every last one of them, joined the pot, along with the remainder of the hard-won hoard in her purse.

"I'm in," she croaked, trying to swallow beyond the growing lump in her throat.

Collectively, they held their breath, all four of them, as Tad, Macy, and Amanda revealed their hands. Macy cursed softly, whacking the table with a fist as he saw his full house beaten by Gardner's four aces.

But Tad was too stunned by Amanda's hand to notice. Four beautiful, magnificent aces, practically guaranteeing him the win and the return of much more than what he'd lost in this mad night of gambling. And all for naught, as Amanda displayed her straight flush, queen high, for one and all to see.

For a long moment, no one spoke. Then Tad pushed himself from the table, stumbling to his feet, Reaching down, he plucked his promissory note from the pot and tossed it toward her. "Congratulations, Miss Sites," he ground out bitterly, his eyes flaming. "You are now the proud owner of a horse farm." He stayed just long enough to sign the paper over to her, duly witnessed by Macy and Widmark, and legally notarized by a groggy lawyer dragged out of his warm passenger cabin into the chill of dawn.

"I suppose this means I might as well give up trying to win you for my mistress," Macy growled, still in awe of her sudden windfall. "You're a woman of no small means now."

Amanda didn't answer. She had yet to utter a single word since she'd won that final hand. She just sat staring at the paper in her trembling hands, the one declaring her the new owner of acres of lush bluegrass land near Lexington and a score of thoroughbred horses. Her eyes wide with shock, her heart beating wildly, she still could not believe this was happening.

Then she started to laugh. "What in blazes do I know about raising horses? For that matter, what do I know about anything but gambling and riding the river?"

"You'll learn," Macy prophesied. "Unless you want to sell the property to me? I can always use another business venture."

"No. I have a home now, a real home for the first time in my life, and a business of my own. I'm not about to sell it sight unseen."

Suddenly she gifted him with a sparkling smile. "Well, Macy?" she asked, wriggling her stockinged toes in pure delight and giving a hearty chomp on her worn wad of chewing gum. "Any wagers on how long it'll take me to get my land legs under me?"

Chapter 2

    As the train taking her from Frankfort to Lexington snaked its way through the Bluegrass region of Kentucky, Amanda gazed at the passing scenery in rapt amazement. Never had she seen land so green, the new spring leaves and fields so vibrant in the April sunshine that it almost hurt her eyes to look at them. Horses grazed contentedly in fenced pastures, some with foals frolicking nearby or nudging their mothers in search of milk. Elsewhere, tiny tobacco plants sprouted from newly tilled soil. It was like viewing a painting, fresh and bright and unbelievably lovely.

    From time to time, in the distance, she glimpsed homes and barns, some grand and sparkling with fresh whitewash, others old and tumbling in disrepair. She could only wonder which she would find as her new home.

    Beyond thrusting a letter into her hands before debarking the riverboat at St. Louis, Tad Gardner had offered little further information about the horse farm called Misty Valley. Grimly, he'd told her its general location and offered the letter addressed to his brother. "This will explain everything to Grant. No doubt you'll need it as proof of your claim, since I won't be returning to do so in person." He'd sighed despairingly. "Cowardly of me, to be sure. But then I've never been strong on facing the consequences of my foolishness, and this has to be the worst of the lot."

It had been a week since that fateful poker game, a long week during which Amanda had alternated between anxiety and excitement. She'd ridden the *Lady Gambler* on to Louisville, where she had bidden her many friends a tearful farewell, boarded another, smaller riverboat to Frankfort, and taken the train southeast from there.

Though Amanda had practically begged Betsy to come with her, her friend had declined. "Get yourself settled first, honey," Betsy had told her. "Find out all about the place and whether or not you're even gonna like it enough to want to stay. Then you give a holler, and I'll come visit for a spell."

Betsy wasn't the only one to offer advice. "Hire yourself a lawyer first off," Macy had instructed brusquely. "Discover exactly what Gardner owned down to the last square inch; make sure there isn't a previous lien on the land or a mortgage on the place. You're going into this blind, Amanda, and you've got to protect yourself right from the start. Not that I think the boy was lying. He was too upset over losing his property for it to have been an act, and the note transferring his holdings to you was legal enough, but he could have been exaggerating its worth."

Everyone had wished her success on her venture, even those who openly envied her newfound fortune. Captain Danson had assured her that if matters didn't turn out well, she could return to her old job anytime she wished. "We'll miss that homely puss of yours," he teased, "and the owners are sure to pitch a fit when they learn you've left us. You've put a pretty penny in their purses these last few years."

Now, as the train chugged slowly to a grinding halt in the Lexington depot, Amanda was almost sick with excitement, half afraid of discovering that Gardner had falsely represented his holdings and hoping desperately that he hadn't. Please, God, she prayed silently, closing her eyes briefly and crossing her fingers for added luck. *It doesn't have to be much, or awfully fancy. Just some place I can call home and put down permanent roots.*

Not altogether sure of what to do first, Amanda arranged to leave her luggage at the depot for the time being. Then, falling back on Macy's counsel, and armed with the name of a reputable lawyer recommended to her by the ticket agent, she headed into town.

"I'm sorry," the attorney's secretary told a disappointed Amanda a short time later. "Mr. Darcy is out of town today, and he doesn't schedule appointments for the weekend. The soonest he could see you would be Monday afternoon, as he usually has to be in court in the morning hours."

Frowning, Amanda tried not to take her irritation out on the man's employee. "I just wanted to obtain information about some property owned by Tad Gardner. Would you happen to know anything about it?"

"Everybody around Lexington knows the Gardner family," the woman assured her. "They've been here since the town was founded, raising some of the finest horses in the country. What was it you needed to know?"

Amanda breathed a sigh of relief, glad to hear that Gardner obviously did hold land here. "Specific directions to the farm, for starters," she replied. "I suppose the rest can wait until I can speak with Mr. Darcy personally."

Though obviously curious, Darcy's secretary set up an appointment for the following Monday afternoon and graciously gave Amanda explicit directions to the Gardner home. "You can rent a carriage at the livery two doors down from the train station," she supplied.

"I . . . uh . . . I've never driven a carriage before," Amanda admitted grudgingly.

"That's all right. You can hire a driver, too, for a little extra. He'll even wait and drive you back into town if you're not staying long." Her inquisitive gaze skimmed Amanda's rather flamboyant attire and brightly enameled fingernails, making Amanda acutely aware that her ruby-colored dress, hastily refashioned from one of her working gowns in an effort to make it appear more decent, was still much too flashy for the average lady.

The woman's attitude, though still properly polite toward a potential client, chafed. With a toss of her dark head, Amanda offered a cool, confident smile. "How long I stay will depend on how much I like my new property, I suppose." She left the befuddled woman to ponder her parting words.

Her driver's name was Willy. Old, black, and wrinkled, he promptly appointed himself as her tour guide, pointing out Lexington's most prominent spots of interest as they passed through town. "Dere's da op'ra house, and dat's da courthouse. Da library an' city hall are on down a couple o' blocks." A smile creased his weathered face as he added, "I don't 'spect dat's of much int'rest to you, though, since da ladies gen'rally takes more to shoppin' dan to gov'ment goin's-on."

Despite her anxiety over soon seeing the farm for the first time, Amanda avidly noted the establishments Willy designated as shops favored by Lexington's most affluent ladies. As soon as the opportunity presented itself, she would have to renew her sadly lacking wardrobe, and she wanted to do it fashionably. If Lexington and Misty Valley were to be her home, she needed to make a proper impression, and her current clothing was not at all suitable for that purpose.

Misty Valley lay north and slightly east of Lexington, a pleasant two-hour ride along tree-shaded roads. The late afternoon sun was slanting lengthening shadows when Willy called back to her. "Here's where da Gardner prop'ty starts. It'll be 'bout twenty minutes or so 'fore we reaches da lane to da house."

What looked like miles of planked fence stretched into the distance as far as Amanda could see. Endless grassland, dotted with spring wildflowers and occasional stands of trees. A narrow brook wandered lazily through the fields. Horses grazed in clusters of twos and threes, unperturbed by the passing carriage. Bees hummed in the wild clover edging the road, and the gentle breeze carried the scent of honeysuckle blossoms.

As well tended as the pastures and animals seemed, Amanda should have been better prepared for her first glimpse of the house. Even when the carriage turned into a sun-dappled lane rimmed by a high flagstone wall and a stately row of huge old oak trees, she was not forewarned, for the house was hidden behind a slight rise. Then, suddenly, it stood before her, proud and grand and gleaming like a jewel in the rose-hued rays of the waning day.

"Oh, my stars!" Amanda declared breathlessly, her large blue eyes trying to take it all in at once.

Never in her wildest imaginings had she hoped to find a home like this. It rose majestically, three and a half stories high, with eight huge, round pillars gracing a wide, porticoed porch and supporting the second-floor veranda. On either side of the main structure a wing extended, each with a flat roof and decorative balustrade. The stark white was broken by a multitude of windows flanked by blue-gray shutters.

As the carriage pulled to a halt below the shelter of the roofed entrance, Amanda gaped in awe at the intricately carved oak double doors. "This is it?" she squeaked, still unable to believe it. "This is the Gardner house?"

"Shore 'nuff," Willy said with a short laugh, enjoying her stunned reaction. "Looks like somethin' God would live in, don't it?"

Amanda had to agree. This definitely resembled heaven.

While Willy unloaded her few bags and placed them by the door, she struggled to gather her wits. In a few moments, she would be meeting Tad Gardner's brother, and she didn't want to give the impression of being weak or featherbrained when she announced to him that she was the new owner of Misty Valley. Regardless of her shock and his, she must stand firm before him, letting him and everyone else know that she was here to take charge of the farm.

After helping her alight, Willy gave the big brass door knocker a hefty rap. "Dey's prob'ly all takin' supper 'bout now," he told her, his black eyes twinkling. "But dis'll bring 'em runnin'."

It seemed forever before the door opened to reveal a tall, thin man in a dark, tailored coat and trousers that, to Amanda's eye, strongly resembled Willy's livery uniform. "Yes?" he inquired stiffly, his gaze swiftly traveling over Amanda from head to toe as a frown deepened the lines in his pale, gaunt face.

For a moment Amanda lost her tongue, wondering to herself whether this was a servant or Grant Gardner. Deciding it must be the butler, for surely in a house of this size the Gardners must employ a full staff, she pulled herself to her full height, stared the man straight in the eye, poked her wad of chewing gum into her cheek, and declared, "I am Amanda Sites, and I am here to see Mr. Gardner—Mr. Grant Gardner."

"Is he expecting you, Miss Sites?" the man replied, both his accent and tone smacking of British superiority as he looked down his long nose at her.

"I'm sure he's not, but you can announce me anyway." Amanda pushed her way past him into the wide entrance room beyond.

Ignoring the servant's indignant gasp, she turned to Willy, who stood grinning on the porch. "Please set my bags inside, if you will. I'll have someone look after them later. And thank you, Willy, for all your assistance." Digging into her reticule, she passed a few coins into his hand as he plopped her luggage onto the floor, barely missing the butler's shiny black shoes.

Though he would have given a week's wages to stay and watch the ensuing encounter, Willy accepted the pay with a nod and departed. "Much 'bliged, miss. And good luck."

"Now, see here, Miss Sites!" the flustered servant began.

"No! You see here!" Amanda interrupted. "I want to see Mr. Gardner, and if you don't tell him I'm here, I'll go looking for him myself." She aimed her most stern glare at him, perfected from years of fending off unwanted admirers. "Now, which will it be?"

The man's eyes glinted at her as if he was contemplating throwing her out the door, baggage and all, but she stood firm, silently daring him to do so. Amanda had faced down many a poker bluff with the same look. It always worked. It did again. "Wait here, please," he grumbled after a moment.

Though he didn't offer her a chair, Amanda availed herself of one anyway, her knees quivering slightly as she lowered herself onto the hard cushion and watched him march down the hall. Looking about, she took a calming breath and began to take stock of her immediate surroundings.

The entrance room, which led into a wide hallway, was not large, but it was furnished grandly. Beneath her feet, veined marble formed an intricate pattern; above her head, a five-tiered crystal chandelier shimmered. Fine lace curtains overlaid with rose velvet draperies matched the bud-embossed wallpaper. Next to her, between her chair and its delicate mate, resided a small cherry stand, polished to a warm glow and crowned with a large bouquet of fresh spring flowers in an exquisite vase. One one side of the door stood a small umbrella stand; on the other, an ornate mirrored coat-and-hat rack.

Farther down the long hall, Amanda could see a broad staircase leading to the second floor, its railing and posts elaborately carved. Everything was shining and free of dust, the smell of lemon and beeswax lingering pleasantly.

She had almost decided that the snooty butler had left her here to rot when he reappeared, still frowning severely. "The master is dining and does not wish to be disturbed just now. Perhaps you could relay your message through me, or try again another day, when it is more convenient."

"Perhaps you could tell your *master* to put his plate aside for the moment and get his well-fed behind out here. Better yet, he might invite me to join him, since I haven't had my own evening meal," Amanda rejoined with a too-sweet smile. "Tell him my business has to do with Misty Valley and his brother, Tad, and that I will not be put off any longer or shuffled out the door by uppity servants."

"Hmph!" the butler huffed haughtily.

"Yes, well, we've all got our trials," she taunted with a distinct lack of sympathy, "and this one is not going to disappear merely to suit you and Mr. Gardner." She waved him back the way he'd come. "Go on, and this time try to be quick about it, will you? I'm tired, I'm hungry, and my patience is hanging by a thin thread. Believe me when I tell you that you wouldn't want to see it snap."

The man returned almost immediately. "This way, please." He led the way down the shadowed hall and through a set of sliding doors into a large dining room, and left her standing there.

This room was more imposing by far, with two gleaming chandeliers, gold-flecked curtains and wall hangings, solid walnut sideboards, china cupboards, and a dining table designed to seat two dozen guests with ease. Twin silver candelabra held six tapers each, a matching compote centered between them.

And seated at the head of the table, as befitted him, was the most handsome man Amanda had ever set eyes upon. With hair as black as her own, glinting emerald eyes, and features so perfect they took her breath away, Grant Gardner was the very image of Amanda's vision of the sublime male. Here, in the flesh, sat a stunning replica of the man her wistful young mind had long ago conjured as her dream lover, her secret fairy-tale prince, the beloved knight of her heart's fondest wishes come to life. To find him suddenly before her, in bold and glorious reality, sent her blood racing wildly to her head, befuddling her brain and flushing her cheeks as she stared at him, helpless to make herself move or speak as her disbelieving eyes drank in the sight of him.

Even seated as he was, half hidden by the table, she could tell that he was tall, broad-shouldered, strong in body—and in determination. It showed in the unyielding set of his square jaw, with that intriguing indentation in the center of his chin; in the stubborn curve of his firm, full lips; in that searing green gaze as he sat watching her, weighing her as the silence between them lengthened.

Amanda's blush immediately condemned her in Grant's estimation. Either the woman was guilty of something, or she had painted her cheeks with rouge. Not yet knowing what she wanted, he could only surmise that his younger brother had somehow embroiled himself in yet another scandal, and that the young woman standing before him was somehow involved.

In this instance, however, Grant could hardly place the blame entirely upon Tad. The woman was beautiful; tall, long-limbed, yet exquisitely endowed. There was a sense of the exotic about her. Perhaps it had to do with the delicate bones of her face, those high, thin cheekbones, framed as they were by her sleek ebony hair. Or her large, slightly tip-tilted blue eyes that appeared so innocent, yet at the same moment as all-knowing as Eve after she'd partaken of the apple in the Garden of Eden. Her slightly trembling fingers were slim and finely tapered, the long, well-kept nails painted to match the garish red gown that clung to her plentiful curves like a second skin and the impossibly high-heeled shoes that made her legs seem endlessly long. She was an enticing package, indeed, though certainly not a lady. Not dressed like this.

Therefore, in Grant's mind, she was guilty before the charge against her was even heard. Whatever mischief she had lured Tad into, she was about to discover that Grant was not nearly as gullible as his younger brother. Whatever her game, he would best her at it and send her fleeing, with her tempting little tail tucked between her legs and very little profit to show for her efforts.

Throughout his silent appraisal, it was all Amanda could do not to swoon at his feet in mute adoration, or to fidget like a nervous peasant called up before the king, either of which would have shocked her friends. This was definitely not what they had come to expect from the normally sensible Amanda, who had yet to meet a man who sent her pulse racing.

At last he spoke. "Chalmers said you need to speak with me about my brother, Miss . . . Sites, is it?"

His tone was imperious and subtly insulting, and it had the effect of a smart slap to her face, bringing her back to herself and her mission. The man might have the face and body of a god, but his manners left much to be desired. Inwardly drawing herself up by her bootstraps, Amanda replied, her voice as cool as his, "Yes, Amanda Sites, and since it appears that you live here, too, I imagine that what I have to say will concern all of us."

"Oh?" Dark brows rose in an arrogant manner as he continued to assess her. "My man also informed me that you arrived with your baggage in tow. Figuring on moving right in, are you?"

"As a matter of fact, I am," she told him. Knowing she would wait in vain for an invitation from this aristocratic cretin, she drew out a chair and seated herself at the table. "Do you suppose I could get some dinner while we talk? I've spent the entire day traveling. I'm weary, hungry, and slightly out of sorts at the moment, and a meal and a hot bath would go a long way toward restoring my humor."

Their wills and their eyes battled for supremacy, until Gardner shrugged, sent her a chilly smile, and reached out to ring a small silver bell to one side of his plate. Silence reigned once more, the only sound that of the ticking of the mantel clock. When a servant arrived in answer to the summons, Grant instructed, "Please set a place for Miss Sites and bring her something to eat."

"Thank you," Amanda said through stiff lips.

Again he shrugged. "My family has long been noted for our courtesy to our *guests.*" He stressed the last word, almost growling it at her. "Would you care for a drink while you await your meal?"

"Please."

He rose, poured a small amount of wine into a glass, placed it before her, and resumed his seat. "Now," he stated, taking a sip from his own glass, "let's get on with the business at hand, shall we? How much do you want?"

Amanda blinked, not certain what to make of his blunt comment, except that it was anything but complimentary. Well, if that was to be his attitude, so be it. She was prepared to defend her rights. "I want all of it," she replied serenely, her face composed as she awaited his response.

He nearly choked on her words. "All of what?" he countered, anger broiling away his controlled demeanor. "What did my brother promise you for your favors? A house? Clothes? Jewels? A life of leisure as his mistress? What, exactly?" he demanded curtly.

She wasn't altogether surprised at his rash assumption, having encountered similar reactions all her life. But she was furious that he dared to take such a superior attitude, all on the basis of his own position and her present outward appearance. "He promised me Misty Valley. 'Lock, stock, and stables,' as he so generously put it."

Grant could scarcely believe the temerity of this woman. By God, she was as bold as brass! Marching up to his doorstep with her ridiculous demands! His eyes swept down to her hand, lying on the table. "I don't see a ring, Miss Sites," he sneered. "Obviously Tad was not so overwhelmed by your charms to have lost his head and married you. And that is the only way you would ever get your grasping claws on a scant square inch of Misty Valley. Even then I would have the marriage annulled and send you packing, so you can forget whatever schemes you've hatched.

"If you're with child, and if you can prove that it is

Tad's, I'll see that he compensates you adequately, for the child's sake alone. But that is the limit of my generosity. When you've finished your dinner, I'll have a man drive you back into town.''

Amanda's eyes blazed blue daggers at him as she clung to the last remnants of her temper, swallowing her gum along with the curse that rose readily to her tongue, forcefully reminding herself to behave in a ladylike manner. ''That won't be necessary, Mr. Gardner. I am here to stay. You see, a romantic liaison is not the claim I am making, sir.'' She let her words rest a moment, then added stingingly, ''Your brother was less enchanted with me than he was with a high-stakes poker game aboard the *Lady Gambler* last week. When his losses multiplied drastically, he desperately wagered the horse farm—and lost it. To me. I am now the new owner of Misty Valley.''

Before Grant could properly digest her startling pronouncement, she dug into her reticule and produced a letter with Grant's name on it. ''This will help explain matters to you in greater detail. Tad asked that I deliver it to you, as he apparently does not intend to return to face you himself.''

Blindly, like a man lost in a nightmare, Grant took the letter from her. Wordlessly, he opened it and began to read. As he did so, the color drained from his tanned face, then rushed back as the truth hit him hard. ''Damn it, Tad!'' he muttered between compressed lips, barely aware of speaking aloud. ''You fool! You thoughtless idiot! Look where your impulsiveness has landed us this time! How could you do such a thing?''

''If it is any consolation, your brother was miserable over losing his inheritance,'' Amanda offered. ''So upset that if it hadn't been for his friend, Mr. Widmark, I fear he might have thrown himself overboard. Certainly, he did not want to be the bearer of such bad news.''

''Where is he now?'' Grant asked gruffly, still perusing the letter written in his brother's unmistakable scrawl.

"I have no idea. He departed the steamer in St. Louis, but where he might have gone from there I don't know."

Grant's head came up, and he speared her with a hot look of pure disgust. "How did you do it?" he snarled. "Did you get him so drunk he didn't even realize what he was risking? Did you dazzle him with those huge blue eyes? Mark the cards? Stack the deck?"

Her fleeting sympathy dissolved into icy rage. Her voice was frosted with it as she returned glare for glare. "I have never cheated at cards in my life, and it certainly wasn't necessary with your brother, since he's just about the worst poker player I've seen in years. So don't try placing the blame on anyone but him. In fact, I tried to talk him out of such folly. There were seven of us at that table, and any one of the others can verify my claim, including Mr. Widmark, who is a neighbor of yours, I am led to believe.

"Now, I can understand your anger and sympathize with the immensity of your shock at losing your family home, but I do not have to put up with your abusive tongue. If you feel you can overcome your animosity toward me, I would be perfectly willing to keep you on as overseer, or manager, or whatever, as I really know very little about running a horse farm, but—"

Grant's caustic laughter cut short her indignant speech. "Oh, woman! You really are something!" he exclaimed derisively. "But it seems I'm not the only one with a surprise coming to him. At the risk of ruffling your fancy feathers further, I have to point out what my dear brother obviously failed to mention. Tad owned only half of Misty Valley. I hold the rest."

"What?" Amanda's eyes flew wide in dismay.

"Oh, yes!" he assured her, his mouth curving sardonically in dark humor. "According to our father's will, the property was split evenly between us. So you see, Miss Sites, you are not quite as prosperous as you thought."

And with barely suppressed fury, in a gesture of defiance at the twist of fate that had brought them together at this time and in this manner, he raised his glass in a toast to her. "Here's to the most unholy alliance heretofore witnessed by man or beast. May it be as mercifully short as it is bound to be distasteful."

He tossed back his drink in one angry gulp, rose, and strode toward the door, intent on leaving the room and her presence as quickly as possible. Before exiting, he spared a final scowl in her direction. "I wouldn't make myself too comfortable here if I were you, Miss Sites. In fact, it will save time if you don't even bother to unpack your traveling bags. You won't be staying long enough to dirty the linen."

"Would you care to wager your half of the farm on that, Mr. Gardner?" she shot back, her pride stung and her eyes flashing.

His gaze swept over her with deliberate disdain. "And what would you wager in return, Miss Sites, to match my bet? Your tempting body, perhaps?" Before she could answer his insult, he taunted cruelly, "Never mind, honey. No deal. You may put a high price on your favors, but they aren't worth nearly that much to me."

Her enraged shriek followed his retreating footsteps, her wineglass shattering against the doorframe, raining glittering shards over the exact spot where he had stood the moment before.

The war was on.

Chapter 3

GRANT left Amanda to fend for herself as best she could, taking himself and a full bottle of Kentucky bourbon off to his private study. There, in complete and morose seclusion, he ensconced himself behind his desk and proceeded to lick his freshly inflicted wounds. Truly, he didn't know whom he'd rather strangle at this moment—his rash, immature brother, or that riverboat tart who was even now dining at his table and drinking his wine, and would soon be sleeping comfortably in one of the upstairs guest rooms.

He had no doubt that the pushy baggage would somehow manage to induce the servants to do her bidding, despite any and all objections to her disturbing presence and her obvious lack of breeding. She'd run roughshod over Chalmers, after all, and he was the very epitome of efficiency when it came to turning away unwanted riffraff. Grant also suspected that she'd choose the best rooms for herself, other than the master suite, of course, which was his. Just the thought of her in his family home, her garish clothes hanging in a wardrobe his dear departed mother had chosen, sleeping in a bed reserved for the finest, most elite guests, was enough to set his back teeth aching with the urge to toss her saucy little rump out the door and kick it all the way back to wherever the nasty little tart had come from.

Well, he would do just that in short order. As soon as he could find a way out of this disastrous mess. With a heart-heavy sigh, Grant poured himself another drink and settled more deeply into the worn leather of his chair, his thoughts now centering on his brother.

At the age of twenty-three, just three years Grant's junior, Tad was still a boy in all the ways that counted when it came to shouldering responsibility and running the family business. Christened Theodore Chadwick Gardner after their great-great uncle Theo, the family's most notorious black sheep, Tad seemed destined to follow in his predecessor's footsteps. The younger son of one of Kentucky's most affluent families, with a lineage that traced all the way back to English royalty, Tad appeared bent on destroying generations of hard work and determination with his thoughtless pranks and reckless actions. He was a man-child whose smile could melt the hardest heart, and who invariably leapt headlong into life before first considering the consequences.

Grant had gotten Tad out of more scrapes in the past ten years than he cared to count. Everything from pilfering apples from a neighbor's orchard and almost setting the barn on fire in his first attempt at smoking, to overzealous carousing with friends that somehow always seemed to get out of hand. He'd had to settle accounts with irate tavern owners, placate angry farmers, pay off hopeful young harlots, even replace a prize mare when Tad had broken her leg racing her through a rainstorm.

Maybe it's my fault he's turned out the way he has, though God knows I tried my best to be both brother and father to him, Grant thought to himself now, trying to understand his sibling's behavior and where he himself might have gone wrong in guiding Tad. *If I'd had more time, been stricter with him, or more patient. If only Dad had lived, Tad might have listened, learned to take things more seriously.*

The Gardner boys had been fifteen and twelve when their parents had been killed. Ironically, the couple had been shot during a rowdy celebration honoring the end of the War Between the States. At an outdoor dance in Lexington, they'd been waltzing when a stray bullet fired by an exuberant drunk had passed first through Harold's body, then Alice's. They'd died in each other's arms.

Though barely in his teens, Grant had become a man that night. From that day on, he'd shouldered the burden of running the farm and raising Tad, stubbornly refusing to sell the property, move in with sympathetic relatives, or be separated from his younger brother. He'd accepted advice from trusted friends, letting them aid him in selecting able hands and a competent manager and accountant to attend to the more involved responsibilities that his father had previously taken upon himself, those which Grant was too young to handle on his own as yet. He listened to counsel about feed crops and new training techniques, learning as he put varied suggestions to practical application. He kept up with his schooling and made sure Tad did likewise, working endless days and far into many a night, pushing himself to excel and achieve every goal toward which he aimed.

Now he couldn't help but wonder if he'd made a mistake in not sending Tad to live with their cousins, or shipping him off to school, where he would have been under stricter supervision, where that wild streak of his might have been squelched at the outset. But that was yesterday's mistake, and now Grant had to deal with today's disastrous result, in the form of one Amanda Sites—gambler, cheat, and beautiful, ebony-haired hussy. A wanton woman with the face of an angel, the body of a courtesan, and the wiles of the Devil's own sister.

Well, she won't get away with her tricks here, Grant promised himself grimly. First thing tomorrow, I'm going to town, and we'll see how legal her claim is or isn't! Casting narrowed eyes upward, as though he could see her in her upstairs bedroom, he muttered, "I wonder how many fools you've lured into your net, you greedy, grasping witch! You won't find it so easy this time, because here is one man who intends to beat you at your own schemes, no matter how much it costs or how long it takes.''

Grant's plans were thrown awry from the start. With a head that felt as if it had been trampled in a stampede, he was awakened before daylight by an urgent summons to the foaling barn. Merry Miracle, one of the prize mares, was having difficulty birthing her foal. Bleary-eyed, cursing himself for having indulged in a drinking spree the night before, Grant dragged himself off to the barn, where he found two more mares in labor. It promised to be a busy and difficult day on the farm, with little time for anything else, let alone a trip into Lexington to consult with the family lawyer.

Meanwhile, exhausted by her travels, Amanda slept undisturbed. She was used to keeping late hours aboard ship and rising late in the morning, so her unconscious mind kept its usual schedule, allowing her to ignore the noise filtering into her bedroom. While farmhands called out to one another in the barnyard, and the household help bustled up and down the hall, she burrowed deeper into her cozy mattress and slept on.

It was nearly noon by the time she finally awakened, and even then it was several minutes before her muzzy mind began to function well enough for her to recall exactly where she was and why. Then, as she remembered, a smile crept over her face, and she hugged herself with delight. "Oh, yes!" she exclaimed to herself on a sigh of utter contentment, her eyes roaming the lovely room with its elegant furnishings. "Yes, Amanda, my dear, fairy tales really do come true!"

The canopied bed upon which she lay was huge compared to the small bunk she'd had aboard the *Lady Gambler*. In fact, the entire room was more than three times the size of her old quarters. Though as soft as a cloud, the feather mattress did not sag in the center, like the one she was used to sleeping on. The pillows were fluffy, the sheets as white as snow; the apricot coverlet matched the curtains, the canopy, and the skirt around the small dressing table across the room.

The furniture was all crafted of the finest oak, with leaves and acorns painstakingly carved into the wooden border of the vanity mirror, across the headboard and footboard of the bed, and over the doors of the immense companion armoire. Mated stands flanked the bed, and on each rested a ruffled doily and a double-globed lamp with delicate cherubs etched into the frosted glass. At the foot of the bed was a large chest, and in the corner of the room nearest the armoire stood a hand-painted silk dressing screen. Next to it was a full-length cheval mirror tilted slightly in its oak frame, reflecting a portion of the brown-and-apricot-designed Persian carpet which covered the central area of the floor.

On the side wall was a door that Amanda knew led to a small, private water closet, complete with a big copper tub and an oak washstand with pitcher and bowl. The chamber pot was ingeniously hidden beneath a straight-back chair which had a hole cut in the lower of its two hinged seats, the cushioned top seat and the cloth draped about the chair legs lending tasteful if insufficient disguise to its intended purpose.

These were luxuries the likes of which Amanda had never before experienced, and she was both delighted and awed by them now, hardly able to comprehend her sudden good fortune. Neither could she believe Tad Gardner's foolishness in risking all this wealth and comfort, or even half of it, on something as fickle as a game of poker. When she'd finally fallen asleep the night before, after practically having to browbeat the household servants into allowing her upstairs and providing a hot bath for her, she would not have been surprised to awaken to discover it had all been just a wondrous dream, to find herself once again aboard the *Lady Gambler*.

But it was real—gloriously real! The bedroom, the house, the farm, and its income. No more long nights of gambling and smiling and fending off lewd advances. No more gaudy costumes or shoes that cramped her feet and made her legs ache. No more squirreling away every dime and dollar, hoping to someday have a tenth of what she now owned. It was as if a huge burden had been lifted from her shoulders, and she wanted to laugh with the freedom from its weight, to shout aloud, to dance for joy that all this was actually hers.

Well, half of it anyway, she reminded herself hastily. There was still Grant Gardner to contend with, and he had made no secret of his anger and contempt for her. Not that she could blame him. It was only natural that Grant would resent anyone, man or woman, who suddenly appeared to claim half of the family property.

Which brought to mind another matter. When the Gardners had jointly held Misty Valley, they had obviously lived together, sharing everything equally. Now that Amanda had come along, she and Grant would have to discuss exactly what they owned cooperatively and how they could direct their combined interests compatibly. Would he be willing to teach her how the farm was run? Would he treat her as a partner, open the business ledgers for her inspection, deal with her openly and honestly, show her even a modicum of respect? Or would he continue to be belligerent and hateful? Would he expect her to run the house, while he managed the horses, shunting her aside as a useless, brainless woman? Would he continue to regard her as a fallen woman, to hold her in contempt?

"Not that I'm complaining, Lord," Amanda avowed aloud to her Maker in her usual offhand manner of prayer. "It's just that having to deal with Grant Gardner is a bit more than I'd counted on. I'm afraid the man is going to give me fits, in more ways that one, and if You could possibly help me out, maybe soften him up some, I'd be grateful. Oh, and by the way," she added with an impish grin as she sprang from the bed and dashed toward the water closet, "he sure is gorgeous! I hope You know what You're doing, puttin' such temptation in my path!"

* * *

Breakfast was long since past, and the luncheon dishes were being carried from the table by the time Amanda had finished dressing and wandered downstairs. With a shrug and a smile, she politely but firmly ordered a light afternoon meal for herself, determined not to let Gardner's staff get the upper hand. "Grits and gravy and a few buttered biscuits will do just fine," she told the bewildered young maid who was clearing the dining table. "And coffee, please."

When her food arrived, she asked, "Would you happen to know where Mr. Gardner is?"

"Yes, ma'am. He's out at the birthing barn."

"Birthing barn?"

"Yes'm. Well, it's rightly called the foaling barn, I suppose, but that's where he's been most of last night and this mornin'." As Amanda continued to give the girl a perplexed look, she explained further. "It's where they stable the mares when they're about to deliver their young, and I guess a couple of them came due during the night."

"I see. But why would Mr. Gardner need to be there?" Amanda asked, frowning slightly. "I mean, is it really necessary? Don't the horses do that sort of thing on their own?" she went on with a wave of her red-tipped nails.

The girl shook her head and gave a little laugh. "You'd think so, wouldn't you? But around here these horses get more help than a woman deliverin' triplets could expect. They're valuable animals, Miss Sites, the bread and meat of Misty Valley, and Mr. Gardner sees to it that they get the very best of care. That's why so many buyers purchase horses from Misty Valley. They know they're getting quality for their dollar here."

The maid's comments gave Amanda much to consider as she ate her meal. From the sound of things, she had a lot to learn about raising and breeding horses. She was woefully ignorant in this area, and it would undoubtedly take some time to learn everything. Thinking perhaps the best place to begin would be by reading up on the subject, and deciding to postpone a tour of the house and grounds until later, Amanda finished eating and went in search of Grant's office. Surely he had some books about the care and breeding of horses.

Several hours later, Grant entered his private sanctum to find Amanda snuggled comfortably in one of two matching leather chairs stationed before the fireplace. Her shoes lay abandoned on the floor, her stockinged feet tucked beneath her, a large volume open in her lap. So involved was she in her reading that she didn't hear him, and he stopped to study her for a moment before alerting her to his presence. Her forehead was creased in concentration, her lips slightly parted, the tip of her tongue caught between her teeth. Midnight-black hair was escaping the haphazard knot atop her head, trailing in tendrils down her nape and temples. She wore an emerald-green dress, the bodice tightly fitted and cut low, exposing a generous portion of the upper curves of her milk-white breasts, the view made even more enticing by the way she sat hunched over the book.

Grudgingly, he once more admitted to himself how incredibly beautiful she was, with a sultry, sensual manner about her that was bound to set a man's mind toward the bedroom. Her features were perfectly aligned in her clean-scrubbed face, her complexion naturally creamy and unmarred, but for a small mole near the corner of her mouth that only served to draw one's attention to her full, pouty lips. With the body of a siren, startling ice-blue eyes, and that mane of tousled raven curls, she was a living, breathing enchantress.

At twenty-six, Grant was a normal, healthy man with all the usual urges, accustomed to satisfying those needs regularly. As his eyes lingered in frank male appreciation, deliberately cataloging Amanda's alluring attributes, his blood began to run fast and hot. Under any other circumstance he would not have been shocked to find himself responding to such compelling beauty, but given his present animosity toward her, it was almost

ridiculous for him to be attracted to her in the same
breath.

Now was definitely not the most convenient or logical time for his wayward body to react so readily and
disobediently, in total opposition to his brain's better
judgment. However, that being the case, he was at least
forewarned. He was going to have to be especially wary
of this woman, lest he, too, fall into her web and find
himself entangled—a spellbound victim of his own lust,
like countless others before him.

Cursing his traitorous flesh, Grant let anger spur him
forward. Striding into the room, he met her startled
look with a sneer. ''Enjoying the pictures in the book,
Miss Sites?'' he commented nastily.

''There are pictures?'' she responded with an arched
brow, meeting him look for look. With an effort, she
managed to settle her leaping pulse, which had begun
playing leapfrog in her chest the moment she looked up
into his magnificent green eyes.

''Don't tell me you can actually read.'' Grant threw
himself into his desk chair, assuming a pose of non-
chalance.

For the second time in as many days, Amanda deliberately restrained her temper, silently admonishing herself to behave with ladylike decorum. ''At the risk of
appearing a bluestocking, yes,'' she answered with ad-
mirable composure. ''I most definitely can read, though
I must admit this text is almost beyond my comprehension.''

The idea of this woman ever fitting Grant's image of
a bluestocking was almost ludicrous enough to bring a
smile to his face. But not quite. ''And what are you
applying yourself to so studiously, if you don't mind
my asking?''

She raised the book for his inspection of the title.
''The Science of Animal Husbandry. Of course, I
skipped to the section dealing with horses. Maybe that's
why it's so confusing. Should I have started at the beginning of the book?''

If someone had just stolen his chair from beneath

him, Grant could not have been more stunned. Not only could the audacious little tart read, but she was evidently set on educating herself in the management of the farm! Oh, but this was too much to bear, coming on the heels of Tad's defection! Spearing her with a glare that should have shriveled her where she sat, he ground out a scathing reply. "Why bother taxing your beleaguered brain, my dear woman? In a few days at most, you'll be on your way. I doubt you'll have much future use for knowledge about the breeding procedures of thoroughbreds."

"Don't bet your bottom dollar on that, Gardner." Her outward calm belied her growing temper.

"Oh?" Now *his* brow arched upward as he leaned forward and asked in a suggestive stage whisper, "Trying to learn some new bedroom techniques for your clientele, perhaps? I'd be glad to supply a few lessons, if you don't mind getting your tasty little neck and rump bitten. Stallions tend to get very excited when they cover a mare, but maybe you like your loving rough."

Amanda launched herself at him like a cat springing at a rat. She was out of her chair and stretched over his desk, delivering a resounding, open-handed slap to his cheek, before either of them realized her intent. Reflex had him grabbing her wrist and yanking her forward, her face inches from his, as papers and ledgers skittered to the floor. Sparks flew from two sets of glittering eyes.

"You are the most disgusting man I have ever had the displeasure of meeting, Grant Gardner," she hissed. Her efforts to pull her wrist from his grasp proved futile. "Let go of me this instant, you beast!"

"But I'm so enjoying the scenery," he said mockingly, his gaze dropping insolently to her heaving bosom and the bountiful display of creamy twin globes as they strained at the edges of her bodice. She was bent from the waist, held captive across his desktop, her chest so near to him that she could feel the warmth of his breath caressing her bare skin. At this angle, Grant had an unrestricted view straight down the top of her dress.

"Damn you!" With her free hand, she tried to push back from him, but couldn't manage to brace herself and gain the necessary leverage. Her palm kept slipping on the loose papers strewn over the polished surface. Realizing her dilemma and taking full advantage of it, Grant relentlessly tugged her nearer, a wicked grin splitting his face as he snagged her other wrist. Sprawled before him like a butterfly pinned to a board, Amanda was at his mercy—and they were both fully aware of how truly caught she was.

"Well, my beauty," he drawled, his emerald eyes sparkling like gems, "what shall I do with you now? Shall I kiss those ruby lips of yours?"

As his lips took aim toward hers, she snapped at him with bared teeth, almost catching the tip of his nose. With fingers curled into talons, she fought to reach his face. Failing that, she snarled at him.

"Watch it, little she-cat," he warned on a gruff laugh. "I bite back." Somehow, while still holding tight to her wrist, his long fingers tangled in her hair, anchoring her head in place. "Now, let's try that again, shall we?"

Every so slowly, tauntingly, his mouth stalked hers, until finally no more than a breath separated them. As his face blurred before her, she scrunched her eyes tightly shut, grabbed one final gulp of air, and clenched her lips against the invasion of his. For endless seconds his mouth hovered teasingly over hers, his nearness generating an odd tingling in her lips, making them tickle and twitch in anticipation of his touch. She heard him chuckle, the sound vibrating across the minute distance that still separated her flesh from his.

Then his lips were searing hers. Hot. Hard. Demanding. The sharp edges of his teeth nipped in silent mandate, his fiery tongue stabbing for entrance. For lack of breath, she complied, opening her mouth to him, and like a conqueror breaching enemy defenses, he boldly staked claim.

A wild quiver lanced through her, sending tremors from head to toe and back again, building into a giant wave that swiftly swamped her senses. In helpless wonder, never having experienced anything like this masterful onslaught, she responded without thinking. Her lips melted, eagerly following his, her tongue dancing like a flame against his. Dizzy with a desire such as she'd never imagined, she mewed in disappointment when his mouth released hers much too soon.

His low laugh sounding against her throat, he sought new territory. "That's it, kitten. Sheathe those painted claws and purr for me. Burn for me."

As his mouth scorched a blazing path from her jaw to her shoulder, she gasped in delight. "Oh, sweet heaven!" she murmured, lost in the delicious torment of his touch, fresh shivers skipping over her skin. His tongue swept out to lap across the upper curve of each breast, then dipped into the deep crevice between them, and Amanda thought she would faint with the pleasure that rippled through her, tightening her belly and pooling wetly at the juncture of her thighs. Through the cloth of her dress, he nuzzled the engorged crests of her breasts, lapping at them, teasing until she arched into his touch as much as her awkward position allowed.

"Good," she heard him say. "Yield to me. Show me how much you want me."

His teeth grazed lightly over her yearning flesh, and a moment later she felt the restraining cloth jerk tight across her breasts. Then it loosened, even as she heard the crisp rip of bodice giving way beneath the pull of those insistent teeth.

She tried to break away from him then, a flicker of sanity filtering through the blissful haze he'd so skillfully wrapped around her, but his fingers were still caught in her hair, still shackling her wrists. "No! Don't!" she objected, her voice weak even to her own ears.

"Yes," he countered haughtily. Then, before she could argue further, his lips captured one dusky nipple, sucking it sharply into the hot, dark cavern of his mouth, and she was lost to all reason again. She felt the pull to the depths of her womanhood, the force of it making her cry out softly. Her breath came in short gasps, seeming to match his rhythmic suckling. Flames licked deep within her, engulfing her, making her writhe with these strange, forbidden desires Grant was calling forth from hidden places in her body and soul.

How far he might have taken her on this mad, rapturous journey was to remain a mystery to both of them. A brief knock on the door announced Chalmers' presence a mere moment before the manservant strode into the room. Which of the three of them was most shocked would have been difficult to determine. Tearing his lips from her passion-swollen breast, Grant abruptly shoved her from him, sending her sliding and stumbling backward off his desk as she frantically attempted to gather her trembling legs beneath her and grab at the shreds of her torn bodice. As luck would have it, she landed smack on her bottom at Chalmers' feet, further stunning the snooty Englishman by giving him an enticing glimpse of her bare bosom before she managed to clutch the ragged edges of the cloth together.

"I . . . uh . . . you said you wanted to be notified immediately when Mr. O'Brian arrived, sir." Redfaced, Chalmers directed his eyes straight ahead of him, stiffly addressing his remark to his employer.

"So I did, Chalmers. Thank you. Please tell Mr. O'Brian that I will be with him shortly." Only the vivid flush around the rim of his shirt collar betrayed Grant's agitation at being caught in such a flagrant display. His voice was as cool and composed as ever, showing none of the acute embarrassment Amanda was experiencing so intensely.

"Very good, sir. Shall I seat him in the entrance hall until you are ready to see him?"

"No. Send him to the main stables. I'll meet him there." Shooting an arrogant look at Amanda, who still sat stunned on the floor, struggling to gather wits enough to move, he added, "First, however, please show Miss Sites the back stairway to the second floor.

We don't want her flaunting her charms any more than need be on her way to her room to repair her person.''

Stung, Amanda scrambled to her feet, shoving aside Chalmers' reluctantly offered helping hand, anger overriding her mortification. "Touch me, and I'll scratch your eyes out," she snarled at the beflustered servant.

Turning on Grant, she pinned him with a look of raw fury. "That goes for you, too, Gardner. Never . . . never lay hands on me like that again, or I assure you, you'll rue the day!''

His lips curled into a smirk, his green eyes narrowing slightly. "Is that a challenge, Miss Sites?"

"No. It's a promise, Mr. Gardner. One I'll take great pleasure in discharging.''

"I'll look forward to it," he assured her calmly. His gaze drifted to her breasts, his smile growing. "Meanwhile, I feel obliged to point out that your . . . uh . . . assets are escaping their limited confines once more.''

On a strangled curse, Amanda stormed from the room, only to stop short in the hall. Barefoot and burning with humiliation, she was nonetheless forced to await the haughty Chalmers, who took his own small revenge and an inordinate amount of satisfaction in delivering her shoes to her—and then, quite leisurely, escorting her to the rear stairway, normally used only by the servants.

Chapter 4

SUPPER that night was a trial. Not wanting to face Grant over the dining table after that disastrous episode in his study, Amanda decided to order a tray brought to her room. Her polite request was promptly denied, in a not-so-polite manner, by Mrs. Divots, Misty Valley's housekeeper, who also claimed a British background and was almost as pompous as Chalmers.

"I will not cater to the whims of the likes of you, and neither will any of my staff," Mrs. Divots said with a sniff, her rather pointed nose aimed toward the ceiling. "Supper will be served in the dining room promptly at seven o'clock, as usual, and if you want your meal, you'll be there then."

Taken aback by the woman's animosity, Amanda stared after her as the housekeeper marched away, her backbone as stiff and straight as a royal guard's. "For crying out loud, you'd think I'd killed someone, the way these people act!" Amanda wondered aloud. "All I asked for was a dinner tray, not the crown jewels! Even condemned prisoners get meals brought to them!"

So, like it or not, Amanda was forced to dine with Grant or go hungry, and she'd always possessed a healthy appetite. At least until the moment she found herself seated across the table from her archenemy that evening. Though the food was well prepared, her dinner companion left much to be desired when it came to being congenial.

Grant took one look at the décolletage of her gown, made only slightly more modest by the lace handkerchief she'd fashioned into a modified fichu and pinned to the neckline of her bodice, and said with sardonic delight, "What is the point in trying to hide what I've already sampled, my dear Miss Sites?"

Clamping down hard on her temper, Amanda asked tightly, "Would it be too much to ask that you try to be a gentleman for the duration of one meal, Mr. Gardner? Or is this the way you treat all ladies of your acquaintance?"

"But you're not a lady, are you?" he countered quickly. "Therefore, you cannot expect to be treated as one."

"And what makes you think I'm not a lady?"

"The way you dress, for one thing. And those lacquered claws of yours. And your atrocious habit of chomping away at that gum, like a cow chewing its cud."

Angrily, she removed the offending gum from her mouth and plunked it onto the rim of her dinner plate.

"Is that better?"

"Hardly." He sighed, eyeing the sticky glob with distaste.

"Fine." Amanda retrieved the gum, and promptly deposited it on the edge of his plate instead, thoroughly enjoying the way his eyes flickered in surprise and dismay.

"As to my manner of dress, Mr. Gardner," she continued, regaining her former composure, "these are my work clothes. I simply have not had the opportunity to shop for more adequate attire since leaving the *Lady Gambler*. In fact, I need to make a trip into Lexington on Monday, and I intend to purchase several items then, if you will lend me a carriage and a driver for the day.''

''If you would agree to take the first train out of town and never return, I'd drive you myself, pay for your ticket, buy you a trunkful of new clothes, and hire a blasted brass band to see you off.''

''No, thank you,'' she replied with a falsely sweet smile. ''The loan of the carriage will be sufficient. I do have another problem you might aid me with, however, if you would be so kind.''

''Oh?''

''Your servants seem reluctant to tend to my needs, and I was hoping you would speak with them about being more cooperative and pleasant to me. After all, I do own half of the property now, and I am assuming that a portion of my proceeds will go to pay their wages. I would hate to have to discharge any of them for lack of respect toward their new employer.''

''Wha—what?'' Grant sputtered past a spoonful of hot soup.

''I said—''

''I heard you!'' With an effort, he strove for a measure of control. ''Miss Sites, you will fire no one. No one. Do I make myself clear? You have absolutely no authority to do so—''

This time it was Amanda who interrupted him. ''I beg to differ, and I suggest that my lawyer will also.''

''What lawyer?''

''The one I'm securing to make certain that neither you nor anyone else tries to cheat me out of what is rightfully and lawfully mine.''

''The way you cheated Tad?''

The only way Amanda could prevent herself from stabbing him then and there was to purposefully lay her fork aside and fold her hands tightly together in her lap. ''I did not cheat your brother. He is the one who so stupidly and stubbornly gambled his inheritance away, against all advice to the contrary. There were three of us equally staked in that last hand. All of us—Tad,

Macy, and I—had an even chance of winning, but the cards fell in my favor.''

"Macy?" Grant leapt at the introduction of this new name. "Who is he? Your consort in crime? Your partner? Do the two of you work as a team to rob your chosen victims? Is he going to come knocking on my door next, demanding entrance?"

Her hands were clasped so tightly together that the blood was no longer flowing to her fingers. Through clenched teeth, she answered, "Have no fear, Mr. Gardner. Art Macy is wealthy enough in his own right. I truly doubt he needs a piddling horse farm to add to his numerous businesses. And no, he is not my partner. When it comes to cards, I rely solely upon my own talents.''

Grant frowned, his eyes narrowing. "Art Macy? The same Art Macy who owns several hotels and whiskey distilleries, and a sizable interest in two major railroads?"

"Among other ventures," Amanda agreed with a curt nod.

"And just how well do you know Mr. Macy, Amanda? Was he a favored client of yours? Your lover? Your benefactor, perhaps?"

Her crystal-blue eyes glittered at him. "I am no man's kept woman. I never have been, and I never will be. I make my own way in the world, quite capably.''

"It would seem so," he admitted snidely. "Of course, it helps that you are so admirably endowed with such flawlessly beauty.''

"My looks have nothing whatever to do with it. My natural talents and the skills I learned from my father are far more important to my former trade than a pretty face.''

Grant's mouth flapped open as he stared at her in horror. "Your father?" he echoed in a stunned voice. "My God! Your father taught you to . . . to . . .''

"To play cards," Amanda supplied, innocent of the mistaken assumption Grant was entertaining at this moment and wondering at his obvious shock. Why was it that everyone seemed to take such offense to the idea of a woman gambling for a living? Certainly it was a darned sight better than a few other professions she might have chosen or been forced to accept in order to feed herself after her father's death.

"He was a riverboat gambler, too, you see," she went on to say as Grant gave himself a mental shake and tried to follow her explanation. "From the time I could crawl into his lap, he taught me everything he knew. I traveled everywhere with him, and quite literally cut my teeth on a deck of cards. Fortunately, I had a talent for it, and by the time he died, the owners of the riverboat had no qualms about hiring me as a dealer in the casino."

Relief flooded through him. Why, Grant wasn't quite sure, except that considering Amanda a scarlet woman was one thing, and thinking that she had been introduced to that way of life by her own father was another matter altogether.

"And that is how you came to meet Tad?" he questioned further. "How is it, then, that you are the one laying claim to Tad's property instead of the owner's of the *Lady Gambler?*"

"It was a private poker game, after my usual working hours, entered into on my own time and with my own money."

"Who invited my brother to join the game?"

"Mr. Macy did, when both Tad and Mr. Widmark expressed interest in playing that night. Why?"

"Are you sure you didn't lure him first into your bed and then into the game, after discovering what a rich, gullible young fool he was? He wouldn't be the first man to fall prey to a pair of ripe breasts and sweet suggestions whispered across the pillow after a night of passion."

Seething with righteous indignation at this last, deliberate slur on her morals, Amanda came abruptly to her feet. For far too long she'd put up with this same obnoxious behavior from too many men, but she didn't have to listen to such abuse any longer. She was a lady of means now, and she could demand proper respect. Glaring down into his handsome, mocking face, she retorted icily, furiously, "Better men than your sniveling little brother have tried, and failed, to get me into their beds, Mr. Gardner. Just because I earned my living gambling does not mean that I place a low value on myself or my body."

Heaping insult upon injury, Grant reached into his pocket, pulled out a wad of bills, peeled several from the roll, and tossed them onto the table before her. "Does that meet your price, Miss Sites? Is that enough to pave my way between your sheets and your thighs? Since the moment we met, you've virtually flaunted your wares beneath my nose. Just this afternoon, you gave me a teasing sample of what I might expect from you, and I daresay you were so hot for it I could have had it all for free if Chalmers hadn't chosen such an inappropriate time to interrupt."

"You filthy swine!" With a sweep of her hand, his money and his glass of wine went flying into his lap. "You arrogant, braying jackass!" She was across the room, and heading swiftly toward the door before he could make a grab for her. "There isn't enough money in the world to get me into your bed or you into mine! You have all the manners and charm of a toad!"

"Beware, Amanda. Toads have been known to turn into princes," he warned. "Perhaps I'll charm you into surrendering your lush body to me yet."

"And maybe pigs will fly! Besides, you're confusing toads with frogs."

With that parting shot, she marched into the hall, barreling straight into Chalmers and almost knocking the two of them to the floor. "Do you make a habit of listening at keyholes, Chalmers?" she snarled at the startled manservant. "It's a darned good way to get a poke in the eye, you know!"

The following day was Sunday, and again Amanda slept late. After her argument with Grant the night before, she had taken the book on animal husbandry to her room and read until the wee hours of the morning. Besides being upset over Grant's hatefulness, she simply wasn't accustomed to going to sleep or rising early. In time, perhaps, she would adjust to a schedule more in line with the others.

The day was lovely, bright and sunny, with a balmy breeze that smelled of spring blossoms. Much too enticing to resist. Though she still lacked the proper clothing, especially the kind required for mucking about in stables and barnyards, Amanda donned her oldest gown and the bedraggled house shoes she normally wore only with her nightshift, and decided to treat herself to a tour outdoors.

She began close to the house and quickly discovered the formal rose garden, much to her delight and confusion. Neither Grant Gardner, with all his cynicism, nor his younger brother, who had seemed so irresponsible, seemed the type to relish such fragile beauty or to care enough to tend to it. Yet someone had planted these bushes. Someone had designed this lovely retreat, carefully plotting where each of the countless varieties would look best, how to space the arbors and trellises and viewing benches along the winding pathways, what added greenery would further enhance the beauty of the garden. And someone obviously worked very hard to keep the flower beds and plants in excellent condition. But who? A hired gardner? The dour housekeeper with her prudish disposition? Or was there another side to Grant Gardner that Amanda had not yet seen, a softer, sentimental side he was hiding?

Just beyond the rose garden was an orchard, the fruit trees alive with fragrant, budding blossoms and the steady hum of honeybees as they flitted from flower to flower, and more butterflies than Amanda had ever seen. Birds serenaded her with glad song, and beneath the thin soles of her slippers the grass was soft and green, the very earth smelling of ripe, awakening soil. Here, tiny wildflowers sprang up in clusters of yellow and violet, blue and pink, vying for the patches of sunlight filtering through the bower of branches overhead.

Amanda was thoroughly entranced. While the rose garden was lovely, the orchard was more private, more naturally cozy and better suited to her taste. It reminded her of an enchanted glade where elves and wood sprites might frolic amid moonbeams and hide beneath giant toadstools. It was the sort of spot she'd always imagined as the ideal place to kick off her shoes, wriggle her bare toes in the grass, sit and while away the hours reading and daydreaming to her heart's content.

She left reluctantly, promising herself that she would return soon, and undoubtedly often in the days to come. But right now there were other areas of the farm to investigate and familiarize herself with.

Behind the house, a summer kitchen, a smokehouse, and a springhouse all stood within convenient reach of the main manor. Off to one side lay another garden, this one freshly tilled and planted, the stakes at the ends of the neat rows proclaiming which vegetables would soon sprout where.

On the other side of the back lawn was an immense barnyard, fringed with dozens of stables and barns and paddocks of varied size and shape. Dirt roads spoked off from the main area, leading toward more distant buildings, and to fields where horses grazed and windmills turned lazily atop several wells, and feed grain even now strained toward the azure sky.

To Amanda's eye, the immediate barnyard resembled a small, bustling town. In all directions there were signs of activity. Everywhere horses were being ridden or led about. Men hurried to and fro, carrying saddles and bridles and tools that were totally baffling to her. Others were busy either emptying or filling numerous wagons with straw, grain, and what smelled suspiciously like manure, used for what purposes Amanda could only conjecture. Near the open doors of the smithy, a huge black man she assumed was the farrier was shoeing a horse. Inside another building she spied a fellow repairing some sort of leather harness.

Entering what looked to be a barn, Amanda found herself standing at the head of a long tunnel flanked on either side with stalls. Outside the double-hung doors of each enclosure a wooden sign declared the name of the inhabitant, and Amanda was intrigued both by the sleek, long-legged animals and by the unique and colorful titles they bore. Names like Nature's Son, Clever Comet, Sure Winner, Star Fire, and Fleet Fellow. Only a few of the stalls were occupied, so Amanda supposed the horses were presently out in the pastures, enjoying the fine spring weather and their daily exercise.

As she walked through two more barns similar to the first, she was favorably impressed by the cleanliness and order. Not only was there less odor than she'd expected, but also nothing was left lying about in the center aisles or the stalls. Everything was neatly hung on convenient pegs and stowed in large wooden boxes, safely out of the way.

When the nameplates began to have a more feminine sound, like Fancy Filly and Siren Song, she guessed that she was now in the section housing the mares. She had yet to encounter one which looked as if she were expecting a baby, and all of the horses Amanda had viewed thus far seemed to be fully grown, which was somewhat disappointing, since she was not really comfortable around the large animals. Raised on the river, she was unfamiliar with horses, and to be truthful, they scared her spitless. If she had to be around them now, she would much prefer to begin her acquaintance with the smaller ones—the babies.

She was peering warily into one of the stalls, ready to leap out of the way if a big head with huge teeth lunged at her, when a voice close behind her demanded loudly, "What are you doing in here?"

"Omigosh!" Amanda shrieked, clutching a hand to her heart, which was at the moment trying to pound its way up past her throat. "Blast you, Grant Gardner! What are you tryin' to do, give me heart failure? You darned near scared the liver out of me!" As she screeched at him, she was hopping around in a fair imitation of an irate Rumpelstiltskin.

He had to laugh, such a sight did she make. "Settle

down, woman! Lord, I don't think I've witnessed such a fine fit since Cousin Nell sat on her pincushion!''

"I'm glad one of us thinks it's so funny! You made me swallow my gum! It's a wonder I didn't choke, what with you creeping up behind me and scaring me half witless!"

"I didn't creep, though I must say you jumped as if you're guilty as sin of something. What were you doing, Amanda? I don't like strangers out here nosing in my barns."

"*Our* barns," she corrected him waspishly, "and I was simply looking at the horses. Actually, I was trying to locate the ponies."

"Ponies?" he questioned, giving her an odd look, rather half incredulous and half suspicious. "We don't have any ponies."

"You don't?" Now it was Amanda who was confused. "But I was sure the little maid who served my breakfast yesterday morning said there were some just being born. Surely you don't get rid of them that quickly. Or did the poor little things die?"

"Wait a minute. I think I'm starting to understand. Are you talking about the new foals?"

Amanda nodded. "Yes. The babies. The ponies. I knew you had some."

Grant shook his head in disbelief, a half smile etching his mouth at the irony of the situation. Here he had been worried about sabotage, and the woman didn't even know the difference between foals and ponies! "You really don't know anything about horses, do you? Amanda, newborn thoroughbreds are called foals. The male foals are called colts; the females are fillies. They are not ponies. Ponies are a different breed altogether, at least to most of us in this business." He was not about to confuse her further by admitting that any adult horse under fourteen hands high was also considered a pony, regardless of the breed.

Her brow furrowed, Amanda considered this for a moment, then asked, "Then you raise thoroughbreds here? And they are a special breed of horse used for racing?''

"And for riding, too," he replied.

"And all of the babies eventually grow to be as big as their fathers or mothers?''

He nodded, though he added for accuracy, "The fathers are known as the sires, while the mothers are called the dams, and the foals usually attain a similar height, yes."

"While ponies stay little all their lives," she deduced.

"Correct, my dear. Now, if your curiosity is satisfied for the day, I have no more time for lesson-giving."

"You volunteered the information, Gardner," she reminded him pointedly. "All I wanted to know was where the foals are."

"Why?" His suspicions were again aroused. Was she really as ignorant as she appeared, or was it an act to make him let down his guard?

"Because I want to see them. Because I'll probably like them better than their full-grown parents. Because I've never seen a newborn animal, except for some kittens once and a nestful of mice." Consciously or unconsciously, Amanda was giving him a look no man could have refused. Those clear, ocean-blue eyes were so guileless, those lush lips pursed into an inviting pout that would have melted Satan's heart.

"All right," he conceded on a sigh. "I'll take you to see the foals."

"No," she told him bluntly, contrarily. "You just said you are much too busy, and I can't expect you to neglect your work to escort me about. Simply point me in the proper direction, and I'm positive I can manage on my own."

The last thing Grant wanted was to have this woman wandering about at will, poking her nose into every nook and cranny of his business, getting underfoot and keeping his men from their jobs. Especially dressed as she was in one of the most provocative gowns he'd seen in the bright light of day. Though the dress had undoubtedly seen better times—now it sported worn spots and several dark stains—Amanda had obviously long since outgrown it. The sleek satin snugged to her torso like a second skin, faithful to every contour, leaving very little to the imagination. A bit of lace had torn loose from around the neckline and was dangling enticingly near the slope of one breast, as distracting and tantalizing as a shiny lure to a hungry trout.

No, it would not do to have Miss Sites meandering about the place, turning his men into slavering, lust-crazed idiots as she went. Even old Clancy, who was seventy if a day, would not be immune to her blatantly displayed charms. Grant would have to see to the matter himself, whether he could spare the time or not—and bear up as best he could until she was safely back in the house and out of sight once more. Better yet, away from Misty Valley altogether, and out of his way for good.

"Oh, Grant!" she cooed, thoroughly enchanted by the two-day-old foal in the stall with its mother. "He's darling! Look at him! Those long spindly legs! That cute, wispy tail! Those big chocolate eyes! Lands, I know women who would kill for eyelashes as long as his! I've never seen anything so adorable." She sighed, her former pique completely forgotten now in her delight over the newborn foal. "It's a shame he has to grow up into such a huge beast when he's so sweet now."

Grant gazed at her speculatively, a wicked emerald gleam born in his eyes. "Amanda, are you afraid of horses?"

He reminded her of a vulture hovering over prospective prey, and she was reluctant to tell him the truth, afraid it would give him a weapon to use against her in the future. "Well," she hedged, "not really so much afraid, I suppose, as . . . as . . ."

"Yes?" he drawled, his lips twitching suspiciously.

"Respectful," she supplied, shooting him a sour look. "I'm not entirely comfortable around an animal that large. Anything that weighs as much as they do and has teeth that big deserves a fair degree of respect, don't you agree?''

He was grinning openly at her now. "I'll be double damned! You're scared spitless of them, aren't you? C'mon, admit it.''

"All right!" she snarled, glaring at him with a frazzled frown. "I've never been around them, I don't know what to expect of them, and they frighten me clean out of my shoes! Now are you satisfied? Does it make you feel better to know that?''

Oddly, it didn't, though Grant was hard put to answer why. His smile melted away, replaced by an assessing, calculating look. "If you have any intention of staying on at Misty Valley, which I will do my utmost to prevent, you'd better plan on getting used to horses real quickly, Amanda, because this is a working farm, and everyone pulls his or her weight around here. Partners share the toil as well as the profits, and I'll be hanged if I'm going to do all the labor while you laze around and do nothing. So think about that while you're contemplating how to spend your ill-gotten gains, my dear. You either earn your keep the best way you can or pack up and move on to more pleasant pastures, so to speak. In other words, no work, no pay, my lovely slugabed.''

Taking her arm, he escorted her from the barn and began leading her up the path to the house at a brisk pace, while Amanda struggled to sort through his comments and decide whether or not to be offended. Had there been some vague, veiled threat hidden within Grant's words? What, exactly, had he meant when he said she could earn her keep the best way she could? Was he referring to her ineptitude with horses? Or was he once again slandering her character, suggesting she either warm his bed or leave? When it suited his purpose, the man was a master at innuendo, as thoroughly exasperating as he was irrefutably handsome.

He was also a wizard at throwing her entire system into disorder, it seemed. Inexplicably, wild tingles were skipping along her flesh, spreading from the spot where his long, callused fingers rested on her bare arm. Though she had no way of knowing it, Grant was experiencing a similar reaction, even as he tried to deny the hot rush of blood to his loins, brought on by the simple act of touching her silken skin.

Her thoughts and emotions in turmoil, Amanda trotted along beside him, a frown wrinkling her brow. More times than not, she surmised with supreme annoyance, life seemed to deal from the bottom of a marked deck, and at this moment she wasn't at all sure how to play the five cards she'd drawn in this newest hand. Misty Valley, snooty servants, thoroughbred horses, and two jokers—herself and Grant Gardner. What a crazy combination!

Chapter 5

THEY were within twenty feet of the house, not a long distance, but too far to head off inevitable disaster when approaching hoofbeats suddenly sounded, followed immediately by the appearance of a young blond woman astride a big bay mare. Horse and rider came racing into the barnyard, drawing to a halt with a theatrical flair mere inches from Grant's chest.

Certain she was about to be trampled to death by those huge, pounding hoofs, Amanda threw up her arms and let loose a shriek that threatened to shatter windows for a square mile. Startled, the horse reared, promptly dumping its unprepared rider into the dust. Only Grant's alert reaction, as he caught the beast's bridle and jerked the animal aside, prevented the unseated lady from being injured.

"Damn it, Annabelle! One of these days you are going to get someone killed pulling stunts of that sort!" Turning the horse over to one of his men, who had come running to help, Grant extended a hand toward his petite visitor, pulling her to her feet.

Despite his harsh words, his touch was gentle as he brushed a speck of dirt from her cheek. "Forgive me for yelling at you, but I don't want to see you hurt, little one. You're eighteen, a woman now, and in spite of the fact that your father spoiled you outrageously, it's time you started to display a measure of maturity, rather than allowing your impetuous nature full rein.''

"It wasn't my fault!" Annabelle gasped, collecting her breath and dusting herself off. She threw an irate glance in Amanda's direction. "I wouldn't have been thrown if that . . . that woman hadn't screeched to the top of her lungs!" Her angry gray eyes widened, then narrowed as she took her first good look at Amanda. "Who *is* this creature, Grant, and what is she doing here?" Annabelle's voice was laced with frozen venom, and if Amanda had ever thought gray eyes warm, she was quickly disavowed of that notion. Annabelle's gaze was as cold and forbidding as an arctic ice floe.

At that moment, caught between Annabelle Foster and Amanda Sites, Grant wished he were anywhere else. Explaining Amanda to his willful fiancée-to-be would not have been an easy task under the best of circumstances. Here, now, it was formidable. Annabelle was in a particularly prickly mood, worse than usual, while Amanda was recovering from her fright, her color high and her blue eyes snapping. There would be the devil to pay, and no avoiding it.

"Annabelle, may I present Miss Amanda Sites, a . . . uh . . . an acquaintance of Tad's," he stammered quickly, earning an incredulous look from Amanda and a not-quite-convinced reaction from Annabelle.

"One of his playmates? Here?" Annabelle inquired tartly. "And you're allowing it?" Before either Amanda or Grant could comment, she threw her pert nose in the air and declared, "Well, at least Tad's return will serve to quell the latest rumor going about the country. I told Patsy I didn't believe a bit of it, and now she'll have to eat her words, the spiteful little gossip. That awful cousin of hers, Ben Widmark, came home with some wild tale that Tad had gambled away his half of Misty Valley, actually lost it in a card game to some

woman cardsharp, of all things! Isn't that the most outrageous thing you've every heard?''

A pregnant silence followed Annabelle's words, broken
abruptly by Amanda's laugh. Full, deep, it resounded
throughout the yard. "Oh, yes!" she chuckled victori-
ously. "Almost as outrageous as the fact that it's absolutely true!"

"What!" The color fled Annabelle's face as she
clutched Grant's sleeve, casting pleading eyes up at him.
"Grant! Say it isn't so!"

"Go ahead, *partner,* deny it if you can." Defiantly,
Amanda dared him to refute her claim.

At Amanda's words, realization dawned anew. "Oh,
God! Not her!" Annabelle wailed loudly, burying her
face in the front of Grant's shirt. "Tell me he didn't
lose the property to this common tramp! This gutter
person!"

"I'm afraid so," Grant admitted gruffly, sounding as
sick at heart as Annabelle. "At least for the moment."
His arms closed about the little blonde, his hand stroking her fair hair. "But, darling, I promise it is only
until I can get to town to consult with Peppermeier and
get this whole mess straightened out."

As Amanda stood seething, cut to the quick by their
hatefulness, their blind readiness to condemn her for
sins she'd never committed and to label her with names
she did not deserve, she heartily wished the two of
them straight to Satan's fiery realm. "Don't make
promises you can't keep, Gardner," she advised him
quietly, pride alone keeping her voice from quavering
and the tears hidden from view. "I'm here to stay, and
all of you will just have to learn to come to terms with
the fact that Misty Valley is half mine. And it will remain mine, come hell or high water, until I willingly
relinquish it."

How he did it Amanda neither knew or cared, or so
she told herself, but somehow Grant managed to calm
Annabelle sufficiently that she agreed to remain for
Sunday dinner. Fortunately, Amanda's own brief fit of

tears, in the secrecy of her bedroom, had not left her eyes swollen or her nose red. Her face was unravaged and serenely beautiful, betraying none of her pain, as she seated herself at the dining table and mentally prepared to endure the worst case of indigestion known to man—or woman. She seemed doomed not to enjoy a single meal in this dreadful house, and though Grant praised his cook's skills, Amanda might have been served sawdust and rabbit pellets for all she tasted of her food.

Grant seemed to be going out of his way to pacify the blonde, being particularly polite and attentive to her, all the while ignoring Amanda. Not at all pleased to be relegated to the position of a piece of furniture, Amanda solved the problem by making her presence known in the most irritating way possible. Relentlessly, with a rhythm that soon began to beat itself into Grant's brain, she drummed her fingernails upon the tabletop.

Finally, unable to bear the noise any longer, he snapped at her, "Must you do that?"

She smiled smugly in return. "No, but it helps to calm my nerves."

"It's not having the same result with mine," he assured her.

"Nor mine," Annabelle echoed, gazing in horrified fascination at Amanda's long, vividly painted nails. "Where on earth did you ever find such a . . . brilliant color?" she choked out, at a loss to restrain herself.

Imitating Annabelle's snobbish tone, Amanda replied, "Why, it's imported from the Orient, of course. This particular shade is known as Chinese Red. I have to go all the way to New Orleans to purchase it."

Evidently, Annabelle could think of nothing to say to that, and if Grant had any comments, he kept them to himself. Instead, they turned the conversation to topics guaranteed to bar Amanda from their discussion.

It also galled Amanda to note how Chalmers and Mrs. Divots fell all over themselves to please Miss Foster, fawning over her until Amanda wanted to gag, while she herself might not have existed. Chalmers gallantly seated Annabelle; Amanda was left to pull her own chair out. The housekeeper offered Miss Foster the choicest pieces of chicken, the most plump biscuits. Amanda made do with a wing and counted herself fortunate to have that. The little blonde's wineglass was topped off every few minutes, as was Grant's, but Amanda had to forcefully request Chalmers to refill hers.

Until then, she held her tongue, but as the manservant bent over her to pour her wine, she smiled up at him and asked softly, for his ears only, "Isn't it hard to breathe, with your nose stuck so far up Miss Foster's skirts, Chalmers? Not that I'm jealous or anything, but I'd hate to see you suffocate in your prime."

Caught off his guard, the man choked, splattering wine over the crisp linen tablecloth as he reddened to the color of a ripe tomato. Flustered to a state such as the others had rarely before witnessed, Chalmers hastened to mop up the spill, then quickly excused himself from the room.

"What did you say to put him in such a dither?" Grant asked, deigning to speak to Amanda once again.

She merely shrugged. offering yet another angelic smile. "I haven't the faintest notion what set him off. You don't suppose he's apt to have a stroke, do you? If he has a weak heart, I'll have to refrain from suggesting a tryst in the rose garden with him."

Mrs. Divots' scandalized gasp was clearly heard from several feet away, and the stained tablecloth received yet another spray as both Annabelle and Grant sputtered into their goblets. The meal progressed fitfully from then on, with glowers exchanged regularly.

When, at last and mercifully, the meal was finished, Amanda stood, set her napkin neatly aside, and announced graciously, "It's been memorable meeting you, Miss Foster. You must come again sometime when you and I can talk privately. Maybe we can trade silly feminine confidences with one another, perhaps rate Grant's kissing skills, or some such nonsense."

With the others gaping after her, she swept regally

from the room, Annabelle's shrill accusations ringing in her ears as the woman lost no time in verbally berating Grant, and he tried valiantly to defend himself.

"Touché," Amanda murmured to herself with a wry laugh. "Two can play this game, Grant Gardner. And I always play to win."

Amanda pried herself from bed much earlier than usual the next morning. While her appointment with Mr. Darcy was not until the afternoon, she had an immense amount of shopping to accomplish beforehand.

She was surprised to find a carriage and driver awaiting her. Apparently Grant was not going to be obstinate about this, for which she was pleased. She was also grateful to be gone from the house without encountering him, though she did pass Chalmers in the hall on her way out. The Englishman sent her a condemning glower, presumably still recovering from his loss of composure the previous day.

Thanks to Willy, Amanda was able to direct her driver to one of Lexington's most fashionable seamstresses, a couturiere by the name of Lenore Lalaine. The formidable dressmaker had an immense bust that rivaled the prow of a ship, a hawk-nose to match, and hard little black buttons for eyes, but for all her indomitable appearance, her long nose did not fly into the air at the first sight of Amanda entering her shop. She simply cast a practiced eye over Amanda's figure, as if mentally measuring her without benefit of a ruled tape, and asked, "May I help you?"

"Yes, please," Amanda replied, surprised that this woman hadn't immediately shown her the door. Perhaps there were some well-mannered people left in the world after all. "I am in need of a new wardrobe, an entire wardrobe, though since I don't ride, I suppose we can eliminate an outfit for that purpose. Also, I willingly admit that I am ready to concede to your superior knowledge in selecting fabrics and styles more becoming to a lady than the gown I am presently wearing."

"I see." The woman nodded and continued her sharp perusal of Amanda's form and features. Her stern lips almost managed an upward curl. "For someone to admit she doesn't ride, in the midst of all this famed horse country, could be considered a dire offense, Miss . . ."

"Sites. Amanda Sites," Amanda supplied with a tentative smile. "And I am fast learning that almost everything about me is objectionable here. However, I am determined to fit in, as a matter of self-honor, since I now own property here and intend to reside in the area."

"May I inquire where in town you are staying, Miss Sites, since we will undoubtedly be making numerous deliveries to your address?"

"I am living at Misty Valley, the Gardner farm."

"I am acquainted with it," Madame Lalaine said, a slightly raised brow the only betraying sign of her curiosity. "Now, then, shall we begin?"

For the next three hours, Amanda suffered being prodded and pinched and pinned and measured. Swaths of fabric lay scattered about like multicolored pieces of a shattered kaleidoscope. "The rose, I think," Mrs. Lalaine would mutter through a mouthful of pins. "Yes, it compliments the tone of your skin nicely." Or, "This blue lawn matches your eyes almost perfectly." Or, "Never wear green, dear. It makes your face look terribly sallow. And whatever you do, stay clear of purple."

Near the end of the session, she advised, "I know you said you don't ride, but might I suggest at least one riding outfit? The occasion may arise when you need it. If you prefer, we can use a less formal style which you could wear otherwise as well, modeled similarly to the split skirts the women out West seem to find so necessary, perhaps with a fitted jacket to match. Also, several casual blouses and skirts might come in very useful from time to time on the farm."

In this, Amanda bowed to the Frenchwoman's expertise, though she did manage to insert various opinions of her own concerning which styles she preferred, the design of sleeve and neckline she liked best, the decorative ribbons and buttons and lace for her gowns. In the process, she surprised the dressmaker as much as she did herself.

"My dear," Mrs. Lalaine told her with just a touch of embarrassment, "you have remarkably discerning tastes, with the possible exception of your nail enamel, which really needn't cause comment as long as you keep to lighter shades to match your new gowns. Actually, the only area in which you fall short is your lack of confidence in your own sound judgment. Certainly you needn't worry about your figure. You have a shape to put most of my customers to shame."

Her figure she had inherited from her mother, Amanda supposed. But her basic ideas of what best suited her were an accumulation of all those years spent traveling with her father and meeting all types of people. From nuns to mistresses, harlots to ladies, royalty to common working women; rich, poor, and in between, they had all influenced Amanda's sense of style. She'd learned from them all, discarding what she disliked or considered lacking, and adopting what she instinctively admired or thought useful.

Likewise, she'd assimilated feminine arts and manners, learned to walk and talk and generally comport herself with a graceful mien, at least for the most part. Yet always, it seemed, some inborn trait, some innate essence peculiar to her alone, seeped through to flavor the end product. Too often her temper made her forget her tongue. Or her willfulness got the better of her, and her ladylike demeanor would slip a notch or two. Or her impish humor would suddenly come to the fore at an odd moment. And her obsessions for chewing gum and nail enamel could not seem to be curbed, no matter what.

By a continual process of observation and imitation, of weaning the ridiculous from the reasonable and the superfluous from the elemental, and suiting them to her own personality, Amanda had eventually acquired a unique and very striking air about her. The result was a compelling combination of chilly reserve and sultry seduction—part lady, part temptress, and all woman. It was an improbable mixture that drove men crazy trying to discover which one she really was, or if by some miracle she was truly all of these things together in one unbelievably lush body.

However, as Madame Lalaine had commented, Amanda sometimes doubted her own judgment, never having had much opportunity to put it to the test—until now. At this moment, it was particularly uplifting to her to have the seamstress praise her good taste, especially since Gardner, his lady friend, and his servants had all sneered so openly at her for the past three days.

As she prepared to leave, attired in a fetching peach walking dress with a smart tucked jacket to match, Amanda's spirits soared. The couturiere had taken the dress straight from her display window, altered it slightly to fit, and presented Amanda with a new ensemble on the spot. She'd also managed to produce a couple of white blouses and two plain skirts, one in pink and one in blue, from her back room, to see Amanda through until more of her clothing could be completed.

"We can't have you walking about town looking anything less than a lady, can we?" Mrs. Lalaine had declared in her crisp manner. "Now, take yourself down to Ada Coletrain's millinery, and I'm fairly certain she'll have a bonnet and gloves and reticule to match. She's also an absolute wizardess at hairdressing, since it invariably helps to sell her hats. Tell her I sent you."

Almost as an afterthought, the dressmaker added, "And don't forget to stop in at the cobbler's shop. He'll grumble a bit and try to charge more for quick service, but he'll fit you with a fine pair of riding boots. Even if you never mount a horse, they're bound to come in handy around the barns and the fields. Much better than ruining a pair of good shoes at every turn."

Amanda paid her bill, put a sizable deposit on the clothing she'd ordered made, thanked Mrs. Lalaine profusely, and left the store feeling like a new person.

Like the lady she'd always known she was within herself, the lady she'd always wanted everyone else to see. For the first time in years, she felt truly lovely. Not stunningly sensual or blatantly displayed. Simply pretty, inside and out. Proud. Fashionable. Respectable. Truly, it was amazing what a tastefully styled new dress could do for a woman!

Stanford Darcy was thirty-three, tall and slim, with a receding hairline and melting chocolate-brown eyes that made Amanda trust him instantly. In all, he was fairly ordinary in looks, except for those eyes. The thing Amanda liked best about him, however, other than the fact that he was a prominent attorney who could advise her well, was that Darcy didn't leer at her. He did nothing to hide his frank admiration, but he didn't make her feel as though he was trying to undress her with his gaze, either. And right from the start, even when he had heard the entire story of how she had come to acquire Tad's half of the Gardner holdings, he treated her with the respect he would have accorded any other lady of quality.

Once Amanda had produced the promissory note, duly signed and notarized, and a word-for-word copy of the letter Tad had sent his brother explaining matters to Grant, Darcy escorted Amanda to the courthouse. There they both put pen to more legal papers, including the legitimate transfer of the deed for Tad Gardner's property into Amanda's name. Judge Harry Latimer stood as witness to the final transactions, as did two court clerks, and Amanda was, finally and indisputably, declared the rightful owner of one half of Misty Valley and a full partner in the business.

When they returned to Darcy's office, after seeing the legal documents duly filed, they found Grant Gardner and his attorney, Roger Peppermeier, awaiting them. As they entered, Grant looked up, cast a fulminating glare in Amanda's direction, then seemed to freeze where he sat. His eyes widened into a disbelieving stare as he took in her new, improved image. They lingered to travel the length of her, from the jaunty feather of her bonnet to the tip of her dainty shoes. Then, as he recovered from the first shock, his lips curled in a derisive sneer. "Behold, a jenny donkey trying to disguise herself as a thoroughbred. It won't work, Amanda. I know you for what you really are."

Both lawyers frowned, and Peppermeier nudged his client. "Now is not the time to be nasty, Grant," he advised softly.

Mr. Darcy introduced Amanda to Grant's attorney, politely seated her, then turned to the other two gentlemen. "Sirs, I assume you have come to discuss Miss Sites' claim to Tad's property."

"Quite right," Peppermeier concurred. "We are preparing to contest it."

"You're a bit late, gentlemen. The lady and I"— Darcy and Amanda ignored Grant's disgusted snort at his use of the term "lady"—"have just come from the courthouse, where the deeds have been lawfully transferred and witnessed by none other than Judge Latimer himself. There is nothing for you to dispute. Amanda is officially an equal partner and co-owner of Misty Valley, which entails fully one half of the horse farm, the house and its contents, and the property on which they stand."

"I think, before you get so cocky, you'd better have a look at this," Peppermeier retorted shortly, leaning forward to place a sheaf of papers on Darcy's desk. "It's Harold Gardner's last will and testament, and there is a clause in it that specifically prohibits the transfer of either Grant's or Tad's property to persons outside the immediate family. According to these terms, Tad had no legal right to sign away his holdings. It also makes such an act null and void." Peppermeier nodded toward Amanda. "I'm sorry, Miss Sites, but I must look after the best interests of my client."

Grant was smiling a particularly superior smile now, while Amanda felt as if someone had just knocked her senseless. Oh, she'd known it had been too good to last! Blast it all! Just when she had begun to feel confident, just when she'd finally found a home for herself! Tears glimmered in her eyes for a moment, before she blinked them back. No, she was not going to give Grant Gardner the final victory of seeing her cry. She might not have Misty Valley any longer, but she still had her pride.

Meanwhile, Stanford Darcy carefully read over Harold Gardner's will, especially the section containing the clause Peppermeier had mentioned. Slowly, a smile crept over his mouth. "Sirs, I beg to differ with your opinion, and I daresay any judge would do likewise. You seem to have misinterpreted the clause. This says, and I quote, 'Neither of my two sons shall sell, trade, bestow, or will their inherited properties to any person outside the immediate family, or said property will revert to the offender's brother, thus negating the legality of any such transaction.' Gentlemen, Tad Gardner neither sold, traded, willed, nor gifted his half of Misty Valley to Miss Sites. He lost it by gambling it away, and therein lies the difference.

"Now, if you would like to take this discussion before the judge, feel free, but his legal interpretation would likely be the same as mine. And if you are especially concerned with the term 'bestow,' I have several texts that define the word as specifically meaning 'to present or convey as a gift,' which Tad did not do."

"Ah, but when Tad put his property into that poker pot, was he not, in essence, exchanging his holdings for equal monetary value? Thus a 'trade,' " Peppermeier argued.

Darcy shook his head. "Good attempt, Roger, but it won't hold up in court, and we both know it. To constitute a trade, both parties must have benefited, and Tad received nothing from the gamble. Only Miss Sites gained from her win."

"We could suggest that Miss Sites cheated him, or at the least took advantage of his inebriated state."

"Nope. Riverboat gambling is a legal enterprise, and anyone entering into it is bound to honor his losses, having no lawful recourse and regardless of the circumstances or reasons for such folly. There is also the matter of the letter Tad sent to Grant, explaining how he happened to lose the property to Miss Sites. A copy of that letter is now on file at the courthouse and is a matter of record, as are the witnessed signatures and notarizations. Unless you could prove she held a loaded gun to his head, you haven't got a leg to stand on, Peppermeier, and that is not likely, with all the witnesses on hand at the game, including our own Ben Widmark, who was present the entire time, as I understand it.''

Peppermeier let out a long breath and sat back in his chair in an attitude of defeat. "I'm sorry, Grant," he told his client. "He's entirely correct. While we could pursue it in court, our chances of winning would be slim to nil, and it would be a long and costly process all for naught." The lawyer cast a glance at the opposing counsel and grinned ruefully. "Now, if Darcy here wasn't such a sharp tack, we might have been able to pull one over on him, but as luck would have it, Miss Sites happened to select a very proficient attorney to represent her.''

"What if I choose to make it known about town that I think Miss Sites all but stole Tad's inheritance, that I believe she willfully manipulated him into that poker game and then cheated him?" Grant asked, glaring at Amanda from beneath gathered brows. "With your reputation in shreds and the entire population of Lexington against you, how long would you want to stay then, my dear 'lady gambler'? Think about it, Amanda. Here and now, I am willing to pay you for the return of my family's holdings. I will offer a fair price for it. You'll still make a tidy profit, in return for which you agree to relinquish all claims to Misty Valley, leave Lexington immediately, and never darken my doorstep again. What about it? Do we have a bargain?''

Amanda was almost light-headed with relief at finding she still owned her portion of Misty Valley. It was her home now, the only one she'd ever had; she wasn't going to let Grant Gardner steal it from under her if she could help it. And she hadn't played poker all her life to mistake a bluff when she heard one. Grant was making one final, last-ditch effort to regain what he considered rightfully his—or Tad's. She wasn't about to bite at such flimsy bait, not when she had him legally cornered. Her low laugh and the humor in her eyes told him so before the words ever escaped her lips.

"No deal, Gardner. Say what you want about me. Bandy my name from here to California, but make sure of your facts before you do, or I'll sue you for slander. You've called me slut, but if pressed to prove otherwise, I can. You've labeled me a cheat, while anyone who has ever witnessed my skill with cards can readily verify that I have no need of such underhanded methods.

"Yes, I made my way as a gambler on the river. I won't deny it, nor do I hold any shame for what is considered by many to be a legitimate, even honorable, profession. My father, rest his soul, was a riverboat gambler, and a better man never walked this earth. So say what you will. I'm not leaving. You can't run me out with your gossip or buy me out with your money.

"With these two gentlemen as witnesses, I will also tell you that I intend to take an active role in the business. As your partner, I will want access to the ledgers, I will want to review the profits and approve the expenses, and if you fail to allow it, I will seek legal retribution. In other words, I'll haul your carcass into court so fast it will make your head spin."

"Don't you even want to hear my proposal?" Grant ground out between gritted teeth, his nostrils flared in suppressed rage. "Think of having, say, twelve thousand dollars at your ready disposal, rather than having to wait for the farm profits to trickle in a little at a time—in the years the business actually shows a profit. That would certainly buy a lot of frocks and bonnets."

Again she laughed, her husky chuckle grating on his nerves. "So will the cash winnings I got from Macy's share of that final pot," she told him. "Not to mention the fact that once the property was deemed legally mine, Mr. Darcy kindly escorted me to the bank, where

I not only opened my own personal account but got a firsthand look at the bank balance for the horse farm. Besides, I'd be more a fool than Tad to even consider accepting such a piddling amount from you when Misty Valley is worth six times that or more. Would you care to sweeten your bid, Mr. Gardner?''

"Would you consider it if I did?'' he responded, knowing full well he couldn't afford to offer more than he already had. While the farm was profiting nicely, a lot of his capital was tied up in horseflesh, or in deals with other owners, or in operating expenses. His actual cash access was barely more than the amount he'd already stated. To advance more would mean selling off some of his prize horses, or letting a prime deal slip through his fingers for lack of funds, or mortgaging his half of Misty Valley to the bank, which he'd rather die than do.

"I doubt a better bargain would make me change my mind, but it would satisfy my curiosity,'' she said.

"Twenty thousand, and that's my final proposal,'' he tendered recklessly, holding his breath against her answer.

"Tempting, indeed, but not nearly enough. Face it, Grant. You're stuck with me, so you might as well learn to like it and save yourself a lot of grief.''

Grant shot her a pained look. "You *are* my grief, Amanda.''

Chapter 6

IT was turning out to be the strangest day. Feeling immensely triumphant at having successfully locked horns with Grant and his lawyer and emerging unscathed, Amanda decided to celebrate with a sinfully large piece of apple pie and a cup of coffee to tide her over until supper. She chose a small table at the front window of the restaurant, where she could watch the passersby, and had just taken the first delicious mouthful when Annabelle Foster approached and promptly invited herself, unasked, to join Amanda.

"Fancy meeting you here," Annabelle remarked, daintily pulling her gloves off.

Setting her fork aside, her appetite fast waning, Amanda replied bluntly, "What do you want, Miss Foster?"

"Several things, actually." Annabelle offered a smile that almost passed for genuine. "I have learned in the last few minutes that you are going to be staying on at Misty Valley."

"Word travels fast."

"Grant told me. It seems your claim is legal and binding." Grudgingly, she added, "Congratulations,

75

Miss Sites. Of course, I've always said that Tad was an irresponsible fool, and now he's proved me correct in the most colossal way, hasn't he?''

"Thank you, I think," Amanda answered wryly.

Annabelle nodded, as if she had just granted Amanda some tremendous boon. "Well, since you will be living at the Gardner home, I thought we should get a few things straight between us. As women, you understand."

Amanda did not as yet understand anything the young blonde had said, but she was willing to listen as long as it took her to finish her coffee.

"Go on, please," she urged.

"I won't deny that it displeases me to have you living in the same house as Grant, especially given your . . . er . . . shall we say, *shady* background, but since there is little to be done about it now, I thought I should inform you, in case no one has thought to mention it to you, and I can't see why they should have, that Grant and I are engaged to be married. He's mine, Miss Sites, and I simply shan't stand for any shenanigans between the two of you. I thought you should know that right off."

The girl's run-on speech finally stopped, leaving Amanda torn between amusement and irritation. "And when is the wedding to be, Miss Foster?" Why did she get this funny little twinge around her heart at the thought of Grant Gardner marrying this hateful little twit? It didn't make any sense. Amanda didn't even like the man most of the time, though she had to admit he was a treat to the eye. Handsome as the devil, and in this instance, the phrase certainly did fit uncommonly well.

"Oh, we haven't set any definite date as yet," Annabelle admitted rather reluctantly. "You see, Grant has several upcoming deals with horse buyers and such that should prove to be very beneficial to the farm, and we are waiting until everything is settled. There is little sense in trying to schedule a wedding trip when the groom will be up to his ears in work, is there? Besides, this way we can plan something truly elaborate, and I won't have to worry about Grant being such a pinch-penny. He's terribly conscientious when it comes to the business, Miss Sites, as I'm certain you will soon learn for yourself. And I'm sure I haven't let the cat out of the bag by mentioning Grant's business deals, because you'd soon learn of them anyway."

Amanda cast a surreptitious glance at Annabelle's ungloved hands, and was irrationally relieved to note the absence of an engagement ring. Was the woman merely trying to warn her off Grant by pretending to be affianced to him, or was there perhaps an unofficial understanding between the two, in advance of a public announcement? Probably the latter; Grant *had* called Annabelle "darling" the previous afternoon, and it did not seem a term he would throw around loosely.

So where did that leave her? And why the deuce did she care? Because, you dunce, you want him for yourself, an inner voice needled. Be honest. The man is everything you've ever dreamed about, or darned close to it. Your most intimate fantasies, your dearest desires, sprung to life. So he's a little surly right now. He's a man, isn't he? He can be won over. It shouldn't be that difficult. You'll be living under the same roof with him, eating at the same table every day, and working side by side. He's already shown a certain attraction to you. Now all you have to do is impress him with your new clothes, your impeccable manners, your quick intelligence, and your ladylike demeanor. Would you really let him slip through your fingers without at least trying to snag him? Could you just stand aside and let this little witch walk away with the man you want without attempting to prevent it? More fool you if you do, and you won't have anyone to blame but yourself!

Having delivered her primary message and believing it received, Annabelle smiled. "You know, Amanda— may I call you Amanda? After all, we are going to be rather intimate acquaintants of a sort, aren't we?—it has occurred to me that since you are going to be a partner in Grant's enterprise, you really should try to improve yourself. You wouldn't want to be an embarrassment to the business, perhaps sour any ventures. It simply would not be beneficial, financially speaking.''

When Amanda failed to respond, Annabelle prattled bravely on. ''As Grant's fiancée, I have decided to bury any personal animosity I might harbor toward you. If you will put yourself into my able hands, I will teach you how to present yourself as a proper lady, and no one need be any the wiser. If you are to be closely affiliated with Grant's business, you will undoubtedly be meeting many of his more affluent clients, and to have you humiliate yourself might also reflect badly on Grant.''

Deciding to play along with the woman for the moment and see in which direction the wind was actually blowing, since she thoroughly distrusted Annabelle's sudden turnabout, Amanda said, ''What would you suggest first, Annabelle? May I call you Annabelle, my dear?'' she asked, mocking Annabelle's own words.

''Of course,'' Annabelle replied a bit stiffly, as if it pained her greatly to concede this small measure. ''Now, let's see.'' She pretended to consider Amanda closely. ''I suppose appearance should be first. While your new outfit is charming, and I know you did your best under the circumstances, the style is not quite right for you, and that color is not at all complimentary. I'd say green or shades of violet would be a better choice. And whoever convinced you to purchase that hat should be shot for fraud. It's really too bad your hair is such a plain black, but if you would get it bobbed, or frizzed to frame your face, I'm sure it would enhance your features, perhaps detract from the length of your nose quite admirably.''

It was a wonder steam was not erupting from Amanda's ears at this point. Only by clamping her jaws together did she keep from screaming. Finally, swallowing all the sharp retorts that stung her tongue, she managed to answer calmly, ''You're so kind, Annabelle, to want to help me the way you do.''

''I consider it my duty, and Mama did teach me that

charity is a virtue and I should try to help those less fortunate than I am.''

A short while later, Amanda found herself being shepherded into another of Lexington's exclusive shops, following meekly in Annabelle's wake.

"Madam, we would like to see some of your latest fashions, please," Annabelle announced. "Bring out your pattern books and your fabric samples."

For the next hour, Annabelle set a pace that would have winded the best racehorse, in the course of it all selecting the most god-awful creations and colors Amanda had ever beheld. Once again Amanda was pinned and poked and measured, and by the time they left the establishment, she had ordered several hundred dollars' worth of clothing she would never think of actually putting on her back.

Annabelle, of course, was ecstatic with her choices, and Amanda was content to let the blonde go on believing she'd pulled the wool over her eyes. Once back outside, however, Amanda quickly made the excuse of having forgotten to tell the proprietress the color of ribbon she wanted on a particularly offensive gown. In a wink, she ducked back into the store, told the befuddled dressmaker to cancel every order she'd just made, and promised to make it up to her by returning soon to purchase more appropriate apparel.

"I just didn't have the heart to offend the poor girl by telling her that her taste in clothing is abominable," Amanda explained with an apologetic shrug. The woman gave a huge sigh, seemingly relieved that she would not be required to sew such ugly gowns, let alone admit to doing so.

Next came a milliner's, thankfully not Ada Coletrain's, where Amanda was forced to purchase two dreadful bonnets simply to pacify Annabelle and continue the ridiculous farce. She vowed to burn them at the first opportunity. Then on to a noted hairdresser's shop. Here Amanda put her foot down, refusing to have her hair bobbed or frizzed. Rather, she studied a few of the drawings displaying various styles, and promised to consider the idea further.

Well pleased with herself, Annabelle was grinning like the Cheshire cat by the time the two women parted company. Though tired from her full day, Amanda was likewise content, chuckling to herself at how irate Annabelle was going to be when she discovered that Amanda had not been as gullible as she'd appeared. The thought was enough to keep a smile on Amanda's face all the way home.

After the warning she'd given him, Grant wasn't exactly surprised to walk into his study-cum-office the following midmorning to find Amanda going over the accounting ledgers for the farm, but he was irritated. The baggage certainly wasn't wasting any time in poking her nose into his business. This, coming on top of the unproductive few hours he'd just spent, was not making his day very pleasant thus far.

To make matters worse, Amanda was looking particularly fetching this morning, in a more demure sort of way. It was disturbing to Grant to discover that, even with her hair tucked up into a haphazard bun and her blouse buttoned almost to her chin, he still found her attractive. No, more than merely attractive. Seductive. Sensual. Vibrant and compelling. Damn it!

"I see you've helped yourself to the books," he grumbled as a means of greeting. "You might have given me the courtesy of asking first."

"You weren't here. Chalmers finally admitted, after I threatened to tromp on his freshly shined shoes, that you'd ridden over to Ben Widmark's. Did you have any luck finding out where Tad has gone?"

"No. All Widmark could tell me was that the two of them got off the boat at St. Louis, as you had said. They took a hotel room, which Widmark paid for, and stayed together for two days, during which time Ben tried and failed to convince Tad to come home. On the third morning, Ben awoke to find Tad gone. He spent hours trying to track him down, then gave up and decided to come home alone. He told me that Tad rambled on about possibly heading out West, or down to New Orleans, even suggested joining the cavalry or some such nonsense, but nothing definite enough to give any indication as to where he actually might have gone.''

"I'm sorry," Amanda told him sincerely.

"What have you to be sorry about?" he returned sarcastically. "You got his land, his money, his home. What more could you possibly steal from him? Maybe it's a good thing he's not around to lose anything else to you."

"You don't need to be so hateful about it. After all, I did try to talk him out of wagering everything."

"So Ben Widmark mentioned. You seem to have made quite an impression on those two young pups."

Amanda shrugged. "That's hardly my fault. Now, if it wouldn't pain you too terribly, would you mind telling me where the rest of the ledgers are?"

"As a matter of fact, yes, I would mind. I also mind that you are seated in my chair, behind my desk, in my private study, in my house, on my land."

"All of which is half mine now," she reminded him. "Half of this chair, this desk, this room, this house, and this land," she mimicked.

Resentment flared in his eyes. "This is not going to work, Amanda. You know that, don't you? There is no way the two of us can live and work together compatibly. We're bound to come to blows sooner or later."

"Probably sooner," she concurred. "What do you propose we do about it, short of one of us moving out? Shall we split the property down the middle?" she suggested saucily. "One room for you, one for me? The left half of each barn mine, the right yours? The north end of the dining room and table reserved for you and your guests, the south for me and mine? Would that solve the problem well enough, do you suppose?"

As ridiculous as her idea sounded, the more Grant thought about it, the more sense it began to make. "It just might work at that," he mused.

"Oh, for crying out loud, Grant! I was joking!" Amanda couldn't believe he'd actually taken her silly suggestion seriously.

"I realize that, but it does have some merit. At least it would keep us from tripping over one another at every turn, or constantly invading each other's territory. It might be worth a try, anyway."

"Lord have mercy, I don't believe I'm hearing this! With all your other faults, until now I thought you were a fairly intelligent man. With every word you utter, you are fast proving me wrong, Mr. Gardner."

"Haven't you ever heard that old saying about necessity being the mother of invention, Amanda? No, don't scoff," he said quickly, seeing she was about to interrupt. "Think about it for a moment. As things stand now, we are literally living in each other's pockets, and I, for one, am not a bit pleased about the situation, as I'm sure you know."

"I think you've made that abundantly clear to one and all," she sneered. "But the idea of physically dividing the property between us is sublimely stupid."

"It was your suggestion."

"In jest, Grant. You're the one who is actually considering doing it."

"Out of necessity," he reminded her. "And desperation. As crazy as it sounds, it might be the only way you and I can reside together without one of us killing the other."

It wasn't going to work. Amanda knew it as well as she knew her own name. But argue as she might, she could not convince Grant of this, now that the idea had taken root. Next she knew, the entire household was in an uproar. Ground chalk was hauled into the house by the bucketful, and Grant was directing its placement like a general commanding his troops.

As the master suite was on the opposite side of the upstairs hallway from Amanda's set of rooms, it was a simple matter to run a line straight down the central hall, leaving one side to her and the other to Grant. Downstairs was another matter altogether, and the ser-

vants merely shook their heads in confusion as Grant
set about devising property lines.

"I get my desk," he declared adamantly. "It's been
mine for over a decade, and I'll be damned if I'm going
to give it up to you now," he told her. "You may have
the escritoire in the reading room."

"How gracious of you," she commented tartly.
"And am I expected to use it there and cart every book
and account back and forth from one end of the house
to the other each time I need access to them?"

"No," he decided after a minute's thought. "As
much as I hate to do it, we are going to have to share
the study. We'll have the smaller desk moved into my
office, and split the room down the center."

"All but the bookshelves," she agreed, knowing it
would do no good to argue with him at this point. He
was like a man possessed, or in great fear of being
possessed, and nothing short of an earthquake was going to deter him. "That section of the room should
remain neutral territory."

"Fine, but only one of us may use it at a time."

"Heavens, yes!" she taunted, rolling her eyes toward
the ceiling. "God forbid we should chance to brush
elbows! Are you quite certain it will do to have our
clothing laundered in the same tub?" He was acting as
if she were a leper, and Amanda was quickly taking
offense.

"Don't be childish, Amanda," he answered sharply.

"Childish? Me? Lord love a duck, but look who's
talking! You're the one running amok here, dashing
chalk dust down the hall runner and across the center
of the dining table! Are we to split the household staff
between us also? Are they allowed to cross the lines
without fear of reprisal? And what is to be the punishment for invading enemy territory, Captain Gardner? A
tongue-lashing? A fine of a penny an offense? Getting
sent to bed without dinner?"

"A fine will do nicely."

"This is asinine! Has it entered your feeble mind yet
what people are going to say when word of this gets

out? Everyone is going to think you've come unhinged. That, or they're going to believe you're scared to death of me.''

Her verbal dart pricked a bit close to the mark for comfort. A good part of his reason for doing all this was to have as little contact with her as possible. A defense of sorts, no matter how puny or silly, against her charms, though Grant was loath to admit it aloud. To his mind, it was similar to fencing the mares away from the stallions, and vice versa. Amanda Sites was too attractive by far, and if he couldn't make her leave, he had to have some means of keeping her at a distance, this being the best way he could come up with for now.

Ignoring her taunt, Grant suggested, ''Perhaps we should agree to dine separately, at different times.''

''Perhaps you have taken leave of your senses. If we're going to do that, why not mark the linens and table service, for goodness' sake! His and hers glassware and china—how cozy!'' She stalked to the sideboard and poured herself a goblet of wine, downing half of it with one toss of her delicate wrist.

''You're on my side of the room,'' he pointed out.

''Then move the dratted liquor cabinet onto the chalk line, and be sure to put half the contents within my reach, because you are surely enough to drive a saint to drink, let alone a mere woman! And don't try to palm that dreadful sherry off on me either. I want an equal stock of your best bourbon and gin.''

''Next you'll be wanting to share my cigars,'' he commented dryly, thinking to himself that the day he viewed her as a mere woman would be the day blood ceased to flow in his veins—blast it all, anyway.

''Why not?'' she exclaimed, throwing up her hands in defeat. Then, reconsidering, she said, ''On second thought, if I do decide to take up smoking, I'd much prefer a pipe. After all, if it was good enough for President Jackson's wife, surely it's good enough for me. And I do feel a sense of sisterhood with the lady, since she, too, had to endure the unfair slander of her good name.''

It was a royal pain in the neck, and ludicrous in the extreme, to have to stay on ''her'' side of the house; and she should have expected that Grant would have his spies watching for any violation. Chalmers and Mrs. Divots, most especially, were on constant patrol to make certain that Amanda stayed within her own boundaries. Then there was Annabelle popping in every whipstitch, giddy with delight over this latest, if odd, development. It suited the young woman's purposes nicely to have Grant and Amanda maintaining separate areas, even if they were still living in the same house. At least the demarcation of territory was limited to the house, primarily because it was so impractical as well as nearly impossible to do so outside in the yards or the stables.

Only by exercising the full range of her patience and employing her sporadic sense of humor did Amanda manage to keep a lid on her temper. She took to amusing herself by deliberately and deviously crossing the mark, making a game of seeing how often she could do it without getting caught, and leaving behind some small token of evidence, primarily to annoy Grant.

First it was little things, like a book misplaced or a hair ribbon dropped on his side of the hallway. He'd rail at her, and she would smile sweetly at him and say, ''I wondered where that got to. I swear my things just seem to walk off by themselves these days.''

Once, he actually discovered her perfumed handkerchief tucked beneath his bed pillow. The scent haunted him until he finally located its source, then continued to torture him throughout the long sleepless night, as he envisioned all the fascinating places on Amanda's body where this same intriguing cologne might be lingering.

The following morning, he returned the handkerchief to her, a smirk edging his smile. ''Sending intimate messages my way, Amanda?'' he asked tauntingly. ''Are you trying to say you want into my bed?''

''Only if it's the last one left in the house and you're not in it at the time,'' she answered saucily, snatching the square of cloth from him and mentally berating herself for her own foolhardiness in placing the handkerchief there to begin with.

Grant found her next memento less amusing. Upon arising from his desk chair, he discovered that his trousers were inclined to stay seated. The cause, to his disgust, was a glob of her chewing gum stuck to the chair, and consequently to the bottom of his pants! ''Amanda! I'm going to tan your hide!'' he yelled, knowing she was lurking somewhere close, though providentially for her, out of sight. ''And when I've finished with that, I'm going to buy an entire case of chewing gum and stick every piece to your head! You'll have to shave yourself bald in order to rid yourself of it!''

After that, he found no more gum, though she did leave sassy little notes around the house. They read, ''I've been here. Ha!'' Or, ''Catch me if you can!'' signed ''Magic Mandy.''

For the convenience of the servants, Grant had decided they would continue to dine together, and at dinner she would intentionally provoke him. An ordinary meal became a trial of patience.

''Would you pass the salt, please, Grant?''

Minutes later: ''May I have the rolls, please?''

''I really hate to ask, but I need butter for these.''

Followed shortly by ''Is there any cream left in that pitcher?''

By the time she requested the peas, in that oh-so-pleasant tone she'd adopted, Grant was ready to thrash her. In lieu of that, he rose and methodically placed every dish on the table in a semicircle in front of her, well within her reach.

''Now,'' he asked through his teeth, as his own meal grew cold on his plate, ''is there anything else you think you might possibly need?''

"Actually," she said sheepishly, turning laughing blue eyes on him, "I was wondering if we might exchange seats. Mine seems to have a lump in it."

"You are the only lump in it!" he declared vehemently, his fingers itching to fit themselves around her throat.

She began taking daily walks through the horse barns, simply because she knew it irritated him so. There she wandered about at will where there were no boundaries, stopping to watch him while he worked, asking innumerable questions, and leaving him no place for peace and privacy, despite his original intention to keep their lives as separate as possible.

When he would retaliate in kind, blatantly borrowing an item from her desk or pilfering from her side of the liquor cabinet, she would ignore the infraction, which made him even more put out with her. She could at least have the common courtesy to pretend to be upset, couldn't she? After all the times and ways she'd irritated him?

He even went so far as to hang one of his shirts in her armoire, in plain sight. Later that same day, much to his astonishment, she appeared before him, modeling her newly acquired garment. "The sleeves are a bit long, but otherwise it fits just fine, don't you think?" she asked with a bright smile.

To his mind, it fit more than fine. The soft material clung to her breasts with seductive faithfulness, while the collar drooped enough to offer an enticing view of her endowments. Grant found himself practically panting. Even a cold dip in the pond did nothing to dim his desire.

Throughout the inconvenience of the chalk lines, and the mutual pranks they pulled on each other, Amanda continued to hope that it would not be long before Grant realized how thoroughly silly all this was and regained his normal senses. When was he going to admit that this idiotic plan of his was doing little good? That it was only serving to make them more aware of each other than before?

A week into this foolishness, the fat really hit the fire. Storming into the study, Grant strode boldly up to her small desk, where she was studying last year's sales records. Determinedly ignoring the fact that she was once again wearing his shirt and the way his body immediately responded to the sight of her in it, he demanded loudly, "What do you mean by telling Mrs. Divots she is dismissed? The poor woman came to me in tears and said you tried to fire her."

Looking up from her papers, Amanda replied tersely, "Tried, my foot! As of half an hour ago, she no longer works here, and it's not as if I hadn't warned you both. And 'poor Mrs. Divots' is the devil in disguise! The woman has been outrageously disrespectful, especially so since I threatened to dismiss her the first time. I gave her every opportunity to keep her position, Grant, but she refused to listen to reason."

"Why?"

"Because she's a stubborn old bat and as dense as a doorknob, I suppose," Amanda retorted, wondering why she couldn't be in the same room with this man without getting hot flashes and cold chills, and alarmingly short of breath.

Through clenched teeth, Grant grated, "No, Miss Simpleton. Why did you fire her? What, specifically, did she do to deserve such treatment, after having been in my employ since I was a boy?"

"I don't care if she's been here since the earth cooled. She is belligerent, she incites the other servants to behave likewise, and she's overstepped herself for the final time. Perhaps you haven't been aware of it, though I can't see how you're not, but she grumbles whenever I request even the smallest service. She glares openly at me, and points her nose so far into the air that if she were to walk outside in the rain, she would drown instantly.

"I have to practically beg before someone finally consents to clean my rooms or change my bed linen. One of my new white blouses, of which I own only two, now has the perfect imprint of an overheated iron on the back of it; and my chamber pot goes a disastrous amount of time between dumpings, which is not the most pleasant thing in the world to have to put up with—unnecessarily, I might add, merely because your housekeeper wants to take her spleen out on me for some reason I still cannot fully fathom. Shall I go on?''

Though he'd known the housekeeper disliked Amanda, he'd had no idea just how far or how spitefully the woman had carried her animosity. Also, a good portion of the fault lay with him, since the servants were only mirroring his own attitude toward the new co-owner of Misty Valley. His conscience tweaking uncomfortably at him, Grant offered, ''I'm sorry, Amanda. I'll speak with her.''

''No.'' Amanda shook her head, not at all mollified. ''What's done is done, and I don't think either she or I will ever be able to abide one another. Pension her off, if it makes you feel better about letting her go, but I'll not have her here any longer. Moreover, I've already promised her position to one of the lesser maids, one who is more to my liking and fully capable of assuming Mrs. Divots' duties.''

''Half of her pension will come out of your profits,'' he reminded her.

''It will be worth it to have that she-demon off my back.''

''All right. I'll go along with you on this,'' he said, relenting. ''But be advised that Chalmers is my man-servant. While he serves the entire household, I reserve the right to maintain his employ, so don't think you'll be rid of him as easily.''

''I couldn't be so fortunate,'' Amanda quipped. A sly smile crept over her face, her blue eyes lighting impishly. ''Besides, I'm beginning to enjoy nettling old Chalmers. He's rather cute when he gets his back up, isn't he? Almost as much fun to rile as you are.''

Chapter 7

SUDDENLY there seemed to be an inordinate amount of activity, an air of expectancy pervading Misty Valley, that even Amanda, in her ignorance of the workings of the farm, noticed. "What is going on?" she asked Grant one evening as he literally gulped his supper down, anxious to get back to his outdoor tasks.

"Pardon?" His concentration was obviously elsewhere, and he'd scarcely spoken a word to her all through the meal, which, regardless of his continued dislike of her, was not usual.

"What's going on around here?" she repeated. "Everyone seems to be running about like chickens with their heads cut off. Is something special happening?"

"You might say that. We're trying to get ready to take two of our best colts to Louisville in a couple of weeks, to run in a race. We've been training them for years, and now we're about to find out just how well they'll run against our competitors' entries."

"Is this a particularly important race?" She was guessing, thinking it must be, since everyone seemed so excited and horse racing was a fairly common event to her mind.

"One of the biggest, and a chance to really prove ourselves to the entire racing world on our own home ground. You see, they've held races in the East for years, Belmont and Saratoga in New York, and at Pimlico in Maryland, but this is only the second season for the Kentucky Derby. As breeders and owners, we Kentuckians have gained a fair amount of fame for our thoroughbreds. We've raced and sold our horses in almost every state, raised countless winners, and now we aim to make a permanent place for ourselves in the racing circuit, to bring the best of the sport to us, where these magnificent animals are being born and bred. And on a more personal level, if our two colts do well in the Derby, Misty Valley will gain even greater acclaim."

"Which will mean more sales and breeding agreements for the farm," Amanda concluded.

Grant nodded, giving her an assessing look. "You know, Amanda, regardless of what else I may think of you, I must admit that you have a remarkably sharp mind for a woman. Your grasp of business matters amazes me."

"That's a backhanded compliment if ever I've heard one." She didn't know whether to be flattered or insulted. "Either I'm supposed to be brainless merely because I'm female, or I'm expected to be doubly so because I'm attractive in the bargain. Is that about the size of it?"

"Not really," he assured her with a wicked grin. "But being a beautiful, intelligent tart is something else entirely. Not a common combination, I would think."

"Unlike you, who are naturally bigoted, shortsighted, and arrogant to a fault," she quipped, matching his insincere smile.

Returning the topic to horses once more, Amanda said, "I want to go with you to the races in Louisville. It will give me the opportunity to view yet another aspect of the business firsthand."

Holding his hands out before him, as if to ward her off, Grant declared, "Oh, no. Definitely not, Amanda. You've invaded my life quite enough, thank you. At least leave me this small part of it to myself, and trust me to look after both our best interests. There will be buyers there looking to make deals, owners wanting to discuss stud fees, some very affluent and influential people who can have a great impact on the business. At the risk of hurting your feelings, you would be more a detriment than an asset, and I will not place the farm's reputation at risk merely to satisfy your whims.''

''Are you afraid I would embarrass you?'' she asked, altogether too calmly.

''I don't think it. I know it.''

''Fine. I don't need you to get me there, and I most certainly do not require your permission. If you don't want to take me, I'll travel to Louisville on my own.'' She rose from the table. ''Now, if you will excuse me, I think I'll go compose a letter to a friend of mine who lives in Frankfort and ask if she would like to attend the races with me.''

''One of your fellow 'passion flowers'?'' he sneered.

She had to laugh despite herself, not only at his phrasing, but also at its application toward Ruth Whittaker. ''I truly doubt that Mrs. Whittaker has ever thought of herself in those terms, or that anyone else has, except perhaps her husband. The lady has a full head of silver hair, looks like the grandmother she is, and is the model of decorum. Though I imagine she was beautiful in her youth.''

Once again Grant found himself on shaky ground. ''Not Ruth Whittaker, the senator's wife?'' he questioned haltingly.

''Uh-huh.'' Amanda nodded pleasantly, enjoying Grant's discomfort. ''Do you know them? I stayed the night at their home when I got off the riverboat in Frankfort, since the train didn't leave until the following morning. They're delightful people, aren't they? Especially Ruthie.''

Grant wanted to be sick. He'd met Senator Whittaker and his wife, though they were not close acquaintances. To learn that Amanda was on friendly footing with them came as quite a blow. How could this common hussy, this riverboat piratess, even be on speaking terms with them, let alone a guest in their home? It was incredulous! It was revolting! It was too much to be believed!

Knowing she was pushing her luck, but unable to resist one final jab, Amanda placed the salt within Grant's reach. "Here." She chuckled. "Maybe this will make the 'crow' a little tastier, since you seem to be having such difficulty digesting it."

In the days that followed, Grant was much too busy getting his horses ready for the upcoming race to have time to argue with Amanda. In fact, the closer the big day came, the less she saw of him. He didn't even notice when she replaced his cook with the French Creole chef Mrs. Lalaine had recommended, though the dinner fare immediately went from flavorless to spicy. He not only failed to comment on her newly delivered wardrobe, but said nothing of the fact that Stanford Darcy had been out to the farm twice in the past week, with no apparent business to conduct except perhaps to pay court to her.

If Grant appeared oblivious to all this, Annabelle certainly was not. She raised a ruckus when she learned the old cook had been dismissed, and fumed silently each time Amanda wore one of her flattering new dresses. "And where are the gowns you ordered when I took you shopping?" she inquired tartly.

"Never to see the light of day, unless some other poor blind fool decides to order the likes of them," Amanda replied scathingly. "I certainly shan't. Surely you didn't think I was that gullible, Annabelle."

"What else was I to think?" the blonde asked, both miffed and befuddled. "After all, those clothes you arrived in did not display even the smallest smidgeon of decorum, though they did display almost everything else you own."

"Jealous, my dear?" Amanda taunted, deliberately eyeing Annabelle's endowments, which in truth were not all that lacking.

"Hardly. Why would I be, when Grant says he likes me just as I am?"

That stung, though Amanda would never admit it. She retaliated by saying cattily, *"Like* is such a bland word, isn't it? On a par with 'nice.' Quite dull and ordinary in describing a person's feelings. Like. Grant likes mashed potatoes. Grant likes a clean house. Grant likes Annabelle's bosom. Ugh! Personally, I'd prefer a more enthusiastic response from a man. Especially when Grant *loves* his horses. He cherishes his home. He adores strawberry jam."

"He *hates* you." Annabelle gloated.

"It's still better than 'like.' ''

Annabelle also criticized Amanda for firing Grant's cook. "What did Grant say about it?"

"He hasn't noticed yet, I don't think," Amanda admitted.

"Well, when he does, your goose is really going to be cooked," Annabelle predicted nastily.

"At least it will be cooked with some flavor. My lands, where did that man find all these stuffy English servants of his? And why in God's name did he bother?"

"The Gardners hail from a very prestigious English background," Annabelle was proud to announce. "Why, Grant has a cousin who is married to a duke. When he and Tad were small, the family took a trip to England. I believe they hired Chalmers and the others while they were there and brought them back to America on their return."

"And their British relatives are no doubt still laughing over having duped them into doing it. I have to hand it to those Englishmen. They might have lost a couple of wars to us, but they're still winning a skirmish now and again, aren't they?"

Annabelle also had a few choice comments on Darcy's apparent interest in Amanda. "Though you chose to decline my advice on your clothing, heed my words now, Amanda, for your own good. The man is only attracted to your money."

Amanda almost choked on the laugh that erupted from her throat. "Sweet heavens! How refreshingly novel!"

"Scoff if you want, but mark me well, and don't say I didn't caution you. While women like you are undoubtedly accustomed to a certain amount of attention—all the wrong sort, I might add—men seldom court your kind; and if they do, there is some other motive behind their actions. In this case, your newfound riches. Out of the kindness of my heart, I am giving you this warning. As my mother would put it, 'Why bother to buy the cow when you can get the milk for free?' "

"And have you always heeded her advice, Annabelle? Even with Grant?" Annabelle's furious blush told the tale. "Ah, I see," Amanda cooed, though she suddenly wanted to cry as she envisioned Annabelle and Grant in an intimate embrace, both enthralled by passion. "Been letting him sample forbidden fruit, have you? Isn't that a bit risky in advance of the nuptials?"

"You're a fine one to talk," Annabelle huffed, dismayed at how much she had revealed without uttering a word.

Amanda shrugged, as if it didn't bother her one whit. "But I'm not the one in the habit of giving the milk away for free, dear girl."

Annabelle's face twisted in hatred. "That's right. I forgot. You make your customers pay for it, don't you?"

Though Amanda's eyes narrowed at this latest insult, she managed to squash her anger and hide her hurt, and answered casually, "All men pay eventually, one way or the other, I suppose, when you boil it all down. Whether it's a new bauble to his mistress or a fancy gown for his wife. Now let me give you a little advice my father passed on to me. 'A wise woman gives her man quality for his time and attention.' The man who tastes my wares will get cream, not milk—cream so fine and rich it'll turn to butter on his tongue. He'll never have to settle for less."

* * *

"Chalmers, can you come in here for a moment?" Amanda called from the study, where she was trying to make sense of her book on animal husbandry.

"Yes?" The manservant's disapproving gaze scanned the floor, where Amanda's shoes once more lay discarded. He also noted, discreetly, that she again had her stockinged feet tucked beneath her in the chair.

"Don't frown like that, Chalmers. It'll give you more wrinkles than you already have. Besides, I assure you my stockings and my feet are clean. Your precious chair is in no jeopardy."

"Was there something you wanted, Miss Sites?" he requested with a sniff.

"Oh, yes! Do you know anything about horses, Chalmers? Mr. Gardner is much too busy these days, or I would ask him. Well," she corrected herself hesitantly, "maybe I wouldn't ask him about this. It's a bit awkward, you see, but I must ask someone, and you, old chap, are summarily elected. So, do you know anything about horses?" she repeated.

"As a matter of fact, I pride myself on my knowledge of them," Chalmers bragged, puffing up like a rooster. "In my years here, I have taken it upon myself to educate myself on the subject, since it is the master's trade and stock."

"Good. Because I can't make heads or tails of this section without someone to explain it to me," Amanda admitted candidly. With scarcely a pause, she pinned him with an earnest gaze and asked, "What, precisely, is a gelding?"

"A ge—gelding?" he croaked. The poor man's eyes bulged, and his Adam's apple bobbed several times.

"Yes, Chalmers. A gelding. Now, I understand that there is a procedure involved that somehow renders the animal neither male nor female, but it's all a fog to me. What do they do to the beast, and why is it necessary?"

Finding his tongue at last, Chalmers stared down at her in dismay. "You are quite serious, aren't you?" he asked in acute embarrassment and not a little amazement. For a woman of ill-repute, Miss Sites was proving somewhat dense.

"Of course I am. Otherwise, why would I bother to ask? Now, can you explain it to me or not?"

After taking a deep breath to fortify himself, Chalmers said, "When a stallion proves too hard to handle, too temperamental, or he simply cannot keep his mind on racing because he is continually wanting to mate with the mares, it is usually thought best to castrate him, which generally solves the problem forthwith. After that, he is incapable of mating, and gives no thought to the matter."

"And castrating involves what?" Amanda prompted.

"Depriving the animal of his . . . his . . . reproductive parts," Chalmers stammered, heat creeping up his neck.

"Which parts? To what extent, and by what means?"

Lord help him, he could not believe he was having this conversation with this woman, or that she was so convincingly mystified by something which should have been common knowledge to her. Of course, they were talking about horses here, not men, and that was probably what was confusing her. With this in mind, Chalmers blurted, "The same parts that make a man a man, Miss Sites. Horses are not much different from men."

"Which tells me exactly nothing. I repeat, Chalmers, which parts and how?" By now she, too, was blushing madly, the two of them looking like a set of matching bookends.

"His . . . his gonads, miss. They cut them off."

"I beg your pardon?"

As well she should! "His testicles. The stones and the pouches behind his . . . his . . . well, hang it all, his tallywhacker!"

"Oh, my!" Amanda's eyes looked like twin blue moons, her cheeks flaming. "By gosh, I'll bet that hurts!"

"I wouldn't know," Chalmers snapped, then relented somewhat. "I would imagine it does, however."

She was still trying to grasp the entire concept and

having difficulty envisioning it. While she knew the basic structural differences between a man and a woman, had even blundered into a few intimate situations during her unusual childhood, and had never been sheltered from the sort of talk that was rampant in barrooms and gambling halls, she'd never gotten more than a quick glimpse of a nude man. Never long enough to truly study his various parts all at a time. And Chalmers hadn't hit on a word she'd understood until he'd mentioned the tallywhacker, since no one Amanda knew had ever used the proper terminology for such things. "Does the poor thing get to keep his . . . his thingamabob?"

"Yes."

"And if one sees a horse standing in a field, how does one readily determine a mare from a gelding from a stallion?"

Chalmers sighed deeply and rolled his eyes heavenward as if seeking advice—or rescue from this unbelievably idiotic situation. "A mare has no 'thingamabob,' as you so delicately put it. The other two, of course, do. And while the stallion has all the required male parts, the gelding is missing some of his."

The light of knowledge registered at last in her eyes. "Oh! Those floppy things that wobble around behind his . . . That's what they remove?"

"Basically, yes, though there is a bit more to it than that."

"I see—I think. Well." Amanda cleared her throat and strove to compose herself. "Thank you for being so kind, and for taking the time to enlighten me, Chalmers. As embarrassing as this has been for both of us, I want you to know that it was not done maliciously. I am endeavoring to learn all I can about the farm and the horses, and too often Mr. Gardner's texts are just too advanced for me to follow without help."

Surprisingly, Chalmers smiled at her, the first smile she'd seen cross his stern face. "I am glad to have been of aid, Miss Sites. Please do not hesitate to ask if you need further help, although I cannot guarantee I will know all the answers to your questions."

He excused himself then, but at the door he halted. "One more thing. I must apologize if I gave the impression that I thought your feet might soil the cushions. I am sure you are a very clean young lady."

He left her completely confounded by such high praise. It took several seconds before it dawned on her that stuffy old Chalmers had actually called her a lady. And, by golly, it sounded as if he'd really meant it!

Though up to his ears in preparation for the Kentucky Derby, Grant was not quite as unobservant as Amanda might have thought. He had indeed taken note of her pretty new dresses and the way they enhanced her voluptuous figure, hiding and accentuating her delicious body at the same time. He'd even noticed that short, sassy fringe of curls across her forehead, a new and quite charming style that drew attention to her tip-tilted blue eyes and peeked out from beneath the brim of her bonnets so perkily.

The change of cooks, and the resulting change of menu, had not gone unheeded. He'd simply been too busy to challenge her on it, aside from the fact that he was enjoying the tastier meals.

He'd also been disturbingly aware of Darcy's visits, and wasn't at all sure he liked the lawyer sniffing around Amanda's heels. Grant had bombarded Chalmers with questions about the lawyer's purpose in coming, justifying his queer feelings of jealousy by telling himself that he just didn't want her and Darcy coming up with any more schemes to further jeopardize the farm.

And now, inexplicably, there was this sudden turnabout in Chalmers' attitude toward Amanda. What the devil was going on? How in heaven's name had the wily woman managed to win the stiff-lipped Englishman over? Naturally, Chalmers was being annoyingly close-mouthed, keeping his thoughts and his reasons to himself, and no amount of discreet prodding could get him to let loose with a morsel of enlightening information. For the first time in his recollection, Grant was so put out with his stodgy manservant that he was tempted to ship his very British behind back to England's foggy shores. The rotting traitor!

Yes, Grant had noticed a lot of things, just as he was now very much aware of Amanda's dainty little toes wriggling back and forth against each other within the confines of her stockings. Her shoes, of course, had been discarded almost since the moment she had ensconced herself behind her desk, mere yards from his. And he would have had to be blind not to notice how she caught her delectable pink tongue between her teeth as she tried to concentrate on her studies, or be deaf to ignore those provocative sucking sounds she made in the process. All in all, she was fast driving him mad.

"This isn't working at all, is it?" he asked abruptly.

"What?" Her head bobbed up, those intriguing blue eyes turning his way. "What isn't working, Grant?"

"This whole insane idea of dividing the house down the center."

"I hate to say this, but I told you so."

"Yes, but you failed to mention that in the process of trying to ignore you, I was only bound to be even more aware of you. It's like deliberately placing yourself in full view and smell of a freshly baked chocolate cake and trying to pretend you don't want a piece of it."

She grinned across at him. "Well, I can't say I've ever been compared to a chocolate cake before, but I must admit it makes me sound awfully tempting."

"Oh, you are, cupcake. Believe me, you are."

"And wonderfully aromatic."

"I can't really tell from this distance. Shall I cross the line and come closer?"

She gave a flirtatious little shrug of her head that set the fringe over her forehead wagging. Rather than answer directly, she added to her list of comparisons. "And sinfully delicious?"

"Now, that I would dearly love to discover, my lovely Miss Sites."

He was leaning over her now, his lips a mere breath from hers. She was playing with fire and knew it well, but she couldn't seem to stop herself. Since the last time he'd kissed her, she'd dreamed of feeling his lips over hers once more, wondered if the magic had all been an illusion or if it had truly been as marvelous as she remembered.

"Shall I start with a nibble of neck, or a lick of earlobe, or a taste of those pretty, pouting lips?" He seemed to consider for a moment, then murmured huskily as he closed the tiny gap between their mouths, "The lips, I think. Definitely the lips."

It was heaven! From the instant his warm, firm lips claimed hers, it was like riding a whirlwind, and when his persistent tongue invaded her mouth to duel with hers, lightning hit the pit of her stomach and sent sparks flying throughout her tingling body. For the longest time, only their mouths touched, until her aching flesh burned for his special caress.

When she thought she'd surely die from want of closer contact, his fingers wound themselves into her hair, sending her midnight tresses tumbling over her shoulders. This one small concession to her wishes brought a low moan of gratitude and yearning from deep in her throat. He chuckled knowingly, his thumbs edging the sensitive rims of her ears to send shivers rippling and gooseflesh peppering her skin. His teeth nibbled at her quivering lips, taking small, tantalizing bites as her own mouth sought more intimate contact with his once more—a desire which was denied her as his lips trailed the turn of her stubborn jawline, then sought the sweeter territory of her throat, nuzzling the lace of her high collar aside.

"So prim and proper these days," he whispered between tiny, teasing kisses. "Like some naughty-minded little nun who is trying to deny her natural sensuality behind her drab habit."

His fingers had just found the topmost button of her blouse when Chalmers entered the study with the tea Amanda had ordered earlier. "Harrumph!" the servant grunted, announcing his presence. As Grant groaned aloud and pulled back from Amanda, a frown drawing his brows together above stormy emerald eyes, Chalmers declared haughtily. "Sir! You are over the designated line!"

Amanda's tinkling laughter rang clear, if a bit wobbly. Flashing Grant an impish grin, her eyes and cheeks aglow as she hastily gathered her hair into a loose knot at the back of her head, she agreed. "He certainly is, the sneaky devil! Assess the proper fine, Chalmers."

"Damn the dratted line!" Grant retorted testily. "And damn you, Chalmers, for skulking about in the hall like some infernal spy! For two cents I'd replace you and send you packing across the Atlantic."

He couldn't believe it when his manservant sent him a challenging half smirk and promptly predicted, "You can try, sir, but Miss Amanda would only hire me back again, and you'd be stuck with me nonetheless."

"By God, Chalmers, you . . ."

"He's right, Grant," Amanda interrupted with a chuckle. "Accept defeat graciously. Chalmers and I have made it our life mission to hound you evermore, probably into eternity. Isn't that a perfectly lovely thought?"

Chapter 8

WHEN Amanda wandered downstairs the next morning, she found the household staff busy sweeping away all the chalk lines dividing her part of the house from Grant's. Chalmers was wearing a particularly satisfied smirk. Grant was already out at the barns, apparently confident that his orders would be promptly and efficiently carried out.

"The master has spoken, I see," Amanda quipped.

"Indeed," Chalmers answered, droll humor making his eyes twinkle. "Does the mistress have any further instructions?"

Amanda stopped short, and for one long, silent moment she searched Chalmers' face for any sign of malice. Finding none, she let herself relax once more. She did want to clear the air between them, though, to avoid any unnecessary altercations in the future. "Chalmers, that word, however respectfully meant, does not have pleasant connotations for me, and if you ever dare to address me in that manner again, I will promptly knock you flat. And should I every marry, the same holds true for the term 'madam.' There are too many people around here who would like to think of me in a bad light, and I do not want to set myself up for further ridicule.''

He had the grace to color, and rushed to apologize. ''I meant no offense, Miss Sites, and I do understand your reasoning. How would you care to be addressed?''

''Most of my friends simply call me Amanda, or Mandy, and I would not mind your doing so at all. But if your English sensibilities require more formality, I much prefer to be called Miss Amanda than Miss Sites, which makes me feel like a withering spinster.''

''Miss Amanda it shall be, then.''

''By the way, is Chalmers your first or your last name?''

''It is my surname, miss.''

''And what is your given name, or is that an impertinent question?''

''More personal than impertinent, I suppose. I've never told anyone here my given name.''

''Is it that awful? Surely your parents didn't think so, or they wouldn't have labeled you with it.''

This was the closest she'd come to seeing Chalmers actually fidget, as he shifted from one foot to the other. Finally, his decision made, he admitted, ''It's Reginald. When I was small, they called me Reggie.''

Amanda smiled at him. ''Reggie. I like it. It suits you admirably. I can't imagine why you chose not to use it.''

'' 'Chalmers' just seems more fitting to my position,'' he told her. ''But if you prefer, you may call me Reggie.''

This was a grand concession on his part, she knew, a mark of his newborn esteem for her. She returned his gesture in kind. ''Reggie it is, but in order not to lessen your authority over the other servants, I'll still call you Chalmers when they are within hearing.''

Not only was Chalmers softening toward her, but the remainder of the household staff seemed to follow suit, now that Mrs. Divots was no longer around to inspire them to rebellion. Even a few of Grant's farmhands seemed more willing to accept her these days, though this presented a different set of problems.

All of the hands who worked around the barns and with the horses were men. Many were young. And they, too, had heard the rumors about Misty Valley's new owner. While many of the older hands, those who had been in Grant's employ for years, merely resented her, purely because they thought she had somehow swindled Tad's inheritance from him, some of the newer men presented an annoyingly cocky attitude whenever she was around. They strutted. They preened like barnyard birds. The ogled her as if she were the latest addition to the henhouse. And many didn't even bother to sugarcoat their attraction to her with even the smallest measure of gentlemanly regard. They simply stared with hot, hungry eyes that frightened Amanda more than she would admit.

For the few who befriended her, Amanda was grateful.

There was Patrick Dooley, a handsome, fire-haired young scalawag only a year out of Ireland's emerald fields, with a brogue that delighted Amanda every time she heard it. He had a ready wit, a sunny smile, merry blue eyes, and more blarney than ten men should have claimed. He also possessed an abundance of horse sense for a man so young. Not that Amanda was any judge of this, but she'd overheard Grant praising Paddy, as he was known, to his manager. Because of his uncanny rapport with the animals and his slight stature, Paddy was Misty Valley's most valuable jockey. He trained with the colts daily, and he would be riding one of them in the upcoming Kentucky Derby.

Then there was Clancy, also from Ireland, and as ancient as stone. The wizened old codger had stolen Amanda's heart the first time he winked at her with his rheumy green eyes. Had it been anyone else, she might have taken offense, but Clancy's gaze had been frankly appreciative without being the least bit indecent. He'd merely been admiring her beauty and acknowledging it.

Another favorite was the resident stableboy, an orphaned lad of no more than ten. Timmy's friendly, freckled face drew a smile from Amanda even on the gloomiest day. Aaron, the smithy, with his bulging black muscles, would have scared her spitless if he hadn't reminded her so much of her friend Amos from the *Lady Gambler*. Aaron was as gentle as he was strong, slow to anger and extremely shy, with a voice like distant thunder.

There were a handful of others who, though not as amiable, were at least respectful to her. It was the men who glared at her with naked lust or unveiled hostility who made Amanda uncomfortable, and she couldn't help but wonder if she had Grant Gardner to thank for their inhospitable reception of her. How was she supposed to maintain a position of authority over these men, her employees, when Grant had undermined her status from the very first day?

"Miss Mandy! Miss Mandy!" Timmy's shrill voice called her from her dark thoughts. She glanced around to find him waving at her from the foaling barn. "Have you seen the new little filly that was born last night? Boy, is she purty!"

Amanda laughed and ruffled his hair when she got near enough. "I'll bet that's what you say about all the girls!"

"Girls?" he groused, wrinkling his freckled nose at her. "Yuck! I wouldn't never say that about no girl! I was talkin' about the new foal."

"Remind me to ask Mr. Gardner what he's doing about your schooling, Timmy. Your grammar is atrocious."

His face drooped until she expected his freckles to melt from his chubby cheeks. "Okay. No more talk about school—for now. Show me this filly that has you so excited."

The foal was darling, and Amanda could have watched it for hours, but Timmy had something else he wanted to show her. With much less enthusiasm, Amanda followed him to the stable where the mares were kept. "You gotta see this one, Miss Mandy. Mr. Gardner bought her a couple o' weeks past, but she just got here this mornin'. That's why she's in her stall all by herself and not with the other mares yet, 'cause we got to let her have time to get used to her new home."

Amanda took the obligatory peek into the stall, noted the size of the horse enclosed therein, and was ready to leave. "She's very nice, Timmy."

"Aw, you didn't even get a good look at her," he complained loudly. "Why don't I get a piece of carrot or somethin' for you to feed her so she can see how friendly you are?"

"Oh, Timmy, I don't think that's a very good idea right now. She looks terribly nervous, and you just said she has to have time to settle in."

"Now, don't be fibbin' to the lad, Miss Amanda," Paddy piped up from the next stall, surprising both Amanda and Timmy with his presence. "Ye're skeered o' the wee beast, and well ye know it."

"Wee beast?" Amanda echoed. "That animal is five times my size and outweighs me by at least a ton."

"More likely half that amount," Paddy corrected, coming to stand next to her. "Ye know, 'tis a shame fer ye to be so afeard of such a fine animal, both o' ye bein' such bonny lasses and all. Give her half a chance, and Toe Dancer'll prove to ye how silly ye're actin.' Why, if ye were to give her a wee friendly pat on the nose, ye'd be mates fer life."

"Or I'd be missing a hand for life," Amanda grumbled, unconvinced.

"Gee, Miss Mandy, couldn't you try it just once?"

She wanted to do this about as much as she wanted the measles, but when she looked down into Timmy's hopeful eyes, she couldn't find the heart to disappoint him. "All right. Just once. But if she bites me, I'm going to take a willow switch to both of you."

Paddy grinned. "I'm shakin' in me boots."

Amanda was. Her knees had turned to water, and her mouth had gone suddenly dry.

Paddy called the mare over to the door of the stall

and stood holding her halter and soothing her with soft words and gentle pats. "All right, now," he said. "Jest reach out yer hand and stroke her nose with yer fingers, nice and easy like. Talk to her. Tell her what bonny eyes she has, how pretty she is."

Hesitantly, her heart in her throat, Amanda touched the tips of her fingers to the mare's nose. When nothing disastrous happened, she stepped nearer, stretching to make one long stroke. Then another, as Toe Dancer nuzzled into her touch. "You certainly do have beautiful eyes," Amanda crooned shakily. "And you do seem to be a very well-behaved lady, as far as I can tell on such short acquaintance."

The mare nickered, as if she were acknowledging the compliment, and Amanda laughed along with Paddy and Timmy. The animal then nudged at Amanda's hand with her muzzle, demanding more attention. Though momentarily startled, Amanda stood firm, more amazed at the velvet feel of Toe Dancer's muzzle than anything else. "Why, it's so soft!" she declared in a whisper. "Like the down on a baby duckling."

"Scratch between her eyes and up on her forehead. That'll make her purr like a kitten."

"Truly?"

"No, but she'll love it jest the same."

Timmy then showed her how to hold her hand flat and give the horse a piece of carrot. "That way she don't get your fingers by mistake, 'cause she likes ya now and wouldn't bite ya a'purpose."

"I'll take comfort in the thought," Amanda said dryly, still a little shy of something with teeth half the size of her thumb.

By the time she headed back to the house, Amanda was ridiculously pleased with herself. She had actually touched a full-grown horse for the first time in her life. It wasn't a great stride, but it was a beginning toward conquering her fear of the big animals, and she was so proud at that moment she could have burst with it.

As she passed Grant coming through the door from the opposite direction, she was beaming from ear to ear. "And what has you so deliriously giddy?" he asked.

"I petted Toe Dancer!" she announced on a girlish giggle. "I really truly, petted her. She liked it, too, and she didn't try to bite me once!"

Executing a delighted little twirl, she ran into the house and up the stairs, leaving Grant to shake his head in amusement, thinking how much like Timmy she had sounded just now. "You'd have thought someone handed her the moon!" he said chuckling. "Sometimes there's simply no figuring that woman."

Three days prior to the race, Grant, Paddy, the handlers and trainers, and the two colts left for Louisville by train. Fortunately, the thoroughbreds need not be ridden the distance, but they would still require time to overcome the fright of the trip, and perhaps gain some practice time on the track at Churchill Downs.

The day before the Derby, Amanda set out for Louisville, by way of Frankfort, where she was to meet Senator Whittaker and Ruth at the train station and travel on with them. They would all stay overnight in a hotel and be fresh for the races the following afternoon.

As she reached the bottom of the staircase, Amanda was surprised to find Chalmers waiting for her at the front door, his own bag at his feet and a stubborn tilt to his jaw. "What is all this, Reggie?" she asked.

"You are not stepping one foot out of this house without me in attendance, Miss Amanda. I am coming with you. It's simply not proper to have you cavorting about the countryside unescorted."

"Cavorting?" She chortled. "Why, I've never cavorted in my life, Reginald, and I doubt I'll start now. Besides, aren't you the least bit hesitant to be seen out and about with me? People might get the wrong impression and assume that you and I are 'cavorting.' After all, you don't look like anybody's nanny to me."

"Propriety still requires that you not travel alone, and I will not see you risking life and limb and possible attack by going off by yourself. And you flatter me if you think anyone will think that you and I are doing anything improper, Miss Amanda. As if you would have an old coot like me!''

"So you have appointed yourself my guardian and protector?''

"Quite so, miss.''

"That's one of the sweetest things anyone has ever done for me, Reggie. Thank you.'' She reached on tiptoe to plant a swift kiss on his cheek. "Shall we be off, Mr. Chalmers?''

Ruth, as flighty as always, almost missed catching the train before it pulled out of the Frankfort station. She and the senator boarded at the last second and fell panting into their seats across from Amanda and Reggie. When they had regained their breath, Amanda performed the introductions, presenting Reggie only as her good friend, Mr. Reginald Chalmers.

It was Reggie who hastened to inform them that he was but a lowly servant. To which Amanda promptly disagreed. "Reggie is our majordomo, and he runs Misty Valley with all the aplomb of a general directing a war. Without him, everything would fall to rack and ruin within a week.'' She ended by wagging a finger at Ruth Whittaker and warning, "Don't you dare try to steal him from me, either, Ruthie. I don't trust that gleam in your eye.''

The trip was very pleasant and relaxed from then on, with Reggie and Frank Whittaker discussing the next day's race and England's most interesting regions, and the ladies talking of fashions and household management. Amanda had already written to Ruth previously, explaining how she had arrived at Misty Valley to find that she was not sole owner of the property, and what a shock it had been to both her and Grant Gardner, so there was no need to go into any of that with Reggie listening.

Ruth, bless her heart, had taken care of making advance reservations at the Brown Hotel for the three of them, and upon their arrival they even managed to snag the last available room for Reggie. "Gracious, am I glad you thought to reserve our rooms ahead of time," Amanda declared, surprised at the number of people milling about in the lobby. "I had no idea it would be this busy."

"I've heard rumors that there may be close to ten thousand people in attendance just for tomorrow's race," the senator advised them. "I do believe Kentucky is on its way to being properly recognized for its high standard of excellence, not only in the breeding of quality horseflesh, but for our outstanding tradition of Southern hospitality."

Weary and not wanting to fight the crowds, they dined in the hotel dining room, shared a quiet drink afterward in the parlor of the Whittakers' suite, and retired to their respective rooms. From Reggie, Amanda learned that Grant would undoubtedly be spending his night closer to the track and the horses, although he did have a room at another downtown hotel if he chose to make use of it.

Much to Amanda's dismay, Reggie additionally informed her that Annabelle Foster was also conveniently registered at Grant's hotel, a fact that did not settle well with Amanda. Nor was it conducive to a restful sleep. All night long, images of Grant and Annabelle entwined on a bed kept tormenting her in her dreams, and she was blessedly relieved to see the sun come up at last.

While the sun rose as usual that morning, it did not shine. The day was overcast, threatening rain and a muddy track if the downpour did not hold off until after the race. Even Amanda was aware that running a horse on a wet track could spell disaster, and she figuratively held her breath as the designated hour approached.

When she, Reggie, and the Whittakers arrived at the track, Amanda as a listed owner was directed to the Gardner viewing box, where eight seats were sectioned off. These chairs were reserved for her and Grant and their invited guests, but when her small party of four arrived, only one place was not already taken. The other seven were already occupied by Annabelle Foster and her personal friends. Grant, still busy with the horses, had yet to appear.

Though angry, Amanda was loath to make a fuss in public. She was about to seek seats elsewhere, but Ruth Whittaker had other ideas. With a shake of her head, she motioned Amanda forward. "Go on, dear," she whispered insistently. "Don't be backward, or they'll walk right over the top of you every time."

Reggie's lifted brow told her he was of the same mind as Ruth.

Feeling like a sailor impressed against his will, she pushed ahead. "Excuse me, but I believe you have our seats." She inclined her head toward Annabelle in greeting. "Annabelle, I'm afraid a few of your friends will have to move, as half of this box is reserved for me and my guests."

"Your guests?" Annabelle echoed, peering past Amanda. "Why, it's only Chalmers, and none of us are going to give up select seats to a servant."

"You certainly shall, you obnoxious little twit!" Amanda was past caring what the others might think now. Annabelle was behaving like the spoiled brat she was, and Amanda was having none of it. "Servant or not, today he is my guest." She paused before delivering the coup de grace. "As are Senator and Mrs. Whittaker, who are patiently waiting to claim the other seats in my area."

Annabelle's neck craned to see beyond Amanda and Chalmers, her mouth falling open in shock as she recognized the illustrious senator and immediately tried to make amends for her impolite behavior. "Oh! Ma'am, sir, I'm so dreadfully sorry! I didn't see you standing there. Of course. Please. I'm certain we wouldn't want to put you out." Quickly, her hands fluttering like sickly moths, she motioned four of her friends out of their chairs.

As she and her guests claimed their rightful places, Amanda deliberately omitted introducing Annabelle to the Whittakers. Chalmers was in a royal miff and refused to even look at the girl, and Amanda thought that Annabelle would be fortunate if the Englishman ever admitted her through the doors of Misty Valley again.

"F—fine weather we're having," Annabelle squeaked from across the aisle that separated the seats into sets of four. Her remaining two friends, a young man and woman who were obviously impressed by sitting in the same section as the senator, nodded eagerly in concurrence.

"It's going to rain at any moment," Ruth returned dryly, as if to deliberately point out how silly the blonde's remark was.

"What I meant is, it's nice not to have the sun beating down on us," Annabelle answered lamely.

They ignored her. To her credit, Annabelle took the hint and stopped trying to make conversation, though the moment Grant came hurrying into the box, she hastened to introduce him to the Whittakers.

After greeting the senator and gallantly kissing Ruth's hand, Grant spied his servant. "Chalmers, what on earth are you doing here? If I'd known you wanted to come, you could have ridden up with the rest of us."

"No, sir. Then Miss Amanda would have been left without a proper escort, and that simply would not have done at all."

"Ah, I see." At last, Grant turned to Amanda. "You do have a way about you, Amanda. Will you soon have me eating from your hand, too?"

"If you'd like," she quipped pertly, earning a giggle from Ruth, a glare from Annabelle, and a quizzical look from Grant.

The first, and less publicized, of the day's two scheduled races was about to begin, and they all settled onto the edge of their chairs. "Oh, dear! I forget what number Gallant Lad is wearing," Amanda intoned nervously, eyeing her crumpled program with dismay. Though this primary run was for two-year-olds and not nearly as esteemed as the race to follow, they did have a horse entered, and it was important to the farm that he do well in his own event.

"Six," Reggie supplied shortly, his gaze glued to the horses gathering behind the starting line.

"And Paddy's colors?"

"Emerald green," Grant answered with a wry smile. "What else? But Eddy is astride Gallant Lad. Paddy will ride Sultan's Pride in the Derby race, though our colors are the same in both."

His attention never wavered from the thoroughbreds behind the starting rope. "Blast! Eddy's having a time of it trying to control Gallant Lad. The colt doesn't like being sandwiched in between the others like that, and I can't say that I blame him."

The horse settled down, the jockeys hunched forward, the air was thick with rising tension. Then two of the animals leapt forward in anticipation of the gun, precipitating a false start. All were called back to begin anew, and the audience wilted as one. It took three starts, and finally, suddenly, the thoroughbreds were streaking down the track, throwing clouds of dirt behind them as they ran.

The crowd came to its feet, as though by standing it could not only see past the dust but urge its favorites on to greater speed. Squinting, nearly choking on her own excitement as well as the billowing dust, Amanda leaned over the rail and might have fallen if Grant hadn't grabbed hold of her waist. A tingle sizzled through her at his touch, though she suspected it was more an instinctive move on his part than anything else. His concentration was entirely on the track and the horses now on the back of it as he peered through the field glasses he held in his other hand.

"What's going on? I can't see!" she exclaimed fretfully.

"He's doing fine. Near the center of the pack and moving up on the inside. Right where he should be about now."

His arm tightened reflexively as he murmured encouragement to his jockey. "Good, Eddy. Now you're coming up to the turn. Don't lose control. Keep the pace, boy. Keep the pace. Wait. Wait for the course to straighten. Wait for the opening.

"Now!" he yelled, nearly scaring Amanda out of her shoes. The horses were heading down the home stretch, hell-bound for the finish line. Amanda got a glimpse of green flashing past, snapping the paper tape stretched across the track, but her mind didn't have time to register the fact that Gallant Lad had won before Grant caught her up in a rib-crushing hug that threatened to bend her stays.

"We won! By damn, we did it!" he crowed, his jewellike eyes glittering into hers. Then he was kissing her, in front of God and Annabelle and everybody, kissing her hard and well, too exuberant to care who might be watching. By the time his lips released hers, Amanda didn't have a breath left in her body. She simply hung in his arms, dazed and bedazzled, knowing in her heart that he would come to his senses much too soon to suit her, and that when he did he would thrust her aside in favor of the fair Annabelle.

While he didn't actually push her away, he did set her firmly on her own two feet and say rather sheepishly, "Gad! I'm sorry, Amanda. I guess I got a bit carried away for a minute."

Pulling her tattered pride around her, she replied quietly and with great dignity. "I think you'd do better to apologize to your intended, Grant, or you may have to court another bride. Annabelle looks quite put out at you."

"Put out" didn't begin to describe Annabelle at this moment. "Furious" was too mild to adequately express the look on her mottled face. "Rabid" was the word that came to Grant's mind as he confronted his fiancée-to-be. Too angry for words, Annabelle didn't say anything. She let loose with an enraged shriek, slapped him smartly across the face, and stormed out of the box with her skirts twitching madly behind her.

Grant collected his winning purse with Annabelle's handprint still vividly impressed on his cheek, while Amanda politely declined to accept it at his side, as was her due as dual owner of the winning horse. He'd made enough of a spectacle of her as it was—and they still had the second, more important race yet to get through. God help her if they won that one! She was very much afraid he would end up breaking something considerably more valuable than her ribs before this day was out—her heart, for instance.

Chapter 9

THE main race, the one being billed as Kentucky's version of the Belmont Stakes, was about to begin. Eleven of the finest three-year-old thoroughbreds were gathered at the starting line, ready to run their proud hearts out for a sliver of glory for their owners. Among them was Sultan's Pride, carrying ninety-six pounds of pure Irish magic on his back. Cadging a quick look through Ruth's opera glasses, Amanda thought that Paddy, in his brilliant green silks, must look more like a leprechaun at this moment than a real one might.

As before, the excitement built to a fever pitch, sweeping Amanda along in its path. When the starting gun fired, she jumped a foot off her chair, then groaned in anguish as a false start was declared. Long, agonizing minutes later, the horses had once more been brought to order. As one, the crowd held its breath. The start was good, the horses bursting across the mark, the jockeys clinging to their backs like circus monkeys.

Afraid to blink lest she lose sight of them in the melee of charging horseflesh, Amanda kept her eyes on Paddy, his slight body hunched into an emerald ball atop Sultan's sleekly muscled form. Then, as if slit wide with a giant sword, the heavens opened with a gush of cold rain. No teasing sprinkles, no warning breeze, but a full-fledged torrent that drenched everything within seconds. In a heartbeat, Amanda was soaked to the skin, straining to see through the downpour as the track immediately turned from dust to ooze.

"Two more minutes!" Grant growled, pounding a fist on the rail. "If it had held off for two more blasted minutes, the race would have been over!" He, too, cupped a hand over his forehead to shield his eyes from the rain, his field glasses almost useless at this point.

"Sultan's fourth back, with another horse between him and the rail," Amanda told him, ignoring the streams of water running down her back. "Is that good or bad?"

"Both," he answered tersely, watching as the horses hit the stretch at the back side of the course, almost to the point where they'd started and close to two-thirds of the way through the race. "He can't stay hemmed in where he's at. He's got to be able to break out for the final burst."

On the far turn, Paddy saw his opening and urged Sultan's Pride to the outside. Grant nearly exploded with frustration. "Dammit, Paddy! What in Hades are you doing, boy? How many times do I have to tell you to stick to the inside and save those few precious seconds?"

"It was the only place he had room to move, sir," Chalmers put in breathlessly from behind them.

They watched anxiously, hearts beating frantically, as Sultan's Pride edged up past the third runner, then drew even with the second colt. With barely fifty feet to go before reaching the finish line, Sultan's Pride burst forward, now nose to nose and running stride for stride with the leading horse. The crowd was going wild, screaming and waving like escapees from an asylum, uncaring that they were half drowned by the continuing deluge, Amanda yelling just as loudly as the best of them.

Her program was in sodden tatters as she beat Grant repeatedly on the arm with it, her voice growing hoarse as she hopped up and down and shouted for all she was worth. "Go, Sultan! Go Paddy! C'mon! C'mon! C'mon!"

The horses dashed past, their churning hoofs throwing clods of mud into the stands, spraying the spectators. Amanda took little notice. Sultan had taken the lead by half a head! He was going to win!

So quickly that Amanda was not quite sure how it happened, the colt on Sultan's right flank stumbled and went careening into Sultan's Pride, sending him off his stride just enough for the second-place horse to charge ahead of him across the finish line, winning the Derby by a nose. Sultan and Paddy came in second, a mere sneeze behind, still off-balance. Then, as everyone watched in horror, Sultan went to his knees and tumbled, dragging Paddy with him as he skidded uncontrollably in the mud. The horse that had originally bumped into Sultan was also down with his jockey, while the remaining eight, unable to maintain more than a modicum of control on the slippery track, thundered overtop of the fallen horses and their riders. Before all was said and done, two more animals were down, squealing in fright and pain, while the crowd gasped in mutual concern.

Grant, his face white with worry, was over the rail and running down the track toward Sultan's Pride before Amanda could gather her wits. She stared after him, hands clasped tightly to her mouth, rain trickling steadily down her face. "Oh, please let Paddy be all right! Please don't let Sultan be hurt too badly!" She was scarcely aware of Chalmers tossing his coat around her shivering arms, or of his own prayer echoing hers.

Sultan's Pride was up, shaking like a wet dog, before Grant reached the spot where they had fallen. Paddy, free of the stirrups, was slower to rise, carefully placing most of his weight on his left leg as he attempted to grab the fractious thoroughbred's reins. "I'll get him!"

Grant called. "Stay put until we can get a doctor to see to you."

Paddy might have argued, except that his ankle was already swelling to twice its normal size. Limping and hopping, he managed to get himself to the inner edge of the track, where he plopped abruptly onto the grass and put his head in his hands, the portrait of abject misery.

The next half hour was one of the longest and most uncomfortable of Amanda's life. Not about to let Grant shoulder all the responsibility alone, she made her way to Paddy and with Chalmers' aid helped the jockey to shelter under the stands. Frank Whittaker, bless his soul, had somehow located amid the spectators a doctor, who determined in short order that Paddy's ankle was not broken, merely badly sprained.

It was better news than they had expected, much better than others were to receive that day. While Sultan's Pride had suffered no more than a bruise to his flank from the flying hoof of another animal, two of the other thoroughbreds were not as fortunate. To everyone's dismay, one had a torn ligament and would be out of racing for the remainder of the season, if not for good. The other had broken its foreleg and had to be put out of its misery. One jockey had a mild concussion, another a cracked rib, a third a broken arm. All in all, it was a dismal day for the racing community, and Misty Valley was lucky to come away as well as it did.

Much later, after Grant had checked Sultan's Pride from head to hoof and turned him over to his handlers, Ruth shepherded the sodden little group to the hotel for a change of clothes and hot toddies. There they took stock and counted their blessings.

"It could have been much worse," the senator pointed out. "At least none of the riders was seriously injured."

"Thank God for that, at least. Those poor horses didn't fare nearly as well," Ruth put in.

"And Paddy's ankle might have been broken. At least now he can still ride, as soon as the swelling goes down.'' This from Amanda, who cast a wan smile at the forlorn jockey, now seated across the Whittakers' receiving room from her with his leg propped up and encased in an ice-filled towel. He was wearing a borrowed shirt and a pair of the senator's trousers, rolled at the cuffs. Frank had also loaned Grant a set of dry clothes until he could get to his own hotel to change.

"We almost won," Paddy said miserably. "We should have won, if it hadn't been fer thet blarsted rain."

"Placing second is not precisely a defeat," Chalmers mocked dryly, the Englishman in him wanting the last word over the young Irishman.

Grant agreed. "Chalmers is right. We came in second in the Derby, and that is no mean accomplishment by anyone's standards. The fact will long remain in many a mind that we might have won if the other colt hadn't fallen into ours. That certainly will not be bad advertisement for the business. Best of all blessings, Sultan's Pride was not severely injured. By the time the Preakness is run in two weeks, he'll be in prime condition for the race, and then we'll see what he has to prove to us and the rest of the sporting world."

"We have another race in just two weeks?" Amanda asked in surprise. "Where?"

"In Maryland, and the Belmont Stakes two weeks after that in New York. Those are just the major races in which I've decided to enter Sultan's Pride," Grant explained. "There are several lesser events during the season where I want to try out Gallant Lad again, as well as a couple of our faster mares. Betweentimes, I'll be meeting with buyers, setting up the summer auction for our yearlings, and keeping an eye out for additional thoroughbreds to round out our own stable."

"My, what a busy man you are!" Ruth gushed in her guileless way. "Quite as busy as my Frank. And how fortunate you are to have Amanda to help you, since she has such a remarkable head for figures. Of course, you already know that, I'm sure. And the way she kept her wits today, pitching right in to help, with nary a whimper about the rain and mud ruining her gown! Well, I'd say that was very commendable!''

Grant nodded and offered his thanks to everyone once more, but most of all to Amanda. As Ruth had pointed out, his new partner had proved to be very helpful today. Much to his surprise, though he'd had little time to contemplate it then, she'd kept a cool head throughout the crisis. Unlike many ladies of his acquaintance, she had not wailed, or pretended to feel faint in an attempt to draw attention in her direction when it was so desperately needed elsewhere. Instead, she'd rushed to Paddy's aid, and tried to restore a measure of calm and order in the midst of the chaos.

Even at this moment, though she had gone to her room and changed into dry clothes, her hair was still damp and mussed; yet she seemed more concerned with Paddy and the horses than herself. While it rankled a bit to admit it, he had to give credit where it was due. "I appreciate the way you helped out today, Amanda," he told her sincerely.

She grinned at him. "You're welcome, Grant. I'm glad I could be of service, but I must admit that if you had attended Paddy and left Sultan's Pride to me, rather than the other way around, I wouldn't have managed nearly as well. Poor Sultan might still be standing in the rain, while I might still be gathering the nerve to approach him.''

Grant gave a shake of his head. "Amanda, what are we to do with you and your ridiculous fear of horses?''

"Not a thing," she hastened to tell him. "I am quite satisfied to go on just the way I have been, thank you. You work with the horses, and I'll learn about them from my books, and admire them from a safe distance.''

"One of these days soon, I'll see you in a saddle," he predicted confidently. "And tending to the horses firsthand, with all the enthusiasm you devote to learning the accounts.''

"I'll see you crocheting doilies first!" she retorted smartly, much to everyone's amusement but Grant's.

For Amanda, being in Louisville and this close to the river was almost like coming home. The wave of homesickness that swamped her was totally unexpected, but very real. When Art Macy walked through the hotel dining room at supper, she almost cried, feeling both happy and morose at once.

He spotted her immediately, as if he'd been looking for her, a wide warm smile splitting his face as he approached. "Amanda, my one and only love," he teased, bending over her hand to kiss it. "I couldn't believe my luck when I saw you at the races this afternoon, and then you disappeared before I could get to you. I've been searching for you ever since."

Her answering laugh was husky with tears. "You're as full of blarney as Paddy is, I swear! Come sit with us," she invited, oblivious of the dark anger gathering in Grant's eyes.

Macy seated himself next to her, squeezing an extra chair into the small space around the crowded table. "Who's Paddy? Another of your many admirers?"

"Hardly. He's our jockey, the one who rode Sultan's Pride today." She went on to introduce Macy to their fellow diners, learning that he already was well acquainted with Senator and Mrs. Whittaker.

"Ruth, you're as ravishing as ever. If Frank ever throws you over, I'll be waiting with open arms," Macy told her, making the older woman blush and giggle like a schoolgirl.

"Whatever would we do about Lorna?" Ruth bantered back, reminding Macy of his ever-faithful wife.

"A minor detail," Macy assured her with a wink.

"I'm not certain your wife would see it quite that way," Grant inserted dryly.

Not taking offense, Macy laughed. "I'm sure you're right, Gardner. She'd probably have my head on the chopping block right alongside her chickens'." Cocking his head, Macy studied Grant more closely. "Gardner," he repeated. "Why is that name so familiar to me?"

Not wanting any unpleasantness to mar the evening, Amanda kicked Art beneath the table. To her immense embarrassment, Macy frowned, picked up the trailing edge of the tablecloth to peer under the table, then commented slyly, "Clipping my ankle would have been much more effective, Mandy dear, if you'd had your shoes on. Though if distracting me was your objective, the sight of your dainty toes does almost as well."

As Amanda glared at him and turned pink to the roots of her hair, Macy snapped his fingers. "That's it! I have it now. Gardner is the name of the young pup you won the horse farm from." Turning to Grant, he asked, "Some relation of yours, I suppose?"

"My brother," Grant supplied shortly, his emerald eyes spearing daggers at Macy.

"And how is it that you and Mandy have become acquainted?"

"We're more than acquainted, Art," Amanda said with a sigh. "We're business partners, much to Grant's dismay. You see, Tad forgot to mention that his older brother owned the other half of the horse farm he lost to me that night at the card table."

"Well, this is getting more interesting by the minute." As coffee was served, Macy brought out a cigar. Before lighting it, he inquired of Ruth. "You don't mind if I smoke, do you?"

Casting him an irritated glance, Amanda said waspishly, "You might ask me if I care, Macy."

"But, darling, after all the nights we've spent together, I already know you don't mind."

Amanda could have died where she sat. Gaping at Macy in speechless mortification, she could have curled up into a smoking ball and disappeared into cinders. Across the table, she heard Ruth gasp. Chalmers seemed to be either choking or clearing his throat. The senator, discreet as always, said nothing. Grant was glaring holes through both her and Macy.

"Macy!" she croaked out. "For pity's sake, can't you see what everyone is thinking? Will you please make it clear to them that we were only playing cards together?"

"Well, of course we were. What else could they have th—Oh! By thunder, I do apologize, Amanda. Me and my thoughtless tongue!" To the others, he added, "You see, Amanda is one of the few people I know, man or woman, who can give me a truly challenging game of poker, and I've found it a very pleasant and lucrative way to pass the time on my business travels. Which reminds me. I happened to notice that the *Lady Gambler* is tied up at the docks. Would anyone care to go down to the river and spend an evening at the tables?"

Despite being furious with him, Amanda was delighted to hear that the *Lady Gambler* was in Louisville. Suddenly she couldn't wait to see her friends, her "adopted family"—dear little Betsy, Captain Danson, Amos, Nettie. In the past month she'd missed them more than she would ever have thought possible. "Oh, I would dearly love to see everyone again!" she said plaintively.

"Well, then, let's be on our way." Macy reached for her elbow to help her from her chair.

Shaking his hand away, she snapped, "After all you've done and the awful impression you've given, I wouldn't let you escort me to a dog fight, Art Macy!" She turned to Chalmers. "Reggie, would you be willing to go with me? I'd love to have you meet all of my river friends."

"Reggie?" Grant echoed, his gaze flying between his faithful servant and Amanda. "You are calling him Reggie these days?" he asked irritably. "Getting a bit familiar, aren't we?"

"That is entirely between Reggie and me," Amanda said with a sniff.

"Why don't we all go?" Ruth offered soothingly,

before a full-blown argument could ensure. "I'd like to try my luck at the blackjack table again. I was just beginning to get the hang of it the last time."

Bowing to his wife's wishes, the senator arched a brow in Grant's direction. "Coming with us, Gardner?"

Grant nodded brusquely, a snide smile curving his mouth. "I wouldn't miss it. For weeks now, I've longed to see Amanda in more familiar surroundings."

Captain Danson was thrilled to see her again. "My, just look at you! Such a grand lady!" he exclaimed. Only Amanda heard the disparaging snort Grant gave on hearing this assessment.

"Hab ya come back, 'Manda?' Amos boomed, wrapping his big brown arms around her in an exhuberant hug, his black eyes shining with glee. "Is ya fed up wit dat smelly ole hoss farm?"

Now it was Amanda's turn to snicker. "Oh, I think I can stand it a while longer, Amos. No, I just came for a visit, because I missed all of you so dreadfully." Tears misted her eyes as she returned his embrace.

Upon seeing her friend, Betsy let loose a squeal that threatened to burst every eardrum on board. On heels so high they resembled stilts, her petite yet buxom body bouncing within the tight confines of a revealing, gaudily sequined gown, she came running. "Mandy! I declare! If I saw a ghost I couldn't be more surprised! Don't tell me that Gardner scalawag left you two broken-down nags and a pile o' debts, or I swear I'm gonna bust out bawlin' right here!"

The tiny blonde's comments about Tad, as well as her garish appearance, did nothing to endear her to Grant. One glance at Betsy's paint-covered face, her frizzy mop of curls a shade surely never created by nature, and he immediately labeled her a grasping, nasty-mouthed tart—probably even worse than Amanda, judging by his first impression.

In response to all they'd witnessed thus far, Chalmers said in an aside to Grant, "It would seem that Master Tad made quite an impression with the crew on his last trip upriver."

"You're fired, *Reggie*," Grant hissed.

Having overheard this exchange, Amanda declared, "Pay him no heed, Reggie. You'll always have a place with me."

"As will every other man who comes her way," Grant sneered, earning himself several killing glares.

While Ruth headed for the blackjack table, Chalmers made a beeline for the faro table, declaring it had been "a frightfully long time since I've had the pleasure of thrashing anyone at the game."

Macy and Senator Whittaker preferred poker, dragging Amanda and Grant along in their wake. "We can't have a decent game with just the two of us," Macy argued persuasively. "Besides, you haven't seen the game properly played until you witness our Amanda at it."

"But I came to see Betsy and the rest of my friends, not play cards." Amanda argued.

"Then we'll request that Betsy play for the house, and that will solve that. Except for the fact that you two will gab all through the game, and I'll likely lose every dime I own for lack of being able to concentrate."

"It will serve you right," Amanda grumbled, still not ready to forgive him for that disastrous blunder at the dinner table.

This was what Grant had been waiting for, an opportunity to see Amanda in action. Everyone seemed so in awe of her skill with cards, and this would be his first chance to see it for himself, if there was actually anything worth witnessing. He still had his doubts. Gamblers came and went, and only a rare few amounted to anything. Usually their reputations were more fabrication than reality, and he suspected this was the case with Amanda. She might be good, but she was more a novelty than all else. She was like a store-window display—a beautiful attraction and addition to the game, more looks than talent, though she had to be able to play reasonably well in order to carry on the image she was portraying.

As they began, he had to admit that she presented a very professional front, if one discounted the wad of gum she was busily chewing. She didn't fumble with her chips or her cards, or ask silly, irritating questions about the worth of either. Without a qualm, she agreed to the suggested stakes and the various rules the others wanted to follow. First to deal, she shuffled the cards with practiced speed, offering them to Grant for the cut, then proceeded to deal them swiftly and without mishap. Not once did she have to ask what the bet was up to, or fail to put the correct ante into the pot, or need to inquire whose was the winning hand, though she consumed a fair quantity of warm beer as the game progressed.

While Betsy was also obviously used to playing the game, the vivacious little blonde would occasionally lose track of which cards had been played or whose turn it was. Not Amanda, no matter how swift the play or how much of her attention was on the conversation she and Betsy were concurrently conducting. She always seemed to know precisely what was going on, what possible hands were showing, and what cards were yet hidden in the deck. And she had the best poker face Grant had seen in years, never letting the others guess her hand by the emotions on her face or in her eyes, though she chatted animatedly, laughing and smiling as she exchanged information with Betsy and other friends who stopped by their table during the course of the evening.

By the time Ruth wandered back to the table, yawning widely and informing them that it was time to head back to the hotel before they all turned into pumpkins, Amanda had collected an impressive stack of chips. The senator had not fared as well. Nor had Betsy, who declared she was glad she'd been playing with the riverboat's money instead of her own. Grant had broken about even for the night. To Amanda's delight, and Grant's, though he wouldn't admit it aloud, Macy was the big loser.

"Mandy, honey," Macy drawled sleepily, "one of these days I'm gonna learn not to play against you, or you're gonna end up sending me to the poorhouse. Then Lorna will kill me for sure."

"Not likely, though I must admit it has a certain appeal." She sighed, as if debating with herself, then leaned down to give him a swift peck on his check. "You have all the charm of a snake, Macy. So tell me, why do I still like you, despite it all?"

"Could it be that you love me?" he asked hopefully, his eyes adoring her face.

"Only in your dreams, Macy. Go home to your wife while she'll still have you."

After a lengthy farewell, a few parting tears, and promises to write, Amanda left Betsy standing on the deck. "You come visit me real soon, Bets! I mean that!"

"I promise! And don't you let no one, especially that smooth-talkin', highfalutin new partner of yours, take advantage of your generous nature, y'hear?" Betsy directed a suspicious glare at Grant, the last of several hostile looks the two had exchanged all evening. It was abundantly clear that neither of them liked or trusted the other, despite Amanda's hopes to the contrary.

"Great! You're inviting more riffraff into my home," Grant grumbled, as the carriage pulled away from the docks.

"Betsy is not riffraff, and I resent your saying so. Besides, I can invite anyone I want. Misty Valley is my home, too."

"More's the pity."

"Now, children," Ruth chided from her side of the carriage, where she nestled her head into the warmth of her husband's shoulder. "Can't either of you say anything nice to the other?"

"Well, you do play a decent game of poker, Grant," Amanda admitted grudgingly.

"So do you—for a woman."

"Are you ready to admit that I didn't rook your brother?"

She felt his shoulder, so near to hers, rise in a shrug. "It's possible. I'm not thoroughly convinced of anything, except that you're a born tease and you drink entirely too much."

"I can handle it."

He laughed, low and tauntingly. "Is that why your hand is on my thigh right now? Because you're such a tease and you think you can 'handle it'?"

"Aargh!" She screeched at him, her elbow jabbing hard into his ribs.

"What's this?" he grunted, grabbing at his abused side. "Macy insults you and gets kissed. I make one small comment and get my ribs broken!"

"There's a vast difference, to my mind."

"Really? What might that be?"

"Because I don't . . . because I . . . because . . ." Her voice faded to nothing as tears gathered, threatening to choke her.

"I'm waiting to hear this profound difference, Amanda."

She simply shook her head, refusing to speak. He could wait until hell froze solid. She was not about to admit what she had almost blurted out in the heat of the moment—what had suddenly struck her with the impact of a hammer to her heart!

For weeks now, she'd been trying to find an excuse for her intense attraction to Grant, labeling it as illogical desire, based in part on her silly adolescent fantasies of a handsome, charming prince—a fairy-tale lover who had unexpectedly appeared in human form to tantalize her, though Grant was more aggravating than charming most of the time.

But she couldn't fool herself, or her heart, any longer. The reason she took such offense to Grant's comments and criticisms, the reason they hurt so much more coming from him, was because she was desperately, stupidly, head over heels in love with him!

To admit this to herself was terrifying enough. But to confess it to him? Merciful heavens! What a calamitous revelation that would be!

Chapter 10

No sooner had they all arrived back at Misty Valley than they were bombarded by visitors to the farm. Several interested buyers arrived, many staying two or three days at a time, trying to get in ahead of the yearling auction to be held later in the summer. In the past, Annabelle had helped serve as Grant's hostess, working closely with the household staff to ensure that each guest was graciously received and lacked for nothing.

At the moment, however, Annabelle was still angry with Grant and undoubtedly thought that leaving him to fend for himself at this crucial juncture would teach him a well-deserved lesson—which was now both a blessing and a hazard, depending on who was viewing it. Up to his eyebrows in work, Grant couldn't tend to his guests' comforts as well as show them around the farm. He couldn't even spare the time to go over to Annabelle's, apologize on bended knee, and beg for her assistance. He was stuck with whatever good or bad Amanda might accomplish in conjunction with Chalmers and his small army of servants.

For her part, Amanda was as nervous as a bachelor

at a spinsters' convention, afraid she was going to make some unpardonable blunder at any given moment. Yet at the same time she was thrilled to have this opportunity to prove to Grant that she could, indeed, fit into his elite society—all without benefit of Annabelle's interference. With Chalmers to guide her through the intricacies, she threw herself headlong into the challenge, hastily assuming her mantle as the rightful mistress of Misty Valley—while Grant walked around like a man holding a lit stick of dynamite, just waiting for the inevitable explosion.

What Grant didn't expect, and probably should have, was that within minutes of meeting Amanda, his fellow horsemen were enthralled by her. Unlike the majority of their female acquaintances and relatives, Amanda was forthright to a fault. She did not posture or pout or put on airs. She had no need for meaningless compliments, admitted that she had never swooned in her life, and was refreshingly blunt when asked to express an opinion. Completely unaware of her previous employment, and therefore unbiased toward her, they accepted her for the lady she seemed to be.

When it became obvious to them that she was serious in her attempts to learn about horse raising and breeding, they readily included her in their conversations and made every attempt to explain whatever it was that she did not understand. All things considered, they were very flattered to become her teachers, and were much less miserly with their trade secrets than they would have been with a male beginner to the business.

It boggled Grant's mind to come up to the house and find Amanda on the porch with three prospective buyers, all of them sipping cool drinks in the shade and discussing, not fashions or the latest craze in dancing, but the merits of grazing versus graining. Or the possibilities of someday being able to vaccinate the horses against various strains of disease.

"That's a right smart filly," one Missouri farmer told him, alluding to Amanda. "She sets a fine table, too.

I'd latch onto her b'fore somebody else takes a mind to.''

Upon leaving, another said, "I'll be back, but you make sure Miss Amanda's here when I come. I told her I'd send a couple of books from my own personal library, and I'll be looking forward to discussing them with her.''

For her part, Amanda found that if one made sure the men had a clean, comfortable place to sleep, a hot bath, a nourishing meal on the table with pie for dessert, and plenty of coffee and brandy and cigars afterward, they were as content as pigs in a puddle. They didn't care how many questions you asked, or how uneducated those queries might be, as long as they came away feeling brilliant about their answers. These men loved expounding on the subject of horses, and once you got them talking, you could simply settle back and take note, mentally absorbing all they had to teach and learning from their mistakes along the way. And if you got three or four of them started at once, all the better; you got several different opinions in the process. It was like being the only student in a class full of professors.

Even the few women who accompanied their men did not present a problem. Most of these ladies were used to listening to their husbands talk about horses from sunup to sunset, and many were likewise interested in the subject. Those who weren't still divulged valuable tips on everything from frugal methods to stretch household finances to the best way to remove tarnish from table silver, and Amanda was open to any and all suggestions. One wife even showed her how to cross-stitch embroider, something she had always wanted to learn.

On one occasion, Amanda and Grant found themselves entertaining three families, adults and children, who had all arrived together. Grant arranged a riding tour of the farm, graciously including the women. When Amanda declined to join them, Grant smirked and explained, "Miss Sites doesn't ride. She's much more at home on a riverboat.''

At dinner that night, he seemed to go out of his way to praise the other women on their riding skills. He was particularly attentive to the guests throughout the meal. Afterward, when the children had been sent to bed and the adults had gathered in the parlor for after-dinner drinks, the men foregoing their cigars and brandy in favor of joining the ladies, Grant suggested slyly, "Amanda, why don't you favor us with a selection on the piano?"

Glaring at him, Amanda replied, "You know I don't play, Grant."

"Oh, that's right," he said, smiling. "You don't sing, either, do you? Well, never mind. Perhaps Mrs. Page will do the honors this evening. Her talents in the finer social graces are known far and wide." Turning to the woman in question, he asked politely, "Rosemary? Would you be so kind?"

With a confused frown and some embarrassment, the lady nodded. "If Miss Sites has no objection, of course."

Despite her anger at Grant and his blatant efforts to humiliate her, Amanda had to admire Rosemary Page's expertise. The woman's fingers seemed to woo the sweetest melodies from the ivory keys, her vibrant alto voice a beautiful accompaniment to the music. By the time the final notes died away, Amanda had almost forgotten her pique toward Grant—until he spoke into the silence that followed.

"Amanda, dear, would you care to demonstrate a few of your own talents now? Perhaps entertain us with some card tricks?"

She whirled on him, her face flaming and her eyes ablaze. The man seemed determined to be especially hateful this evening. He deserved no less in return. "I have a better idea," she suggested snidely. "Why don't you show everyone how completely brainless you are by sticking the lighted end of a cigar into your mouth and letting the smoke roll out of your ears?"

For several long minutes, no one spoke. Then, with a hasty clearing of his throat, one gentleman said, "You know. I think I could use a good cigar about now, and a sip of brandy, if the ladies wouldn't mind doing without our company for a time."

The men departed en masse, Grant's parting shot ringing out behind them. "Miss Sites, please try to remember to serve sherry to the ladies. Unlike you, few of them have a preference for warm beer or whiskey."

Left alone with the other woman, Amanda was fighting tears. To her surprise, Rosemary Page approached her and put a comforting arm around her shoulders. "Why is Grant so intent on being obnoxious to you?" she wondered.

On a deep breath, Amanda confessed, "He resents the fact that I won my half of Misty Valley from his brother in a poker game. You see, previous to this I earned my living as a riverboat gambler." Fully expecting to hear gasps of horror from the women, Amanda was ill-prepared when they chuckled in obvious appreciation. Thinking they had misunderstood, Amanda assured them, "It's no jest, ladies."

"Oh, we believe you, Miss Sites. Our humor is more toward the irony of the situation, and Grant's behavior, than at you, my dear. You see," Rosemary continued, with a wave of her slim hand to include the other two wives, "Harriet was a barmaid before she married James, and Charlotte met William when he tried to run her family off his property. They're traveling gypsies."

At this, Charlotte nodded, "My given name is actually Sharla, not Charlotte. And Will always brings me along on these buying ventures because, with my background and the reputation gypsies have for recognizing prime horseflesh, I am a much better judge of which animals to purchase than he is."

"I, on the other hand," Rosemary claimed, grinning, "was formerly known as Merry Rose, finest tavern singer Natchez-Under-the-Hill has ever known, or likely ever will again. So you see, Amanda, our circumstances are not all that different from yours, though very few people are aware of it, outside of our closest friends and families. As far as society knows, we are, and always were, ladies of the highest rank—and the joke is on those, like Grant, who believe this."

"They see what they want to see, and are blind to all else," Harriet contributed. "And who are we to tell them otherwise?"

Amanda was dumbfounded. "Grant is the only one I wish I could convince," she said at last. "He is determined to think the worst of me, no matter how hard I try to prove that, regardless of my upbringing and my lack of social graces, I am still a lady. He considers me a tart, and refuses to believe anything else."

"He will in time," Charlotte predicted with a knowing smile. "Oh, he'll fight it all the way, but if you have patience enough to wait it out, he'll see the light in due course."

Harriet laughed. "Another of your fortune-telling prophesies, Sharla?"

"Have you ever known me to be wrong before?" Charlotte challenged.

"No," her friends responded as one.

"But there's always room for miscalculation," Rosemary added prudently, "and Grant Gardner is a particularly stubborn man, I fear."

Charlotte merely shrugged, her smile complacent. "Time will tell. Meanwhile, I could do with a drink, and I don't mean sherry, either. That swill is enough to rot your tonsils."

Harriet agreed. "Have you got any good Kentucky bourbon stashed away, Amanda?"

"For myself, I could use a little of that beer Grant mentioned," Rosemary said, "though I prefer mine cold."

Amanda grinned. "Coming right up, *ladies.*"

In between playing host, Grant was getting Sultan's Pride ready for the second important race of the thoroughbred's budding career. Paddy's ankle was improving, and it looked as if it would be well by the time they left for Maryland. Trainers and handlers and grooms all were having a particularly busy time of it, and Misty Valley was a beehive of activity.

In the midst of it all, Annabelle suddenly decided she'd better stop pouting and make herself available for an apology. If Grant wouldn't come to her, she would come to him for it. She arrived at Misty Valley early one morning, three days before Grant was scheduled to leave for Maryland, and shadowed his footsteps from breakfast till supper, tempting Amanda to ask the woman if she planned to go to the outhouse with the man. He couldn't draw a breath that Annabelle hadn't already breathed, and his ears must have been ringing from her constant chatter. Several times Grant politely suggested that the blonde leave, that he had no time to devote to her now, but she refused to take the hint.

When Annabelle appeared early the next day as well, Amanda took pity on Grant. She had never been one to hold a grudge for long, and her temper had cooled in the wake of his decent behavior since the departure of their guests. She was feeling very generous toward him as she played on Annabelle's feminine ego, cornering the gullible girl with a plea for help—after first alerting the new cook to her scheme, enlisting her full sympathies, and giving her the day off.

"Annabelle, I simply don't know what to do!" Amanda wailed. "Our cook has disappeared, there are meals to be prepared, and I don't know a ladle from a butcher knife! Grant will stand for leftover pork for dinner, perhaps, but he'll want something more substantial for supper, I'm sure. Do you happen to know how to cook any of his favorite dishes? Do you think you could show me how to prepare them?"

Annabelle spend a good portion of the day slaving away in the kitchen, pleased as punch at being able to prepare a special meal for Grant, and positive that this would bring about the apology she was still anticipating. Though she accepted the help of two kitchen maids, to pare vegetables and wash the pots and pans, she summarily barred Amanda from the room, unwilling to share her culinary skills or the praise that would surely be forthcoming from her grateful fiancé.

In the interim, she was out of Grant's and Amanda's hair, for which both were immensely thankful, and supper did turn out to be divine. Annabelle got her praise, if not the long-awaited apology. The cook got an unexpected free day.

Amanda found a fresh-cut rosebud on her pillow when she turned down the coverlet, with a note that simply read; *Thank you. Grant.* She pressed the flower between the pages of her favorite book of poetry.

If Annabelle was proving a pest, Stanford Darcy was taking lessons from her. Every time Amanda turned around, she was practically tripping over the man—or Grant was, which was even worse. "Doesn't that man have a home of his own to go to?" Grant complained when Darcy's carriage pulled up for the third time in five days just as lunch was being put on the table. "If he doesn't stop this nonsense, he's going to eat me out of mine, and run the legs right off those poor horses of his."

"Well, you could always sell him a couple of good pacers and get some of your money back," Amanda joked.

"Maybe I'll offer him our cook instead. Has it occurred to you that he always manages to arrive at the start of the noon meal and he never leaves until just after supper?"

"Are you suggesting he comes for our food, rather than the delight of my enchanting company?" Amanda cocked a dark brow at him. "Between you and Annabelle, who claims he is only after my money, perhaps I'd better start checking my mirror for wrinkles."

Grant gave her a grin that reeked of male arrogance. "Offer him the cook and see what happens. I dare you. Better yet, let it be known that you'll be expecting nothing less than a marriage proposal and an expensive engagement ring to seal the bargain, and see how fast that blue-nosed lawyer will run in the other direction."

"I have a better idea. Why don't you mind your own blasted business and let me tend to mine?"

"But your business is my business," he reminded her. "At least it used to be my business until you came poking your nose into it and made it yours. Or something to that effect. Hell, I'm so confused these days that I don't know if I even have any business of my own anymore. Maybe it's all yours, and nobody's bothered to tell me."

"Have you been nipping the brandy on the sly?"

"You know I haven't, or Chalmers—excuse, me, *Reggie*—would have tattled by now. That's what I mean, Amanda. No more Mrs. Divots, the old cook replaced, Chalmers charmed out of his socks, Paddy singing your praises in that god-awful brogue of his, and now Darcy sniffing at your skirts. Where is it all going to end? Whatever happened to my nice, peaceful life? The one I had before you started tampering with it?"

Chalmers ended Grant's diatribe by announcing Darcy. The lawyer was already entering the room when Grant hissed loudly, "And for God's sake, put your shoes back on, Amanda. We don't want the man's imagination running wild while he ogles your toes!"

Grant had a few final items he had to discuss with Amanda before heading into Lexington to meet the train for Baltimore, but he couldn't find her anywhere in the house or the barn. Finally, Chalmers suggested he try the orchard, and that was where he located her.

She was lying under an apple tree, her shoes tossed carelessly into the grass beside her, staring up through the leaves toward the sky and humming lightly to herself. As he watched, strangely hesitant to disturb her, a butterfly fluttered past her face. She chuckled, lifted her arm, and waggled her fingers, and to Grant's amazement the butterfly landed lightly on her upraised palm.

"My, but you're a pretty thing!" she crooned softly. "Just look at all your beautiful colors and intricate designs. If nature had given me a gown such as yours, I'd want to show it off to the world, too.''

It crossed Grant's mind that nature had, indeed, blessed Amanda with an equally intriguing body, in a form and texture just as marvelous to behold. At this moment he couldn't imagine anything more lovely than Amanda dappled in sunlight, her eyes glowing like stars, her long black hair spread out upon the vivid green grass.

He spoke, and the spell that bound this bewitching tableau in place was broken, his first words sending the butterfly skittering away and bringing Amanda into a more upright position. ''I've been looking for you.''

''Oh? Whatever for?'' Modestly, she rearranged her skirts about her legs and began to wind her hair back into its undone knot.

For the life of him, Grant couldn't recall those last-minute instructions he'd wanted to relay to her. They seemed so trivial now. ''I wanted to say good-bye,'' he admitted to her and to himself, knowing that this was the primary reason he'd gone searching for her after all, no matter what else he'd told himself.

Her dazzling smile was his reward for such honesty. ''I'm glad you did. I have something I wanted to give you.'' Digging into the pocket of her skirt, she cautiously brought out a small piece of green and handed it toward him. ''Be careful of it, now, so you don't break it. I wish I knew a way to protect it. They're so terribly fragile once they dry completely.''

As he bent toward her, she dropped a tiny four-leaf clover into his palm. ''It's for luck, you know,'' she went on to explain when he didn't say anything. ''I found it just this morning, and I wanted you to have it in time for the trip—and the race.''

Confusion and disappointment mingled in the look he sent her. ''Have you changed your mind about coming?'' Her plans had been to follow a few days later, with Chalmers once again in tow.

''Oh, no! I wouldn't miss it! I just wanted you to have all the luck you could carry with you.'' Her eyes twinkled merrily as she laughed up at him. "We gamblers are superstitious that way, you know."

He smiled back. "So are we horse racers. Why do you think there is a horseshoe tacked above each of the stable doors?"

She nodded. "Open side up, to catch and hold good fortune. Paddy explained it to me."

"So tell me, do you have a special charm or something you carry with you to the card table?"

She grinned sheepishly. "Yes, it happens that I have a gold coin, from the very first pot I ever won. I keep it with me wherever I go, not to spend, but to assure myself that I am never completely without funds."

"Wherever you go?" he asked, intrigued. "Even now?"

Nodding, she admitted, "Even now."

"Where do you keep it? Certainly not in your shoe." His eyes were teasing her as he leaned closer, coming to his knees beside her. "Tucked securely away in the depths of your bodice, perhaps?"

It bemused him how comments of this sort always made her blush. He would have thought her long past such girlish modesty, and had to wonder how she managed to produce the color on demand—or why she bothered.

"Will you show it to me, Amanda?" he murmured, his voice seduction itself, dark and deep and compelling. "Can I hold it in my hands, warm from lying next to your sweet, steamy breast?"

Dear God, why did her bones always seem to turn to jelly whenever he looked at her this way? Why did her insides begin to quiver like leaves in a storm? Of their own accord, her hands came up to shield her breasts, as if he could see through the cloth that covered them from his view.

His fingers brushed hers aside, "No. Let me do it. Half the fun is in the discovery," he urged, and she knew he'd thought she had been about to unbutton her blouse to him, but she could not seem to find her tongue to tell him otherwise. One by one, his fingers dealt deftly with the small pearl buttons that lined the front of her blouse, his eyes holding her mesmerized all the while. Then the thin material was being pushed aside, along with the top of her petticoat. Only her lace-edged camisole hid her rose-tipped breasts from his view as he gently nudged her backward onto the soft bed of grass once more.

With the lightest of touches, like a brush of gossamer wings against her longing flesh, he traced the lace with his fingertips, as if savoring the moment of unveiling. Then, unable to bear the waiting any longer, he tugged at the ribbons, and her camisole parted to bare her breasts at last. And there, nestled into the curve of the left one, was her gold coin, shining up at him like hidden treasure upon a treasure, rising and falling with the rapid cadence of her breath. Gently, as if not to disturb it from its resting place, his lips came down upon the coin, his tongue tracing the outer circle, where it met her skin.

"Warm gold against hot white satin," he whispered. "Topped by a crown of pink that puts the blush of the most perfect rose to shame."

His breath danced across the crest, making it peak even more, as if begging for his touch. "Oh, please," she moaned, her hands coming up to clutch at his head and urge his lips nearer to her aching nipple. "Please."

She gasped aloud as his hot, moist mouth claimed its prize, closing over the pouting nub and suckling greedily, drawing it ever deeper into his fiery grasp. The world seemed to spin beneath her, her breath coming in short, labored pants as she arched into him, her only thought to get closer still. His warm, hard hands spanned her waist, moved up over her ribs, felt her heart pounding against his palms as he cupped her breasts and made love to them with his lips, his tongue, his teeth.

Somehow his shirt had come undone, Amanda knew not how or when, and as he slid slowly upward, his lips blazing a path toward her waiting mouth, his bare flesh slid tantalizingly along hers, the dark mat of hair on his chest teasing against her sensitized breasts until she nearly screamed with the pleasure of it. "You are so exquisite," he breathed, and she gloried in the wonder she heard echoing in his voice. "A masterpiece of feminine sorcery. Created to bewitch a man. Fashioned for his hands, his lips, his desire. Made, above all else, for love."

His lips claimed hers, devouring them. His tongue made a swift invasion of her mouth, stealing the breath from her lungs, his hard torso refusing to allow her more as it lay over hers, crushing her breasts and caressing them in the same movement. His work-callused hand caught the hem of her skirt, tugging it upward, baring her legs in long, seductive strokes that edged ever higher toward the delta of her silken thighs. As his body lay so intimately over hers, she could feel his manhood, hard and stiff against her leg, straining toward her through the restriction of his trousers.

Never had a man touched her in this way. Never before had she allowed it, but it didn't enter her love-fogged mind to stop him. Not now, while her senses were screaming for more, every nerve in her quivering body calling out to his. Her head was swimming, her heart pounding like a drum gone mad.

He touched her then—there, where the throbbing was the worst, and even through her pantalettes she felt branded, as though he'd burned her flesh with his. "God!" she heard him groan, though his lips never fully released hers. "You're so hot, so wet for me!" His laugh was short and gruff. "Remind me later to get a good look at these fascinating new underdrawers. They feel almost as soft and sleek as you."

Before she could think to object, his fingers crept inside the loose leg of the short French satin panties she'd let Madame Lalaine talk her into purchasing—and found that pulsating nub of flesh. The searing contact made her lurch and cry out in wonder, in a flash fire of desire mingled with a hint of hesitancy. While her body reveled in the awesome new emotions spiraling through

her like summer lightning, her brain was trying helplessly to signal a warning.

"No, we shouldn't," she protested quickly, tearing
her mouth from his. Her hands pushed ineffectually at
his broad chest even as her fingers entwined lovingly in
the crisp curls there.

"Darling, we must. Don't stop me now and disappoint us both." With practiced ease, he calmed her
with long, drugging kisses, giving no pause to let her
object anew. And when she once more arched into his
touch, mewling deep in her throat, his fingers began
again to work their magic. Stroking, petting, making
her writhe in wordless passion. Only then did he give
her what she pleaded for so urgently, as his fingers made
their foray into the hot, dark recesses of her silken body.

It surprised him to find her so tight. It shocked him
further when her body immediately stiffened and began
to convulse in climactic spasms, when she clutched
frantically at him and screamed her release, only his
mouth over hers preventing all the world from hearing.

As she lay spent beneath him, still reeling within the
spell of splendor, he chuckled and reached for the fastenings of his trousers. "It's been too long between
men for you, my pet. At my slightest touch, you exploded like Chinese fireworks."

His disparaging words filtered through her lingering
haze with the stunning effect of an ice storm in midsummer. "You bastard!" she hissed, pushing him away
so suddenly that he lost his balance and toppled at her
feet. Scrambling up, her face flaming with fury and
humiliation, Amanda kicked at him when he tried to
catch her by the ankle. "Don't you dare touch me, you
swine! You blind, rutting beast!"

"What the devil is the matter with you?" he roared,
lurching to his feet, his hands bunched into fists of
frustration on his hips. "What the bloody hell is your
game, woman? You got your pleasure, and now you're
going to play the tease and deny me mine? Is that close
enough to the truth?"

"You wouldn't know the truth if you stumbled over

it, which you already have, you ignorant imbecile!" she ranted, yanking the straps of her petticoat over her shoulders and drawing the loose ends of her blouse together.

"You're not only being impossible, you're redundant," he pointed out stiffly, his wounded pride bringing arrogance to his rescue.

"And you're a complete and utter ass! Go catch your train, Mr. Gardner, before I give in to temptation and give you the thrashing you deserve!"

"If anyone could benefit from a good thrashing, it's you, Amanda. Someday I'm going to see that you get it. That I promise you. However, it will have to wait for later." He cast a glance at his watch and added scathingly, "I've already *dallied* enough time away, and as you reminded me, I do have a train to catch."

With a strangled squeal of rage, she gave him her back and marched away, once more marring a perfect exit by forgetting to take her shoes with her. Grant stared after her, shaking his head, still trying to figure out what had gone wrong just at that most crucial stage of their lovemaking. One minute she'd been as hot as brimstone, and the next as cold as ice.

A glimmer of gold caught his eye, and he bent to retrieve her lucky coin from the crushed grass at his feet. "Next time, Amanda, my lovely, unpredictable vixen," he vowed as he slipped her talisman into his shirt pocket to rest alongside the four-leaf clover she'd given him. "For now, we'll see how well you fare without your special charm—or what you might do to get it back."

Chapter 11

AMANDA considered not going to Maryland at all, then decided staying home would amount to snipping off her own nose to spite her face. She wanted to be there to see Sultan's Pride run in the Preakness, especially if he and Paddy should win this time around. Grant she would rather not see, but Amanda was realistic enough to know that she would have to face him again sometime, and it might as well be while she was still angry with him, since her anger served as a fair defense against his devilish charm.

Thinking of charms reminded her of the second reason she resented Grant just now. The wily rat had taken her gold coin. She was sure of it. When she'd realized it was missing, she'd gone back to the orchard to find it, searching in vain. Though it might be lost somewhere on the path to the house, Amanda was willing to bet her bottom dollar that Grant had pocketed it, and she was going to hound the living daylights out of him until he gave it back, if it took the rest of her life—or his, whichever was shorter.

And the way she was feeling toward him now, he was living on borrowed time.

The third, and perhaps the most important, reason Amanda chose to travel to Baltimore was that she was sadly in need of advice. While she knew that what she and Grant had done in the orchard was not sufficient to bring about a pregnancy, there was another matter about which she was not as certain. None of her childhood adventures, her reading, or her gossiping with Betsy and the other girls had ever fully explained what constituted loss of virginity. Her adopted riverboat family, recognizing her innocence, had chosen to shield her from the most intimate facts of life, even in the midst of their own, often ribald behavior.

Certainly this was one question Amanda did not feel free to ask Chalmers. Nor was there anyone else she might ask, at least not anywhere around Lexington. Though a local doctor might advise her, Lord only knew whom he might tell.

Going to Baltimore would be the perfect solution. There must be a hundred physicians in a city that size, and the likelihood of ever again seeing the one she chose would be next to nil. Not that the man could do anything to remedy the situation if she learned she was no longer a maiden, but at least she would know whether or not her momentary lapse of common sense had rendered her as soiled as she was stupid. And if Grant had ruined her for marriage to another man, gelding would be too good for the randy buzzard!

This time, she and Chalmers checked into the same hotel where Grant was staying. In fact, Grant had made advance reservations for them there. Making an appointment with a nearby doctor was child's play compared to dodging Chalmers, who faithfully dogged her every step. Amanda finally had to resort to claiming a stomach ailment in order to justify a trip to the doctor's office, and Chalmers, dutiful as always, sat in the waiting room while she spoke with the physician on the other side of what she was positive was a very thin door. Still and all, she was grateful the Englishman hadn't insisted on accompanying her inside the examining room.

In the end, red-faced but relieved, Amanda was pleased to discover that she was still as pure as driven snow, at least technically speaking. The doctor even proved to have a sense of humor about it all, sending her on her way with a huge bottle of chalky tablets guaranteed to counter her bilious stomach and provide a sufficient and harmless alibi for Chalmers at the same time—the only problem being that Reggie insisted on seeing her chew the blasted pills after every meal, as directed.

The fake illness did provide her with the perfect excuse to order a meal sent to her room that evening and avoid Grant until the next day at the racetrack. Even then, he stayed with Paddy through the preliminary races, coming to the stands scant minutes before the start of the main event. By this time both of them were too excited about the upcoming contest to be bothered with personal bickering.

"How does it look, sir?" Chalmers inquired, just as nervous as they were.

"Sultan is in prime condition and eager to run. Never better."

"And Paddy?" Amanda asked stiffly, still seething over her last encounter with Grant. "How is his ankle?"

"We've taped it just in case he should get a good bump, but he claims it feels fine."

"And no chance of rain today," Chalmers added on a breath of relief.

Another thing that made Amanda feel better was that Annabelle had not come to Baltimore. It seemed the two people who had remained seated with her at the Derby were Annabelle's cousins, who had been acting as her escorts that weekend. To her parents' minds, Baltimore was simply out of the question, too far to travel to since a proper chaperone was not available for the trip.

The race began, and all outside thoughts flew from their heads, the three of them concentrating solely on Paddy and Sultan's Pride. Once again, emerald green was the color of the day. They had drawn a better starting position closer to the inside of the track this time, Sultan bearing the number two slot. This pleased Grant immensely. Amanda also thought it boded well for them, since two had always been one of her luckiest numbers.

As the starting gun went off, she instinctively reached for the spot where her gold coin usually rested, muttering an oath as she failed to find it. Darn Grant anyway! If they lost, she would blame it all on him for taking her charm!

As if to borrow a little of her good fortune back from him, she reached out and grabbed his sleeve as the horses went streaking down the track. She felt him stiffen, sensing his frown rather than actually seeing it, with her gaze riveted on their horse. "What is it?"

Above the noise of the crowd, he leaned into her and yelled, "Sultan is almost too eager for it. He wants out of the pack, and it's too early yet to allow him to run full out. Paddy is having a devil of a time trying to convince Sultan of that, though."

Wanting to see for herself, miffed that he could view the race much better with his field glasses than she could with her naked eye, Amanda yanked the binoculars from his grasp, uncaring that she almost tore his head from his shoulders as she brought the lenses to her own eyes. She ignored his choked bellow of protest, ignored also the way the strap of the field glasses, still wrapped around his neck, was practically strangling him. His head was forced toward hers at an odd angle, his eyes nearly bulging by the time he managed to disentangle himself and stand upright once more. With a final glare, he turned his attention to the race.

Amanda could now see it for herself. Sultan seemed to be straining at the bit, impatient at being held back when all he wanted to do, all he'd been taught to do, was to run like the wind. To his credit, Paddy kept him down until the final turn was made. They were running on the inside, second from the front, when the lead horse angled a bit too wide for the turn. With nothing but open space before him, Sultan broke free, his long, powerful legs pumping. Magnificent to behold. Making it all look so effortless and deceptively easy as he forged onward toward the finish line.

One length ahead. Two—as the crowd went wild! Ladylike demeanor abandoned, Amanda was leaping about like a mad frog, screaming to the limit of her lungs, just as crazy as the rest. Behind her, Chalmers was yelling like a banshee, uncaring for once of the spectacle he might be making of himself. The grin on Grant's face widened with each ground-eating stride Sultan look, his chest expanding with the prayerful breath he held. As Sultan crossed the finish line a full four body lengths ahead of his nearest competitor, that breath exploded from him in a wild whoop of pure exultation.

Once more Amanda found herself whirled about in his hard embrace, giddy as his arms squashed her ribs together. Briefly, she wondered if he was paying her back for nearly decapitating him minutes before. Their laughter blending, Grant crushed her against him—to the accompaniment of Chalmers thumping them both on the back in his own excitement as they all shouted their joy.

"We did it!"

"We won!"

"God, what a glorious moment! I wish I could freeze it and keep it fresh forever."

By the time Grant thought to release her, Amanda was gasping for air, and funny yellow spots were dancing before her eyes. But she hadn't been this outrageously happy since she'd won Misty Valley. This trip, she was at his side as he went to collect his prize money, watched proudly as he accepted the coveted trophy, posed with him and Paddy and Sultan's Pride as a Baltimore newspaper photographer snapped their picture, recording their moment of triumph for posterity. It was a victory they would cherish always, no matter how many more were to come in the future.

A celebration was in order, and personal animosities were put aside, temporarily forgotten. In honor of the win, and of all the hard work that had gone into making it possible, Grant treated the lot of them, trainers and handlers included, to the fanciest supper in the grandest restaurant Baltimore had to offer. Even the two stablehands who had been left behind to guard their prize stallion had supper catered to them, minus the accompanying champagne the rest of them indulged in so freely. Sultan's Pride was even more valuable now, and Grant was taking no chance of anything happening to him.

If Amanda had been giddy with joy before, she was more so now, as the night wore on and her glass was refilled time and again despite her objections. While her tolerance for beer and whiskey was remarkable, champagne went straight to her brain. Perhaps it had something to do with the bubbles; Amanda didn't really know. All she knew was that she'd never been able to drink much of the stuff without getting tipsy.

Besides making her head spin, it had the odd effect of making her blood warm drastically. Soon her flesh would burn, as if with fever, and become so sensitive to touch that the brush of her own clothing against her skin was almost intolerable.

As the evening progressed, Grant made certain that Amanda's champagne glass was never empty. Amid the laughter and gaiety of the celebration, it was ridiculously easy to do so, and she was consuming far more than she would ever believe, he was sure. Her laughter turned to giggles, not the irritating high-pitched noise that so many women affected, but a low, throaty ripple that seduced the listener, and Grant most of all. Before too long, she began to fan herself with her hand. Her face became attractively flushed. Her eyes sparkled like brilliant blue topaz, much more bright than normal. She was definitely assuming the glad glow and carefree attitude that marked a mild state of inebriation, though her speech had not yet begun to slur and she was still fairly steady on her feet.

Which was exactly what Grant wanted. He wanted her relaxed enough, happy enough, to willingly follow his lead, but not so drunk that she would be oblivious to what she was doing or unable to participate fully. Hiding a wide grin, he patted his vest pocket, feeling the raised shape of the small gold coin. Maybe it was lucky after all, to him as well as to her. When his conscience gave an ugly twinge, telling him he should be ashamed of himself for what he was planning, and for the underhanded method he was employing to achieve his ends, he justified his actions easily. She'd teased him since the moment they'd met; she'd only be getting what she deserved, what she'd been asking for all along. And this time he'd be getting what he wanted, too. After all, it wasn't as if she were some untouched innocent.

When Amanda started to fidget and pluck at her dress, as if to cool the skin beneath it, Grant judged that she'd had enough to drink. If he didn't want her senseless, it was time to go. Nudging Chalmers, he said, "I'm going to take Amanda back to the hotel. I think she's had enough revelry for one evening."

"Oh, fine," the gentleman agreed. "I'll come along."

"There's really no need for you to curtail your fun so early," Grant told him. "Some of the men are going to see if they can get a game of cards going, maybe find some other amusing ways to spend their bonuses. I'm sure they wouldn't mind if you tagged along."

"What about you, sir?"

"I think I'll turn in early. I didn't get much sleep last night for thinking about today's race." It wasn't really a lie, just not the whole truth. When he turned in, it wouldn't be to sleep.

"Well, if you're sure it won't be an inconvenience, sir," Chalmers said, weakening.

"I'm positive." Before Chalmers could change his mind, Grant collected a rather woozy Amanda and left.

All the way to their hotel, she cuddled sleepily next to him in the carriage, inflaming his ardor even more. He could only hope he hadn't misjudged and let her drink too much. This was definitely not the time to have her pass out on him.

She started to squirm, and he asked, "What's the matter, pet? Too warm?"

To his stunned delight, she admitted outright. "Lands, yes! I should have known better than to consume so much champagne. It always makes my skin feel as if it's on fire. I can't wait to get back to my room and be rid of these clothes. I swear they're chafing the flesh right off me!"

This was more than he could have hoped for, and he almost shouted with glee. Damn! If he'd known the bubbly brew would affect her this way, he'd have served it to her sooner. He'd heard of various foods which were touted as having strange results on people, arousing them and making them react oddly. Prickly, sensitive skin. Heightened sensuality. Amorous behavior. Amanda wasn't merely tipsy, it seemed. Either she was having an adverse skin irritation to the champagne, or it was acting as an aphrodisiac on her system! And unless he missed his guess, it was the latter, for she was practically rubbing herself against him and purring like a cat in heat!

Their hotel boasted an elevator for the convenience of its patrons, and it was all Grant could do to prevent Amanda from embarrassing the young man operating the conveyance, as she kept attempting to unbutton the top of her dress on the way up to their floor, then all the way down the hallway. By the time he gently pushed her into her room, followed, and locked the door behind them, she had her dress half off, her shoes discarded, and one stocking dangling from her fingertips. She was staring at it and giggling, as if it were the funniest sight in the world.

Flopping onto the bed faceup, she wriggled her toes and declared, "Ooh! I feel sooo good! Except for these dratted clothes!" she qualified, immediately resuming her attempt to remove them, but having difficulty with the fastenings.

Laughing with her, Grant approached the bed. "Here, my passion princess, let me assist you, or you're liable to get yourself so tied up in them, it will take an army to get you free again."

"Passion princess!" she trilled, lifting her arm at his instruction and watching, fascinated, as he pulled her sleeve loose from it. "Oh, Grant! You say the silliest things sometimes!"

"Do I?" he returned dryly, shaking his head at her and smiling to himself. One way or another, tonight was going to prove very interesting!

With nary a murmur of protest, she allowed him to undress her, until she lay gloriously nude before him, clad in only a rosy blush and her streaming black hair, resembling nothing so much as a mythical sea siren. Looking down at her, Grant could understand why sailors had been lured to such as she. Amanda was perfectly formed, from those wavy midnight tresses that flowed halfway down her back, to her heart-shaped bottom with an enticing dimple in each taut cheek, to her dainty toes, the nails of which were painted a pale pink, an erotic sight that sent Grant's temperature soaring higher than mercury on a midsummer afternoon.

Milk-white flawless skin, pert uptilted breasts, hips that flared out from an impossibly small waist and melted into incredibly long, beautiful legs. Exotic eyes that hinted at sensual secrets, and lips as soft and full as rose petals. Everything a man would ever dream of; all he could ever desire.

As he began to rid himself of his own clothing, she watched, her misty gaze adoring him. All the while her hands rubbed at her own skin, teasing him with the thought of what they would feel like caressing him, arousing him to the point that he had difficulty divesting himself of his trousers.

When he came to her at last, she opened her arms wide to him. "Take me! I'm yours!" she declared on a giggle, borrowing a line from a risqué novel she had once filched from one of her father's mistresses.

"You will be. Soon," he promised, hoping her amusement would abate enough that she would not view his amorous advances in a ludicrous light. Laughter was one thing, ridicule quite another.

He needn't have worried. The champagne, combined with the feel of his flesh stroking hers, soon had her writhing in ecstatic torment. Every kiss, every caress, had her begging boldly for more. "Yes! Touch me! More!"

He teased her unbearably, employing his tongue and teeth, nipping playfully, bathing away the small hurt with wet, warm kisses, until no spot on her body had not felt the fire of his touch. Likewise, he urged her to caress him, surprised at the light, tentative exploration of her trembling hands, the look of dawning delight on her face, almost as if she were discovering it all for the first time. As a sensual ploy, it was very effective, the most erotic he'd ever experienced, sending his passions spiraling. She was good—smart enough to know that there was nothing as provocative as innocence on the verge of surrender, nothing that would bring out a man's urge to conquer more quickly or more forcefully.

Her nose nuzzled into the fur on his chest, her tongue slipping out to lap at the flat nipples hiding there, her lips lingering to suckle at them as he had done to hers. She sighed and rubbed the length of her body along his, enjoying the light abrasion, the difference in texture between his skin and hers. Her fingers found his swollen manhood, and she stroked it lightly, lovingly, laughing seductively as it jerked against her palm. "So soft, yet so hard. You're beautiful, Grant. So incredibly fascinating."

His answer was to curl her fingers more tightly about his throbbing member, at the same time capturing her lips in a searing kiss that left them both panting, arching into one another. "Tell me you want me," he urged, needing to hear her admit it after all her teasing.

"I want you," she gasped, as his fingers found the proof of her claim, delving into her hot, honeyed body, feeling her quiver in reaction. His lips traced a tantalizing path across her chest, finally claiming the rosy crest of her breast. She lurched, her silken chamber clutching more tightly at his fingers. "Oh, mercy! How I want you!" she whimpered, almost weeping in her intense need.

He moved over her, nudging her thighs apart, settling her legs about his hips when she seemed incapable of doing so herself. "Look at me, Amanda," he demanded huskily. "I want you to know who is making love to you. I won't be just any other man, some nameless face in your bed. Say my name. Let me hear it come from your lips as I make you mine."

As he plunged into her quaking body, his name emerged on a startled exclamation. Her fingers caught his forearms, curving into talons that bit into his skin. Her eyes clenched tightly, her breath coming in short, shallow pants.

And then he knew. Knew what he had never expected to discover. Her innocence had been real. She'd been a virgin. The act, the deception, had been the other way around. This riverboat cardsharp who dressed the part of a trollop, this hoyden with the body of a courtesan and the smile of a fallen angel, had never known a man's body until now. Until his.

"You should have told me," he said, stunned,

his body still held tightly within the hot depths of hers.

She shook her head, her lashes fluttering open, her eyes finding his. "It's all right. Please. The hurt is nearly gone." She pulled him down where she could reach his mouth. "Kiss me again. Love me," she murmured, her lips trembling against his.

He could not have denied her at that moment if his life had depended upon it. Once his lips touched hers, the flames which had been banked flared anew. Tenderly he kissed her temples, whispered softly in her ear, caressed and petted her until she was arching into his touch, bringing him deeper inside her. And then he was moving over her, in her. Long, smooth strokes that sent desire crashing through them like waves driven by a hurricane wind. The splendor built ever higher until at last they rode the crest of passion—and this time her ecstatic cry was one of rapture, blending perfectly with him.

"I love you." She sighed on a final shudder, her dewy lashes drifting shut as she snuggled into his arms and pillowed her head on his shoulder.

She slept then, cradled in his embrace, while Grant wrestled with his conflicting emotions. Shock, shame, indignation. Guilt and confusion. All mingled with the tingling remnants of the most spectacular night of lovemaking he'd ever known. In the end, anger salvaged his bruised pride, spurring him to leave her bed. Tomorrow they would talk. Tomorrow he would wring an explanation from her, one that would let him live with himself and what he had done this night.

Taking care not to wake her, for he had yet to sort through this emotional tangle and did not want to face her until he could speak with her more calmly and rationally, he gathered his clothes from the floor and dressed. As he pulled on his vest, her coin fell from the pocket, yet another reminder of his devious maneuvering. It was hers, her talisman against bad luck, and if he had not taken it from her, perhaps she would still have her virtue, the innocence he'd so arrogantly stolen from her.

Carefully, he placed the coin on the stand near the bed, where she would see it when she woke. He could not replace her purity so easily. Would that he could! But he could return her charm, and perhaps some of the good fortune she'd lost with it.

Chapter 12

THE first thing Amanda noticed when she began to awaken that morning was that Grant was gone. She was alone in her hotel bed, with only sweet memories of the night before to warm her. And what marvelous remembrances they were! None of her fantasies, or the bits of information she'd gleaned from her women friends, had prepared her for the wondrous reality of lovemaking such as she'd discovered with Grant. It had been so breathtaking, so much more magnificent than anything she'd ever expected! Even now she felt aglow with lingering pleasure, her longing pulsing anew as she recalled the splendor of his touch, his lips, the scent and feel of him, the power of their desire, the rapture that had burst upon them.

Though disappointed that he had not stayed with her until morning, she wasn't really surprised. His sense of propriety most likely would not allow them to be discovered together in such a compromising situation—at least not until he had broken off with Annabelle and announced that he and Amanda were to be wed.

Feminine instinct assured her that Grant did not love Annabelle. The relationship between the couple seemed so lackluster matched against the fiery passion he and Amanda had shared. She could not imagine Grant, or any reasonable person, actually preferring a dull partner over an exciting one—especially after last night. Why, that would be like settling for plain vanilla ice cream when the strawberry flavor you craved was yours for the asking!

It wasn't until she rolled her head on the pillow that she realized two very disturbing facts. Her head was pounding fit to fall off, thanks to all the champagne she'd drunk the previous evening. The pain was excruciating—but nothing compared to the intense agony that struck her heart when she saw the glimmer of gold on the night table near her head. Her coin! Waves of the most powerful anguish she'd ever felt poured through her.

"No!" she whispered. "Oh, dear Lord, no!" Tears sprang to her eyes, her heart twisting within her breast. As if to torment her further, crisp images of their lovemaking flashed through her mind—Grant's hands exploring her naked body; hers caressing him so intimately; long, tantalizing kisses that had burned into her very soul; that hurtful-poignant moment when he'd made her his, and the glory they had shared soon after; Amanda admitting her love to him.

It dawned on her now that he had never responded in kind, that all through their loving he'd not once told her of his love for her, though he had praised her beauty, her body. What a fool she'd been! Such a crazy, stupid fool, to hope that he might care for her when she'd known deep down that all he truly wanted was her body. The bare truth was, he probably didn't love either her or Annabelle, and they were both demented to think otherwise. Amanda's own emotions had momentarily blinded her, since she could expect no more from Grant than the night of pleasure he'd offered her—and stolen for himself in the bargain. Well, it would be many a day before Amanda was that gullible again! He wouldn't find her such an easy mark in the future!

But how humiliating that, just the day before, she'd

been so relieved to learn that she was still a virgin. No longer could she make that claim to purity, and she had no one to blame but herself. And that dratted champagne that had weakened her will and her reasoning. And Grant for the rotten rutting beast he had proved to be time and again, until he'd finally achieved his goal of getting her into his bed—or hers. It really didn't matter much now, did it? The deed was done.

But it did matter. Terribly. And it hurt almost more than she could bear. Damn the man to hell and back! He'd taken from her the most treasured gifts she had to give a man, her chastity and her love. And what had he given her in return? A gold coin. Her own token. Oh, what irony! Paid for her services like a common whore! Paid with her own coin!

There on that lonely bed in that solitary room, with the mocking golden symbol of her downfall held tightly in the palm of her hand and her virgin's blood still staining her thighs, Amanda cried as she had never cried. Bent double with the pain that racked her, that speared to the depths of her being, she sobbed out her heartbreak. Her tears fell like rain, her muffled wails those of a wounded animal, until she had no more voice for her agony, nothing but this horrible ache inside her.

When Grant pounded on Amanda's door, he got no answer. When he located Chalmers in the hotel dining area having breakfast, Amanda was not with him. Nor was she anywhere else to be found, and neither of them had the vaguest idea of where to begin looking. Finally they thought to check with the desk, in the hope that she might have left a message, only to discover that she had checked out early that morning. The desk clerk recalled that she had ordered a carriage; he thought she'd been bound for the railway station, but couldn't be certain.

"Why would she leave without saying anything?" Chalmers mused, concern furrowing his brow. "Where could she have gone?"

"Home to Misty Valley, I hope," Grant responded

brusquely, again wondering just what was going through Amanda's head. Was she as disgusted with herself as he was with himself? Was she being eaten up with guilt? Remorse? Anger? Did she even remember any of it, or had the alcoholic haze dimmed her recollection of last night's activities? No, that didn't make sense. If she didn't recall what had happened, why would she have run this morning, unwilling to face him?

"Oh, hell and damnation!" he muttered. "There's no use trying to second-guess the woman! Let's go home, Chalmers. Undoubtedly we'll find her there ahead of us."

By the time they'd seen to gathering everyone together and making all the proper arrangements for Sultan's Pride, Amanda had a half day's start on them. They arrived home, tired and bedraggled, in the early morning hours of the following day, while the rest of the household was still sound asleep.

After stabling Sultan, Grant went off to his own bed and slept until almost noon. When he finally roused, it was to Chalmers' summons. "Sir, something is dreadfully wrong with Miss Amanda," the manservant informed him.

"At least you've found her," Grant grumbled, still half asleep. Then, as Chalmer's words registered more fully, he became alarmed. "What do you mean, something is wrong with her? Is she ill?"

"I don't know, sir. She says not, but it looks as if she has been crying, and Cook says she didn't eat a morsel last night, or this morning, either. When I asked what the matter was, Miss Amanda simply shook her head, gave a sad little smile, and refused to say. Perhaps you can get her to tell you what is wrong."

Grant could surmise what the problem was, and he had to agree that it was high time he and Amanda had a talk. "I'll be right down, Chalmers. Where is she now?"

"In your study, sir, just sitting there staring out the window and looking lost." He started to leave, then remembered. "Oh! I might tell you that she saw a doctor in Baltimore the day before the race for a stomach ailment of some sort. He gave her some pills for it. You don't suppose the medication has had an adverse effect on her, do you? Should I send someone for Dr. Lowell?''

''Not just yet. I think I'd better speak with her first.'' Grant dismissed Chalmers almost absently, his mind preoccupied. This was an interesting bit of news. Amanda seeing a doctor prior to their—well, their assignation, for lack of a better word. But perhaps it was a fitting term after all.

Mentally, Grant ran through the list of possible reasons she might have had for seeking out a physician. First, she might well have had an upset stomach. If she had, what did that indicate? Pregnancy? Had she gone to bed with him as a means of trying to palm some other man's child off on him?

But that was preposterous. She'd been a virgin, as he very well knew. The most practiced whore could not have faked the pain he'd caused her, or the blood staining the sheets beneath them, which he had seen with his own eyes. Or had she, with the doctor's help, wangled to pull the wool over his eyes?

No. He'd felt the barrier of her maidenhead, the resistance and the tearing as he'd broken through, and known it for what it was. That had been no bag of chickens' blood, no false rending contrived to seem the real thing. Which brought him back to his original question. Why had she seen that doctor? Could it have been because she intended to seduce him, just as he had set out to seduce her, and wanted to secure some sort of protection against conceiving? If so, why? And who had been luring whom to bed, when all was said and done?

By the time Grant entered his study, he had worked himself into a fine state of confusion. ''Amanda, we have to talk,'' he said with false calm.

''Why? Will it fix anything?'' She turned on him with smoldering fury in her eyes, and something that resembled hurt. ''What's done is done.''

"Will it help if I say I'm sorry, how dreadfully I regret what happened?"

"Oh, by all means!" she mocked. "Why not rub salt into the wound? Regrets and remorse are just what every woman wants to hear afterward from the man to whom she gave herself! Would you also like to tell me how ignorant and inadequate I was as a bed partner?"

"That's not what I meant at all. I simply meant that I'm sorry if I've caused you distress, but in my own defense, how could I have known? You should have told me you were a virgin."

"Really? When would have been an appropriate time, do you think? After all, it's not something that comes up in the course of general conversation, now, is it? 'Please pass the potatoes. May I have the salt? Oh, by the way, I'm a virgin.' Or should I have worn a sign about my neck? Had it stamped across my forehead? Taken an advertisement out in the *Lexington News?* Had fliers printed for you and all of your snobby friends who judge and condemn all on the basis of a first meeting, never bothering to look below the surface to discover the true person beneath?"

"If you're trying to make me feel like a worm, you've succeeded. Still, all things taken into consideration, how *could* I have guessed?" He went on jeeringly. "After all, you were dressed in a manner unbecoming to a lady. You didn't arrive wearing a sign about your neck, or a notice written across your forehead, or—"

"Oh, do shut up!" she hissed, irritated by the knowledge that at least a part of the fault was her own. She'd known better than to drink that champagne. She hadn't done a single thing to discourage him when he'd begun to undress her or make love to her. Of course, her inhibitions hadn't been in prime working order that evening, either. Had they been, she would have thrown him into the hallway on his ear!

"Things being what they are, I suppose I should ask you to marry me," he continued. "It didn't cross my mind to take precautionary measures, and you might find yourself with child because of it."

"You're just a barrel of good news today, aren't you?" She groaned. "Now I have something else to worry about. Thank you very much!"

"Obviously you didn't consider the consequences, either. What *did* you go to the doctor for, then?"

"How could I consider consequences I didn't even know might occur?" she countered angrily. "And Chalmers had no business telling you about that doctor. Furthermore, I wouldn't marry you if I found myself expecting triplets!"

"The doctor?" he repeated, his stubborn look telling her he was prepared to quiz her all day if necessary.

"A stomach ache," she barked, glaring back at him.

"That's all I wanted to know, Amanda. Thank you. Now, as to marrying me, I'd reconsider if I were you."

"But I am not you, thank God!"

"Your reputation is bound to suffer over this, worse than before."

"Yours won't be so sterling either. Have you thought yet what you're going to tell your fiancée? Annabelle is simply going to be ecstatic, isn't she?"

After all the hurt and humiliation he'd put her through, it helped to see him blanch. Still, she relented. "Don't worry, Grant. I'm not going to tell anyone, and if you have half a brain, neither will you. Just be grateful that it happened in Baltimore, where the stained sheets won't cause raised eyebrows and wagging tongues. And if you'd just shush up about it, maybe our own servants won't catch on and blab it to the entire Lexington community."

"Whether anyone knows or not, the fact remains that you are ruined for marriage. What man wants to discover on his wedding night that his bride has been with another before him? That would not be a good beginning to a marriage. And I assume that you will want to wed and have children of your own someday. Who will have you now, Amanda, if you turn down the offer I am making so graciously?"

"Graciously?" she spat back. "You suggested marriage about as *graciously* as you paid me for my favors, Mr. Gardner."

"Would you care to explain that remark?"

"My charm, Grant. My gold coin, lying there on the bedside table when I awoke. Did it satisfy your warped sense of humor to pay me back with my own coin?"

"My God! Is that what you thought? Is that why you ran off?" He was aghast. "Amanda, I would never have done it if I'd had any idea you would put that connotation to it. I simply left your charm so that you might have it again, because I felt bad about taking it in the first place. Because it is yours. Not as a means of payment. Certainly not to cause you any distress!"

Tears glittered in her eyes. "At least I have that small comfort, if you're telling me the truth. It did hurt, Grant. Terribly. I won't even try to deny it."

"Again, I apologize. And with that cleared up, how soon can you arrange to have a wedding gown sewn and arrange—"

"Wait just a minute. Simply because I choose to accept your apology concerning the coin does not mean I agree to marry you. You seem to be forgetting something. Stanford Darcy is not at all put off by me, and he probably sees me in much the same light as you have, never expecting me to be chaste. Maybe I'll just wait for him to propose and accept him instead. Besides, he's probably a darned sight more trustworthy than you, running around behind your fiancée's back, bedding your own business partner."

"You have no guarantee he'll propose marriage, Amanda. Perhaps he just wants a mistress. And you still might be carrying my child."

"Then I'll wait until I'm sure that I'm not. And then I'll wait until I meet the man who will want to marry me because he loves me, not because I might be carrying his child, or because he feels guilty, or because he'd gain the lost half of his family's property back by doing so," she ended scathingly. "Oh, don't think that hasn't crossed my mind in the past few minutes, you low-down snake!"

"It might have crossed yours, but it certainly never entered mine," he denied vehemently. "I offered marriage because it was the honorable thing to do."

"Is that the same reason you proposed to Annabelle? Because you couldn't keep your hands out from under her skirts? My! What a busy fellow you have been, Mr. Gardner, and what a trench you have dug for yourself. Two virtuous young women—well, two whom we know about, anyway—both ruined by you. What a quandary! Which do you marry? The neighbor lady, of whom society already approves? Or the scandalous riverboat gambler, who just happens to own half your business?"

She sneered at him from across the room. "Well, I have news for you, sir. I'm not quite as foolish as I appear. There are other fish in the sea, much better specimens than you. So I am *graciously* letting you off the hook, Grant. Go marry your little blonde, and may both of you get everything you so richly deserve from one another—because I wouldn't have you on a bet!"

For days afterward, Amanda was depressed. Under any other circumstances, she would have given her right arm to marry Grant. She loved him so very much! But he didn't return that love, and unless and until he did, she could not bring herself to accept his proposal, though it nearly killed her to turn him down. It also occurred to her that by doing so she had literally pushed him back into Annabelle's waiting arms, though the young woman knew nothing of what had taken place between Grant and Amanda.

For his part, Grant was as angry as he was relieved. On one hand, as soon as he felt assured that Amanda was not pregnant, he would be free to resume his normal life—or what had passed for normal since Amanda had come on the scene—including his plans to marry Annabelle. In the meanwhile, he would stand clear of both women. God forbid that they should prove to be breeding at the same time, both with his offspring!

On second thought, there was little chance of that occurring at the moment, since he'd not bedded Annabelle since before Amanda's arrival at Misty Valley, and really had little inclination to do so now. For some reason, his desire for his fiancée-to-be had dwindled drastically in the past few weeks, which might prove fortunate before all was said and done.

On the other hand, his pride had taken a severe beating, compliments of Amanda's sharp tongue. How dared that little witch refuse to marry him! Didn't she realize what he had offered her? How magnanimous the gesture had been? What it had cost him to voice it? It would be a cold day in Hades before he proposed marriage to her again, only to have her toss his words back in his face! And longer still if she intended to wait for any other man to come along and do likewise. Foolish woman!

Well, now he would sit back and let her stew in her own pot, and maybe one day he would make her another offer. Oh, not for marriage. She'd thrown that chance away. Next time, he'd offer to make her his mistress. Not for monetary gain, since she seemed to take such offense to the idea of being paid for her services, but for passion. She'd just had her first taste of lovemaking, and if Grant was any judge, she'd liked it, despite the initial discomfort. He was willing to bet that it would not be too long before she wanted a taste of it again. And he would be waiting, like a fox for a rabbit.

Amanda moped about the house like a dog deprived of its bone. Grant was as irritable as a bear with a sore behind. Between them, they nearly had Chalmers tearing his hair out. Then Grant came up with an idea he considered just this side of being brilliant, the perfect way to salve his wounded male pride and take spite on Amanda.

He stalked into her bedroom early one morning, just as the sun was peeking over the horizon, and gave her a resounding crack on her backside with the flat of his hand. Then he stood back, arms folded across his chest, and awaited her response.

It was not long in coming. Jolted from a sound sleep, Amanda jerked awake with a loud yelp. "Oooow!"

Spying Grant and the smug look on his face, she glowered grumpily, rubbing at her smarting posterior through the thin sheet. "Blast your hide! What the devil did you do that for? And what are you doing in my bedroom, you weasel?"

"Rise and shine, Amanda. Today is the day you start earning your keep around here."

"What are you blathering on about? Make sense, or go away," she grumbled, trying to bury her head under her pillow and shut that disgustingly cheerful voice out of her hearing. "Besides, I'm already earning my keep by helping with the accounting."

He ripped the pillow from her grasp and tossed it on the floor. "I meant with your back and the sweat of your brow, my dear, and more muscle than you have between your ears. You said you want to learn how the farm operates. Well, I've decided it's time to teach you."

"Not now." She groaned, tugging the cover to her eyebrows.

"Yes, now, and you are going to learn just the way Tad and I did, firsthand and from the ground up." He grabbed the sheet and yanked it downward, eliciting a shriek from Amanda as she tried, and failed, to retrieve it before it fluttered to the floor.

It was a toss-up as to which of them was more stunned, as Grant stared in disbelief at her sleep-flushed, absolutely naked body! His mouth flopped open, rather like a fish trying to breathe out of water, and it took him several long seconds before he managed to snap it closed again. In the interim, Amanda scrunched up against the headboard, pulled her long legs up tightly against her chest, and used the remaining pillow as a shield against those piercing green eyes.

Grant was the first to find his voice. "Where is your nightdress?" he demanded.

"In the dresser drawer, not that it's any of your business!" she snapped, glaring back at him.

"Why in blazes aren't you wearing it?"

"Because it's flannel, and I only wear it in winter,

and in case it has skipped your notice, it is now late spring and much too warm for flannel nightwear. Does that satisfy you, your lordship?''

"Well, why don't you order some lighter ones for summer, instead of strutting about like a strumpet?''

"I was not strutting. I was sleeping. And no one was here to see or disturb me until you had the temerity to barge in here!''

"What if there was a fire?'' he countered, frustration gnawing at him. Lord, but she was lovely, and alluring, even this early in the morning and completely disheveled. And those pink-enameled toes were as tempting as ever!

"Then I'd either fry to a crisp or drag the sheet along with me out the window, I suppose.''

"Don't be a sass-mouth! Get yourself some summer gowns and start wearing them.''

She stared him straight in the eye. "No.'' Whether she did or not, she certainly wouldn't ever tell him. Let him go around with that hungry look in his eye—thinking of her naked in bed, wanting her until it drove him mad! It would serve him right, the bossy barnyard cock! The insufferable ass!

"What did you say?''

"I said no. They're entirely too uncomfortable. They hitch up in the night and bind about fit to strangle me. I only wear one when it's too cold to go without, and I most certainly will not start now, simply because you command it. You are not my father, my husband, or my boss.''

"Well, I hate to disappoint you, Miss Know-It-All, but I am about to become your boss, which brings us back to why I came in to wake you. You will never learn about raising horses without putting your book learning to practical use. The best way to learn about something is to do it, preferably under proper supervision. You will be the laborer, I will be your supervisor, and I promise that you will learn more about the workings of a horse farm than you ever thought existed or wanted to know.

"Now, get your sweet butt out of that bed, dress it in something appropriate for mucking about in the barns, and haul it down to the breakfast table before you miss your morning meal entirely and have to wait until noon to eat. Your days of lazing about until mid-morning are done, my dear."

"Grant . . ." she began.

He speared her with a stern gaze and asked tersely, "Do you want to learn or not, Amanda? Or was all that talk merely a pretty speech, to impress everyone with your good intentions, but little else?"

She *did* want to learn. And this was her chance to do it. So she swallowed her pride and said, "If you will kindly give me a few minutes of privacy, I will be right down."

When Grant had made reference to mucking about in the barns, Amanda had never dreamed he'd meant it so literally! Just as he hadn't been joking when he'd said she was going to learn the business from the ground up. She soon found herself put to work as a lowly sta-blehand, raking soiled straw out of the stalls, shoveling it into a wheelbarrow, and hauling it out to a huge ma-nure pile some distance from the barn. Later, the waste would be loaded onto a wagon and used as fertilizer on the tilled fields.

Various of the stalls were due for a scrubbing, and when she had finished removing the old straw, Amanda was shown how to scrub the floor and walls of the stall with a long-handled brush and soapy water. Then the grain boxes had to be filled, fresh water hauled inside, and clean straw strewn on the floor.

It was an endless process, a thankless job, and harder labor than she had done in her entire life. If it hadn't been for the wide smirk on Grant's face as he waited for her to object or to refuse outright, plus the expectant grins on many of the other men's faces—added to the fact that little Timmy did exactly the same work as she was doing now, day after day—Amanda would have tossed a shovelful of steaming horse droppings smack in Grant's face. But she'd be double darned if she would give him the satisfaction of hearing her whine, let alone quit over a little honest, if smelly, work. She'd see this through if it killed her, which, by the end of the day and a thousand aching muscles later, she feared it very well might!

"How do you like farm work now?" he asked as he inspected her progress late in the afternoon. "Not quite as easy, or pleasant, as you'd thought, is it?"

"If you have something better to do than to stand around taunting me, please don't let me keep you from it," she told him grouchily, holding back a groan as she shoveled another forkful of soiled straw from the stall.

He grinned at her. "You missed some droppings in the far corner," he instructed gleefully.

"So kind of you to point that out."

"You also have dirt on your face and straw in your hair."

"No more than you have on your boots," she retorted, giving in to the urge and tossing a huge glob from her pitchfork at his feet. "Now, Mr. Bossman! If you don't want the next shovelful right in your mouth, I'd advise you to go away and let me get on with my work!"

"Just for that, I'm not going to give you a massage tonight to ease your sore muscles," he said, frowning at the mess on his boots.

"What makes you think I'd let you that close to me?"

He sniffed, his nostrils flaring at the pungent odor that rose to them. "On further consideration, I rescind the offer." He walked hastily out of range before adding, "Honey, I hate to be the one to tell you this, but you stink!"

Despite the odor and the dirt, and the scratchy straw that invariably found its way inside her clothing to chafe at her skin, Amanda would not have minded the hard work had it not been for having to be so near the horses. While most of the stalls were empty during the day when she was cleaning them and filling the food and water bins, occasionally a thoroughbred would be kept indoors for one reason or another. Amanda lived in fear of having to encounter one of the huge beasts, and flatly refused to enter a stall with a horse inside it.

Since Grant had promptly turned her over to Clancy's care, with Timmy to guide her through her chores, he witnessed none of this, evidently having temporarily forgotten how afraid she was of horses. He never knew how close to tears she came when confronted with them, or saw how valiantly she was trying to overcome her fright. She imagined he would have scoffed, not only at her, but also at Aaron and Clancy and Timmy, even at Paddy when he had the time, for they all took her beneath their collective wing and tenderly tried to help her.

Bit by bit, little by little, they were teaching her how to behave around the animals, how to talk to them and move about calmly and surely.

"It don't help if they know you're scared of 'em, Miss Mandy," Timmy said, sharing his youthful wisdom with her. "Even if you don't know what you're doin', you got to make 'em believe you do. Just like you got to make 'em believe you like 'em and ain't afeard of 'em."

She tried. Swallowing hard, sometimes clamping down on her own tongue to hold back a screech, she tried. She learned how to approach a horse from the front or the side so he knew she was coming and wouldn't be startled. She found that humming or whistling softly helped calm both her and the animals, besides alerting them to her presence. She even got so she could fill the food bins and give them fresh water while they were in the stalls. But she couldn't quite work up the courage to lead one out, or to replace the bedding with the horse in residence. She was still too afraid of being kicked or bitten or stepped on.

As she became better acquainted with them, she began to see that they had different personalities, much the same as people did. She also began to favor a few over others—the nicer ones, the calmer ones, the ones that nickered softly and followed her movements with shy velvet eyes. Those that never bared their teeth at her, or tried to lunge in her direction, or laid their ears back and snorted when she walked past. And once in a while, when she was feeling very brave, she would stop and pet one of her favorites. Just a light pat, or a quick scratch on the forehead, enough to make her feel as if she was edging up on the day when her awful fear would eventually leave her.

Chapter 13

WITH Amanda now busy in the barns, Annabelle reassumed her role as acting hostess for Misty Valley, at least to some extent. She saw that the linens were fresh and the rooms kept ready for the business guests, who were all the more interested now that Sultan's Pride had won the Preakness. She also directed the food preparation, though Amanda presided at the table during the evening meal.

Fortunately, by that late in the day, Amanda was usually finished with her work and had time to take a bath and change into clean clothes that didn't smell of horse dung. But she was also bone tired and aching in every joint and muscle of her body, and had to force herself to stay awake during supper and for conversation afterward, until she could politely excuse herself and drag her weary body off to bed. It was a wonder she hadn't toppled face-first into her soup and drowned by now!

Two things helped stiffen her resolve. The first was Annabelle, who was just waiting for Amanda to abdicate her position entirely. Second was the knowing looks and smug grins cast her way from Grant's end of the table. Amanda would be damned before she would give either of them the pleasure of seeing her falter.

Amanda's added duties also left her little time to entertain Darcy when he came calling. Much too filthy to want to associate with the guests at the noon meal, Amanda took to eating her dinner in the kitchen, or packing a small picnic and wandering out to the orchard to be by herself for a short while. After the first time he joined her there, Darcy learned to sit upwind from her.

"Good grief, Amanda!" he complained. "What has that man had you doing? Your clothes are a fright, there is straw in your hair, and your face is streaked with dirt."

"Yours would be, too, if you'd been cleaning stalls all morning," she grumbled.

"Cleaning stalls?" he exclaimed. "My dear woman, why are you putting up with this? You are his business partner, not his stableboy."

"Precisely. I am his business partner, and as he has pointed out more than once, partners share the work as well as the gains. Besides, I am trying to learn about the horses and how the farm is run."

Darcy gave a short laugh. "The only thing you're learning is that what you feed one end of the horse finds its way to the other. Gardner has you working like a slave, and I'll wager he's relishing every minute of it. Amanda, you are the lady of this house. You should never have to dirty your hands, let alone muck stalls."

"Oh, I don't really mind it so badly, and I am learning more each day. I suppose, if I wanted to complain, I could do my share by keeping the account books and never have to go near the barns unless I wanted to, but I have my mind set on learning everything there is to know about the place."

"Amanda, why bother yourself with it, or the books? Most women would be content to manage the house and shop and sew and visit with their friends. They stay busy and would never think of trying to help run such an enterprise. That's what husbands are for."

"I'm not most women, Mr. Darcy. And in case it has escaped your notice, I don't have a husband."

Darcy's gentle brown eyes took on an interested gleam. "That is another thing I'd hoped to discuss with you, my dear, and since the subject has come up . . ."

He let his words hang in the air, as if waiting for her to either encourage him to go on or discourage him from doing so. When she did neither, he continued. "Amanda, would you consider marrying me?"

As proposals went, Amanda thought Darcy's was almost as weak-kneed as Grant's. Not *Will you marry me?* Or *Would you do me the honor?* Or some flowery and romantic declaration of undying love, but *Would you consider?*—as if one were deciding fabric for a gown or what vegetable to serve with the chicken. Still, with choices as limited as hers, she shouldn't be so picky. She also needn't be hasty, however.

Frowning a bit, she said, "Mr. Darcy—"

"Please," he interrupted. He picked up her hand, then dropped it when he recalled her morning's activities and where that hand had been, though she had washed meticulously before eating her lunch. "Please, call me Stanford. We are, after all, friends. And perhaps more."

"Stanford," she replied with a weak smile, "if we were to marry, would you expect me to give up my half of Misty Valley?"

"Oh, my, no! I would never ask that of you, though I would expect you to consult me on various business matters which I would better understand and could offer advice on."

"Such as?"

"The accounts, any fees or offers or agreements to be signed. Cost estimates. All the sort of things you shouldn't bother your head about."

"I see." And she did. Stanford Darcy was another of those countless men who thought a pretty face covered an empty head. For an attractive female to attempt tabulating to twelve constituted using both hands and a couple of toes, and even then it was an effort, according to Darcy and his ilk. "And do you know very much about horses, Stanford? What is required to breed and train thoroughbreds? What makes a good hunter or racer or show horse?"

"No, but I do know how to effectively cut operating costs and balance accounts with a minimum of effort."

"How nice for you, and how terribly efficient." And how dreadfully pompous and boring! she added silently. "If we were to wed, where would we live?"

"Why, in town, of course. Where else?"

"Not here at Misty Valley?"

"Regretfully, no, though it would make a delightful retreat from the midsummer heat. My work is in Lexington, Amanda, and we would have to live where it was most convenient."

"And what about my work as co-owner of the farm?"

"Your job would be to keep our household running smoothly, to raise our children with love and care, and to make your adoring husband happy at the end of his long workday."

"Of course. Stanford, I would like some time to consider your proposal, if you please. You see, I'm still trying to adjust to my new surroundings, and another change in my life so soon is just too much to contemplate at the moment."

"I quite understand, and I'll do my best not to pressure you, while at the same time I'll also do my best to convince you to accept me."

After a few more alfresco luncheons, with Amanda looking little better than a chimney sweep, Darcy started limiting his visits to the evenings, which suited Grant just fine. The less he saw of Darcy—the less Amanda saw of Darcy—the happier Grant was.

This new arrangement also worked out well for Darcy, allowing him to devote more daylight hours to his own profession without having his courting interfere, though he saw less of Amanda than before. It was not as convenient for Amanda as for him, however. She lost count of the number of times she almost drifted off in the middle of one of his lengthy discourses on law, and fast became an expert at yawning with her mouth shut.

At least she didn't have him hanging over her shoulder all day, for which she counted her blessings and silently thanked Grant. As with Annabelle, a little bit of Darcy went a long way. Despite what she'd told Grant, she would have to think long and hard before accepting the lawyer's proposal, which she very much doubted she would do in the end. Somehow the benefits just didn't stand up very well against the disadvantages, even less than Grant's offer had done.

She wanted more. She wanted love and fidelity and respect, someone who appreciated her for her brains as well as her beauty. She wanted what she couldn't have, what no man seemed willing to give her. And now that she'd experienced passion in Grant's arms, she wanted that, too—the passion, and Grant, and all the rest of the impossible fantasy.

"Amanda." A voice whispered to her in the dark; a hand gently shook her shoulder. "Amanda, wake up."

"Wh—what is it? What's wrong?" She came more fully awake, rubbing her eyes, though it did little to help her see any better in the unlit bedroom. "Grant Gardner, what are you doing in my room at this hour? It must be the middle of the night!"

"It is, but I thought you might want to witness your first foaling, and nature won't wait until morning merely to accommodate you."

"Oh, my, yes!" Amanda breathed softly. "I do want to be there. Thank you for waking me, Grant. I'll get dressed immediately."

He didn't have to wonder if she was wearing a night shift. The shoulder he'd touched had been bare, and the moonlight drifting into the room was just enough for him to see the enticing contours of her upper chest against the white sheet. Blast the woman anyway! Was she deliberately trying to provoke him? Did she realize how many times a day his attention drifted toward thoughts of her and the one night they'd had together? Did she have any notion of how pale and uninviting Annabelle seemed to him now in comparison? How even kissing the young blonde had become almost a chore? How visions of Amanda's lips, Amanda's eyes— Amanda's lacquered toenails—kept interfering with his desire for his fiancée?

"I'll wait for you in the hall. Don't be long," he told her gruffly, leaving the room before he could give in to temptation and join her in her warm, woman-scented bed.

Amanda had never seen any living creature in the process of being born, or any in the throes of labor. As she watched the mare's sides heave with her contractions, with the movement of the foal within her swollen body, Amanda's sympathy went out to her. "Poor thing! That must hurt like the dickens!"

Grant chuckled. "I don't imagine it's any too comfortable, but it will all be over soon."

On her own, the mare decided when it was time to lie down on the fresh bed of straw provided for her. "If you'd like to sit with her, near her head, you might soothe her by talking softly or petting her a bit. Sometimes it seems to help."

Hesitantly, Amanda edged her way to the mare's head and took her place on the floor, while Grant stationed himself more to the business end of things. Huge, anxious, velvet brown eyes stared up at her, as if asking her to make the hurt go away, and Amanda lost her heart. "It will be all right, Starfire," she crooned, petting the animal's sweaty neck. "You'll see."

When the next contraction came, the mare's head rose, then fell as the pain subsided. Twice more, and Amanda scooted closer, so that when Starfire's head lowered, Amanda's leg was there to cushion it. "Is that better, sweetheart?" she asked, as if talking to a hurt child.

"It's fine," Grant answered, shaking his head and laughing as Amanda's head snapped upward. "Oh, I guess you weren't talking to me, were you?" he teased.

More seriously, his eyes darkening with desire, he asked, "What would it take to get you to speak that nicely to me and call me sweetheart?"

"When you give birth, I'll do the same for you, I promise," she vowed with a gaminlike grin.

Whoever had called it labor had certainly termed it correctly, Amanda thought as she watched poor Starfire weather one contraction after another. As the time for the birth grew closer, so did the intervals between pains, and the greater they grew in intensity. With little else to do but watch and try to make the mare feel as if someone cared what she was going through, Amanda stroked her head and talked nonsense to her. Finally she ending up singing every song she could recall, including several Negro spirituals she'd learned from Amos.

At last she heard Grant say softly, "Here we go, Amanda. Prepare to meet the newest addition to Misty Valley."

The mare strained valiantly, and with Grant helping to ease the foal out into the world, it took only a few minutes more. Wet, bloody, with its coat matted down like a drowned cat's, the baby filly was still the most precious thing Amanda had ever set eyes on. Witnessing its entrance, its first breath, was like taking part in a miracle.

With a clean rag, Grant helped wipe the foal clean, and Starfire took over from there. Between them, Amanda and Grant replaced the soiled straw with fresh bedding, Grant explaining the need for extreme cleanliness, especially during and immediately after the birth process, in order to lessen the chances of severe infection to both the mare and her newborn foal. Then, side by side, and with all the pride and joy of parents viewing their offspring, they watched the little filly try to stand for the first time.

It took several attempts, for her legs were so long that they kept getting tangled up, and so wobbly it was like trying to stand on four wet stalks of straw, but she finally made it. As she stood, spraddle-legged and nuzzling her mama's belly in search of her first meal, Amanda sniffled and brushed away a tear. "I've never seen anything as marvelous as this. Oh, Grant, I'm so very glad you came to wake me! This is a moment I'll never forget, if I live to be a hundred."

"I know. I've experienced it a hundred times, I suppose, but each time is brand new, each time a miracle in itself. And this little filly is going to be special. I can feel it in my bones. Besides, look at those legs! I swear she has the longest legs of any foal born to Misty Valley yet. She rather reminds me of you that way." He smiled and tucked Amanda beneath his arm so that her head came to rest on his shoulder. "I think we should name her in honor of you, the first foal to be born with you assisting its arrival. What shall we call her? Leggy Lass?"

Amanda shook her head. "What about Mandy's Miracle?"

"Wait!" Grant snapped his fingers and declared, "I have it! The perfect name. We'll call her Shady Lady."

With a heavy sigh that spoke of more than weariness, Amanda gave a tired little laugh. "Well, why not?" she conceded wryly. "It's what half the world seems to think of me, anyway. Shady Lady it is, and I hope she proves to be the fastest little horse anyone has ever seen. I hope she breaks more records and wins more races than all of your other thoroughbreds combined. Together, she and I are going to show you and everyone else exactly what we *shady ladies* can do when we set our minds to it. Just see if we don't!"

Amanda's muscles were just starting to become accustomed to her new labors when it was time to leave for New York and the upcoming Belmont Stakes. Again, because of the lengthy train ride, Grant was taking Sultan's Pride several days earlier so the animal would have sufficient time to overcome the rigors of the journey before the big race.

This trip, Amanda was also going a few days ahead of schedule. Though she'd heard about its marvels, she'd never visited New York City, and she wanted a few days to explore this grand metropolis, this mecca that beckoned to all nationalities and welcomed thousands more into its embrace each year. She wanted to revel in the swarming sea of humanity that thronged the streets; to sample exotic foods and listen to foreign tongues and search out every treasure the city had to share with her; to immerse herself in all the things she'd never had the opportunity to experience as yet, like art and fine music, the ballet, and so much more. As important as the Belmont Stakes was to the farm, it was taking second place now in Amanda's estimation as she anticipated all the exciting new things New York had to offer.

The racetrack and adjoining stables were out on Long Island, just a couple of miles from the shore. Their seaside hotel opened onto the beach, which thrilled Amanda no end, especially since the weather was warming nicely for this first weekend of June. The Long Island resort proudly offered lawn bowling, croquet, even that new sport called lawn tennis, for its well-to-do patrons, and Amanda was eager to try her hand at each of them, since she'd never had the time or the opportunity to do so before.

She had never considered her childhood lacking, merely different from that of most children. While they ran about in streets and grassy yards, her play area had been bounded, primarily, by the deck rails of a riverboat. There had been those few years during the war when she'd gone to school in New Orleans with other girls her age, but for the most part her father had tutored her once she'd learned the basics, and Amanda's natural curiosity had taken over from there.

If she'd lacked for pets and playmates, she'd gotten to go fishing almost every day she wanted, and she could probably still outspit any boy in three counties, given the proper plug of tobacco. She'd learned those skills and more from her riverboat friends. But now she was going to do some of the things she'd never gotten to before, and she was so excited she didn't know what she wanted to try first!

To add more choices, this year marked America's centennial birthday, and the entire country was preparing to celebrate it in spectacular fashion. New York, not to be outdone, wasn't waiting until July Fourth, but was planning to make an entire summer of it with special events and programs. There were to be sailboat races, horse races, footraces. Parades and galas. Special musical and theatrical presentations. Picnics and fireworks displays and costume balls. The circus was even in town, to stay for several weeks. It was to be one continuous gala the whole summer long, with Amanda fortunate enough to get a small sample of the fun, and she felt like a kid let loose in a candy store!

Early on the first morning of her stay, she and Chalmers were about to take a carriage into the city when they met Grant, who was just returning to the hotel.

"Where are the two of you off to so soon?" he asked. Turning his gaze toward her, he said with a dry laugh. "I thought you'd be sure to revert back to your old habit of sleeping late at the first opportunity."

Amanda shrugged. "I guess you've reformed me. Besides, I don't want to waste a moment of our time here. Reggie and I are off to town to spend the day."

"Shopping?"

"Oh, no," she answered with a shake of her head. "I can shop anytime I want to back home. First we're going to watch the parade, then go to the art museum."

"Without inviting me along?" He made a little-boy-lost face that almost passed for innocent.

"Aren't you going to be busy with Sultan's training?"

"He's already had his run this morning, before the others were out. I don't want to take any chances on him getting injured in a practice with the other horses. Or to give our competitors a true gauge of his abilities beforehand."

"Very wise, sir," Chalmers agreed. "If you're free, we'd be glad to have you accompany us," he offered politely, much to Amanda's dismay. Grant was a bit dismayed himself, when he realized how seriously

Chalmers was taking his new duties as Amanda's chaperon. There would be no shaking him today.

Sensing her reluctance to include him in their plans, Grant asked, "Amanda? If you don't care to have me along . . ."

What could she say, with Chalmers standing there, without looking the shrew? "It's fine with me, as long as you promise not to try giving me orders. You are not my boss today."

The parade was fun, the art museum impressive. Then, since they were on the edge of Central Park, Amanda decided they should wander through and see the sights. "They are supposed to have an animal menagerie somewhere," she told the two men. "And all manner of interesting activities."

"Let's find the stables first," Grant suggested. "It will be easier if we rent horses and ride through the park."

"Sir, do you realize how many years it has been since I have been astride a horse?" Chalmers exclaimed, the horror on his face mirroring Amanda's. "I'm afraid it's either walk or hire a carriage, because Miss Amanda does not ride, either."

"All right. We'll walk," Grant agreed, to Amanda's relief, then spoiled it by adding, "But as soon as we get back to Misty Valley, Amanda is going to learn to ride."

"I don't want—"

"Yes, I know. You're still scared silly, and the last thing you want to do is to get on the back of a horse. But that is the best way to overcome your fright. Learn to master the animal, and you'll also learn to master your own fear."

For now, Amanda preferred to shove the thought to the back of her mind and bury it there. The sun was shining, the park was beckoning, she had the entire day to do as she pleased, and she was not about to let Grant ruin it for her. They wandered the paths and soon came upon a group of girls who were twirling a jump rope.

Amanda's eyes lit up. "Oh! I haven't done that in years!"

One of the girls, hearing her, invited her to join them, and in a wink Amanda had discarded her shoes and new bonnet alongside the path and was gathering her skirts around her knees. Chalmers merely shook his head in mute resignation. Grant exclaimed in disbelief, "You're actually going to do this, aren't you?"

"Of course I am, silly! Don't you ever do anything just for the fun of it? Don't you ever take time out to play?" Then she was dodging beneath the twirling rope, hopping up and down, oblivious to all but the girls and the game.

In her stockinged feet, she leapt over the rope in time to a ridiculous rhyme, which the girls singsonged: "Pease porridge hot, pease porridge cold, pease porridge in the pot nine days old. Some like it hot, some like it cold, some like it in the pot nine days old." Then the chant changed, and the rhythm of the rope became faster as they began to count off the number of days old Amanda's porridge might be. "One, two, three, four . . ."

She tripped on five, the rope tangling about her ankles as she fell laughing to the ground. The girls laughed with her. Grant was frowning as he helped her to her feet. "You could have broken your leg doing such an idiotic thing! Sometimes I think you have all the sense of a five-year-old!"

"And you're a stick-in-the-mud!" she retorted, swatting at a passing bee. She thanked the girls, gathered her hat and shoes, and began to walk on, eager to discover what other adventures lurked nearby. "Don't you ever long to be a child again, Grant? To run barefoot and free through the grass? To lie on your back in a field of flowers and watch the clouds race by overhead and enjoy the fantastic forms they take as they change from ships to dragons to castles in the sky?"

"Being an adult brings responsibilities with it, and we all have to grow up, Amanda. That was the problem with Tad; he never grew up."

"Maybe so, but that doesn't mean you can't let your hair down and have fun once in a while. It doesn't mean you have to turn into an old killjoy. When was the last time you did something for the pure pleasure of it?"

His devilish grin was matched only by the glint in his eyes. "Baltimore, the night of the race. You were there, as I recall, and anytime you'd care to play that game again, I'll gladly oblige."

"Oblige, presumably just shy of the point of obligation?" she answered stiffly.

"Precisely."

Chalmers had no idea of what his employer meant, or why it set Amanda off as it did, but she didn't speak to Grant for half an hour after that. Not until they chanced across four lads who were riding those new-fangled contraptions called bicycles. "I want to try that!" she declared.

"Good grief, Amanda! You refuse to mount a horse, yet you'd dare life and limb on a rickety device such as that?" Grant asked, hoping she would reconsider.

This time, Chalmers had to agree. "Miss Amanda, those things do not look at all safe!"

"Pishposh! You're both a couple of sniveling ninnies! Chicken hearts! I'll bet I can stay on one of those bicycles longer than either of you," she challenged boldly.

"You're on!" Grant accepted, his male pride demanding it. How dared she call him a sniveling ninny! He'd show her! "C'mon, Chalmers, let's go see how much these boys will take to loan us their conveyances for a short contest."

"But, sir!"

"Chalmers, old fellow, would you have Miss Amanda think you weak-willed?" Grant called back as he strode after the boys. "Get on with it, man!"

Twenty minutes later, Chalmers was bruised but triumphant, crowing his victory to his defeated opponents. "Showed you who's an old fellow, that I did! Ninny, indeed!"

Grant, who had come in a close second, was also

feeling ridiculously proud of himself, his chest puffed out like a peacock's and a huge rip in the knee of his trousers. Amanda was still trying to dislodge her skirts from the spokes of her bicycle and muttering to herself. "Dratted thing! I should have known it would be devised to suit a man! Most amusements are!"

They stopped at McGowan's Tavern for a light lunch, walked partway around the lake, and caught the last half of a Shakespearean play enacted outdoors on a makeshift stage. They snacked on ice cream in a dairy building right there in the park, stuffed themselves later on small fruit pies they bought from a vendor's stand, and eventually found the little zoo Amanda had mentioned.

Grant could not recall the last time he'd had such a frivolous, fun-filled day. He'd laughed until his sides ached as Amanda had swatted at the geese that were determined to follow her around the lake path. She was equally leery of the zoo animals, even the goats and llamas, though the monkeys seemed to delight her thoroughly. She deliberately aped their movements and expressions, then giggled hilariously as they mimicked hers. She tossed them gum and tired to teach them how to chew it, all the while totally uninhibited by what passersby might think of her, refreshingly open and honest in her childlike enjoyment. By the end of the day, he couldn't say who had had the most fun— Amanda, who welcomed every new experience with glee, or he and Chalmers, watching her and following where she led.

Chapter 14

THE day was far from finished, however, as Grant was soon to discover. Amanda had made plans for the evening hours. There was a popular theater production at the Cherry Lane Theater which she wanted very badly to see.

"Amanda, your dress is stained with grass and grease from the bicycle, my pant leg is torn, and even Chalmers is looking a bit ragged about the edges," Grant pointed out. "By the time we go all the way back to Long Island, to the hotel, bathe and change and grab a quick bite to eat, it will be far too late to catch the show."

"Which is precisely why we are going to stay in the city, find a decent meal in some nearby restaurant, and proceed directly to the theater from there."

"Looking like vagabond gypsies? We'll be lucky if anyone agrees to serve us. More than likely, the most we could hope for is stale fare from one of the street vendors."

"If I've learned one thing from you and your uppity friends, it is that money has a voice of its own," Amanda argued. "Given the proper incentive, we'll not only get a good meal, but there's a chance we'll even get our clothes freshened. And if we don't, who's to notice in a dark theater? After all, it's not as if we smell or something!''

"Must you see this production tonight? Can't it wait until tomorrow?''

"I have too many other plans for tomorrow. I've signed up for a tennis lesson in the morning while the weather is still cool. Then a group of other ladies and I are going to have a couple of sets of croquet before lunch. Afterward, I need to come back into town to look for a costume for the masked ball the hotel is hosting the night of the race, and I'd hoped to find time to stop by Macy's and catch a peek at the fashion show they're having.

"And tomorrow evening I have to choose between the opera, the ballet, and the symphony, since I obviously can't attend all of them in the short time we are going to be here. Of course, I've seen the opera in New Orleans, and to tell you the honest-to-goodness truth, I thought it all nothing more than a lot of people screaming in a language I couldn't begin to understand or even want to, so I suppose I'll try the ballet this time around and see if I like it any better, since the orchestra will accompany the production anyway. I'm fortunate the season has been extended for the centennial, or I wouldn't get the opportunity to see it now.''

Grant was getting tired just listening to her list the things she wanted to see and do. "Is that all?'' he inquired in droll astonishment. "Are you positive you haven't forgotten to mention anything?''

"Oh, there's plenty more, and not nearly enough time for it all,'' she conceded. "Of course, there is the race on Saturday and the ball that evening. And I'd truly love to take a peek at St. Patrick's Cathedral, though I am aware that it isn't completed yet. It's supposed to be one of the largest and most ornate churches in the world, by the time they finish it. And I've heard the women raving about Tiffany and Company. Lands! Did you know they have some of the most exclusive jewelry in the country in that place? And Mr. Tiffany is noted for his art and stained glass. Even if I can't afford to buy anything, it can't cost much to just look, can it?''

Knowing defeat when it stared him in the face, especially accompanied by sparkling blue eyes and a stubborn little chin, Grant gave in gracefully, as did Chalmers. They found a laundry establishment about to close and bribed the owner to stay open long enough to repair most of the damage done to their clothing. Then they located a rather shabby little restaurant within walking distance of the theater and had a surprisingly well-prepared supper at a portion of the cost they would have spent elsewhere.

Finally the theater, where Amanda sat enthralled throughout the third-rate comedy. Grant wondered whether she realized how poorly it was performed, and decided she wouldn't care if she did know. She was simply having fun, indulging herself as she had rarely had the opportunity to do, and that in itself was enough to make it all worthwhile.

It was entertaining merely to observe her as she watched the show, to see her laugh at the jests she understood and puzzle over those she didn't. It was also an education for Grant to realize all over again just how naive this woman-child was, when some of the bawdier jokes sailed straight over her head. Amanda was a paradox, a lovely, intricate enigma, one he found himself more desperate to solve each day.

There was no avoiding her, for even when she was out of his sight she was never far from his thoughts. At times it seemed the best he could hope for was to survive their encounters. Every day she surprised him anew, and sometimes, like today, she made him look at things in a fresh way, through more innocent eyes, and it was like revisiting his all-too-short childhood and reliving the best parts of it again.

Amanda—woman—child—temptress—sprite. Amanda.

* * *

He made time to go with her the next afternoon. It was worth it just to see the look of reverent awe on her face as she gazed at the immense, still-skeletal cathedral that took up one complete city block. And to observe the size of her eyes as she viewed the array of jewels at Tiffany's.

"If ever you have the money to spend, don't bother with diamonds or emeralds," he told her as they browsed over rings and bracelets, necklaces and tiaras. "As prized as they may be, the blue topaz or the aquamarine better suits you. See how perfectly they match your eyes? And coral to match your lips. Or rubies, like fire against your skin and hair."

To commemorate their visit to New York, he bought her a small window hanging made of stained glass, a colorful butterfly with outspread wings to catch the light of the sun. It reminded him of the day he'd found her in the orchard.

They parted paths for a few hours while Amanda saw the fashion show and searched for her costume. In that time, Grant managed to find an outfit of his own, swearing Chalmers to secrecy so that Amanda might not know how he intended to dress until they met at the ball. They teamed up again and went to supper at a renowned club, coming away vastly disappointed in the place after having eaten such a delicious meal in that dingy little restaurant the evening before.

It was time for the ballet. Amanda was counting on it. The problem was, there was also a major prize fight being featured at Madison Square Garden, which both Chalmers and Grant would have given a fortune to attend. Behind Amanda's back, the two men flipped a coin to see which of them would escort Amanda and which would be free to go to the boxing match. Chalmers won, and with a grin the size of all outdoors, he took himself off for the Garden. Grant resigned himself to a night at the ballet, his only comfort being that it was not the opera, thank the good Lord.

Once again, Grant enjoyed Amanda's pleasure more than the performance itself. At one point he glanced over to find her sitting with her eyes closed, seemingly enraptured by the music. Leaning close, he whispered teasingly, "You can see it much better with your eyes open, Amanda."

"Shhh! I'm feeling the music," she answered softly, reaching out to clasp his hand, her eyes still shut and an angelic smile on her face. "Isn't it lovely? It goes all through you, like a magical waterfall. I could listen to it all night."

At the intermission she came out of her music-induced spell and surprised him by suggesting, "We could go over to the Garden now and probably still catch the major fight of the night if we hurry."

"You knew all along, you wicked little witch!" he said with a laugh.

She nodded, grinning up at him. "Well? Do you want to go or not?"

"Yes, but we can't. It's not a proper place for a woman. Besides, you're enjoying the ballet."

Grabbing his arm, she pulled him out of the theater and into the street. "Hail a cabbie, Gardner. We're going to the fights. Surely, with both you and Reggie to protect me, there's not too much trouble we can get ourselves into."

She was wrong. They found Chalmers and managed to squeeze onto a bench just behind him, with Amanda half sitting on Grant's lap in a space meant for one person. The main bout had just gotten under way.

Having lived on the river most of her life, Amanda was not shocked at the display of violence, not even repelled by it, though she failed to understand why two sane, fairly reasonable men would agree to pound the daylights out of each other for a pittance and the sheer pleasure of it. At least at this match, unlike at some others, the combatants were wearing gloves. Not that it seemed to matter all that much. By the end of the tenth round, both looked as if they'd been pulverized by a millstone, bruised and battered and bloody.

The match ended, the fighter Chalmers and Grant had favored winning, and they were both congratulat-

ing each other on choosing the better boxer when the
man sitting on Amanda's other side clamped a beefy
hand on her thigh and suggested drunkenly, "Let's you
an' me go somewhere an' have us some fun, sweet
face."

Amanda froze. When she dared to move again, she
brushed the man's hand aside, glared straight into his
red-rimmed eyes with her best poker-bluff stare, and
said, "Forget it, fella. I'm with him." She motioned
toward Grant.

"What's going on here?" Grant was just becoming
aware of her predicament, not having heard the man's
comment over the noise of the crowd.

"Nothing," Amanda squeaked.

Her words were nearly drowned out by the man's
claim: "The lady's gonna come with me. You got anything to say to that, mister?"

Grant's answer was a fist in the man's nose.

The man's reply was a clip to Grant's jaw.

Then Chalmers got into the act, and the whole place
erupted in an all-comers-welcome brawl as Amanda
cringed and tried to hide behind the seats. Until her
assailant managed to pull her up by the roots of her hair
and hold her before him like a shield, grinning all the
while like the village idiot. His mistake was in not
making certain she was facing away from him at the
time. Though it cost her the entire side seam of her
skirt, Amanda crashed her knee into his groin, squealing almost as loudly as he did when he let her loose
and she went tumbling to the floor. She crawled her
way to Chalmers' side, where the manservant lay
groaning and half conscious, and it was right about
then that the police arrived to haul all of them, Amanda
included, off to jail.

It was a red-faced, hangdog trio that went before the
judge the next morning, explained sufficiently to get
any charges against them dropped, and headed back to
Long Island after spending an uncomfortable night in
the calaboose.

"If you ever tell anyone back home about this, either

of you," Amanda warned on a growl, "I swear I'll try every one of those hateful maneuvers I learned last night on each of you—and believe me, these New York girls really know how to hurt a man!" She'd spent the night locked up with several of the city's most infamous women, and had learned more in those few hours than she had in all her years on the river.

"Miss Amanda, I'm sworn to silence. I'd rather cut out my tongue than ever tell where we spent last night," Chalmers pledged wearily, gingerly poking at his swollen nose.

"Me, too," Grant vowed. Then he grinned that outrageous grin at her, made even more mischievous by the black eye he was now sporting. "I must say, though, you certainly landed that fellow a telling blow, Amanda. You women can pack a wallop to make boxing look tame."

Paddy, bless his soul, had taken care of properly exercising Sultan's Pride in Grant's absence. They were able to bathe, change clothes, and get out to the track in plenty of time for the race.

After the harrowing escapade of the night before, and the two initial races she'd attended in the previous month, Amanda thought she would be much calmer this afternoon; but the minute she set foot in the owner's box, the excitement began to build. Of the three races she'd been to, this was the most revered and the longest in existence, having been run since 1867. To win the Belmont Stakes was akin to winning the presidential election. It amounted to carving a permanent place for oneself in the annals of racing history.

And that was exactly what Sultan's Pride and Paddy did for all of them that day. From beginning to end, they were magnificent. Brilliant. Magic in motion. Horse and rider acting as one, with only one thought between them. *Win.*

Grant nearly had a stroke when Paddy let Sultan break for the lead on the backstretch, with over half the race yet to go, but the little jockey was reading his mount correctly, could feel Sultan's tension and fierce will clear through his bones. They crossed the finish line alone and with regal pride, scarcely winded, six lengths ahead of the nearest challenger.

This time it was Amanda who threw herself at Grant, clinging like a koala and screeching almost as loudly. If they thought they'd been bombarded by buyers before, it was nothing to what they could expect now. Katie, bar the door! Misty Valley was on the map to stay! Sultan's Pride would reign as king long after he ceased to race, his offspring much sought after for many years to come. And somehow, through the grace of a benevolent God, Amanda had become a part of this winning team. Jubilant, Grant and Amanda went to claim their winning purse, to congratulate Paddy on a spectacular ride, to bathe in the glow of Sultan's triumph.

Much later, so totally exhausted that she felt as if she'd run the race herself, Amanda left the others to their celebration. Slipping away almost unnoticed, she returned to the hotel, locked herself in her room, and fell quickly and gratefully asleep. As she drifted into slumber, she chuckled to herself at her own behavior. "Defeat I can handle. Victory puts me straight to sleep! Move over, Rip Van Winkle!"

Even costumed as she was, Grant would have known her anywhere, been able to pick her out from amid a crowd of a hundred others. As he did now. Standing on the threshold of the hotel ballroom, he watched Amanda toss back the hood of her bright red pelisse, the better to scan the room. Looking for him, he hoped. Adjusting his eye patch, he went to greet her.

"Little Red Riding-Hood, I presume?" he asked slyly, coming up from behind and leering at her as she jumped in surprise.

"And here I was told to beware of wolves!" she scoffed lightly. "No one thought to mention the perils of encountering a pirate, a wolf in sheep's clothing if ever there was one!" She looked him over approvingly.

"Yes, you do cut a dashing pirate, Mr. Gardner, and to think you chose the costume before collecting your black eye, which the eye patch conceals very nicely, I might add."

"I augmented it as an afterthought," he admitted. "But it does fit right in, doesn't it?"

In his turn he perused her costume. "May I say that you look ravishing in red, Red?" he queried with a grin.

"Oh, I don't believe you actually said that!" She grimaced. "Next you'll tell me that you are fully prepared to ravish me, I suppose."

"You stole the words from my mouth."

"As the pirate, you are the thief, I should think."

He clasped his chest, as if in pain. "I am mortally wounded that you would think so badly of me!" he exclaimed dramatically.

"You'll live, and if you don't, please refrain from bleeding on the carpet. The stains are the devil to remove."

"Why, Red, what a sharp tongue you have."

"The better to stab you with, my dear," she returned, sticking the offending appendage out at him in impish delight.

"Don't point that thing at me unless you intend to use it," he warned. "And keep in mind that I have a sword of my own."

"Besides the one dangling from your belt?"

"For shame! You nasty little girl! Does Grandma know you talk this way?"

"Grandma's the one who taught me."

"I should have guessed. Maybe I should meet Grandma. She sounds like a rowdy old gal."

They laughed. They danced. They drank punch liberally laced with liquor, though Amanda steered well clear of anything that even hinted of champagne. She was not about to repeat that particular lesson. Yet as the night wore on she was more and more certain she was doomed to do just that. As they waltzed, the room seemed to spin more than the dance warranted. Her heart wanted to beat out of kilter. Her breath caught in her throat as he seared her with a look, caressed her with his voice.

"If I were an actual pirate, I'd abduct you and have my way with you," he hinted darkly.

"What way is that?" she asked on a whisper, feeling as if she were drowning in his emerald gaze.

"Any way and every way there is possible for a man to have a woman."

"Are there many?" She was flirting with fire, sure to get burned, but couldn't seem to stop herself.

"Enough to keep us both busy the night long, and more."

"Show me."

Chapter 15

THERE, in the midst of the dance floor, Grant stopped, stunned. He stared at her in mute disbelief, sure he had merely imagined her bold words. All through the evening he'd been deliberately seducing her, hoping to get her into his bed before the night was done, to experience that same delirious delight they'd shared but once before. Yet he'd never expected her to yield so soon or so readily to his charms.

Yield? No, that didn't fit the situation at this moment. Amanda had gone beyond that. Somehow the enticing little witch had managed to turn the tables on him, as if she were challenging him now, rather than the other way around. Was she just teasing him again, luring him before she denied him? What game was she playing this time?

"Cat got your tongue?" Amanda taunted softly, her eyes laughing up at him.

From behind, another couple jostled into him, bringing Grant alert to the fact that they were standing still while the other dancers maneuvered around them. Yet even as he automatically resumed the rhythm of the waltz once more, his mind remained focused on the beautiful woman in his arms and the promise in her eyes. "Never promise anything you can't or won't deliver, Amanda," he warned thickly. "Especially favors of that sort. It can prove a very dangerous mistake, particularly if the man you are flirting with is not a gentleman."

Her gaze held his, as sure and bright as candles glowing in a dark night. "Show me," she murmured again, her voice coursing through him like warm whiskey. Bold. Brash. Daring him. Exciting him to a fever pitch.

"With pleasure, temptress." Not waiting for the music to end, he took hold of her wrist and led her hastily from the dance floor, eager to get her alone before she had time to change her mind. "Just remember, you asked for this. Afterward, remember that you wanted it as much as I did. No latter-day laments or accusations."

All the way to her room Amanda argued with her conscience, her emotions and her mind warring within her.

This was wrong.

But it felt so right! She wanted him so much she ached with it.

It was sinful.

Then she was surely damned to hell, but she'd find her own heaven in his arms, in his kiss.

He was promised to another woman.

Yes, but he'd be hers, only hers, tonight—in her bed, with no thoughts of anyone else. She'd make certain of that.

Like all the rest, he wanted nothing more than her body, offering nothing more than a night of passion and giving no thought to her as a person. He didn't even like her half the time. He harbored an abiding resentment toward her, continued to deny her the respect he readily gave other ladies, refused to view her as anything more than a common tart. By offering herself to him tonight, wasn't she about to reinforce his low opinion of her, perhaps beyond redemption?

Irrationally, despite all this, he was the man her heart had chosen. For the first time in her life, she was madly, helplessly, in love. Didn't that count for something? Didn't she have a right to some small happiness, a moment of glory, no matter how brief or one-sided? One night of ecstasy—just one perfect night in the arms of the man she loved, to cherish all the days of her life.

As he swept her into the room with him and gathered her into the heat of his embrace, Amanda had no more time for thought. His lips came down over hers, his arms drew her close against his lean, hard body, and from that moment all she knew was Grant. All she cared to know. He filled her senses to overflowing. The feel of him. The taste and smell of him. His gaze burning into hers as he loosened the ties of her pelisse and shoved it off her shoulders to pool at her feet. His low growl as he claimed her mouth once more, the weight of his body pressing hers back against the closed door.

Before she could quite fathom how he had managed it, he had the top of her dress tugged down, her arms still bound in the sleeves and her breasts spilling over the top of her chemise, framed only by the delicate lace trim. "Peaches and cream, and twice as delectable," he murmured, grazing his teeth across the tip of first one offering and then its twin, laughing softly as they sprang to attention. He wet each with his tongue, then blew gently upon them, hardening them further.

By the time he drew one into the hot depths of his mouth, Amanda was nearly mindless with desire, arching into his touch like the wanton he'd claimed she was, whimpering and squirming against him. From head to toe, breast to belly, she was a mass of quivering need. Tingling. Wanting. Burning.

When his hands found their way beneath her skirts, searing a path from her knees to her waist, her legs threatened to collapse beneath her. Blindly, deftly, his mouth still tugging at her breast, he dealt swiftly with the ribbons at the waistband of her French panties. Before they hit the floor, his palm had replaced them, finding the very heart of her desire. She moaned, her hands fluttering as she made a weak attempt to push him away. "No more. Please."

If he heard, he gave no sign. His fingers continued their foray, undeterred by her entreaty, sending spirals of pleasure dancing through her, firing her blood, building the need until she was filled to bursting with the most intense yearning she'd ever known. Fevered and slick with it. Wild with wanting him. He pressed close, and she felt his manhood, bare and pulsing against her belly. "Grant," she panted. "Please . . . the bedroom. Now."

Groaning, he slid his hands beneath her buttocks, cupping and caressing them with his long, callused fingers. "I can't wait that long," he admitted huskily. "Wind your legs around my waist."

Even as he lifted her free of her panties and wedged himself between her quivering thighs, she gasped, "We can't. Not here."

"We can. Right here. Right now." Looming over her, with that black patch still covering his eye and the other blazing emerald desire, he looked very much a pirate—a pirate bent on reveling in plundered treasure. A shiver of breathless anticipation skittered through her.

In the next instant, he proved his claim.

Hot, hard, throbbing, he thrust into her, and she gasped anew and clenched her legs more tightly about him. Again, and she felt the silken length of him fill her, felt herself open more fully to him.

"That's it, darling," he crooned seductively. "Take me in. Take me all the way inside. Warm me. Hold me. Oh, God, but you're sweet!"

She couldn't have answered if she'd wanted to, for his mouth covered hers then, his tongue forging past her parted lips in imitation of their lower bodies. Her back pressed against the door, his hands beneath her bottom, and her legs wound about his hips, she clung tightly to him and trembled. Time and again she drew him to her, welcoming his invasion as the passion and pressure built within her.

Then, in the space between one frantic heartbeat and

the next, she was catapulted high above the world, taking Grant with her. Soaring on golden wings, while a million brilliant suns shattered all about her, floating slowly back to earth on a downy cloud of wondrous bliss.

Her legs slipped from about him, dangling weakly. Only his strong arms and the weight of his body leaning into hers kept her from sliding down the wall onto the floor. His damp head lay in the crook of her neck, each ragged breath echoing hers.

A short, breathy laugh escaped her. "Lord A'mighty! I'd never have believed it!"

He answered with a chuckle and a nibble at her neck that sent gooseflesh rising along her cooling skin. "I won't bother to ask if you liked it," he said wryly. "It'll be a miracle if half the hotel didn't hear you, and as soon as my ears stop ringing I intend to make you screech like that some more."

"I don't know if I have the stamina," she admitted. "I think all my bones have melted."

"Honey, we've only begun. There's plenty more to teach you." With an ease that amazed her, he swept her into his arms.

Startled, she cried, "Grant Gardner, don't you drop me!" She couldn't help but wonder if his legs were as wobbly as hers.

"Stop your fretting," he instructed, giving her a decidedly wicked grin. "Just reach down, grab hold of the waistband of my britches, and keep them from falling around my ankles, or we'll both be flat on our faces before we reach the bed."

They made their way to the bed, Grant carrying her and Amanda holding his pants up, both of them giggling like naughty children on their way to making delightful mischief.

As, indeed, they were.

By the time the sun broke over the eastern horizon, Amanda had lost count of the number of times and ways they'd made love—often frantically, sometimes lazily. Lingering to explore each other's body. Searching out those many pleasure points, those sensitive, sensual areas that invariably set their pulses racing and their passions rising.

She learned more about her own body in those few hours than she'd ever imagined. And she learned about his—what pleased him, how to tease him to the limit of his endurance. Where to stroke. How to touch. With mouth and hands and body. First following his whispered instructions, then her own natural instincts, letting curiosity and desire guide her movements.

Replete, gloriously exhausted, Amanda lay snuggled in Grant's arms, her head pillowed drowsily on his shoulder as the room lightened with the borning day. She was almost asleep when he asked softly, ''What made you change your mind?''

''About what?'' she murmured, running her fingers through the springy dark hair on his chest, loving the feel of it tickling her palm.

''About becoming my lover—my mistress.''

''What!'' She sprang into a sitting position, her face a mixture of amazement, dismay, and instant anger. ''What did you say?''

Disdain curled his lips as he, too, sat up, leaning over his side of the bed to find his trousers. ''From your reaction, I'd say you heard me just fine, Amanda. I'd also guess I leapt to the wrong conclusions about last night.''

''You're damned right you did!'' she retorted stiffly, gathering the sheet to her chest.

''What was last night all about, then?''

She glared at him and flipped a tangled strand of black hair out of her face. ''Call it a temporary lapse of good sense. Consider it a moment of insanity. Think of it as anything except . . .''

''Except becoming my mistress?'' he supplied, tugging on his pants. He reached for his shirt.

''Yes!'' she hissed. ''Anything except that! And you can rest assured that hell will freeze solid before I let you into my bed again, you low-down snake! You cur! You . . . you bastard!''

"Now, now, Amanda. That's not what you called me last night, love."

"I am not your love!"

He arched a dark brow at her, his expression speaking for him as he denied her claim.

"I'll never be your *love*, or your lover, again, I promise you!"

"And I'll do everything in my power to make you break that vow, darling. That is my pledge to you."

"You can try from now until doomsday for all I care, Grant Gardner! But you lay so much as a finger on me, and you'll draw back a bloody stub! Do you understand me?"

"I thought we weren't going to have any accusations of this sort this morning," he reminded her as he continued to dress. "That was the agreement, if I recall."

"I never agreed to it, *if you recall,*" she tossed back.

"How convenient for you," he drawled. "I believe you're sitting on my sash," he added, referring to the red cloth he'd wound around his waist as part of his pirate's costume.

On a strangled screech, she pulled the cloth from beneath her bottom and threw it at him, blushing as she recalled how he had employed it in their love play the night before. Tickling her with the fringe. Draping it over her like a matador's cape. Binding it around her thin waist, pretending she truly was his captive, and he the plundering pirate.

Oh, Lord! How mortifying to think of such things now, in the bright light of day. Worse, to admit, if only to herself, how much she had enjoyed their games, their passionate pretense. And pretense it had been, for now the fantasy had evaporated like dew on the morning grass. Lovers they might have been, for a few brief, splendid hours, but now they were back to being enemies, rivals, their usual antagonistic selves.

"Will you kindly get your blasted, damned backside out of my bedroom?" she snarled. "I've had just about as much of you as I can stand!"

"That's quite a reversal from what you were saying

just an hour or so ago," he taunted. "Then you couldn't get enough of me, would never get enough of me, would die if I ever stopped. Am I quoting you properly, Miss Sites?"

Her face glowed with her humiliation. "A gentleman would never remind me of those things."

"And a lady would never play the part of a harlot as well as you do, my dear. Nor would she use the language you do, in bed or out."

"You'll live to regret those words, Mr. Gardner," she warned darkly. "Just as I regret ever letting you into my bed or allowing myself to think one decent thought of you! In the last few days, I was beginning to hope you might have a heart after all, even if it is in the wrong place most of the time."

He leaned over the bed, his hands searching beneath the covers, and for a moment she thought, incredulously, that he meant to resume their lovemaking. "What do you think you are doing?" she squealed, swatting at his fingers as they brushed her bare thigh.

"Sorry to disappoint you, love," he said on a sardonic laugh. "I'm merely searching for my missing sock." He retrieved it and bent forward, his unbuttoned shirt flapping open as he planted a swift kiss on her flaming cheek. "By the way, your ever-handy wad of chewing gum is there on the bedpost. Don't forget it, sweets."

Her eyes narrowed to blue slits as she reached out, yanked the sticky gum from its resting place, and smacked it square in the center of his hairy chest. "You can have it." She smirked. "You were eager enough to suck it out of my mouth last night. You may as well keep it."

Grimacing, he peeled the glob of gray goo from his chest, wincing as several hairs came with it and more of the gum stayed glued to his skin. "It's not much as mementos go," he commented lamely.

"Well, it's all you're ever going to get from me."

The intensity of the look he leveled at her almost made her squirm. "We'll see, won't we," he answered softly, seriously. "If our first interlude didn't produce a child, this one might have." As the color fled from her face, he smiled grimly. "Ah, I see that didn't occur to you, did it? Unfortunately, you had me panting after you so furiously that it didn't cross my mind either. And so we wait—again—to see if our foolishness will bear fruit."

"Well, thank you very much for that wonderful lecture, Dr. Gardner! And I suppose all the blame is mine? What about you, you randy goat? You're the one chasing everything in skirts. You're the one with all the experience, with the obliging fiancée. Does Annabelle have to listen to this tirade every time you make love with her?"

"No," Grant replied simply, abruptly taken aback by Amanda's last suggestion. To her confusion, and with no more argument, he gathered his remaining clothes and left immediately, closing the door quietly behind him.

"Well, what was all that about?" she wondered, frowning after him. "All that yelling, and then he clams up tighter than Granny's drawers! Lands, but I'll never understand the workings of that man's mind! And why the bloomin' hell would I want to?" she added grouchily to herself.

As Grant made his way to his room, Amanda's final comment kept echoing in his brain. It was upsetting to realize, so suddenly and unexpectedly, that not once had he gotten so carried away with Annabelle that he had failed to protect the two of them against the possibility of a child being conceived prior to their wedding night. Not once had his body overtaken his mind, as it seemed to do whenever he touched Amanda. And since he had bedded Amanda, his desire for the cool blond woman he was to marry had taken a decided decline, so much so that he hadn't even entertained the thought of making love with Annabelle since then, though Annabelle had hinted along that vein quite boldly several times.

It was a disturbing thing to learn about himself, something that certainly warranted further thought. Was it respect for Annabelle and her family that always made him draw back in time? Did the clandestine nature of their rendezvous make him more alert, more on edge than he was with Amanda, so that he never fully relaxed or let down his guard? Or could it be that there was less passion between him and his bride-to-be than he had admitted to himself until now? Less fire? Dimmer desire? More subdued emotions?

Especially compared with the force of his attraction to Amanda. Lord knew, his body reacted immediately whenever the woman came within ten feet of him. Lately, she had been intruding into his thoughts constantly, to the point where his mind was often off his work, and that in itself made Amanda unique, for this had never happened to him before with any other woman. She was even interfering with his sleep, invading his dreams. Now, instead of gray eyes and blond hair, he had visions of ebony tresses and snapping blue eyes, lips like cherries and endlessly long legs that drew him lovingly into her . . .

With a jerk and a curse, Grant realized he was doing it again. Fantasizing about that raven-haired witch! "Damn you, Amanda!" he growled. In frustration, he aimed a fist at his bedroom wall, fracturing the plaster and wincing with the pain that shot up his arm. "What are you doing to me, woman? What have you done to my calm, well-ordered life?"

As before, when Amanda had rejected his proposal, Grant became more surly than usual. Actually, he was worse than a wounded bear for those first few days following their return home. He barked and grumped and growled at everyone, but most especially at Amanda. The only one he went out of his way to be pleasant to was Annabelle, and Amanda suspected that was only Grant's way of trying to irritate her all the more.

To top it all, Grant remembered his vow to teach her to ride. None too thrilled at the prospect to start with, she was even more reluctant now, sure that Grant was out to make her break her neck. The morning he called her out of the barn, where she was diligently cleaning stalls, and led her to a small corral where a mare stood saddled and ready for her first riding lesson, Amanda immediately balked. Digging the heels of her boots in the ground until Grant literally had to drag her forward, she complained loudly, too scared to care who witnessed her acting the coward. "I'm not going to do this, Grant. You can't make me!"

"You should know better than to challenge me by now, Amanda," he retorted, yanking her toward the horse. "You're going to ride Lady Mist if I have to tie you to the saddle."

With several farmhands helping to hold the leery mare steady, and another aiding him with Amanda, Grant managed to wrestle her into the saddle. "Amanda!" he commanded sharply, releasing her and stepping back, leaving her all alone atop the horse, with nothing to hold onto but the saddle. "Damn it all, settle down! You're frightening Lady Mist, and only making things worse for yourself in the process."

Even through her extreme fright Amanda heard and realized the truth of his statement. Abruptly, she ceased screaming and sat as stiff and still as a statue—a trembling statue. Her eyes were so huge in her pale face that Grant feared she might faint before the lesson began. He softened his tone slightly, using the same firm yet comforting voice he employed with a nervous horse. "That's better. Now, Paddy is going to lead Lady Mist around the corral, and all I want you to do is concentrate on staying in the saddle. Sit up straight and try to relax, Amanda. Keep your feet in the stirrups and just move with the horse. Can you do that, honey?"

"I'm not your honey," Amanda ground out from between clenched teeth.

Grant bit back a chuckle, glad to see that she was regaining her courage, at least enough to bark back at him. "All right, let's try it. Now steady yourself with your thighs and just sit back and enjoy the ride. I'll be right alongside to catch you if you start to fall.''

"Is that supposed to be a comfort?" she retorted.

Paddy urged Lady Mist into a slow walk, and Amanda swallowed a hard lump of fear. "Oh, God! Oh, God! Oh, God!" she chanted, as if reciting an invocation. Then, as tears fell down her cheeks, "I'll get you for this, Gardner! Plan on it! If I live through this, I'll make you pay!"

For fifteen of the longest minutes of her life, Amanda slipped and slid and prayed for all she was worth. Half a dozen times or more, Grant had to nudge her back atop the saddle when she started to slide sideways. Throughout the lesson he clipped out instructions like an army drill sergeant. "Keep your knees in. Straighten your back. Christ, Amanda! You look like a hunchback! If you're having this much trouble riding astride, I'm glad I didn't decide to start you out sidesaddle. Relax, damn it!"

At the end of the lesson, she was holding on so tightly that he literally had to pry her stiff fingers loose and peel her from the saddle. She was drenched with perspiration, panting out tiny whimpers, and quivering so badly she could hardly stand when he set her on her feet. "Come now, Amanda. That wasn't so bad, was it?" He reached out to wipe the tears from her glistening cheeks.

His fingers scarcely touched her face when Amanda's fist flew up and connected solidly with his eye—his good eye!

"Ouch!" He stepped back, his hand flying to his throbbing orb as he glowered at her. "Blast it, woman! What are you trying to do, blind me?"

"It's the least you deserve, you beast! I just hope it turns as black as your other eye, you heartless weasel!" With that, she turned on her heel and headed toward the house, her stride more an unsteady wobble than the angry strut she intended.

Grant glared after her, rubbing his smarting eye. "Darn, that woman packs a whollop!"

He'd forgotten the other men, who had witnessed the entire scene, until old Clancy chuckled softly and said, "Ye know, I'm thinkin' I've heard of black-eyed weasels out West somewhere. Thet I have."

Grant rounded on the lot of them, squinting at his grinning crew. "And if you don't want to join them out there, you'd better get back to work. All of you!" he warned. "And if I hear one more smart remark about this, I'll have your hides nailed to the barn door." The men ambled off, still grinning.

Glowering Grant grumbled, "I'm surrounded by smart-asses! Irishmen and temperamental women alike! It's enough to drive a man to drink!"

Recalling the bottle of cherry brandy in the liquor cabinet, he gave a fatalistic shrug. Well, why not? If nothing else it would help ease the pain still lancing through his swelling eye.

Chapter 16

ANNABELLE took one look at Grant, her first since his return from New York, and exclaimed in horrified amazement, "My stars, Grant! What in heaven's name happened to you?"

"It looks worse than it is, Annabelle," he said.

"But what happened? How did you get two black eyes, for goodness' sake?"

"In a brawl, if you must know. Now, I don't mean to be short with you, but I really am too busy to stand about chatting with you today, Annabelle. I have a million things to do, not the least of which is to give Amanda her riding lesson."

"Riding lesson? Amanda?" Annabelle's face clouded up immediately, a childish pout pursing her lips. "Why can't someone else teach her to ride, Grant? Why must you do it?"

"Call it a debt I owe her." A grim smile curved his lips as he thought to himself, Yes, and while I'm teaching her something useful and helping her to overcome this ridiculous fear of hers, I'll be collecting a bit of revenge on the little witch as well. Two birds with one stone.

"What sort of debt? For what?" Annabelle was fast on his heels as Grant strode out of the house, headed for the barnyard.

"Nothing you would understand, dear. Don't worry your little head over it."

Fuming, Annabelle stopped short, her stony gray eyes glaring daggers into Grant's back as he proceeded into one of the barns. Spying Paddy nearby, holding the reins of what she presumed to be the horse Amanda would ride, she changed course. Perhaps her energies would be better spent prying information out of the hired help, since Grant was being so stubbornly uncooperative this morning.

Meanwhile, Grant searched the stalls from one end of the barn to the other. When Amanda failed to materialize, he cornered Timmy. "Where is she?"

"Wh—who, sir?" Timmy stammered, his face turning almost as red as his hair.

"You know very well who. Miss Amanda. Where is she hiding?"

"I . . . I can't say, sir." Timmy's chubby freckled cheeks quivered in his halfhearted attempt at a smile.

"Now, Timmy," Grant said calmly, but with enough force to make the boy realize just how serious he was, "I think I'd reconsider that answer, if I were you."

"But, sir! I promised!"

"It's for her own good, son. She's got to learn to ride sometime, and it might as well be now." In a lower voice, that of one confidant to another, Grant suggested, "You don't have to tell me. Just point out where I might find her. That way you really wouldn't be breaking your word, would you?"

Timmy considered for a moment, then nodded and reluctantly pointed toward the upper hayloft.

Grant grinned and ruffled the lad's hair, and headed directly for the ladder leading into the mow. As he climbed, he called out, "You might as well show yourself, Amanda. I know you're up there. You can't hide from me forever."

He'd almost reached the top rung when her small fist

swung out at him, once again aimed for his face. This time, however, Grant was ready for her. Making use of her own momentum, he caught her arm, ducked into her swing, and quite without warning, Amanda found herself slung headlong across his shoulder like a sack of grain, dangling several terrifyingly long yards above the barn floor.

"Aah!" she shrieked, the air puffing out of her belly and the world starting to spin. Pounding on his back with her fists, wriggling like a fish on a pike, she yelled frantically at him, "Put me down! Grant! Have you lost your mind? Let me go!"

With one hand on the ladder and the other arm anchoring her legs, Grant settled for giving her a sharp shake. "Enough, Amanda! You're going to have us both on our heads in a minute if you don't stop fighting me. Now, you have a choice. You can either settle down right now or continue to make a fool of yourself, the way you did atop Lady Mist yesterday."

His words had enough truth in them to sting her pride. She had made quite a spectacle of herself the day before, but it wasn't her fault! Drat it all! Why couldn't the man see that she was truly afraid? It wasn't easy to master such fright, especially with someone else pushing you into it before you were ready!

Her hurt feelings, added to the fear of falling, kept her still until Grant had both feet planted on solid ground once more. Then, incensed at his arrogance and his lack of compassion, she became a writhing tigress once more. Still dangling face-first, Amanda clawed viciously at his back. When that brought nothing more than a grunt from him, she resorted to the ultimate defense and sank her teeth through the fabric of his shirt into the flesh over his ribs.

This time she gained a response, though not the one she wanted. Rather than release her, he let loose a yelp and swatted her smartly on her backside, hard enough to bring tears to her eyes. "So help me God, Amanda, do that again and you won't sit for a week!"

Just as he was approaching the doorway out into the

barnyard, from beneath his arm Amanda caught sight of Annabelle outside. "Oh, dang!" she cursed softly. The last thing in the world she needed right now was to have Annabelle see her like this!

"Wait!" Grabbing frantically for the doorframe, Amanda held tight, yanking Grant to a halt and almost launching herself off his shoulder.

"What?" he asked tersely, backstepping to keep his hold on her.

Nearly choking on her pride, Amanda forced the words from her throat. "Please. I'll behave. I'll get on the blasted horse. I promise. Just let me down, Grant."

He was silent for so long that she thought he wasn't going to bother with an answer. Finally he said, "If I put you down, you'll walk out there and mount that mare, and not give me any more sass or trouble for the duration of your riding lesson? And do everything I tell you to do, without question or argument?"

"Yes. On my honor."

"And what is that worth, Amanda?"

She was tempted to bite him again, just barely resisting the temptation. Her better sense came to her rescue. "I swear it on my father's grave, Gardner. Is that good enough for you? Now, will you please put me down? The blood is rushing to my head, and I think I'm about to faint!"

More carefully than she expected, certainly more gently than she deserved after biting him, he slid her slowly to her feet. So slowly, in fact, that it became an erotic act in itself, her belly slithering intimately along his, her legs tangling with longer, stronger limbs, feeling every muscle, every tendon, even the hard pulsing of his heart against hers as her chest mashed up against his. Their eyes caught and held for a long, breathless minute, his darkened to jade as his lust flared.

Then, as if the moment had never been, he pulled back from her, his tone harsh and commanding as he said, "All right, you're free. Now, get out there and see if you can conduct yourself with a modicum of decorum for a change."

"Louse," she muttered, starting out ahead of him.

She'd taken two steps when he caught her arm. "Did you say something, Amanda?"

Recalling her promise, she executed a neat salute and retorted irritably, "No, sir! Certainly not. You must be hearing things, sir!"

"Of course," he agreed with a false smile. "And chickens have lips, too."

Amanda puzzled over that last comment all the way across the yard. Did chickens have lips, or not?

By sheer determination alone, she made it through the following session without bursting into tears. Valiantly, she swallowed every cry that rose in her throat and every curse that entered her mind, though in her private thoughts she boiled Grant in hot oil the entire while. Still and all, by the end of the riding lesson, she was no longer quite as unsteady on the beast. At least she didn't feel as if she were going to tumble to the ground at any given moment, and was giving God's ears a slight reprieve from her continuous pleas for mercy.

To his credit, Grant never left her side the whole time, and even managed to convince her to let loose of the pommel and take the reins for a few minutes toward the end, though Paddy retained a firm hold of the lead rope and kept the docile little mare to an even walk throughout. Strangely, amidst her fright and anger, Amanda felt braver with Grant there. A bully he might be, but somewhere deep down inside herself, Amanda trusted him not to let her fall, knew he would protect her from hurt, at least physically. Just having him near lent her courage she did not have on her own, and a word of encouragement or praise from him was worth more than an ace-high royal flush in a high-stakes poker game. And that was something rare, indeed!

Amanda was sitting in the orchard in her favorite spot, listening to the bees hum and the birds chirp, and soothing her frazzled nerves. She wasn't hiding, precisely, for her riding lesson was finished for the day, but she'd had enough of Grant's bossy ways, and Annabelle's snooty airs, to suit her for a spell. All she wanted right now was to be by herself. And she wasn't sitting, exactly, either. More to the fact, she was slumped against the trunk of an apple tree, more on her back than on her aching bottom. Riding wasn't the most pleasant of activities, in more ways than one—and this on top of the hearty smack Grant had administered!

She was trying to read a book of poetry, one of her favorites, but today, for some reason, it wasn't holding her interest as it had in the past. Then she felt something fuzzy brush against her leg, and she froze, half afraid to look and see what it was.

Oh, sweet Lord! Snakes weren't fuzzy—were they? But mice were, and so were rats! Then again, she thought, trying to calm her racing heart, so were kittens and bunnies. Again the thing touched her leg, higher up this time, as if to make its way beneath her skirts!

Drawing on every ounce of courage she could muster, Amanda lowered the book just enough to peep over the top edge. A burst of nervous laughter caught her unaware, startling the small downy creature as much as it had frightened her just a moment before. There, peering up at her with big hazel eyes, was the cutest, sweetest baby duckling Amanda had ever thought to see. Covered in downy yellow fluff, with a bright orange beak and webbed feet, it was only as big as her hand, and quivering fit to lose its feathers, or what passed for feathers. It let out a tiny squawk, puffed itself up, and stared back at her. Then, quick as a wink, it darted under her skirts!

"Oh, no, you don't, you little rascal!" Amanda squealed. Tossing the book aside, she slapped lightly at her skirts, giggling as the duckling raced over and around her bare legs, tickling as it went. Finally, she managed to capture the little mite in a wad of cloth. Carefully, not wanting to startle it any more than she already had, she crept one hand inside and gently brought the bird back out where she could get a better look at it.

As she held the duckling at eye level, in the palm of her hand, the two of them once again took each other's measure. "I don't know where you came from, you imp, but if you have a penchant for chasing about beneath ladies' skirts, I'd bet my last dollar you're a boy duck!" she told it with a tinkling laugh. "Now, what are you doing wandering around all by yourself? Did you lose your mama?"

The duckling blinked and cocked its little head sideways, as if in answer to her query, or asking one of its own. "Oh, you're a sweetie, you are," Amanda crooned. With one finger she gently petted its downy back, and the baby duck made an odd little sound and settled itself more comfortably in her palm.

"Like that, do you?" Amanda was enchanted. "Tell you what, little man. You can stay here with me as long as you agree not to make any more forays into forbidden territory. What do you have to say to that?"

The tiny creature answered with what Amanda interpreted as an affirmative quack. Then it hopped down into her lap, cuddled into a ball of fluff, tucked its head under its minuscule wing, and promptly went to sleep.

Then and there, Amanda lost her heart. She'd never had a pet, at least not for long. Though she'd once tried to keep a kitten on board the riverboat, it had run off the first time the boat docked. The one and only canary her father had bought for her had died from the river drafts in a week's time, and she hadn't had the heart to get another only to chance having it die, too.

Now to have this small creature appear out of nowhere and curl up so trustingly on her lap was like being offered a rainbow to hold in her hand. Of course, she knew she couldn't keep it. It had a mother somewhere on the farm. But for just a little while, she could pet it and cuddle it and take comfort from its warmth.

It was getting on toward dinnertime when Amanda reluctantly decided to return to the house. Gently, she dumped the duckling off her lap. laughing as he waddled drunkenly and tried to shake himself awake. "Well, tyke, this is where we part company, much as

I regret it. And if my dinner is waiting, yours probably is, too. Maybe we'll meet again sometime, if you ever get back this way.''

In no great hurry, since she suspected Grant had probably invited Annabelle to stay for dinner, and also knowing that there was every possibility that Darcy would show up at any moment, Amanda sauntered toward the house at an easy pace. She'd gone perhaps a third of the way when she heard a rather loud quack behind her. Stopping short, she turned, and sure enough, there was the duck, faithfully dogging her footsteps.

"Say, now! This won't do, you know,'' she told her feathered friend, trying to look stern. "You just waddle on home. You've been gone a long time, and your mama is undoubtedly worried sick over you.''

He cocked his tiny head again, as if considering her words or begging to go with her. Amanda's heart gave an odd twinge, but telling herself it was for the best, she turned her back and resumed her trek toward the house.

Again, more loudly and sounding quite put out with her, the duckling quacked. This time Amanda whirled around with her hands on her hips. "Lands, but you're a stubborn thing!'' she commented, shaking her head at him. "If I wasn't sure it was impossible, I'd swear you were related to Grant, and a more muleheaded man never drew breath.''

The duck just stared at her, then waddled toward her. "No! Now shoosh!'' She flapped her arms at him in an attempt to turn him away. He stopped and looked up at her in a sad, confused sort of way that tore at her heartstrings.

"Oh, piddle!'' She sighed resignedly. "All right, come on. I guess it won't be much out of my way to take you down by the duck pond and see if we can locate your mother.'' With that, she scooped him up and hurried toward the pond, scolding and petting him all the way.

A few minutes later, she set him down again, just a

few feet from his fellow ducks. "Go find your family," she instructed firmly. "And from now on, don't go wandering off, or some hungry fox is liable to have you for lunch!"

Much to her dismay, as soon as she turned back toward the house, the little duck began to follow. For the life of her, she couldn't seem to discourage him, and no mother duck came running out of the flock to claim him and urge him back into the fold. In the end, he followed her clear to the side porch, quacking and flapping his tiny wings furiously in an attempt to follow her up the steps.

"Hell's bells and little catfish!" she swore. "Do you have any idea what a nuisance you are? What am I supposed to do with you now? If I leave you out here, you're bound to either get stepped on or carried away by some chicken hawk. Don't you have an ounce of sense in that fluffy little head of yours?"

Quack.

"Oh, horse feathers!" she grumbled, relenting. "I never thought I'd see the day when I'd get adopted by a duck! I don't look anything like your mama, and we both know it, but I know when I'm licked! You win, Sweet Cheek! Lord knows, Grant is going to have a fit, but he'll just have to get over it. If I can stand you, so can he! And you're a darned sight cuddlier than those huge horses he keeps. That's for sure!"

Amanda was walking down the upstairs hallway, on her way to breakfast the next morning, when she met Grant coming out of his room. He nodded a greeting to her, paused to let her pass ahead of him, then suddenly bellowed, "What is that thing doing in my house?"

Confused, Amanda turned. Then she realized the problem. There, waddling calmly along behind her, was Sweet Cheek. She'd forgotten to close the door to her room, and the duckling had immediately begun to trail her. And Grant was staring at it as if it were a creature from the moon!

"Oh, for heaven's sake, Grant! Don't tell me you're afraid of a little duck!" she sniped. "He's just a baby. And don't holler at him. You'll frighten him." Stooping, she collected her new friend in her hand. "Won't he, Sweet Cheek?" she crooned.

"Sweet Cheek?" Grant echoed, his voice cracking on the words.

"Yes. I think the name fits him admirably, since he's so adorable and has what Chalmers would call 'a lot of cheek' for a creature as small and defenseless as he is."

"So do you, my dear, for even daring to bring that bird inside," Grant observed. "Now, kindly take him out again, where he belongs, and leave him there."

"I can't."

"Why not, pray tell?"

"Because he's adopted me."

"Well, let him adopt someone else, preferably another duck."

"I tried that last evening, but none of the other ducks seem inclined to claim him, and I can't just let him wander about outdoors on his own."

"You can't?" Grant cocked a dark brow upward and waited for her answer.

"No, I can't. He's liable to get eaten, or trampled by one of your precious horses."

"Then feed him, keep him as a pet. Have Clancy build you a pen for him outdoors, but you can't keep him in the house."

"No." Amanda's chin went up a notch and stayed there as she stared Grant straight in the eye. "He'll get lonely for me. He loves me."

Grant ran a hand through his hair in frustration and groaned. "Amanda, do you have any idea what a mess that cute little duckling could make of this house, these floors? He'd have sh—duck droppings strung from one end to the other in no time. If you don't believe me, go take a look around the henhouse, or the edge of the duck pond. It's not the most pleasant sight—or smell. Certainly nothing you'd want on the bottom of your slippers."

"I'll train him. Like a puppy," she insisted stubbornly. "I'll get some butcher's paper and lay it down and teach him to use it."

"Easier said than done," Grant told her, "especially since I've never heard of anyone doing it before with a duck."

"Then I'll be the first, won't I?"

"Not in my house, you won't."

"Then I'll do it in *my* house."

"Your house *is* my house, you little twit!"

"Nice of you to admit it," she snapped back. "And don't scare my duck, or I'll give you another black eye!"

"That would be a neat trick, since I already have two, thanks to you. Plus a bruise on my side in the exact shape of your teeth!"

"Then I'll just have to find another part of your anatomy to maim, won't I?" With that foreboding promise ringing in his ears, and a too-smooth smile that set his hackles rising, she trotted blithely down the stairs to breakfast, taking Sweet Cheek with her.

From then on, everywhere Amanda went, Sweet Cheek was sure to go, just like Mary and her little lamb of nursery-rhyme fame. He accompanied her to the stables and barns, playing in the straw as she cleaned the stalls, riding on her shoulder or waddling along behind her as she went about her various chores, snoozing comfortably atop her bare feet as she worked at her desk. The duckling even ate at the table with her and slept on the pillow next to hers, much to Grant's disgust.

"Keep that bird off my dining table, Amanda," he ordered the first time she brought Sweet Cheek to supper. "He probably has lice or mites by the dozen!"

Wrinkling her nose at him, Amanda replied, "I've bathed him and checked him thoroughly, and he's probably cleaner than you are."

"The only way I want to see a duck on my table is

plucked and roasted, and that's exactly what's going to happen to Sweet Cheek if you persist.''

"You touch one downy feather on his body, and I'll take a gun to your favorite horse,'' she retorted. Of course, she'd do no such thing, as she didn't know one end of a gun from the other. Still, it made a good threat.

"That would be cutting off your nose to spite your face, wouldn't it? After all, those horses are Misty Valley's livelihood.''

"Well,'' she said thoughtfully, "perhaps I'll reconsider and pepper Annabelle with buckshot instead. Would that better suit you, Grant?''

"Hardly.''

He threw her and Sweet Cheek a dark look as the duckling gobbled up a piece of bread Amanda offered him from her plate. "That's disgusting. Chalmers, can't you talk sense to this woman? I can tell by the look on your face that you are no more thrilled with her pet than I am. Since you are in charge of running the house and usually do so with such meticulous results, why haven't you done something about that creature?''

Chalmers continued refilling Amanda's wineglass, gently shooing the duck aside, careful not to touch the bird in the process. "Miss Amanda has threatened to fill my shoes with bird droppings if I do, sir,'' he admitted stiffly.

Grant stared, nonplussed, then burst out laughing. "She certainly has you dancing to her tune, doesn't she, Chalmers? However, I sense you are somewhat disenchanted with her. Is the bloom off the rose, as they say? Are you once more beginning to see our resident 'lady' gambler for the charlatan she truly is?''

Chalmers' face drew into a haughty frown. "No, sir. I simply do not care for her keeping her pet in the house, though I must say she is good about cleaning up after the thing. Even if she does let it sleep with her,'' he added in an undertone.

"Oh?'' Grant looked half amused and half put out at this latest bit of news. "Lucky duck, to win himself such favor. What has Sweet Cheek got that I lack, if I may ask?"

"Manners, for one thing," Amanda countered with a false smile. "I do wish you and Chalmers would stop talking around me, as if I'm not present to speak for myself. It is extremely rude and quite exasperating."

"I stand corrected, Miss Conduct," Grant answered with a slight nod and irritating arrogance. "And since you are suddenly so bent on proper etiquette, might I point out that your charming pet is presently drinking from your water glass?"

Chapter 17

ALMOST the only time Sweet Cheek did not accompany Amanda was during her continuing riding lessons. Each morning, bright and early, Grant assumed the role of Amanda's teacher—and tormentor—convinced that this was the surest way to cure her of her fright of horses. "If you can learn to master your mount, to feel confident in your ability to control her, then you will also master your fears," he assured her. "This is for your own good, Amanda. In the end, you will thank me."

"If I don't yield to the temptation to strangle you first," she vowed.

She was already proud of herself, however, no matter how much she hated the lessons and Grant's superior attitude. It was a monumental accomplishment merely to be able to mount the mare on her own, using the mounting block, and not have the animal shy away from her—or to spend several minutes talking herself out of the urge to run back into the house and lock herself in her room for the remainder of the day. Though her stomach remained tied in knots and she was constantly wiping nervous perspiration from her hands and brow, she no longer felt as if she were about to burst into tears at any moment simply because she was astride the beast.

Besides, Lady Mist was proving to be a very gentle, docile, patient horse upon which to learn. No matter how unskilled Amanda was or how many mistakes she made, regardless of the confusing signals she often gave the poor animal, Lady Mist took it all in stride. This further enabled Amanda to progress, if slowly, and now, two weeks from the start of her lessons, she was riding the horse around the corral on her own, without anyone leading her or standing by to catch her if she fell. Of course, she had yet to try a gait faster than a plodding walk, and she was anything but graceful or relaxed.

"As soon as you learn to ride with confidence and some semblance of skill," Grant told her, "we will see about removing you from your more menial duties. Once your fear abates and you can handle the horses with calm, firm assurance, we can advance you to other training positions, such as grooming and saddling, and later perhaps helping to exercise them. But as long as you communicate fear to them, it simply won't work, and you'll keep mucking stalls."

"Have you ever considered a career in the army? Personally, I think you'd make a wonderful officer. That way you could holler at people all day and boss them around to your heart's content, and get paid for doing it. It would be perfect for you."

"Quit stalling, stop sassing, and get mounted, Amanda."

For the next hour, she rode nervously around the corral while Grant showed her how to handle the reins to make her horse turn in the direction she wanted. Over and over, he drilled her. Stop. Walk. Right. Left. Left. Left. Until Amanda was almost dizzy, and wondered if poor Lady Mist was also.

Then Grant decided it was time to instruct her on the various gaits and how to get the mare to advance from one to the other. For this, to her dumbfounded dismay, he mounted behind her in the saddle. "All right, now, Amanda," he ordered gruffly, nudging forward until she feared he meant for their two bodies to merge into one, "pay close attention while I demonstrate." His big hands closed over hers on the reins, the better to direct them. "Watch what I do with my hands. Feel how I move my legs, where my knees are."

How could she not? Lord, the man was so near she could feel his heart beating against her back, his breath wafting tendrils of hair on her nape! His thighs were all but melting into hers, not to mention the telling bulge in his britches that kept nudging into the small of her back.

Later, Amanda could scarcely recall any of the things he'd been trying to teach her. But the shape of him was indelibly imprinted against her backside, and her mind was rioting with sensual images and emotions. By the time they dismounted, she was drenched in desire. Her pulse was beating erratically, her knees had turned to custard, and she couldn't seem to breathe properly.

Throughout the lesson, Grant had said nothing to indicate that he was similarly bothered, but as he helped her to the ground, his hands lingered at her waist. "Now, wasn't that cozy?" he teased, his eyes dark, his nostrils flared as if to catch the scent of her arousal. "And we get to do that all again tomorrow, and the next day, and the day after—until you learn to direct the horse on your own. It could prove to be very interesting on several levels, don't you agree? Especially as slowly as you are learning."

"Fry in hell, Gardner," Amanda snapped, thrusting his hands from her. "Take your little games and play them with your fiancée, but don't expect me to be amused. You can taunt and tease me until you turn blue, but you'll be tormenting yourself as well, and all for nothing. I will not be your mistress."

"Tomorrow, my dear." His words followed her retreat. "Don't be late."

Angry, frustrated, and close to tears, Amanda turned and glared at him. "Stanford Darcy proposed marriage to me," she informed him tartly. "Did you know that? He is waiting for my reply. Anytime I want, I can accept his offer. I can be the wife of a respected man, Gardner. I don't have to take second place in anyone's life. Especially not yours. So tamp that in your pipe and smoke it!"

She'd thrown down the gauntlet, was verbally challenging him, though he wouldn't give her the pleasure of seeing how her words had jolted him, couldn't even be sure why they did. All he knew was that the thought of her wedded and bedded by another man brought an unexpected pain, somewhere in the region of his heart. "Are you going to accept him, Amanda? Do you dare? Or are you just having fun dangling the poor fellow on your string?

"You'd be terribly mismatched, you know," he continued imperiously. "Particularly now. Darcy would bore you witless within a month, and you would probably be the death of him in the end, since he considers a rousing debate in the courtroom the height of excitement. He wouldn't have the slightest idea what to do with a passionate woman like you."

"Then I'd just have to teach him, wouldn't I? It could be quite entertaining."

"You can't teach what you don't fully know, darling. And I haven't begun to educate your properly yet. But I will. Rest assured that I will, Amanda. Meanwhile, we'll continue with your riding lessons, and you can keep Darcy hanging on a bit longer while we do." He waited until she began to walk away again, then added spitefully, "I might warn you, love, that if you decide to accept Darcy's proposal before I am ready to let you go, I'll be forced to tell him that I've bedded you. Twice."

"And Annabelle would be sure to hear about it as well, Grant," she reminded him, never breaking her angry stride. "You'd be hanging yourself with your own noose, so don't try to threaten me. Don't *ever* try to threaten me again!"

* * *

A few days later, she was topping off the feed bins, Sweet Cheek cuddled in the pocket of her work apron, when she heard a terrible commotion start up at the opposite end of the barn. Curious, she went to investigate the disturbance. There, in a far stall, she found Paddy, Aaron, and Grant all trying to subdue a very agitated colt.

Grant approached the young animal warily, his voice as soothing as velvet. "Now, Challenger, settle down, boy. It's not as bad as all that. Aaron here just wants to fit you with another set of shoes. We've been through all this before, and you know it's nothing to get so riled up about." He made a grab for the lead line dangling from Challenger's halter, but the horse shied away at the last moment, his eyes rolling wildly as he reared up on his hind legs.

"Damn!" Grant swore softly, ducking hastily away from the flailing hoofs. "You're getting to be more trouble than you're worth, Challenger. I'm beginning to think the only way to get you to settle down may be to geld you, you big dumb beast! And with your bloodlines, I'd really hate to resort to such drastic measures, especially when it won't guarantee results."

"I can talk to Clancy about puttin' a wee bit of somethin' in his feed to calm him," Paddy suggested quietly, not wanting to disturb the horse any more than he already was.

"It may come to that," Grant agreed, "but I hate to chance it. One never knows exactly how much or how little an individual animal can safely take into his system, and these thoroughbreds are particularly unpredictable that way."

From a safe distance outside the stall, Amanda asked, "What happens if you try everything and still can't get him to behave?"

"Then I'll just have to sell him for what I can get out of him and have done with it."

"Dat or shoot da ornery critter," Aaron muttered, eyeing the colt with disgust. "Dis fella seems set on

gibin' me trouble ever' time I'se got to fit new shoes
to him. Nice as pie any oder time, but a debil when it
comes to bein' shod. He don't seem to know he's
s'posed t' lib up to his name by challengin' other hosses
on da track, not by gibin' me fits.''

Grant made another try for the lead line, but again
Challenger was having none of it. With a shrill neigh,
he lunged away, his teeth bared in warning, his nostrils
flared and quivering.

''You are the stupidest piece of horseflesh I've ever
encountered,'' Grant grumbled, retreating once more.
''I may just take Aaron's suggestion after all.''

Amanda had crept cautiously forward and was now
standing next to Paddy just outside the stall's closed
half-door. She'd completely forgotten about Sweet
Cheek until he suddenly tumbled from the confines of
her pocket and went dashing between the slats of the
door into Challenger's stall. In a blur of yellow fluff,
the duckling streaked through the loose straw, headed
directly for the fractious colt.

Without thinking, intent only on saving her beloved
pet, Amanda yanked at the stall door, frantic to open
it. ''No!'' she cried, stumbling inside. ''Sweet Cheek!
No!''

Challenger gave a startled neigh, dancing and rearing
nervously, his hoofs crashing down perilously close to
the small, defenseless duck even as Grant grabbed
Amanda and pulled her away from danger, his hand
closing over her mouth to keep her from crying out
again and further distressing the crazed horse. Then,
just as everyone was certain the poor duckling was
about to be trampled, Sweet Cheek let loose with a
series of small but imperious *quacks*, his tiny head tilted
up toward the fretful horse.

For an instant, Challenger seemed to halt in mid-
motion, his forefeet frozen in the air. Slowly, as if controlled by unseen forces, he carefully let his hoofs fall
harmlessly to the earth. His ears pricked forward and
his eyes seemed to bulge as he lowered his huge head
to stare at this newest intruder.

As Challenger's nose edged ever closer to the little duckling, Amanda cringed, sure the horrid beast meant to eat her precious Sweet Cheek before her eyes. Her shriek came out as no more than a pitiful moan, muffled by Grant's hand. She and the others watched in helpless fascination as Challenger's lips quivered and parted to reveal those big, hard teeth. Just as Amanda was about to scrunch her eyes shut, not wanting to witness such a terrible tragedy, Challenger nuzzled the baby duck curiously, sending the ball of fluff tumbling beak over downy bottom.

Before anyone could actually comprehend what he was seeing, Sweet Cheek righted himself, marched brazenly up the Challenger once more, and gave the horse a sharp peck on the muzzle with his beak. Then he quacked out another command and stood his ground.

Poor Challenger seemed confused. He shook his head, sending his mane flying, and stared at the duckling. Sweet Cheek responded by waddling unconcernedly through Challenger's forelegs as the befuddled horse craned his neck to look beneath his own belly at the bossy little bird.

Amanda held her breath, watching in disbelief. The three men did likewise. No one spoke, no one moved, as Sweet Cheek wandered about beneath Challenger's bulk. Each time the duckling brushed against the horse's leg, Challenger would twitch noticeably, but not once did he attempt to kick out. And when Sweet Cheek finally settled onto a tuft of straw near Challenger's head, the big animal heaved a mighty sigh, nuzzled the duckling ever so gently, and accepted a reciprocal stroke from the little orange beak. Within seconds, Challenger calmed, the muscles beneath his sleek coat relaxing visibly, his ears flopping drowsily, his eyelids half closed.

"Amanda, honey," Grant drawled softly, removing his hand from her mouth at last, "I want you to call Sweet Cheek over here now. Do it very quietly and calmly. We don't want to upset Challenger again."

"What if he won't come to me?" she whispered

back. "I've never had to call him before. He just seems to follow wherever I go."

"Then get his attention and walk out of the stall. Walk slowly, and head straight for Aaron's shop."

"Why?" Amanda's look was pure suspicion.

"Because, as crazy as it sounds, I think Sweet Cheek is the key to Challenger's best behavior. It's happened before, though we've never seen it here at Misty Valley. High-strung thoroughbreds that are difficult to handle suddenly forming an attachment of some sort to another animal—be it a cat or dog or even another horse—and calming considerably when their newfound friend is near. However, I've never heard of one taking a liking to a duck before," he added with a confused shrug. "I'm betting that if Sweet Cheek follows you, Challenger will trail along behind as docilely as a little lamb."

She stared at him, incredulous. "If you're trying to be funny, I fail to see the joke, Grant. And if by some strange chance you are serious, I think your mind is coming unhinged. I've never heard such a wild tale."

" 'Tis true, Miss Amanda," Paddy assured her with a quick nod. "To be sure. I've seen it b'fore with me own two eyes."

"And what happens if you're wrong?" Amanda asked, not sure she believed either of them. "What if that is not the case, here and now, with Challenger and Sweet Cheek? Suppose the horse bolts and runs right overtop of me? You might be willing to bet on my life, but I sure as Hades am not!"

Jerking loose of Grant's hands, she marched out of the stall, intent on getting away from the lot of them before they got her killed. She hadn't gone a dozen paces when she heard a sound that made her heart begin thumping madly in her breast and beads of cold sweat pop out on her brow. Chill bumps raised all along her arms and skittered from the top of her skull to the base of her spine. Behind her came the steady clip-clop of Challenger's hoofs, accompanied by Sweet Cheek's intermittent quacking.

Either he sensed her near panic or he saw the shiver that racked her lean frame. Grant's voice lent her some small courage as he called out softly from close behind. "You're doing fine, Amanda. Just keep going, darling. Slow and easy."

She didn't have much choice in the matter. Her only hope of ridding herself of this strange entourage she'd suddenly collected was to steer a course toward the blacksmith shop and pray Challenger did not become nasty on the way—or once they got there.

Luck was with her. They reached the farrier's without mishap, but as soon as Amanda started to leave, and Sweet Cheek to follow her, Challenger began to stomp and snort with renewed vigor. "You'll have to stay until Aaron has finished," Grant told her.

"Oh, no," Amanda replied, eyeing him malevolently. Scooping Sweet Cheek up, she plopped the duckling into Grant's hands. "Sweet Cheek can stay, but I'm leaving."

Sweet Cheek had other ideas. He set up a squawk fit to wake the dead and promptly tried to take a chunk of flesh from Grant's finger. "Ouch! The blasted pest bit me!"

Meanwhile, Aaron and Paddy were having a time of their own, trying to calm the fractious colt. Things were fast going from bad to worse when Grant dumped the wriggling duck back into Amanda's arms, led her unceremoniously to an overturned nail keg at the entrance to the smithy, and firmly commanded, "Sit down, shut up, and stay put, or I swear you'll find duck soup and horse steak on your supper menu tonight."

She sat.

Immediately, Sweet Cheek stopped squawking and settled down.

Challenger calmed as well, and Aaron got on with the job of replacing the colt's shoes.

Afterward, Amanda led the way back to Challenger's stall, feeling much like the Pied Piper of Hamelin. This trip, Sweet Cheek preferred to sit on Amanda's shoulder, where he could ride facing his new equine friend.

All went well until Challenger decided to get playful. Coming up close behind Amanda, the colt nudged her shoulder with his nose. Unprepared, she lurched forward, and would have gone sprawling if Grant hadn't caught at her arm to keep her upright. Whirling around, frightened and angry and thoroughly fed up, she found Grant laughing at her. Likewise, Challenger tossed his big head, bared his teeth, and whinnied—and for the life of her, it seemed to Amanda that the horse was laughing, too! Even Sweet Cheek was making odd chirruping noises she'd never heard him make before, rather a cross between a hiccup and a chuckle.

Amanda wanted to give them all a good shaking! Instead, to her own surprise as well as Grant's, she began to laugh, weakly at first, and then more heartily. The sound rippled merrily from her throat. To her further amazement, she found herself stepping forward, her hand outstretched until it met with Challenger's nose. As the horse nuzzled into her touch, she sighed shakily and petted him. "They should have named you Trouble," she quipped.

Hesitantly, she slid the lead line from Grant's hands into her own. "I'll take him the rest of the way, if you want," she offered shyly.

"Are you sure?"

"Not really, but I have Sweet Cheek to protect me. Besides, if a defenseless baby duck can stand up to this huge beast, then I should be able to do so, too. Perhaps Sweet Cheek can help me cure my cowardice."

"You are not a coward, Amanda. A coward runs from what he fears. It takes a lot of bravery to face up to your fears instead, and meet them headlong." His hand came up, his fingers gently caressing the contour of her cheek, a contemplative look on his face. "No, my sweet little gambler. When it comes to something that counts, something you truly want, you'd rather fight than flee, wouldn't you? I honestly think you'd wager against the Devil himself if you felt you held the better hand."

"Only if I was sure I could win. I'm not a fool, Grant."

"No," he agreed softly. "You're a very smart, very beautiful woman—and that's an extremely dangerous combination, my dear. Maybe that's why you continue to intrigue me so. It's like being fascinated by flames, knowing they can either warm you or burn you, wondering just how close you dare come to them without risk of being consumed."

After the incident with Challenger, Amanda did, indeed, feel braver around the horses—as long as little Sweet Cheek was by her side. Also, as Grant had promised, she was relieved of her stall-mucking duties and elevated to grooming status, now that she no longer feared being in the stalls with the animals and could freely touch them without such paralyzing fright, though she did so now with a good measure of caution and a great deal of respect. Even her riding skills began to improve drastically.

Meanwhile, she was still studying Grant's books, learning all she could about caring for the horses and managing the farm. She bombarded Grant with questions, and when he was too busy, she asked Paddy or Clancy. Additionally, she carefully reviewed all the ledgers and accounts, checking on payroll and purchases and expenditures, learning where and when they bought feed, which crops they grew themselves, and how and when they were harvested. She maintained a separate accounting ledger of her own, and at the end of each week she compared it with the one Grant kept, just to double-check all the tallies and to make certain she was doing things properly.

From the start, she caught small errors, pointing them out to Grant when she did. Invariably, her sums were more correct, and calculated in half the time it took him to figure them. It seemed her talent for numbers was not restricted to cards, and was proving more valuable to the farm with each passing day. Before long, Grant put her in charge of figuring their employee payroll. Next, he turned the accounting books over to her completely, much relieved not to have to spend his time and energy in that direction, though he did check the accounts thoroughly each and every week.

"Don't you trust me, Grant?"

"Sure. As far as I can see you, and half as far as I could throw you," he responded with a wry grin. "While I will allow that we are getting along better these days, and you are becoming an unexpected asset to the farm, I haven't forgotten how you came to own half of Misty Valley to begin with, my dear."

"You still think I rooked your brother, don't you?" she answered, frowning. "Are you afraid I'll do the same to you?"

"No, but as the saying goes, an ounce of prevention is worth a pound of cure. I simply don't intend to give you the opportunity to do so."

"Cheating you would mean cheating myself, Grant."

As he continued checking the accounts, his reply was a droll "I'll sleep easier knowing that you realize that, Amanda."

"Grant?" She was leaning over his shoulder, watching him work.

"What?" When she didn't respond immediately, he looked up from his papers, one dark brow arched in question.

With her chin tilted imperiously upward, she promptly wrinkled her nose, crossed her eyes, and stuck her tongue out at him.

He laughed. "Is that all you have to say, you homely puss?"

"I thought it sufficient."

"Not at all."

Without warning, his arm snaked around her waist. In the next instant, she found herself on his lap, his desk chair tilting precariously beneath their combined weight. "I've warned you before, you sassy imp, not to point that tempting tongue at me unless you intend to use it." His fingers gently closed about her chin, bringing her face close to his, her lips within reach.

"And I know exactly how you should employ it, my sweet Amanda."

Warm, firm, commanding, his lips plied hers—and hers answered. With easy pressure, he parted her lips and tugged her tongue into the heated haven of his mouth, there to tangle intimately with his own. Between her silken thighs a heavy throbbing was born, the rhythm matching the suckling motions of his mouth and the mad drumming of her heart. His fingers left her face, drifting downward, following the curve of her delicate throat, pausing briefly at its base to note her pounding pulse; going on to etch the heart-shaped bodice of her gown, delving beneath the sheltering fabric in search of succulent fruit—teasing, tempting, until she shivered in delight and growing desire, and her arms tightened around his neck.

His other hand left her waist to find its way beneath her skirts. Hard. Warm. Work-callused. And familiar— much too familiar!

On a groan of despair and self-disgust, Amanda tore her mouth from his. Her hands came down to push at his chest. "No! Blast it, Grant! I told you I was having no more of this from you, and I meant it! Now, let me up!"

"And if I refuse?" he taunted, his eyes glowing like emerald coals, his smile that of a wolf toying with a mouse. "Honey, you're so hot for me, you're ready to ignite like dry tinder. Why deny yourself—and me?"

Her hands fell from his chest, and for a moment he thought she would surrender to their mutual desire. Then she repeated, her voice as chilled as winter, "I said, no! I'm warning you, Grant! I know I've never seen you geld one of your stallions, but I'm sure I could make a fair stab at wounding your manhood if you persist!"

It was then that he felt the slight prick through his trousers. Only his eyes moved as he cautiously glanced down to find the point of his own letter opener aimed directly at a most treasured part of his male anatomy. "You wouldn't," he muttered, hardly daring to breathe.

"Try me," she bluffed, her eyes meeting his with bold intent even as she prayed he could not feel how she was trembling inside.

Slowly he withdrew his hands from her clothing, holding them out at his sides in a gesture of defeat. "Fine. You're free. Take your weapon and go, you hellion!"

Hastily, she scooted off his lap and tossed the dagger-shaped opener back onto the top of his desk. For several seconds they stared at each other.

"Why, Amanda?" he asked with a curious frown. "Why are you being so stubborn now, when you know what pleasure we can bring one another? It's not as if you have a reputation to preserve, after all."

"For which I have you to thank," she reminded him stiffly.

"Then why?"

It was providential that Chalmers should knock on the door at that moment to announce Annabelle's arrival.

Amanda flashed Grant a grim smile. "That's why. Your reason has just appeared, to discuss wedding plans, no doubt. And if you want to enjoy your honeymoon with her, you'll keep your paws out from under my skirts, you faithless fiend!"

Chapter 18

ALL was not roses and bliss at Misty Valley. The tension between Grant and Amanda was as thick as river fog, affecting more than just the two of them. As if their mutual, growing attraction was not disturbing enough, there were other business and personal matters influencing their lives. It was creating havoc for everyone.

Regardless of the fact that she wanted Grant, that she loved him more than she'd ever imagined it was possible to love any other human being, Amanda was stubbornly resisting her desire for him—and his for her. Which, in turn, only made Grant more surly than usual. She was a constant irritant to him, an itch he couldn't scratch, one that only got worse with each passing day. Consequently, his temper flared. Predictably, hers ignited to match his. And poor Chalmers was once again stuck in the middle of the fray.

Additionally, the entire farm was in a tizzy trying to get ready for the midsummer horse auction. Several business transactions were at crucial stages, with major decisions and a great deal of money hanging in the balance. Again, Amanda was the crux of Grant's problems, and he was not above letting her know that he was none too happy with the situation.

"Damn it, Amanda! I can't negotiate with these people with one hand tied behind my back! I can't consult with you before each and every decision I'm forced to make on the spur of the moment!"

"Hogwash! It's not as if I'm asking for any more consideration than you would concede to any other partner you might have. You're just being ornery because I happen to be that partner. Well, mister, that's something you are going to have to learn to live with. Misty Valley is half mine, and I deserve some say in the business deals that take place. If these little delays are so bothersome, then include me in the conferences, and we can all decide the terms together."

"When hell freezes over!" he retorted hotly. "The last thing I need is you jeopardizing delicate negotiations by flaunting your 'assets' around in front of potential clients."

"Your stupidity is showing again, Grant. Not to mention your asinine bigotry. Merely because I am a woman does not preclude my having a brain. Need I point out that I am far superior to you when it comes to balancing the farm books?"

"Simply because you have a flair for figures does not make you a genius at business matters, my dear."

"And merely being a man doesn't make you one, either. Now, just to make things perfectly clear to you, and to avoid any further misconceptions along these lines, I won't mince words with you. Either I attend the meetings with you and learn firsthand all that is involved in each agreement, or you can kiss the deals good-bye, Mr. Almighty Gardner. I refuse to sign anything you bring to me after the fact; and as my partner, you can't buy, sell, or trade so much as a bale of straw without my approval, and we both know it."

"You can't do this to me, Amanda!"

Her answering smile was that of a cat licking canary feathers from its paws. "I just did."

"It's blackmail!"

"Discuss it with your attorney. In the meantime, I believe you have a meeting set up with Andrew Hastings next Friday. I suggest you resign yourself to including me in that discussion. I also suggest that you decide to behave decently toward me then, as behooves a gentleman, or I shall make you rue the day you were born."

"I already do. I have since the moment we met. You have done nothing since but make my life miserable!"

"Ha!" she shot back. "You don't know what miserable is—yet!"

Amanda had him over a barrel, and there was little he could do about it but fume. It grated him to admit that the little witch held the future of Misty Valley balanced on her slender, enamel-tipped fingers. To top it all, the greedy, grasping piratess had the law on her side! Either he involved her in the talks, or she could foul several lucrative deals, while including her might well have the same result.

It was like making a pact with the Devil. Any way he turned he was bound to lose. The woman was making a fool of him, on a personal level and now in his business ventures, and if there was anything Grant hated, it was being made to look foolish. Lord! If Tad had to lose half the farm to a woman, why couldn't it have been to a nice, tractable old lady who would keep her nose to her knitting and out of Grant's way? Why did it have to be this female vixen? This stubborn, delectable, gum-chewing, gambling goddess?

To further frustrate matters, Annabelle had taken it into her head to publicly proclaim her engagement to Grant at the upcoming centennial celebration in Lexington on July Fourth, and nothing Grant could say would dissuade her.

"Darling, it's the perfect time," she argued, sweetly but with a determined glint in her eyes. "All our friends will be there. We can announce it during the raffle for the picnic dinners, when you bid the most for my basket. It will be such a lark, so unique and unexpected.

Of course, Mother will still insist on having a betrothal dinner later, but . . .''

"With half the county already aware that we intend to marry, how can you say it will be unexpected?'' he responded brusquely.

"Oh, Grant! Don't be such a stick-in-the-mud! That's precisely why I want to announce it this way. If our marrying is no surprise, officially declaring it in this manner certainly will be. It will add to the day's festivities. People will remember it for years to come.''

"I'm sure they would, if only because it lacks the decorum of the normal engagement announcement.''

"You're a fine one to talk!'' Annabelle huffed. "Half the town is whispering behind their hands, wondering what is going on between you and that trollop you have living in the same house with you! Why, you can't imagine the comments I've heard, the questions I've had to counter because of it!''

"Ah, finally we come to the real reason you're in such an all-fired hurry to announce our betrothal to one and all, when we already discussed waiting until Christmas to do so. You want to hush the gossips.''

"Yes,'' she admitted more softly, "but it's more than that.'' Annabelle ducked her head, her cheeks rosy with embarrassment as she refused to meet his look. "I'm not positive, but I suspect I may be with child. If I am, waiting would not be a good idea.''

Grant was dumbstruck. Until this exact moment, hearing those fateful words falling from Annabelle's lips, he hadn't realized how totally disenchanted he'd become with her these past months. Even before that, before Amanda had ever appeared, he'd made countless excuses to delay announcing his intention of marrying the blonde, always finding some plausible reason to put it off. Now, finally, when it was far too late, he suddenly realized why. The truth of the matter was simple. He didn't love Annabelle—hadn't for some time, if ever.

Upon reflection, he had to admit that he'd initiated their relationship with the same sane reasoning he applied to a business venture, with more calculation than passion, if he were honest about it. She was cultured, a lady born and bred; beautiful, if spoiled; young enough and healthy enough to bear him several children, among them hopefully a couple of sons to help him carry on the horse farm; and marriage between them would almost ensure added acreage to the farm, since Grant and the Fosters were neighbors.

Yes, he'd desired her, but even that had been more of a convenience than anything else. Once he'd decided to marry her, it had been easier to sweet-talk Annabelle into his bed when he wanted a woman than to make those long rides into town to visit a brothel on the occasional Saturday night.

Of course, he'd been surprised, the first time, to discover that his bride-to-be was not a virgin. Well, actually, she was, but not to the full extent that most young women were. As Annabelle had tearfully explained, she'd had a riding accident as a young girl which had ruptured her maidenhead; and after having a doctor friend confirm that this was, indeed, possible, Grant had not doubted Annabelle's story.

Just as he did not doubt her now, though it pained him to accept the fate he'd brought down upon his head. He'd thought he'd been so careful, so cautious in taking measures not to get her pregnant whenever they'd made love. Obviously, he'd not been careful enough, and now he was neatly caught in his own trap—obliged to marry her whether he wanted to or not, to make good his half promises to a woman he didn't love, didn't even desire any longer. All because he'd been hasty and randy and careless. At this bleak juncture, the only good thing about this whole unfortunate mess was that he might soon have the son he'd wished for.

"You say you're not positive," he told her. "How long before you can be sure?"

She gave an agitated shrug. "I don't know. A couple of weeks, I suppose."

With the Fourth of July just a week away, he could now understand Annabelle's rush in wanting him to publicly declare his intentions before everyone. As it

was, their wedding would have to follow an embarrass-
ingly short engagement period if Annabelle were to
prove pregnant after all. Tongues would surely wag,
and brows would rise when the baby arrived several
weeks prior to the acceptable time, but at least they
would be married. He would have done the honorable
thing by her; their child would not bear the stigma of
being labeled a bastard. Certainly, they wouldn't be the
first couple to have precipitated their vows. And given
time, the gossip would die down and be all but forgotten.

"All right. We'll announce our betrothal at the centennial," he agreed, feeling as if a mountain had just
settled on his chest. For Annabelle's sake, he forced a
note of cheer into his voice and a slight smile to his
lips. "I'll come by and speak with your father beforehand, and officially get his permission to marry you.
Then we'll go to town and choose an engagement ring
for you. You'll want to show it off to your lady friends,
I'm sure."

With a squeal of delight, she launched herself at him,
twining her arms about his neck and lifting her radiant
face for his kiss, "Oh, Grant! Thank you! You won't
regret it! I'll make you the best wife you've ever wished
for!"

Little did she know how much he already regretted
it. And why, as Annabelle's lips met his, did his heart
yearn toward an ebony-haired siren with eyes the color
of a midsummer sky?

In this extreme state of emotional turmoil, it took
very little to light the fuse to Grant's temper. Two evenings later, Stanford Darcy managed it without even
trying. All it took was for Grant, tired, disgusted,
downhearted, to step onto the dark veranda and find
Darcy and Amanda entwined in a fervent embrace on
the far swing. He exploded with the force of an overdue
volcano blast.

"Darcy, get your hands off her!" he raged, his long
strides taking him to where the couple sat. One big

hand came out to snatch hold of the lawyer's collar, literally yanking the man to his feet and away from Amanda. "What the hell do you think you're doing, you simpleminded, pencil-pushing little runt? I could tear you apart with my bare hands, with no effort at all," he taunted, giving Darcy a sharp shake. "And all the excuse I would need is your trespassing on my territory."

"Amanda in—invited me," Darcy squeaked out through the tightening band of his shirt collar.

"Oh, I'm sure she did," Grant intoned, menace in every syllable as his gaze found hers. She sat huddled at one end of the swing, staring at him as if he had just lost his mind, her lips parted in soundless astonishment. "However, she did not have the freedom or permission to do so."

At last Amanda found her tongue. "Permission?" she echoed angrily.

The fury in his eyes and his sharp command stopped her short as he barked out, "Shut up, Amanda. I warned you what would happen if I caught you letting Darcy sniff too closely at your skirts, didn't I?"

Before she could answer, he gave the hapless attorney another shake. With his teeth bared, he snarled, "Amanda is mine, Darcy. And she'll be mine until I decide otherwise. Now, if you're still confused, let me spell it out for you—"

"Grant! No!" Amanda wailed, springing at him.

With ridiculous ease, he shook her loose of his arm. "I've had her sweet body beneath mine," he continued as if she'd never tried to interrupt him. "Several times, in fact. I'm her lover. Her only lover. And I don't intend to share her with anyone, let alone the likes of you.

"Now," he said, releasing the smaller man suddenly and giving him a shove toward the veranda steps, "I'd heartily suggest you tuck your tail between your legs and slink back to town like the spineless vermin you are. And be forewarned that if I catch you around here again, I'll tear you limb from limb and throw your broken body to the vultures.''

As Darcy scurried for his carriage with the utmost haste, not even bothering with a farewell, Amanda exclaimed, ''Grant! For God's sake, the poor man didn't do anything more than kiss me! How could you do this to him? To me? You had no right! No right!''

With clenched fists, she pounded on his stiff back, until he whirled about and caught her wrists in his hands. ''I claimed the right for myself. Just as I intend to claim you, my fickle, philandering puss—anytime, anywhere, and any way I want.''

With no more warning than that, he swung her into his arms and marched into the house with her, Amanda's irate shrieks piercing his eardrums every step of the way up the long staircase. ''Put me down, you overbred brute! You muleheaded beast! Damn you, Grant Gardner! I won't let you do this!''

He strode into her room, slammed the door shut with a vicious kick of his boot, and tossed her onto the bed in a flurry of skirts, his fingers already ripping at the buttons of his shirt. ''You can't stop me, Amanda, and in a few minutes, you won't even want to try. You'll be begging me to make love to you.''

She tried to scramble off the other side of the bed, but he caught her skirts and dragged her back, then sat on them as he proceeded to tug off his boots. ''You arrogant jackass! You rutting dog!'' she screamed, her fingernails raking red welts down his bare back. ''I'll kill you for this!''

''You might try,'' he said imperiously, ''for about ten seconds. But in the end, you and I will die together, in that heart-stopping moment when we become one with each other, when nothing else in the world matters except touching that elusive piece of heaven only the two of us can grasp together.''

He was looming over her now, gloriously naked, his muscles already gleaming with a fine sheen of perspiration as his hands tore her clothing from her, baring her body to his searing green gaze. Then his lips claimed hers with bold demand, smothering her protests, his hands holding hers to the bed, away from his burning flesh.

Still far from helpless, she thrashed beneath him, bucking and heaving in an effort to throw him off-balance. Failing that, she tried to bring her knee crashing into his groin, but he anticipated her move and settled his own strong legs between hers. Tearing her lips from his, she groaned, "You great oaf! You'll pay for this! In blood!"

True to her promise, when his lips closed over hers once more, she bit him. For just an instant he drew back, startled. Then he leaned forward, a devilish smile etching his mouth—and administered an answering bite to her lower lip. He laughed when she yelped, her tongue snaking out to lick at the slight hurt.

As if to further teach her a lesson in bedroom manners, he proceeded to pepper her mouth, her throat, and her shoulders with tiny, stinging nips of his sharp white teeth, soothing them afterward with warm, wet laps of his tongue and soft, teasing kisses. By the time he reached her breasts, Amanda's senses were swimming. Her protests had long since diminished, replaced by breathless whimpers of desire. Held fast, she could do little but arch her body toward his, as a delectable offering for his delight.

"Say it," he demanded, his teeth lightly grazing her pouting nipple.

Too far gone to deny his command, too crazed with desire to care about anything but satisfying this fierce need that only he could quench, she whispered, "I want you, Grant. God help me, but I need you more than life itself!"

Her reward was his hot mouth closing upon her yearning breast. Tugging, suckling, fanning the fire in her veins and sending shafts of white lightning to the very center of her being.

Her body strained toward his, her wrists pushing against the restraint of his hands. "Please. I want to touch you."

His fingers released her, free now to travel their own course down her quivering body. Teasing, tantalizing, tracing a blazing path toward the heart of her desire. Finding, at last, the moist heat of her. Lingering and stroking her there until she was crying out to him, brazenly returning caress for searing caress, each building the other's passion to a smoldering summit just this side of ecstasy.

Only then, when they were both trembling mindlessly with intense yearning, did he join his body with hers. Amanda's release came instantly, with an awesome force that ripped the breath from her body and sent ripple after ripple of rapture coursing through her. Her spasms triggered his, and with a primal roar from the depths of his soul, he joined her on a glorious journey through cascading stars and swirling clouds that caught them up in their mad tempest and tossed them far into the sparkling realms of splendor.

As her mind drifted toward full consciousness once more, gradually easing its hold on the final, echoing chords of passion, the first thing Amanda became aware of was Grant's hand gently stroking her bare side. From ribs to calf, his fingers trailed easily over her pleasure-misted flesh, raising a ridge of gooseflesh in their wake. "I hope this sets to rest any ridiculous ideas you might be harboring about resuming your lukewarm relationship with that insipid lawyer," he said, a veiled note of steel underlying his softly spoken words.

Immediately, she felt her hackles begin to rise in response to his arrogance. "Oh, I believe you put a stop to any future courting from Darcy," she answered tartly, pulling loose from his arms and gathering the bedcovers over her torso. "I hope you are very proud of yourself, Grant. If my reputation was tarnished before, it is in tatters now, I'm sure. That was your primary objective, wasn't it? To make sure everyone in three counties is aware of what a terrible tart I am?"

"Actually, I didn't give it a thought," he admitted readily, arching a dark brow at her clumsy attempt to cover herself, while he lay on the majority of the blankets. "When I saw him kissing you, I reacted entirely on instinct. The only thing I could think of was to get him away from you—and keep him gone for good. That and impressing upon both of you the fact that you are solely mine."

"First let me say that you have the instincts of a charging bull. Second, at the risk of my forever wounding your male pride, while you might have impressed Darcy, you failed miserably on my account."

"Oh, I did, did I?" he challenged. "That's funny. I distinctly recall you wriggling and moaning beneath me not five minutes ago."

Her face flamed at his blatant reminder of the way her body had so readily betrayed her. "I won't bother to deny it, Grant. But one night does not a mistress make."

"Three nights," he corrected her smugly. "And countless sessions of lovemaking."

"Well, I hope you enjoyed them, darling," she purred spitefully, "and I hope you remember them fondly, because your romps in my bed will henceforth hinge upon my whims, not yours, and I wouldn't hold my breath hoping for a repeat performance if I were you. Also, regardless of what you wish, I do not now, nor will I ever, consider myself your 'territory,' your possession, or your mistress, exclusively or otherwise."

"Is that so?"

"Indeed, it is." Even as she spoke, her feet were lashing out at him, catching him off guard and off-balance as she promptly kicked him off the edge of her bed onto the hard floor. Before he could recover, she reached into the drawer of her bedtable and produced a lethal-looking pair of scissors, brandishing them at him.

"Now, just trot your naked carcass out of my room, and think twice before trying to sneak back in here in the dark of night, as you seem to have a penchant for doing now and then. I'll whistle when I require your services again, my handsome obliging stallion. Until then, kindly keep your randy desires under control and your interference in my affairs limited to business only."

Rage battled with contempt in the look he gave her. "If you think for one moment those shears you're waving about will keep me from you, you are sadly mistaken, Amanda. Besides, it isn't so much me you are fighting as your own lusty nature, and for that there is no cure but a man between your thighs."

As he gathered his clothes, he continued scathingly. "I don't mind playing the stud for you. It suits my purposes nicely, in fact. So I'll just wait until that itch you have becomes too much for you to bear, and you'll come panting after me like a she-cat after a tom." At the door, he paused just long enough to add a final, cutting remark. "You've tasted passion now, my sweet, and I'm willing to bet you're well and truly addicted to it. We'll see who whistles first, shall we?"

The blades of her weapon were still quivering in the splintered wood of the closed door, Grant's retreating footsteps yet echoing in the hallway beyond, as Amanda dissolved in a furious fit of tears.

Chapter 19

    As Grant rode toward the Foster home the following morning, on his way to formally ask his future father-in-law for Annabelle's hand in marriage, he thought about all he'd said and done the night before. He'd behaved in a manner unbefitting a gentleman, to say the least, threatening Darcy, blurting out private bedroom matters, and nearly attacking Amanda afterward, not to mention the hateful things he'd said to her, merely because she'd hurt his pride. Thoroughly ashamed of himself, he admitted, if only to himself, that he'd behaved like a lust-crazed animal. He hated to think what might have resulted if Amanda's passions had not risen to match his own. He'd acted like the hotheaded stud she'd labeled him, and he deserved nothing less than to have his hide tacked to the barn door and left to dry.

    To make matters worse, Darcy was sure to spread the news that Grant and Amanda were lovers. In one inconsiderate moment of anger, Grant had let his tongue overrule his good sense, and now several people would pay for his indiscretion. What little respect Amanda had managed to glean from the townspeople in the past few weeks would be destroyed. His own reputation would fare better, of course, merely because he was a man and these things were to be expected, but explaining this to Annabelle and her family would certainly prove embarrassing, particularly now, with their engagement announcement in the offing. The rumors would be flying, and he'd be fortunate if Annabelle didn't demand his head on a platter, which was well within her right, since of them all she was the most innocent victim in this mess.

Thinking of Annabelle—innocent Annabelle—triggered another thought in Grant's head, one that had been nagging at the back of his beleaguered brain for the past two days and suddenly popped through the fog into the clear light of day. So disturbing was it that Grant abruptly pulled his horse to a halt, stunned by the revelation that had just occurred to him.

If Annabelle were pregnant, as she claimed she might be, she would have had to conceive the child sometime before Amanda's arrival at Misty Valley, for since then Grant had not lain with her. According to his calculations, the last time they'd made love had been the middle of March, unless Annabelle had become pregnant earlier—and it was currently the end of June. The girl would be at least three and a half months along in her term by now, and it suddenly didn't make much sense to Grant that she would still be uncertain as to whether or not she was with child.

He was no doctor, but something was not adding up properly here. Surely if she were that far along, Annabelle would have had some indication before, some symptoms like the nausea he'd always heard plagued women in such a delicate condition, or fainting perhaps. And shouldn't her waistline and tummy be starting to expand a bit? Also, why hadn't she mentioned the possibility earlier, when she first suspected it? Why wait until now, and suddenly be hell-bent on getting publicly engaged?

Something smelled mighty fishy, and Grant was just suspicious enough not to want to fall into a trap unaware, especially with his emotions all in turmoil. Maybe, having admitted to himself that he really didn't love Annabelle and didn't want to marry her if he didn't have to, he was unconsciously searching for a way out of a commitment to her. Then again, it would be a hell of a situation if he were to marry her, only to discover too late that she wasn't pregnant after all, but had merely been trying to hurry their marriage along.

As he resumed his ride, Grant decided that before speaking with her father, he and Annabelle were going to have a long, serious talk. The little blonde had some explaining to do before he would be convinced that she wasn't up to some sort of feminine trickery.

Upon arriving at the house, Grant immediately asked for Annabelle. When he was told she was out at the stables and would be sent for at once, he told the servant not to bother. He would go for her himself. What the two of them needed to discuss was best said in private, away from prying eyes and ears. He would take her for a short walk, and they would straighten matters out between them.

If he'd thought the housemaid seemed a bit nervous about his plans to locate Annabelle himself, it was nothing to the reaction he got from the old estate manager. "Sir, why don't you just set yourself down out here in the yard, and I'll go inside and find her for you," the man said, casting a nervous glance behind him at the stables. "Matter of fact, why don't I have Miss Annabelle meet you in the gazebo? No need for you to go mucking about in there and get the shine off your boots."

With a laugh and a confused shake of his head, Grant declined the offer. "What's gotten into you, Sam? You know darned good and well that I spend most of my day inside barns and stables, and I can't remember when I last worried about getting straw dust or manure on my boots." He edged his way around the fellow, who seemed reluctant to let him past.

"Uh, Mr. Gardner, sir. I really don't think this is such a good idea, if you'll pardon my saying so."

"Whyever not?"

"Well . . . uh . . . Miss Annabelle won't want to be caught looking all grubby and such, you know."

"She'll get over it," Grant assured him. "Besides, it won't be the first time I've seen her with her hair straggling and horsehair on her clothes."

With a determined stride, Grant continued through the open doorway before Sam could voice any more lame excuses. Inside, all was shadowed and silent, save for the quiet shifting of hooves against straw. The hard-packed dirt floor muffled his footsteps as he made his way down the dusty aisle toward the stall where Annabelle's favorite horse was kept.

Then, before he could call out to her, he heard her soft laugh from the hayloft above his head—followed by a low, masculine groan. Bits of hay sifted downward through the cracks in the upper floorboards as something shuffled overhead. He heard a bump. A muffled squeal.

Before he reached the top rung of the mow ladder, Grant knew what he would find—knew why the Fosters' servants had been so reluctant to let him near the stables. There, bare-assed as the day she was born, and as slender as the last time he'd seen her milk-white body, was Annabelle—happily and energetically copulating with an equally naked young stablehand. Both were so involved in their mating that neither took note of his presence.

Until he spoke. "My, my! What have we here?" he jeered softly. "A little morning romp in the hay between mistress and servant? How common of you, my dear girl."

"Oh, my Lord!" Annabelle shrieked in alarm. Not knowing what to do first, she started to shove her lover from atop her, then changed her mind and tried to hug him to her in a vain effort to shield her nakedness. "Grant! What are you doing here?"

"Offhand, I'd say witnessing your infidelity, my sweet," he answered mildly. It crossed his mind, for a mere second, that he was taking Annabelle's defection much more calmly than he had Amanda's comparatively innocent spooning with Darcy the previous evening. Why this should be so eluded him at the moment.

Crossing his arms over his chest, he stared down at the two of them, his mouth quirking in ill humor as the young fellow tried to move away and Annabelle held him fast, peering warily over his shoulder. "Really, Grant! Your humor is misplaced. Besides, I defy you to tell me that you have not engaged in similar activities with that strumpet you claim is your partner!"

"That's a case of the pot calling the kettle black if ever I've heard one," he responded snidely, "and quite beside the point. Just now I'm more interested in hearing precisely how long this has been going on between the two of you. Or between you and God knows how many other men, for that matter," he added.

"Well, I refuse to tell you anything of the sort—at least until you have been decent enough to remove yourself and allow me time to dress. We can discuss this unfortunate episode then."

"Unfortunate episode?" he echoed, his brow arching. "Why, Annabelle, I consider this the most fortunate meeting of our relationship. You can't imagine how glad I am to discover the fickleness of your nature prior to committing myself to you for a lifetime. Of course, you realize this means we will not be getting married. I certainly can't have a wife who's not to be trusted around my farm help."

At this juncture, the stablehand managed to yank himself loose of Annabelle and tried to scramble, buck naked, toward the ladder. He hadn't managed two yards when Grant's boot came down upon his backside, pinning the hapless youth to the floor. "Stay put, or you'll be going down a hell of a lot faster than you came up," Grant warned darkly. "No one is going anywhere until I get some answers."

Meanwhile, Annabelle had reached hurriedly for her discarded clothing and was jerking it on without thought to the seams or the prickly hay imbedded in the fabric.

At any other time, Grant might have laughed at her

haste, if not her false modesty. He might also have pointed out to her that she had pulled her underdrawers on backward and her camisole on wrong-side-out. However, given the circumstances, his self-esteem was a bit dented and his mood correspondingly sour. After all, everyone knew it was one thing fo a man to be unfaithful—almost expected actually—but quite another for a woman.

"Now," he continued, "let's get on with this, shall we? Exactly how long have the two of you been consorting in dark corners?"

"Since . . . since he raped me the first time," Annabelle stammered, her face going from pink to glowing red.

At this, the fellow in question denied the charge quite loudly. "I did no such thing! Why, I would never have even looked . . ."

Added pressure from Grant's boot cut him short with a grunt. "Come now, Annabelle. You can't believe I'm that gullible," Grant sneered. "I've seen with my own eyes how gladly you accepted his advances today, and those delighted little moans of yours were not born of pain. I realize that getting caught with your pants down puts you at some disadvantage, but the least you owe me is the truth. How long?"

"Since that tart moved in with you," she claimed poutily.

Another reflexive jerk from beneath Grant's boot gave lie to Annabelle's words. Nudging the fellow, Grant put the question to him. "How long, lad?"

"Since just after Christmas last, sir. And that's the honest-to-God's truth."

"I see. Have you anything to add, Annabelle?"

A pleading look entered her eyes. "Grant, please! You must understand! I was so sure you would present me with an engagement ring over the holidays, and when you didn't, I was beside myself with disappointment."

"So you salved your wounds by having an affair with your stablehand. How quaint. Then, to compound your sins, you have the gall to claim you are carrying my child, all the while cajoling me into agreeing to announce our engagement earlier than planned. Tell me, Annabelle, are you or are you not breeding? If so, since when and by whom?''

Annabelle promptly burst into tears. Whether her emotion was real or feigned, Grant did not know. Neither did he care. Coming upon Annabelle and her lover had dealt him quite a blow, fortuitous though it might prove in the end, and he could not find an ounce of sympathy for her. Not while he was busy feeling so dreadfully ill used and trying his damnedest not to show it! Blast it! He'd trusted Annabelle, and she'd betrayed him!

"I didn't lie to you about that, Grant. You must believe me! I am going to have your child."

"Forgive me if I doubt that, my dear," he told her, a distinct bite to his words. "However, I am curious to know how far gone you are. You certainly don't look as if you're carrying a child. Judging from what I saw just a few minutes ago, I'd say your breasts and waist are as small as ever."

"You are a vile beast!" Annabelle sobbed.

"So I've been told before. How long since your last monthly flow, Annabelle?"

Her face flamed anew at his blunt question. Nevertheless, she drew herself up proudly and announced, "I've missed two, if you must know."

He sketched a slight bow in her direction. "Thank you, dear. That's all the proof I require. Since I've not bedded you in more than three months, I believe we can safely assume the child is not mine. I hope you and your young lothario are very happy together."

He turned and started back down the ladder.

"Grant! Wait!" Annabelle called after him. "Please! You can't leave me like this! You can't! What will I possibly say to Father?"

"Whatever suits you best, Annabelle. That is entirely your problem."

Grant was brooding. Feeling lonely and abused and betrayed. Up to his eyebrows in self-pity. And soused to his back teeth! After leaving Annabelle's, he'd ridden into Lexington, and hadn't started back home until he'd sampled the whiskey in every tavern in town. As he rode toward Misty Valley, depending in large part on his horse's sense of direction, he lamented all the disasters that had befallen him, listing them aloud.

"First Dad and Mother died. That started it, I guess. Then I had the farm and m'self and Tad to look after, and ole Tad was always gettin' in some trouble or other. Shoulda known better than to send that scamp to N'Orleans, 'specially with that Widmark friend of his. Shoulda known he'd come to grief.

"An' now he's gone, too. Didn't he know I'd f'rgive him anything, no matter how bad? Sure I'da been mad, but hellfire! He's my brother, an' I'd never have turned him away. Now I don't know where he is, or how he is, or even if the danged fool is still alive! Damn it all, anyway! Why does ever'body I love go away an' leave me? First my family, and now Annabelle, though I really didn't love her, I suppose—not like I should've. An' I've even lost half my home an' farm an' horses, too! How much is one man s'pposed to take?"

He gave his horse a companionable pat on the neck and continued his maudlin conversation as if the animal were actually listening to his complaints. "An' then who comes waltzin' into my life but that two-bit female bam—bamboozler.'Manda. A true tart if ever I saw one! All strawberry icin' over a heart of pure stone!" Grant laughed drunkenly at his own poor pun.

"Did you know she had the nerve to call me a stud? No, I guess I called me a stud. She called me a stallion. A handsome stallion, at that. Well, I guess tha's not so bad after all, is it, ole boy?" He gave the horse another pat. "Sort of a compliment, act-chally, if you think about it the right way. An' she's one fine filly, too, even if she ain't the lady she thinks she is."

He gave a snort. "Lady! Ha! Tha's a laugh! I'm beginnin' to wonder if I even know what a lady is anymore! On the one hand there's 'Manda, who shows up

dressed like a strumpet an' paints her toenails an' cracks
her gum an' cusses like a mule skinner when she's
mad—an' she turns out to be a virgin, of all the in—
incredible things you might imagine! An' on the other
hand, there's sweet little innocent Annabelle, the belle
of Lexin'ton, product of one of the finest Southern families, with the most impec—impec—best of manners.
Why, butter wouldn't melt on her tongue, an' she
wouldn't say 'shit' if she had a mouth full of it, an' she
goes to church every Sunday like clockwork—an' she's
more of a whore than 'Manda is, by God! Cuckolded
me, she did. Me! An' with 'er stableboy!

"Now, tell me, what the hell is a man s'pposed to
make of that? I'll tell you what," he went on in answer
to his own drunken query. "He's s'pposed to take warnin', tha's what. Warnin' that all women are Jezebels
at heart, given half the chance. Fickle as the day is
long, an' 'bout as trustworthy as a rattlesnake! They're
trouble, I tell you. Mean-hearted trouble, all of 'em!
But I got me a plan to get even, one that'll get the farm
back an' make both o' them gals sorry for treatin' me
so shabbily. You just see if I don't!"

By the time Grant arrived home, toppled off his
horse, and stumbled into the house, he was into his
third, full-voiced, off-key rendition of "On Top of Old
Smoky," warbling fit to wake the dead about "false-
hearted lovers" and how there wasn't a "girl in ten
thousand that a poor boy can trust."

He was halfway up the staircase, hanging onto the
banister for dear life, when Amanda appeared at the
top of the stairs, and Chalmers at the foot of them.
Chalmers sent Amanda a pained look, obviously em-
barrassed to have her witness Grant in such a condition.
"It appears the master has imbibed too freely this evening," he offered lamely.

"The *master* is as drunk as a skunk with its head
stuck in a whiskey barrel," Amanda corrected him
dryly.

"The *master* begs to differ," Grant told them both,

vainly trying to place his foot squarely on the next step. "I am not drunk."

"You could have fooled me," Amanda assured him.

"I'm merely a bit sloshed at the moment."

"I stand corrected, which is more than you seem capable of doing just now," she added, watching him slump into a sitting position. With a grin, she walked down to join him there. "Need some help, Grant?"

"The day I need help from a woman is the day they can dig my grave and toss me into it."

"Chalmers," Amanda said with a smothered chuckle, "go get the shovel—and brew a pot of strong black coffee while you're at it, will you please?"

"Witch!" Grant grumbled.

"Yes, well, we all have our cross to bear," she commiserated.

"You don't know the half of it."

"I have a feeling you're about to enlighten me, so why don't we wobble down to the study and you can tell Aunt Amanda all about it?" Half dragging, half supporting him, she led him to the sofa in his office, and by the time they finally got there she was glad to let him collapse.

"I've got to take charge of my life, 'Manda," he told her, peering up at her from bloodshot eyes. "You can see that, can't you? Somewhere, somehow, things got out of control. I've lost ever'thing because of it. My parents, my brother, my self-esteem, half of Misty Valley. Even Annabelle. This can't go on, you know."

Frowning, Amanda nonetheless nodded. "Of course not." What was the man rambling on about? What was this nonsense about losing Annabelle?

"I mean it, 'Manda. I have to get a grip on the reins again. An' you can help me do it."

"If you say so."

He sent her a lopsided grin. "I knew you'd agree. I knew I could count on you when the chips were down." He started to laugh. "When the chips were down!" he hooted, as if it were the most hilarious thing he'd ever heard. "Oh, tha's good!"

Amanda rolled her eyes and shook her head. "Very funny," she agreed.

"An' app-appropriate, too, since we're gonna be gamblin'."

"Gambling? Us?"

He nodded, his head bouncing like a fishing bobber. "Yep. You're gonna give me a chance to win back Tad's part of Misty Valley."

"No, I'm not. Where did you get such a crazy idea?"

"Aw, Mandy! You said you'd help! You can't go back on your word now!" His tone was the plaintive whine of a little boy begging for favors, one Amanda had never thought to hear from the great Grant Gardner.

"Want to bet?"

"Tha's what I've been tryin' to tell you, woman. The bet. The terms. Now, are you gonna listen?"

"Do I have a choice?" she asked drolly.

"Here's the plan. We play a game of poker, and whoever wins gets the whole farm. An' jus' to sweeten the pot, if I win, you have to stay an' be my mistress. How's that for a cha—challenge?"

"Just peachy," she smirked. "But only if you stay on as manager of the place if I win."

"Then the bet is on?"

"Not quite yet. First, explain to me, in terms I can understand, precisely why you are suddenly so willing to risk losing the remainder of your inheritance."

" 'Cause I've reached the end of my rope, don't you see?"

"Actually, it sounds as if you've reached the end of your sanity, Grant."

"That, too," he conceded. "Mandy, I own only half of my own prop'ty. You're set on runnin' the rest of it to ruin, 'stead of lettin' me do wha's best for the bizness. Hell, the men don' know who's in charge 'round here anymore! There are too many chiefs an' not 'nough Indians to suit me, an' it jus' can't go on like this much longer. There can only be one boss, an' if you won't let me buy you out, this is the only way to re—resol—fix it.

"B'sides," he added with a cheeky grin, "a woman's place is in 'er man's bed. Not b'hind a desk."

"Spoken with your usual flair for prejudice," she returned, applauding him. "And what if you lose it all, Grant? What if I win? What will you have done to yourself then? To your precious male pride?"

"Ha!" he mocked with a rueful laugh. "What pride? The little I have left is in the dung heap! My servants don't r'spect me anymore." At this, he slanted a sour look at Chalmers, who was placing the coffee service on the table before the sofa.

His gaze returned to Amanda accusingly. "You ridicule me at every turn, an' now Annabelle has taken up with 'er stableboy!"

"She did what?" Amanda and Chalmers echoed as one.

"Yeah! I caught 'er in the hay mow with 'im jus' this mornin'. Ruttin' like pigs! Only good thing about it was I hadn't gotten 'round to askin' 'er father for 'er hand in marriage. Which is def-initely out of the question now."

"I should hope so!" Chalmers exclaimed. Amanda was too dumbfounded to know what to say.

"An' the joke is on me, 'cause it's been goin' on for half a year, with me none the wiser," Grant bemoaned. "The twit had me halfway to the altar, believin' she was pregnant with my child!"

"Is she?" Amanda squeaked, her heart tumbling into her stomach.

"Pregnant? Yes. By me? No. An' b'fore either of you asks any more stupid questions, let me assure you that my aptitude with numbers is not so poor that I can't accurately calculate the prob—probabilities. There are none. The child is not mine. Even if it were, I wouldn't marry the silly baggage. I'd support the child, but never 'er."

"I'm sorry, Grant. Truly," Amanda told him in a small voice, thinking it was no wonder the poor man had been out trying to drown his sorrows in a bottle.

"Save your pity," he growled irritably. "Jus' break

out the cards and let me try to win back my home, and a portion of my self-esteem with it.''

"Grant, why don't you think about this for a spell? There's no hurry, after all. Take a few days to mull it over in your mind, and I'm sure you'll see the folly of it.''

"No. My mind is made up. Chalmers, you'll be our witness, since I've no doubt you were eavesdroppin' outside the door long enough to have heard everythin'.''

"Sir, if I might point out, your faculties are a bit—uh—dull just now. Perhaps Miss Amanda is right about waiting a while.''

"Listen, you traitorous bag of wind! We are goin' to do this, an' if you won't witness it, I'll get someone else to do it. It might also be in your best interest to pray that Amanda wins, 'cause if I prevail, you may find yourself on the next boat to England.''

"Grant, this is definitely not a good idea," Amanda persisted.

"Wha's the matter, Mandy? Scared you'll lose?'' he taunted.

The thought had crossed her mind, and the absolute last thing she wanted to do was forfeit her half of Misty Valley. Or to be at Grant's mercy as his mistress, at the beck and call of the man she loved more than anything on earth, only to be shoved aside with less consideration that last week's newspaper when he was through with her. To live on the edge of her nerves every day, just waiting for him to tire of her and kick her out. Offhand, Amanda couldn't imagine a worse fate for herself.

Of course, the chances of her ever winning Grant's heart were slim even if she didn't go through with this nonsense, if she remained half owner of the farm and Grant's partner. Heartache was bound to be hers either way. The only difference was, if she lost she'd also lose her self-respect, as well as her newfound wealth and stability. Whereas if she won, she would be twice as wealthy—and as Macy had once told her, with wealth came respect, reluctantly though it might be given. And respect was the one thing Amanda had always craved and never received much of.

The icing on the cake was the thought of being Grant's boss. Though vindictiveness was not normally in her nature, the idea of paying Grant back for some of the nasty jobs he'd made her do, the way he'd forced her to learn to ride despite her numbing fear of horses, was almost too delicious to pass up.

Besides, in his inebriated state, her chances of losing were practically nil. So what if it wasn't fair to take him up on his bet when he was half stewed for mourning the loss of his precious Annabelle? He was the one being so almighty insistent about this stupidity, wasn't he? He'd only be getting what he'd asked for—and scarcely half of what he truly deserved. After all, as the saying went, "All's fair in love and war."

Amanda's only problem was trying to decipher which applied in this instance—the love part, or the war.

Chapter 20

SUCH a wicked smile curved Amanda's lips that a chill raced down Chalmers' backbone, especially when she turned to him and cooed, "Bring the cards, Reggie. Master Gardner is long overdue for his comeuppance."

"Miss Amanda, are you sure about this?"

"I've never been more positive about anything. And get that worried look off your face. I'm not about to cheat your dear, drunken employer. You can stand by and watch as I fleece the poor sod fair and square. In fact, I insist that you do."

She poured Grant another steaming cup of black coffee and thrust it at him. "Drink up, Gardner. I don't want you falling asleep in the middle of the game."

A fresh deck of cards was promptly, if reluctantly, produced by the frowning Chalmers, as well as the necessary markers. Each began with an equal number of chips, agreeing that the first to lose all of them would lose the poker game. The contest began, the two opponents seated opposite each other across the low tea table, in deference to Grant, who could barely maintain an upright position on the sofa, let alone move to a more convenient spot.

At Amanda's insistence, Grant dealt first. To her delight, she found herself holding four deuces, easily winning the first hand. It seemed to set the tone for the night, for with each progressive hand, more of Grant's chips found their way to her side of the table, though few of hers strayed in his direction. Amanda's God-given talent for keeping track of the cards played held her in good stead, while Grant's drink-fogged mind lagged.

Additionally, she was extremely grateful that she'd worn gloves when performing her farm chores, for she'd collected few calluses to interfere with her play. Touch was an all-important sense for a professional gambler, giving him the advantage of having a "feel for the cards" that most occasional players lacked. By touch alone, she could tell if even one card was missing from the deck. Many were the times, in the past, that she'd caught fellow players trying to introduce marked cards into play, her sensitive fingertips alerting her to tiny bumps or pinpricks or rough spots on the cards; or to a trick known as "playing both ends against the middle," where certain cards had been minutely shaved along the center edge, making them slightly uneven and usually detected only by an experienced gambler.

Another favorite trick employed by unethical gamblers was the use of a "shiner," this being anything that reflected the cards as they were dealt, a small mirror, a polished watch, even a ring or "lucky" gold coin. Amanda had never resorted to this type of trickery, though she remembered one game when she had glanced at the fellow playing opposite her and realized that his entire hand was reflected in the lenses of his spectacles.

She recalled that incident now, as Chalmers placed a newly lit lamp nearby. Not only did the added light make it easier to see one's own cards, but Amanda was suddenly aware that the highly polished top of the tea table also reflected each and every card in her hand—

and in Grant's, who was half reclining over the table for support, and not being at all careful of the way he was holding his hand. Gathering her cards in such a manner that they would not be obvious to her opponent, Amanda cast a hasty glance at Grant. He seemed unaware of the inadvertent advantage offered them, as did Chalmers.

For a full ten seconds, Amanda's conscience tickled her. In all her days, she'd never deliberately cheated anyone at cards, and now seemed a poor time to start. She really should say something to the others. Shouldn't she? After all, Grant was already so sodden that playing against him was tantamount to shooting fish in a barrel! Still, if she ignored the reflection, simply didn't look and pretended to herself it did not exist, she wouldn't be cheating, would she? But ignoring this providential advent was like trying not to notice a beckoning green oasis in an otherwise barren desert! It was altogether too tempting!

Then again, why bother? She hadn't asked for this unexpected benefit to be thrust beneath her nose. And if Grant had half his sense about him, he'd be as aware of it as well and readjust the angle of his hand so that she could not see his cards. It certainly wasn't any of her doing! Besides, he was the one who had insisted on this gamble, who'd egged her into it when she really hadn't wanted to take him up on his ridiculous wager.

Of course, if she didn't say anything, the game would not be fair, though it really wasn't fair from the start, given Grant's liquored condition. She was bound to win regardless, and heaven knew the arrogant ass deserved to be taught a lesson in humility!

Amanda longed to be the one to teach him that lesson, if just this once! The opportunity was before her, and it was simply too good to pass up! She would win his farm from him this night, by fair means or foul. Then, for however long it took, she would have him at her mercy. One way or another, she'd enlighten the man to some very basic facts—a primary fact being that women were not placed upon this earth purely for the pleasure of men like him. That they had just as many brains as, if not the brawn of, their male counterparts. That they had feelings and emotions which were not to be toyed with carelessly. Most importantly, perhaps, that a woman need not be born on a satin pillow, or have a lineage resembling royalty, to be a lady.

Later, when he'd had sufficient time to reconsider his faulty reasoning and his biased opinions, she would hand his half of the farm back to him, with no other payment required but that he allot her the respect she demanded and deserved.

With that resolve to keep her conscience from pestering her further, Amanda proceeded to beat her unsuspecting opponent in short order. For every hand Grant took, she won eight; and with the final show of the cards, she topped his ace-high straight with a full house of lowly fours and sixes.

At the exact moment of his defeat, just as Amanda reached out to rake in the winning pot and the last of his chips with it, and Grant finally realized that he had lost the game, a sudden bolt of lightning startled all of them. Even Chalmers, usually so unflappable, gave a surprised jump as the room lit up as brightly as midday. On the heels of this unearthly brilliant light, the entire house shook with a tremendous roar of thunder, rattling long and violently.

Amanda reacted with a terrified shriek, her hand jerking spasmodically to sweep dozens of chips onto the floor. Cards appeared to fly through the air, as if tossed aloft by a magical, unseen hand.

Grant's anesthetized state, greatly reduced by coffee and the later hour but not totally dispelled, did little to prevent him from jolting upright, an unforseen movement which almost dislodged him from the sofa. "Good God, that was close!" he exclaimed, even as he thought it eerily appropriate that the lightning should strike just when it had, precisely at the instant of his doom.

"Grant! Don't blaspheme! Not now, for heaven's sake!" Amanda pleaded breathlessly, still clutching a hand to her thudding chest. Shaken to the soles of her bare feet, she, too, wondered if this was some sort of omen from above—perhaps God's way of voicing His disapproval over her less-than-honorable method of winning this poker game.

An admission of guilt was on the tip of Amanda's tongue when Grant drawled sarcastically, "Getting religion at this tardy date, my dear? A bit after the fact, isn't it?"

"What exactly are you implying, Grant?" she inquired stiffly, shelving her ready confession now that her fright was lessening and her anger on the rise.

"Nothing," Grant replied disgustedly, sinking back onto the sofa cushions with a tired sigh. "I'm just feeling spiteful and mean, though you must admit I have ample reason for my black mood. This hasn't been one of my better days."

"That isn't my fault."

"No, but I wish now that I'd kept your lucky coin for myself, instead of returning it to you. Perhaps then my own fortune would have been brighter, and you might not have fared as well tonight."

"It wouldn't have made a whit of difference," she assured him without sympathy. "At any rate, it's far too late to consider such things now, isn't it? The farm is mine."

She rose and stood looking down at his forlorn figure. "Both Chalmers and I tried to tell you that you would regret this, Grant, but you wouldn't listen. Now it is time to pay the piper, and I do hope you aren't going to try to weasel your way out of our bargain come morning, when you fully realize the extent of tonight's folly. Also, since you have succeeded in turning Darcy against me, I'll have to go into town and hire another lawyer to act on my behalf, I suppose."

"That won't be necessary. I'll have Peppermeier draw up the papers to transfer the deed into your name, and Chalmers can witness them."

"Isn't that a little like trusting the fox to guard the henhouse?" she asked suspiciously.

"No. The man is scrupulously honest, or he and I

would have found some way to gain Tad's part of the farm from you long ago. You have my word on it, Amanda.''

''I'd also like your word that you won't attempt to renege on our agreement that you stay to manage the farm for me, Grant.''

He nodded bleakly, the portrait of a man with his pride trampled beyond redemption, and suggested wearily, ''Would you like it signed in blood, my dear?''

With a satisfied smile, she replied, ''The sweat of your brow will suffice—for now.''

If Grant thought that having Amanda as a partner was bad, it was nothing compared to having her for his boss. The woman was Attila the Hun reincarnate! First she took to calling him Mr. Gardner, sweetly suggesting in the most infuriating way that he should reciprocate by calling her Miss Amanda, as properly befitted their new status. Merely for spite, he continued to call her everything *but* Miss Amanda or Miss Sites.

The moment the title was deeded into her name, she promptly took over the master suite. Grant entered the house later that day to find Chalmers and two maids transferring all of his personal belongings into one of the spare bedrooms at the far end of the hall. Stunned, outraged, he could do little about it other than vent his spleen, which he proceeded to do.

''Not wasting any time, are you, my sweet?'' he commented angrily.

''Is there any reason why I should?'' she retorted in an exasperatingly superior tone, her pert nose edging upward. ''Just count your blessings that I didn't tell Chalmers to remove your things from the house entirely. By all rights, you should be housed in the manager's quarters. However, I didn't want to have to bother with finding the old manager new lodgings. This seemed to be a reasonable alternative, and much simpler all around.''

''You have my undying gratitude, madam,'' he replied snidely.

"Don't get uppity with me, or I might reconsider my choices, Mr. Gardner," she warned. "And don't ever call me madam again! Also, I should tell you that if you take it into your head to visit my rooms without my prior request, you will find yourself sleeping with your horses."

"Rest easy, Amanda. I don't bed with barracuda."

"Then your tastes are improving since Annabelle."

Merely dining at the same table with the woman was a trial for Grant. Throughout the meal, she interrogated him on the day's happenings, down to the smallest detail. Did the new racing saddle they'd ordered arrive? How soon would the grain be ready for harvest? Had he recruited the additional men necessary to execute the task? How were Frances Turner's mares progressing with their breeding, and when would they be able to return the animals to their owner, contract fulfilled? Had Paddy been exercising Gallant Lad and Sultan's Pride regularly?

Grant took to answering in terse, one-word replies whenever he could, and invariably escaped with a roiling case of indigestion for his efforts.

Word of the exchange of ownership spread like wildfire among the farmhands. A few of them quit outright, refusing to work for a woman, most specifically this woman. Most stayed on, assured that their positions were secure, their salaries to remain the same, and orders still filtered down to them through Grant, as in the past. As far as they were concerned, not much had changed beyond the hand that doled out their pay. They considered Grant still very much in charge.

There were a couple of men, however, who took it into their heads to challenge Grant's authority, now that he no longer owned the farm. A sound thrashing behind the barn soon made them realize the error of their ways, though Grant came away from one such encounter sporting a set of bruises, which he had to explain to Amanda's satisfaction.

"You should have sent the man to my office and let me deal with his insubordination," she said.

"I handled it, Amanda."

"I can see that. What does the other fellow look like?"

Through a split lip, Grant awarded her a smile that reeked of male confidence. "Let's just say he can now whistle better than you, through the enlarged gap in his front teeth."

"I do hope this type of behavior is not going to become commonplace."

"So do I," Grant conceded. "It's damned rough on the knuckles!"

They'd scarcely had time to accustom themselves to their new roles when July Fourth was upon them. Previously, Amanda had planned to spend the day with Darcy, at the centennial celebration. When the morning arrived, and Darcy didn't, despite the polite note of apology she'd sent him, she resigned herself to attending the festivities alone. Obviously, an apology for Grant's behavior, minus any real explanation of the matters Grant had introduced that fateful night, was not enough for the lawyer.

For Grant's part, his plans had changed only insofar as he no longer intended to announce his engagement to Annabelle Foster. He and Paddy were still entering one of their previously untried fillies in the holiday race. It might prove a bit awkward explaining his reduced status to his friends and neighbors, but it would still be an opportunity to exchange new ideas on breeding techniques and the latest innovations in racing and training.

Discounting the day he'd spent in town getting drunk, most of which remained a blur, this was the first time Grant or Amanda had been to Lexington since his heated exchange with Darcy. Consequently, though Amanda had experienced her share of public censure many times before, Grant was shocked to find his own reception equally cool upon their arrival together. As they rode down the crowded streets, acquaintances openly shunned them. Ladies hastily pulled their skirts aside, as if fearing contamination. Former friends pretended not to see them, turning aside to gaze raptly into the nearest store window, or to strike up a sudden conversation with the nearest person. Many a glower and whisper followed their passage.

Grant was stunned. What the devil was going on here? These people were his neighbors, his boyhood friends, folks he'd known since birth! So he'd met with a reversal in finances. Did that warrant such rebuff? Such out-and-out rudeness? Certainly he wasn't the first in the area to lose his property. It had happened to many others he knew, especially during and since the war. And they hadn't been ostracized by their fellow members of society. Even his own brother, if Tad were to suddenly appear, would be welcomed back to their bosoms. But this, this was simply beyond Grant's comprehension.

"What's wrong with all of them?" he muttered beneath his breath. "Lord, you'd think I'd murdered someone, the way they're behaving."

"This your first encounter with snobbery?" Amanda questioned snidely, seething inside and feeling wounded despite having half expected this treatment from the elite citizens of Lexington. "Well, get used to it, Grant. I sincerely doubt it will get much better as the day goes on. Look on it as a lesson of sorts, one of the facts of nature that seems to have escaped you until now. There are a lot of 'fair-weather friends' in this world, those who will bend over backward to speak to you when you are in favor, or in the money, and won't give you the time of day when you're in trouble and in need of their support. If you're very lucky, there will be a few who are tried-and-true, who value your friendship regardless of your wealth or position or lack thereof, those who actually treasure your companionship more than your bankbook."

"Is this what you have had to endure all your life?" he asked in dismayed amazement.

"For the most part," she replied evenly. She added pointedly, "You've treated me no better. Still don't. But I consider myself fortunate. There are a number of people I can count on through thick and thin, people who really care about me, as I do them. Whatever else I might lack, I'll always have Betsy, and Amos, and Macy, and Ruth Whittaker, to mention a few. When they look at me, they don't see my clothes or my nail paint. They see me, the person I am inside. And that goes both ways. I love them for who they are beneath the outer coverings, and they know, without a doubt, that they can come to me at any time, and I'll do anything for them that is within my power.

"That's friendship, Grant." She waved a hand at the crowd of onlookers. "This bunch of snooty acquaintances, who at this moment wouldn't spit on you if your hair were on fire, doesn't begin to measure up against the real thing."

Amid curious stares, Amanda alighted, leaving Grant and Paddy to go on to the fair grounds, where they would ready the filly for the race. "Will you be all right?" Grant inquired, frowning at the glares they were garnering.

"As long as they confine themselves to malevolent looks and don't decide to tar and feather me, I'll survive," she quipped, sounding much more brave than she actually felt. "Don't forget, Mr. Gardner, I've had a few more years of this to contend with than you have. It's nothing new to me."

"You can't mean to tell me it doesn't bother you," he remarked in disbelief.

"No. It's not something that gets any easier to stomach; you merely get used to having to deal with it."

As she made her way slowly through the milling throngs, Amanda tried to ignore the whispers and condemning looks thrown her way. Eventually, as luck would have it, she chanced across Stanford Darcy. On his arm, as bold as brass and looking as smug as the devil on Judgment Day, was Annabelle Foster.

Tossing her blond curls and poking her nose so far into the air it was a wonder she didn't kink her neck, Annabelle sniffed. "Come along, Stanford. I'm sure neither of us wants to breathe the same air as this hussy who employed her wicked ways to wreak havoc with so many lives. If not for her, I would be engaged to Grant at this very moment, and you, dear man, might still be ensnared by her dubious charms. Not to mention how she has managed to hoodwink *both* the Gardner sons out of their inheritance, though God knows the blind fools undoubtedly deserve it, even if their parents are, no doubt, spinning in their graves as I speak.''

Amanda somehow curbed her tongue until the couple began to walk away. Then, almost choking on self-righteous anger, she called out loudly, "Watch out for her, Darcy, that she doesn't faint on you. It's said that women with child tend to do such things and have to be coddled in their delicate conditions.''

A gasp arose from those close enough to hear. Annabelle stumbled and turned to face Amanda, her face livid. "You vindictive witch!" she shrieked. Although lace gloves sheathed her hands, she came at Amanda with clawed fingers. "You jealous Jezebel! I'll scratch your eyes out for that! I'll scar your face so badly that no man will ever want to look at you again! Slut! Whore!''

Standing her ground, Amanda caught Annabelle's wrists, struggling to keep the maddened girl's hands clear of her face. "And what are you, Annabelle? Queen of the cuckolders? Crowned betrayer of trust?''

For several tense seconds they tussled, as a curious crowd collected to watch. While neither gained much advantage over the other, Amanda did hold Annabelle at a safe distance until Darcy managed to pull the hysterical blonde away. "I've also heard that breeding women become very emotional," Amanda concluded cattily. "Most especially after having mated with their stablehands.''

As Darcy held fast to his bundle of writhing, screeching fury, Amanda calmly took her exit past astonished onlookers, who were too shocked to do more than stare after her with gaping expressions.

She'd gone perhaps half a block when a woman came up next to her, matching her angry strides. "Nicely done, Miss Sites,'' Madame Lalaine commended. "Most especially since Miss Foster and that devious lawyer have been perpetrating gossip all over town, telling everyone that you and Mr. Gardner are lovers, and that Grant threw Annabelle over for you and ran Darcy off Misty Valley with threats of bodily harm. Not to mention the most recent tidbit, that you supposedly now own the entire horse farm—this from several reliable sources.''

When Amanda failed to respond, she went on. "I wasn't sure you'd have the nerve to put in an appearance at today's festivities, after all the rumors I've heard bandied about this past week, but I'm glad you did. It shows spunk, girl, and that's something I've always admired.''

"I thought perhaps Darcy would be telling tales,'' Amanda admitted, "but I had no idea Annabelle would be spreading such atrocious lies to cover her own misdeeds. While I never expected the reaction to be pleasant, I didn't think it would be this bad, either.''

The dressmaker shrugged. "All will pass eventually. You just have to wait it out, let the furor die.''

"How can it die with Annabelle Foster running off at the mouth like a clapper in a duck's tail, and Stanford Darcy swearing gospel to every inane accusation she spouts?''

Mrs. Lalaine gave a rusty, grating laugh. "I've waited many a year to see that sassy young woman get a proper set down, and the wait was well worth the end result! Bide your time, and everything will work itself out. You've just planted some mighty strong seeds in quite a few fertile minds, and I have no doubt they'll take root. By nightfall, one and all will have heard the story, and everyone with fingers or toes to count upon will be marking the months until Annabelle Foster's figure begins to expand, proving your claim. How far gone is she, do you know?''

"A couple of months, I suppose. All I really know is that Grant caught her coupling with her stablehand, and the child she carries is definitely not Grant's. Her infidelity so devastated him that he got roaring drunk, only to come home and rope me into a gambling match, each of us betting our half of Misty Valley as the winnings.''

"Ah, so that's how you came to own the rest of the property!'' The seamstress nodded. "I wondered. There have been a dozen different versions, everything from you giving him free and unlimited right to your fair body, to the promise to bear him his first son.''

"Saints alive!'' Amanda exploded. "Doesn't this town have anything or anyone else to talk about?''

"Not at the moment, my dear. Your current escapades are morsels too juicy to reject just now. They're better than a dime novel, and everyone is nearly salivating for the next installment.''

"So what do I do?''

"Go back to the farm, proceed with business as usual, ignore the gossip, and wait for someone else to commit some faux pas more delicious than yours,'' the woman advised. "However, that is for tomorrow. Today you must brave it out, which I am more than willing to help you do. Come and let me introduce you to some of my friends, women who have minds of their own and the will to use them instead of following the crowd like dumb sheep. Thank *le bon Dieu* there are still a few of us left, eh?''

"Aren't you afraid that being seen with me will hurt your business?'' Amanda asked.

"Sweet girl.'' Madame Lalaine chortled. "This city has but a handful of dressmakers, of which I am the undisputed leader, if you will pardon my pride in saying so. My business will flourish, if for no more reason than everyone will assume I know the best and most recent gossip. I'll be turning customers away at the door!

"And lest you get the wrong impression, I am not befriending you for gain. Quite simply, I admire your fortitude in the face of such stubborn prejudice. Lexington society, crude though it is by Parisian standards, is nonetheless as cliquish as a nunnery, but with much more snobbery, of course. It has certain accepted standards to which one must strictly adhere, and more than its share of straightlaced prudes amidst the more likeable of its number. It also holds the peculiar belief that horses are next to gods on the list of created beasts, and woe be to the person who dares to differ. Which reminds me—have you put those split skirts I made for you to their proper use and learned to ride yet?''

Chapter 21

WHILE Amanda allowed herself to be taken beneath Madame Lalaine's benevolent wing, Grant was experiencing his own problems. Fully a dozen of his formerly close associates had made a point of snubbing him, actually turning their backs and walking away as he'd approached them. Overnight, it seemed, he'd become a social pariah, though his offenses did not seem to warrant such extreme reaction, at least not in his own estimation. Yes, he'd lost the farm. True, he'd bedded Amanda. But people were behaving as if he'd grown horns!

As he watched a group of his fellow horsemen walk off, completely ignoring him, four other men appeared at his side. "Don't mind them," one told him sympathetically. "They're put out with you now, but they'll get over it sooner or later."

Grant sighed. At least if Frank Hanover was still speaking to him, as well as Jarod Spelling, Bobby Ray Joseph, and Larry Duff, he wasn't a complete outcast. "What the devil is all this, Frank?" he asked. "Surely my financial setback isn't the only reason they're treating me as if I've contracted the plague—or the fact that

I bedded Amanda Sites before Darcy could work up the nerve to do it.''

They all gave him odd looks, but it was Jarod who spoke for them. ''Actually, it has more to do with the ungentlemanly way you broke off with Annabelle Foster when everyone was well aware the two of you would eventually marry. Bedding your business partner was bad enough, but to set Annabelle up for ridicule was the thing that really put the bur under their tails.''

''What the hell else was I supposed to do after catching her in the hay with her stableboy?'' Grant demanded heatedly.

''What?'' the four echoed with varying degrees of astonishment.

''Jesus!'' Larry said on a whistle. ''Annabelle?''

''Grant, she's been goin' all over town tellin' every livin' soul that you dumped her flat for the 'black-haired hussy,' I think is the way she worded it. Among other vile accusations. Then, when you suddenly signed the farm over to Miss Sites, the rumors really started flyin'. Most folks are wonderin' what hold Amanda has over you. Some claim she must be carryin' your child, while Annabelle swears the woman's an honest-to-God witch who's cast her evil spell on you. Others have gone so far as to suggest she's your half sister, or some such incestuous nonsense—and don't think that didn't set the Christian community on its ear!'' This from Bobby Ray.

''Damnation! How stupid can folks be?'' Grant roared. ''Here I was trying to be a gentleman by not telling tales on Annabelle, and what do I get for my efforts? I was even willing to let people believe she'd broken off with me, if that's what she wanted to tell everyone. But this is too much! The truth of the matter is, Annabelle's been carrying on with her lover since the first of the year, and, fool that I was, I didn't suspect a blasted thing! I also might point out, in case it's slipped your notice, that Amanda Sites hadn't even appeared on the scene at that point.

''As if that wasn't offense enough, our dear Annabelle tried to rook me into announcing our engagement, with a hasty marriage to follow, I suspect, on the pretext that she was carrying my child. When, in reality, the babe is not mine at all!''

"Holy Moses!"

"No kiddin'?"

"Why, that lying little . . ."

"Bitch," Grant supplied coldly. "I suppose, when her condition becomes evident, she'll tell everyone the child is mine, and my name will be even blacker than it is now."

"Is that a possibility?" Jarod asked boldly.

"It would be," Grant readily admitted, "if I hadn't stopped bedding her before Amanda showed up at my door. Annabelle confessed to me that she's only a couple of months along, so you figure it out, boys. God, I can't believe what a fool I've been! Hell, she wasn't even intact when I slept with her the first time, so heaven only knows how many men she's really had! And to think I was going to marry her! I truly would have been the world's biggest ass then!''

"What about the farm?" Bobby Ray questioned.

Grant let loose a derisive snort. "Purely the result of wounded pride and a drunken spree, the combination of which brought about my downfall. Seems I'm no better at gambling than Tad is, and probably more stupid, everything considered."

"Meaning?"

"Thinking to gain total control of the farm, I made the mistake of challenging the infamous Miss Sites to a game of poker. Needless to say, I lost, and am now reduced to managing my former business. My only legitimate excuse is that I was so inebriated I could scarcely find my ass with either hand at the time."

"And she took unfair advantage of your less-than-astute condition," Frank guessed. "Isn't there anything your lawyer can do about that?"

"Apparently not. Peppermeier himself drew up the papers and witnessed the exchange of deed."

"Gad, Grant! What are you going to do now?"

"There's little I *can* do, for the moment." He sighed.

"Except try to quell most of Annabelle's more vicious claims. For the rest, I'll just have to bide my time and hope something will happen to change my current situation for the better, though I can't imagine what it might be."

"Well, for a start, the boys and I can help spread the word for you," Larry offered. "I for one don't believe in kicking a man when he's down, particularly if he's not entirely at fault."

"Yeah," Bobby Ray concurred. "It ain't right for you to shoulder all the blame in this. Tarnation! It's enough that you've lost your home to that woman gambler, and that on top of what Annabelle's done! Personally, if I came up against that much trouble with women, I'd be seriously thinkin' about runnin' off and joinin' the Foreign Legion!"

For the first time in almost a week, Grant laughed outright, clapping his friend on the shoulder. "I'll keep it in mind as a final alternative, Bobby Ray."

"Meanwhile," Jarod suggested with a huge grin, "let's go find the beer tent. All this talkin' has me parched."

"You buyin'?"

"Hell, why not?" came the answer. "Come on, fellas. It's as good a place as any to start some gossip of our own and get old Grant here off Annabelle's hook. While we're at it, if we put our heads together, maybe we can even think of some way to help him get his farm back from that female cardsharp."

The return ride to Misty Valley late that night was quiet, if not pleasant, until Grant broke the tense silence. "The fireworks display went well, don't you think, Amanda?"

She shrugged. "I suppose so."

"Did you enjoy the day at all?" he pressed. For his own part, he was feeling much better. His best friends hadn't all deserted him after all, and the filly had easily won the afternoon's contest, further proving his ability to breed and train some of the best racehorses in the country. His trampled ego was fast recovering, and his gloomy mood with it.

Again Amanda's reply was unusually subdued. "It wasn't an experience I would care to repeat any time soon, thank you."

"Don't tell me you're heartbroken over finding Darcy keeping company with Annabelle."

"Hardly!" she retorted with an unladylike snort. "Were you?"

"Actually no, though it does make me a bit uneasy wondering what she's up to now, and why the two of them are consorting with one another like thieves in the night." When she failed to comment, he went on. "I heard about your confrontation with them."

"I'll just bet you did. I think the entire town knew about it ten minutes afterward."

"Did you know that Annabelle is going around trying to convince them that you're an evil witch capable of casting spells on unwary men?"

Amanda's smile was sour. "Well, that certainly explains the odd looks I was getting from some of the gentlemen today."

This brought a frown to Grant's face. "What sort of looks?"

"Rather a mix between fascination and caution, though a few brave souls managed to work up enough courage to approach me."

"For what purpose?"

"My, we're nosy this evening, Mr. Gardner!" she returned with sugary sarcasm.

"What did they say to you, Amanda?" he insisted darkly.

"Nothing I haven't heard before, I assure you, unless you count the young man who made it painfully obvious that, considering the state of his bank account and mine now that I own Misty Valley, he wouldn't mind courting me. He seemed more relieved than anything else when I politely told him I wasn't interested."

"And the others?"

"Oh, they were even more candid, to varying degrees. It seems they had the impression I would be willing to exchange my favors for even more money than I now possess, since word has spread that I'll lie with any man with coin in his pockets. Now, where do you suppose they got that idea?" she asked mockingly.

Grant cringed, well aware that he had greatly contributed to this low opinion of her, primarily by shooting off his big mouth to Darcy. Darcy and Annabelle had picked up where Grant had left off, and the damage was done. "A few of the ladies seemed willing to accept you," he pointed out, trying to salve his conscience. "I saw you with the Lalaine woman and some of her group. That's a start."

"Yes," Amanda conceded. "They've invited me to join their literary group. And one sweet old lady told me she'd save a seat for me in church if I'd care to attend."

This brought Grant's eyebrows arching upward. "Are you going to accept?"

"I don't know. She belongs to the Presbyterian church, and I've never attended anything but Catholic services."

"You have?"

"You don't have to look so shocked, you know!" she complained. "I spent four of my most formative years in New Orleans, after all!"

"I'm sorry. It just came as something of a surprise. Somehow, I've just never thought of you . . . well, in church."

"I have a revelation for you, Gardner. I have a difficult time picturing you in church, too."

He decided not to take offense. "Yeah, I know. You probably think of me along the same lines as I do you, naked and panting in a big feather bed!" The grin that accompanied his comment was pure deviltry.

"Actually, I rarely consider you at all," she fibbed, not about to admit to him how close to the truth he'd struck. "But when I do, it's usually in a very deep river—with rocks tied around your neck!"

* * *

The most demoralizing aspect of working for Amanda was having her hand Grant his wages, like any other employee. It almost killed him to accept the plain white pay envelope from her, though she did have the grace to give his to him separately, at dinner, rather than in full view of the other farmhands and servants. At least he was spared that humiliation.

Another irritating thing she seemed bent on was having him saddle her mare for her whenever she wanted to ride, a service she insisted that he, and he alone, perform. No matter how busy he was or what he was doing at the time, he would have to stop and prepare her horse. Most maddening was that she did it primarily to aggravate him, and took such notable pleasure in reminding him that he was now at her beck and call.

One thing leading to another, they had some very hearty disputes about where she should ride and with whom.

"You are not experienced enough to go gallivanting all over the countryside by yourself," he told her bluntly. "The bald fact is, you're still such a novice in the saddle, you shouldn't be allowed past the barnyard, with or without an escort."

"I am not a child, Mr. Gardner." Ignoring his disgustingly male look as he dragged his hot gaze deliberately over her figure, she snapped, "Must I remind you that I own this property? I do not need your permission to ride anywhere upon it."

"No, but a little common sense would be nice for a change."

"If I feel I need an escort, Paddy can accompany me."

"Paddy is busy with training, as am I. We don't have time to act as your nannies whenever you decide to make a nuisance of yourself."

"Then I'll simply have to hire a man especially for that purpose, won't I?" she crooned, her eyes shooting daggers at him.

Throwing his hands up in disgust, he conceded the argument. "All right! You win! I will make the time, whether I can truly spare it or not, to accompany you on your little jaunts around the property. But don't come crying to me when things start to fall apart around here for lack of attention."

They also argued heatedly when Amanda decided to raise their customary stud fee to what Grant considered an exorbitant figure. "I'm telling you, Amanda, it's too much. Our customers will simply refuse to pay it. And the horse breeders' association is going to have fits with you over this."

"I hope it throws them all into apoplexy," she replied waspishly, her anger rising as she recalled the recent meeting she'd attended in Lexington. First they'd ignored her throughout the meeting, as if she were invisible. Then, after they'd adjourned, several of the randy old coots, with a few of the younger ones thrown in for good measure, had promptly availed themselves of the opportunity to proposition her! And they'd had the nerve to act offended when she'd told them all to take a running jump off a short pier! To frost that particular cake, Grant had laughed himself silly when she'd related the incident to him upon returning home.

"Ah, Amanda, you are truly one of a kind," he said between snickers. "I'd have given my last dollar to see the looks on their faces when you told them that! Still, you're not doing yourself any favors by offending them, you know. That is definitely not the way to win friends and influence your fellow horsemen."

"And accepting their lewd invitations would have been?" she'd countered angrily. "Frogs will grow hair sooner! Anyway, if they can behave rudely to me, they deserve no less than the same in return, and the faster they realize it, the better!"

Now she'd decided to raise breeding fees, as well as the price of Misty Valley's foals, all without bothering to advise the other members of the association or to discuss the matter with any of them, as was considered polite and proper procedure among the elite group.

"We have proven winners, Grant," she argued. "The time to up the ante is when you hold the best hand. In a couple of years Gallant Lad and Sultan's Pride are going to be in such demand that we'll be turning down the offers.''

"As you said, that is still a couple of years away. What makes you think you can get away with raising fees now?''

"After the racing season they've just had, this farm's name is on the tip of everyone's tongue. Now. At this moment. And while they may not be servicing mares yet, we have other stallions from the same lineage or better. The bloodlines are there, and we'd be fools not to take advantage of that.''

"Isn't that just like a woman?'' Grant mused, half annoyed and half laughing at her. "Give her a little knowledge, and she thinks she wrote the damned book!''

He soon ate those words when their customers agreed, without much fuss, to the higher fees. Once again, it was a case of Amanda at her bewitching best— sweetly, swiftly, and competently presenting her arguments. And their clients believing every honeyed word that fell from her lips, their money practically flying from their pockets into her waiting hands. It was a talent of hers that Grant had to admire, even while it irked him mightily.

They came to loggerheads again when Amanda decided to redecorate the parlor more to her liking and make a number of minor improvements to some of the other rooms as well. Grant was outraged. This was his family home with which she was tampering! The house his grandfather had built, and the house his grandmother and mother had filled with love and warmth and the finest furnishings! How dared she suggest changing things, even if she did own it all now?

"There's not a blamed thing wrong with this house just the way it is,'' he claimed. "It's exactly the way I like it.''

"Well, it isn't the way I want it,'' she told him flat out. "I have a perfect right to change anything I wish.

And the parlor draperies will be the first to go. They're old and faded from the sun."

"I'll have you know that my grandmother spent weeks searching for just the right material for those draperies. She sent all the way to England for the fabric, and paid a seamstress a plentiful sum to sew them up to her satisfaction."

"I don't give a rat's tail if they came from Buckingham Palace! They are ready to fall from their rods. There comes a time when everything has seen its better days, Grant, and this is that time. I am also going to have the cushions on the divan and chairs recovered."

"My mother embroidered the design on those cushions herself," he pointed out angrily.

"And a fine job she did of it, too," Amanda admitted, "but the edges are fraying badly, and it's making the entire room appear shabby. However, if they hold such sentimental value for you, I can always move them upstairs, where they won't be seen by everyone who comes visiting, and buy new furniture."

"And spend even more money in the process, as well as turn my home into the likes of a bordello, I suppose. What do you plan on replacing the cushions with? Something with red velvet and gold tassels? Do you plan on ordering a few very large mirrors as well? Perhaps cover the dining table with green felt and start a gambling hall? Bring in a few girls to entertain our overnight guests and hire a piano player?"

"I might at that, if you keep giving me such wonderful ideas," she taunted with a nasty smile.

"I hope you realize that the stables require painting before the summer auction, and the foaling barn is in need of repair, and the fence along the south pasture has several rotted fence posts, and there are other necessary business expenditures we need to make." He stressed the word "business."

"I have taken that into account," she assured him. "The farm will not be neglected, Grant. With the expectation of a higher yield this year, the price of feed grain and hay should be lower. If that, plus the higher fees we've been charging lately, doesn't offset the cost, I intend to use my personal funds for my redecorating projects.''

''I still don't like the idea any better,'' he complained. ''You're going to ruin the place. I just know it. Misty Valley has held a position of high standing in the community since my grandfath first bought land here and built this house. Now you come along and can't wait to undo all their fine work. It makes me sick to think what this place will look like when you're done with it.''

''Well, please go air your laments to someone else for a while,'' she answered with a weary sigh. ''I'm tired of hearing you do nothing but whine.''

Chapter 22

WHEN Art Macy, accompanied by Amanda's riverboat cohort, the tiny blond Betsy, pulled the carriage to a halt before Misty Valley's front entrance two days later, Grant almost died on the spot. His first incredible thought was that Amanda did indeed intend on turning his home into either a gambling establishment or a house of ill repute!

Before he could recover from his shock at this unexpected arrival of two of his least favorite acquaintances, and make a total ass of himself, he noticed that the girl was limping badly, her pale little face screwed up in pain. A small grain of gentlemanly sympathy rose within him then, and recalling his formerly impeccable manners, which his mother had pounded into his thick head, he hurried forward to aid the approaching couple. Explanations could come later, when Amanda's friend had been made more comfortable.

"Macy, Betsy, welcome to Misty Valley," he said with a polite nod. "Come on inside, and I'll send for Amanda. She's probably in her office." Reaching out uncertainly, he offered, "May I assist you, miss?"

"Better not, Gardner," Macy suggested. "Betsy's

broken a couple of ribs, and she's a bit reluctant about chancing further discomfort to them. It's best to let her creep along at her own pace.''

"Thanks anyway," Betsy said with a grimace.

By the time they reached the door, Amanda was there to greet them. Her delighted smile immediately melted into concern. "Betsy, honey, what's happened to you?"

While Grant's mind immediately leapt to the conclusion that one of Betsy's customers must have beaten her, Macy grunted out a terse explanation that had a much more devastating effect. "The *Lady Gambler* blew up in the water on the Fourth of July. I thought you would have read about it. It was in almost all the papers.''

"Oh, my God!" Amanda's face drained of color, and for a moment Grant feared she might faint at his feet. He reached out to steady her as Macy gently led Betsy to the nearest chair and helped her into it.

"We haven't had much time to keep up on the news lately," Grant commented. "And no one's been to town for several days, so I'm afraid this comes as a real surprise to us all.''

Frowning, he studied Amanda's stunned features. "Are you all right, darlin'?"

"I'm fine," she answered on a deep, shaky breath, hardly aware of the endearment. With an effort, she shoved aside the still-echoing remnants of shock and rushed to kneel at Betsy's side, taking the girl's cold hand in her own. "How bad was it?" she asked, almost afraid of the answer.

"Bad," Betsy replied on a sob, her big brown eyes filling with tears. "Real bad. Amanda, Amos is dead! So is the captain, and old Nettie. And pretty Ella Mae is all burned and crippled up! Oh, Lord, Mandy! It was so awful! Like a trip into hell!''

Amanda's own tears dropped onto Betsy's trembling hand. "Oh, Betsy, I'm so sorry! But you're here now. You're alive and you're here with me. I'll look after you, and you'll soon be well again. I promise, Bets. I promise. Sweet heavens, but I'm so thankful you survived!''

"It's nothing short of a miracle," Macy put in. "That boat went up like a ball of fire, and when the smoke settled, there wasn't much left but splinters.''

"How did it happen?" Grant asked.

"The owners were hot for a centennial race, from what I gather, and no amount of arguing was going to change their minds. The damn fools! Then, to compound their stupidity, they crowded the riverboat from stem to stern with twice the passengers she usually carried. Over a hundred people died in the explosion, or drowned trying to make it to shore. Eighty more were injured—burned and battered, limbs torn off. God, it was a mess! A bloody mess!''

"Were you aboard?" Amanda questioned, her eyes anxiously looking for some sign that the man had been injured as well.

"Fortunately, no. It so happened that the explosion took place not a mile from my plantation. Lorna and I were hosting an outdoor barbecue at the time, when out of nowhere it sounded like the world blew up! Hellfire, part of the paddle wheel put a hole through the roof of my smokehouse, the pieces flew so far!''

"Naturally, we all went traipsing down to the river to see what had happened." Macy rubbed a hand over his face, his eyes bleak with remembrance. "If I live till eternity, I'll never forget the sight of all those charred and burning bodies floating on the water! And the sounds! Those poor souls who weren't already in their Maker's hands, moaning and screaming in pain. It's something I never want to witness again.''

"Me, neither," Betsy echoed softly, "but I sure am glad you were there that day, Macy. If not for you and your friends, a lot more of us might have died. And your wife was so kind to me. I'll never be able to repay you folks for savin' me.''

"We were glad to do it, little one," Macy told her with a sad smile. "I just wish we could have saved more of them." A teasing glint came to his eyes as he added, "But next time you decide to drop in on us, feel free to use the front door, instead of landing yourself in the tree branches and screeching like a banshee. It's a darned sight easier on your bones, not to mention my nerves!"

Macy stayed overnight before making the trip back to St. Louis. While the women were upstairs settling Betsy into one of the bedrooms, he related more of the grisly details to Grant. "I'll be having nightmares for a good month at least," he swore. "And Lorna has said that Betsy cries out almost every night with her own tormented dreams. You will take good care of her, won't you? I know Amanda will, but I need to know that you will make the poor girl feel welcome in your home."

Grant gave a short shake of his head and sent the older man a wry grin. "My word doesn't carry much weight around here anymore, Macy. You see, Amanda owns the whole farm now. But if it will ease your mind any, I'll do all I can to make sure Betsy gets the best of care."

On a gruff laugh, Macy exclaimed, "Land sakes, boy! Don't tell me you were fool enough to play poker with that woman! Shoot! I thought you were a hell of a lot smarter than that!"

"Not when I'm drunk."

"Well, I'm right sorry to hear that, son. But all is not lost. If you play your cards right, excuse the expression, you can have that little cardsharp eating out of your hand in no time flat. She's in love with you, you know. I can tell it by the way her eyes light up when she looks at you."

"Don't confuse love with spite, Macy. Amanda's got more malice in her than a snake has venom."

"Don't all women? Look what Eve did to Adam, and it hasn't stopped since. Still, you mark my words. She loves you. All you have to do is convince her that you feel the same. Get her to marry you, Gardner, and you'll get your property back and have the best darned wife a man could ask for.''

More likely a life sentence with a mean-mouthed she-devil, Grant thought to himself with a shudder. Obviously, Art Macy didn't know Amanda all that well after all. That, or Amanda had never shown him the nastier side of her personality, the part she reserved for people she detested—and most especially for Grant Gardner. Marry her? When mares gave birth to chickens!

Chickens. Geese. These species of fowl were ten times better than ducks any day of the week! At least in Grant's estimation, with Sweet Cheek paddling about underfoot constantly. The little bird was fast turning into a pampered monster. He looked like one these days, too, now that he was getting older and starting to trade his baby fluff for real feathers. The duckling was molting, losing tufts of down by the fistful. He was a mottled mess, half naked, with pin feathers poking out every which way and the remainder of his chunky little body looking as if he had a bad case of mange.

Even now Amanda refused to confine him to the out-of-doors, where he belonged. ''Land sakes, Grant, have a little compassion, will you? He'll catch cold with only half his feathers.''

''Show some sense, Amanda,'' Grant retaliated in kind. ''It's mid-July and hotter than Hades. The only thing that critter is bound to catch is the sole of my boot if he doesn't stay out from under my feet.''

As if he understood Grant's words and resented them, Sweet Cheek dashed up to Grant, snatched hold of his pant leg, and gave it a vicious tug. ''See that?'' Grant declared with a glower at the minuscule bird. ''If not for my boot, he'd have taken a chunk out of my ankle! He's a menace!''

Amanda merely laughed at him. ''He just doesn't seem to like any man very much,'' she explained with a teasing smile. ''If it's any consolation, he's taken several nips at Darcy in the past, and he caught Chalmers fresh out of bed one morning and bit him on the big toe. Sweet Cheek prefers women, which I suppose is natural for a boy duck.''

''Drake,'' Grant corrected with a sneer at both of them, as Amanda picked the little duckling up and cuddled it close to her, uncaring that she was getting duck down all over the front of her dress.

''I beg your pardon?''

''Male ducks are called drakes, Amanda.''

''Thank you. I'll try to remember that.'' Following a brief pause, and with a smile that would have put Eve to shame, she asked too sweetly, ''And what are male humans properly called, Grant, according to your superior knowledge in that area?''

''Men,'' he supplied shortly.

''Oh.'' Her lips pursed with ill-concealed humor. ''I was hoping to hear something a bit more fitting and descriptive, like horn-tailed lechers, or randy-minded panters and grabbers.''

''Very funny, Amanda. Keep pushing, sweetheart,'' he warned, his emerald eyes gleaming as they skimmed her delectable form. ''One of these days soon, I'm going to take you up on those countless invitations you're always making.''

''I haven't issued any as yet.''

Grant laughed. ''You think not? With every look, every step you take, that husky vibration in your voice, you're sending out signals a blind man could read. And I'm not blind. Or deaf. Or too old to answer your siren's call. So beware, darlin', and don't say I didn't warn you.''

Grant soon resigned himself to the fact that Betsy was here to stay, at least for some time to come. Not only had she sustained broken ribs in the disastrous riverboat accident, she also had a badly bruised hip and assorted lesser scrapes and burns. All in all, she had escaped lightly, though it would be many weeks before she fully recovered.

In addition to her other responsibilities, Amanda was now overseeing Betsy's nursing care. Consequently, and almost without a second thought, she relegated a number of Grant's previous duties back into his capable hands.

It was then, in the middle of their hectic preparations for the upcoming horse auction, that Grant was made aware of the escalating unrest among his neighbors and the town merchants alike. His reception at the Fourth of July celebration had been just the start of future problems regardless of the few friends who were trying to help him overcome the slander to his reputation, and Amanda's confrontations with the horse breeders' association hadn't helped soothe ruffled feathers.

The first indication came when their usual grain supplier suddenly canceled their fall order without explanation or forewarning. When Grant rode into town to confront the man, the merchant was downright hostile. "I don't do business with whores and pimps," he told Grant flatly, and promptly locked his doors in Grant's stunned face.

Then, when Grant bought paint for the barns, the store owner demanded the money up front, before he would load the order onto the wagon. "Cash on the barrel head, Gardner," he said gruffly, not at all his usual congenial self. "Misty Valley's account is closed from here on out. No more buyin' on credit and payin' at the end of the month."

"Since when?" Grant retorted angrily.

"Since that *woman* took over the farm and started invitin' all the riffraff onto the place. If she wants to start a brothel, she should do it openly and honestly like the rest of 'em, not try to disguise it behind the workin's of the horse farm."

He got the same reaction when he tried to order new fencing for repairs to the pasture. "Sorry, Grant," the red-faced clerk muttered, "but Mr. Eplinger won't put the order in unless you pay for it first. Guess he thinks he might not see the money otherwise."

Humiliated and enraged, Grant left and went directly to Peppermeier's office, stomping into the attorney's private quarters unannounced and mad enough to tear heads off. "What in blue blazes is going on around here? I have merchants all over town refusing to credit Misty Valley's accounts, and long-standing orders being turned down, and all I'm hearing by way of reasons is some ridiculous nonsense about harlots and whorehouses! Damn it all, I haven't got time for this stupidity!"

Peppermeier waved him into a chair. "Well, son, I was going to ride out to the farm in the next couple of days, but you've saved me a trip. Frankly, I'll admit I wasn't looking forward to explaining such delicate matters to Miss Sites."

"Then you are aware of the situation," Grant surmised. "Which is more than I was until now. Oh, I knew the community was up in arms about Annabelle and that incident with Darcy, but I thought they'd take it all in stride and simmer down soon. Guess I was wrong. But why? Is there something else going on I should know about?"

"Mostly the same old song and dance," Peppermeier said. "Only now there are a few new stanzas being added to the tune."

"Such as?"

"For one, Annabelle Foster's father stopped by to see me yesterday. Seems his daughter is claiming you got her 'in the family way' and are now refusing to do the gentlemanly thing about it. Foster wanted me to tell you that, while you are the last man on earth he'd want for a son-in-law, he is bound to see that you claim responsibility for the act and make a suitable monetary settlement for the child's support."

"With what?" Grant demanded. "I own no more than the clothes on my back. Besides, the baby isn't mine, and I'll be double damned if I'll pay for someone else's dalliances."

Peppermeier nodded. "I related those same thoughts to Foster yesterday, and he was not over-thrilled, I assure you. I have also been approached by several irate members of the horse breeders' association, and they, too, are displeased, though not so much with you as with Miss Sites. She seems to have a particular knack for irritating people in high places, doesn't she?''

"To put it mildly," Grant agreed with a disparaging grin.

"Well, she's done a fine job of it this time around. Whether she's the owner of Misty Valley or not, the title does not automatically guarantee her membership in the association, and those fine fellows are not about to let her become part of their group. Her application for admission is being summarily blackballed, by unanimous vote, and heading the motion is none other than our own Mr. Foster."

"Why am I not surprised to hear this?" Grant said. "But I did expect better from some of the other members. While I realize Amanda didn't endear herself to them by raising the breeding fees without first consulting their illustrious fellowship, it seems she is unfairly bearing the brunt of Annabelle's hatefulness and my foolishness."

"More than you know, Grant. Word has it that she is welcoming other 'unsuitable types' to Misty Valley now, that she's sent numerous invitations to other gamblers and ladies of shady reputation, with plans to start up an establishment of, shall we say, unscrupulous intent."

Grant nodded sheepishly. "I'll admit the same thought crossed my mind when Betsy first arrived, especially with Amanda so set on redecorating the house. I wondered—very briefly, mind you—if she was going to turn my home into a fancy gambling hall. But I've since calmed down and realized that I was leaping to all the wrong conclusions—in this case, simply because I don't like Amanda's previous occupation or her former associates."

"There's more," the lawyer warned. "To reinforce the rumor, many of the association members are claiming that she has tried to buy their votes by offering herself to them. Favor for favor, so to speak."

"That's ridiculous! They're trying to save face, when

they all know exactly the opposite occurred! It galled them to have Amanda turn them down to a man.''

"Yes, I've heard that side of the story, too," Peppermeier said. "She wasn't very diplomatic in her refusal, was she? However, with Stanford Darcy also insisting that Miss Sites flaunted herself at him regularly and several times invited him to her bed, the good citizens of Lexington are not looking kindly upon her just now. I have to warn you, it will probably get worse before it gets better. To date, resentment has been restricted to the surrounding region, and you've seen the result. But heaven only knows how fast gossip will travel to the ears of those farther afield, and when it does it's bound to have a detrimental effect on your other business dealings. I think you ought to be prepared for several broken contracts in the near future.''

With a defeated groan, Grant let his head fall into his hands. "Damnation! This is all I need! There must be a way to put a stop to it, short of meeting Darcy at twenty paces and sewing Annabelle's lips shut!''

"Well, if I come up with anything, you and Miss Sites will be the first to know," Peppermeier assured him. As Grant prepared to leave, the lawyer said, "By the way, Grant, it would appear that someone, perhaps a misinformed visitor or a disgruntled employee, is adding his own fat to the fire, with many a listener ready and willing to believe that Amanda is collecting her former colleagues around her for some illicit purpose.''

"And the rumor probably began with me," Grant conceded miserably. "I seem to recall making a few heated remarks along those lines to one of my men, and God only knows who might have overheard me. Meanwhile, Amanda has done nothing more threatening than to take in a friend of hers who was wounded in that riverboat explosion in St. Louis and desperately needs her help. Now, if that's some sort of evil collaboration, I'll dance naked down Main Street!''

"Only if I can sell tickets to the event." Peppermeier chuckled. "Also, coward that I am, I will leave it to you to explain this latest state of affairs to Miss Sites, while I try to discover some way out of this predicament you two have gotten yourselves into—though at the moment I doubt even a public proclamation in the *Lexington News* would sway social opinion in your favor.''

"If that's all the choice I have, I might yet resort to it,'' Grant avowed. ''If nothing else, it would air more soiled laundry than mine or Amanda's. Some of the dirt is sure to splatter a few of the more ardent gossip-mongers—the exalted Fosters, for instance. Thanks for the suggestion. I'll keep it in mind.''

"Grant, it was said in jest,'' the astounded attorney blustered. ''I wasn't serious.''

Grant answered with a sardonic grin. ''I was.''

Chapter 23

IT was a couple of days before Grant told Amanda what had transpired in town. To begin with, he, like Peppermeier, was not fond of having to relay the information to her, and wasn't certain how to word it when he did. She was sure to be upset, her tender feelings dreadfully wounded, and he was truly dismayed at the thought. Thus, he put it off as long as he could, hoping in vain to find a logical and simple solution to the problem in the interim.

When she mentioned taking Betsy into Lexington to purchase some new gowns for her friend, Grant knew he had stalled long enough. There was no getting around it now. She had to know before she encountered the volatile situation herself, firsthand and unprepared for it.

Amanda exploded, her first wave of fury directed at the snooty members of the horse breeder's association. "Why, those lying, hateful old bags of wind! Those sniveling, slithering lice off a river rat's tail! Those—those horses' asses!"

Leaping from her chair, she began to pace the office, pausing at each pass to jerk open another desk drawer and riffle through the contents. "Blast it! Where did I put that packet of chewing gum!" she railed, her features clouding further.

When she failed to find it, she yanked open the lid to Grant's humidor and grabbed one of his cigars. "Forget the dratted gum!" she exclaimed. "If ever there was a time to begin smoking, it's now!" Cigar in hand, she stomped toward the door.

"Where are you going?" he called after her, unreasonably grateful that she was venting her hurt with hot words rather than tears.

"To the barn, to curse at the horses! Maybe I'll even shovel out some stalls while I'm at it, because if I don't work off some of this anger, I'm going to either explode or kick tail!"

Trotting after her, he couldn't help but grin at the mental image of her booting each and every member of the breeders' association in their respective posteriors. "You can't smoke in the barn, Amanda," he reminded her.

"Then I'll curse in the barn and smoke in the yard! And after that, I'll probably have a few healthy belts of your best bourbon, just to top off the evening!"

"Good. Maybe if you get drunk enough, I can talk you into playing some poker and win back the farm from you."

"Ha!" she retorted. "Even then I could beat you without working up a sweat, Gardner. I've been drinking beer from the age of three and whiskey since I turned fourteen, and I've never become so addled that I couldn't play a darned good game."

"How about some champagne instead?" he suggested tauntingly. "Then I could probably win more than the farm from you. In fact, chances are you'd give me everything I wanted for free!"

"I wouldn't recommend trying it. In my present mood, I'd shoot you before you could get your pants undone!"

Privately, Grant wondered if he didn't deserve a good blast of buckshot, since his stupidity and big mouth had no doubt bolstered the latest rumors, as well as a good deal of the earlier gossip.

In the barn, he stood by, grinning like an idiot and watching as she did indeed tackle cleaning the stalls, muttering to herself and cursing imaginatively all the while. When she finally tired, he followed her into the barnyard and politely lit her cigar for her, wisely tamping down the urge to laugh when she drew in the first lungful and promptly went into a spasm of coughing. He did, however, give her some helpful advice and a few hearty whacks on the back to aid her breathing.

"You're supposed to puff gently on it, honey, not try to suck the smoke clear down to your toes. Try drawing a bit into your mouth and holding it there for a moment, instead of actually inhaling. Then let it out again."

Never one to quit, she managed the next few puffs without mishap before crushing the cigar out. "Ugh! How do you stand those awful things?" she asked, pulling a face. "They taste like they're rolled with horse manure instead of tobacco."

"Don't let the local tobacco growers hear you mouth such obscenities about their product, or you'll have them just as miffed at you as the horse breeders are now."

"Those yellow-bellied varmints aren't half as furious with me as I am with them," she claimed righteously. "It might take me a while, but I'll find some way to get back at the lot of them. And that nasty little snit you were engaged to, too!"

"Almost engaged to," he corrected mildly.

She waved his objection aside.

"And what about Darcy? Doesn't he deserve some of your ire?" Grant went on.

"I'm still thinking that one over," she said, sliding him a sideward glare. "After all, he only did what you'd expect a jilted beau to do, after you tattled to him about the two of us. If either of you needs a good lesson in keeping your mouth shut, it's you, Grant Gardner! I wouldn't have half the problems I do now if not for you and your wagging tongue!"

"Well, someone else has been flapping his jaw

lately," he informed her. "Perhaps even one of our own employees, if Peppermeier is right. Someone who is embellishing comments he may have overheard and adding his own opinions."

Amanda nodded miserably. "There's a rat in the woodpile someplace," she agreed. "Darn! I hate to think that any one of the people who work for us actually dislikes me enough to collect his wages from me and spread lies at the same time he's taking my money! It makes me feel so . . . so used!"

"None of us likes to be made a fool of, Amanda. If it helps you feel any better, I intend to find out who the culprit is. And if it is one of our workers, you can have the pleasure of personally dismissing him and watching while I throw him, or her, off the property."

While Grant went about discreetly narrowing his list of suspects, Amanda did her best not to display her vexation to one and all. In fact, in the next few days she made a deliberate effort to be pleasant and courteous to all of her employees, reasoning that perhaps just being nice would win the guilty party over and make him realize that she wasn't the awful person he assumed she was, thus quelling any further rumors.

Her plan went all wrong, though she had no way of knowing how wrong until it was much too late. It happened as she was on her way from the foaling barn, where Grant was busy making the necessary repairs. With ears still ringing from all the sawing and hammering the men were doing there, and her mind occupied with other matters, she was paying little attention as she took the shorter route to the main stable, one that led behind the blacksmith shop.

When the man suddenly stepped in front of her, barring her path, Amanda knew at once that she was in trouble. His name was Dell Erkel, and he was one of the workers who had leered at her since the first day she'd arrived. Why she hadn't thought to fire him before now was beyond her. But hindsight being better than foresight, it did little good now. "Well, little missy," he crowed, a maniacal gleam in his eyes, "whatcha doin' back here all by yerself? Lookin' for ol' Dell, were you?"

With an immense effort, she faced him down, instinctively knowing that to show her fear of him would be the worst thing she could do. "Get out of my way, Erkel, and go back to work. You don't get paid to stand around doing nothing."

"Oh, I plan on doin' somethin', all right," he assured her with a grin so evil it made the fine hairs on the nape of her neck stand on end. "I plan on gettin' me a piece of what the boss's been havin' all along."

Slowly, without taking her gaze from his, Amanda backed away from him. Out of the corner of her eye she spied an iron pipe propping open the rear window of the smithy. If only she could reach it, she would have a weapon to use against him! "Erkel, I'm warning you," she told him, praying to keep his attention focused on her words and not on the way she carefully edged toward the pipe. "If you lay a hand on me, you'll regret it."

He chuckled, a menacing sound that seemed to echo through her brain. "I'm gonna lay more'n a hand on you, girlie, and you ain't gonna do nothin' to stop me. Are you? You think I ain't noticed the way you look at me sometimes? And the way you strut around this place, makin' sure every man within sight takes notice? You're like a match lookin' for the tinderbox, and I'm just the fella to show you how it's done."

Behind her back, Amanda's trembling fingers wrapped themselves around the pipe, and she thought she'd faint with relief. Her heart was pounding so loudly that she could barely hear the man's threats above the sound of it. As he lunged toward her, she jerked wildly at the pipe. It tore loose from its mooring, the weight and length of it sending her stumbling forward with her own momentum even as the window of the smithy slammed shut, muffling her first terrified shriek.

Erkel seized the pipe, wrenching it from her grip,

but not before she landed one good blow to his leg. With one brief grunt of pain, and a glare that promised retribution, he tossed the metal bar aside as if it were no more than a straw. Above her frantic screams, he growled, "You shouldn't have done that. It don't pay to make me mad, 'cause then I tend to get mean."

He grabbed for her again, catching her arm, his grip so strong she feared he would tear her limb from its socket. Tears of agony blurred her vision as he threw her to the ground, coming down hard on top of her, cutting short her shouts for help as the air was crushed from her lungs. Before she could regain her breath, a beefy hand clamped over her mouth, reducing her shrill yells to muted whimpers.

His other hand was under her skirt, his knees wedging their way between hers, when the tines of a pitchfork pressed against his side claimed Erkel's attention. Shaking his head like a man throwing off a bad dream, Erkel focused slowly on the huge black man wielding the weapon. To Amanda's horrified amazement, Erkel laughed aloud. "Go ahead, nigger," he taunted. "They'll hang you so fast you won't have time to feel the rope around your neck!"

Though all three of them recognized the truth of Erkel's threat, Aaron did not back down. "I've sent my boy for Master Gardner, Miss Amanda," he told her calmly, keeping an even, threatening pressure on Erkel's ribs.

Almost before the words were out of his mouth, Grant and several other men came tearing around the corner of the building. "You can back off now and let him up, Aaron," Grant said, murder in his eyes. "I'll take over from here."

"See, boy? What'd I tell you?" Erkel sneered, mistaking Grant's intent, somehow arrogantly thinking Grant's anger was directed toward Aaron rather than toward him. He levered himself to his feet, "The boss knows—"

Grant's knuckles smashing into his mouth made Erkel swallow the rest of that comment. A second blow followed the first, this one meeting the man's midsection, making him gasp for air and double over. As Grant continued to thrash Amanda's attacker, Aaron pulled her free of the fracas, swiftly turning her over to Paddy's supporting arms, without which she would have crumpled into a sobbing heap.

Within minutes it was over, and Grant was barking out his final commands. "Get your belongings and get off this property, Erkel, while you still can. And if I ever find you within ten miles of either Misty Valley or Amanda, you'll consider yourself lucky if you rot in jail. Because the alternative is a grave somewhere in the middle of one of my fields, where no one will ever find your stinking body until someone gets to wondering why the hay grows taller there than anywhere else."

While his men helped hurry Erkel on his way, Grant turned his attention toward Amanda. Her frightened sobs now reduced to residual hiccups, she stared at him through glazed blue eyes. "Damn it, Amanda!" he cursed. His anger still not fully spent, he vented the remainder on her, uncaring at the moment whether she truly deserved it or not. Coming upon them like that, with Erkel poised over her, had scared him more than he wanted to admit. There was no doubt in his mind what would have happened if Aaron hadn't heard her screams.

"How many times do I have to remind you to take care around the men? How many ways must I say the same thing before it finally sinks through that feeble brain of yours?"

"It—it wasn't my fault," she stammered through chattering teeth.

"Well, who but you was stupid enough to go traipsing about behind the smithy, out of sight and sound of safety?"

"I . . . I . . ."

"Precisely. You. And you almost got raped for it!"

Anger and the most intense resentment she'd ever felt

finally loosened Amanda's tongue. "That was your fault as much as anyone's!" she screeched back, much to his astonishment. "You were the one who treated me like dirt beneath your boots, who refused to allot me even the smallest amount of respect from the moment I arrived. And you made certain the men knew it. How was I supposed to overcome that, Grant? Tell me why the hired hands should act any differently toward me than you did, when you were their revered leader who taught them to despise me from the outset! You set the example for the rest of them to follow! Only a handful dared befriend me and disregarded your opinion that I was a cheat and a harlot. The rest have simply mimicked your own behavior."

The validity of her words struck Grant a reeling blow, forcing him to face the result of his actions, his resentment, and his undisguised prejudice that had brought them both to this point in their lives. It was not a pretty picture she'd painted for him to see, or an easy thing to accept about himself. But it was true; he'd partly admitted it to himself earlier, and now he realized he had yet to fully resolve and accept the truth in his own heart and mind.

"Amanda, I'm sorry," he began, reaching for her as he attempted the most painful apology of his life.

She winced and jerked back from his touch, as if he'd offered her a handful of writhing serpents. Though her instinctive reaction was more a lingering result of Erkel's attack than a rejection of Grant, he had no way of knowing that.

"Fine. Have it your way for now, Amanda," he responded flatly. "We'll talk later, when you're more receptive to my company."

Grant had a lot to think about, mostly having to do with his own vile behavior and the resulting repercussions. The more he considered them, the more guilty he felt. If not for him and the way he had treated her, Amanda would not have had to endure such scathing censure, at least not to such an exaggerated extent. Nor would she have risked being raped by one of his own employees. If only he'd accepted her presence more gracefully from the beginning. If only he hadn't constantly taunted and tormented her. And if he'd only had the common decency to keep his hands off her, she'd still have the right to refute the claims against her character, with her head held high.

But no. He'd robbed her of that God-given privilege when he'd so thoughtlessly stolen her purity, and again when he'd blurted out those intimate admissions to Darcy, and consequently to all of Lexington. Now he had to think of a way to make things right again, for both of them, and he wasn't at all certain how to go about doing that.

Amidst the turmoil in his mind, two individual, seemingly unrelated thoughts kept recurring. One was Peppermeier's jest about taking out an advertisement in the newspaper. The other, more disturbing by far, was Macy's suggestion that Grant marry Amanda. Yet the more he considered each idea, the more they began to merge in his brain, until he could scarcely separate them.

Suppose he did marry her. Would becoming his wife raise her standing in the community? Would people respect her any more than they did now? Perhaps, since Misty Valley would then revert to his ownership, by right of marriage, and he would regain his own social rank once more. Also, with Grant already a long-standing member of the horse breeders' association, a position he still held even now, denying Amanda admission would be a dead issue.

Of course, that still left Annabelle's allegations to set to rest, as well as Darcy's. If nothing else, time should tell the trick there, when Annabelle eventually produced a child who bore no resemblance to Grant. As for Darcy's tales, they could reasonably be explained away as jealousy and wishful thinking on the part of a rejected suitor. And if all else failed, Grant could resort to the final ploy of placing a public announcement of the facts in the *Lexington News*, proclaiming specific

names and dates and places for all to see and speculate
upon.

Yes, the longer he pondered the problem, the cure,
and the probable result, the more certain he became
that marriage was the only solution, disregarding the
fact that he didn't love Amanda, and that she still didn't
qualify as a lady, or what constituted a lady in his estimation. As his father had been fond of saying, Grant
had made his own bed, and now he would simply have
to lie in it. In this instance, marriage seemed the only
gentlemanly, honorable course to take.

This decided, albeit with some dread, all he had left
to do was to convince Amanda.

"Have you lost your wits entirely?" she exclaimed
incredulously. "As recently as yesterday, you were
calling me an idiot and yelling at me. Not a month ago,
you could scarcely stand the sight of me, and I distinctly recall you telling me that I was the last woman
you would ever consider marrying. Now, suddenly, you
can't wait to get me to the altar! Grant Gardner, you
are the most maddening, contrary man I have ever met!
Are you deliberately trying to make me crazy, or is this
a natural talent that comes without any effort on your
behalf?"

"Amanda, if you will just simmer down, perhaps we
can discuss this rationally."

"There is nothing rational about any of this—or
you!" she insisted. "Tell me, Grant, if I married you,
what would I gain that I do not already possess?" she
went on with a wave that indicated the house and property around them.

He knew the answer that would sway her most
readily. He employed it now, like a gambler playing his
high card at exactly the right moment. "Respectability.
The right to call yourself a lady and dare anyone to
contradict you."

"Does that include you?"

"Yes, Amanda," he answered tersely, as if it pained
him dearly to concede this to her. "In addition to the

aforementioned, you would also gain a husband, and eventually, children of your own, something all women seem to desire greatly.''

''Fools that we are,'' she muttered in reply, fully aware that he had omitted any mention of undying love. Leveling a cool gaze upon him, she said, ''You, on the other hand, would get Misty Valley back again, wouldn't you? A rousing incentive for proposing marriage, if ever there was one.''

''That is beside the point.''

''No, I rather think it *is* the point, Grant.''

''Then am I to understand that you are yet again refusing my offer?''

''No, I am merely exploring the credits and debits of it, attempting to see if it is worth my while,'' she countered. ''If we were to marry, what would you expect of me as your wife? With Chalmers in charge of running the house, there would be little left for me to do but plan the meals and see to the comfort of any visiting business clients and their families, which I already accomplish with moderate success. Would you expect me to join a sewing circle, perhaps, to help fill my time? Or learn to play the piano?''

''If that's what you want.''

''I do not want.''

''Then what would you prefer to do? Out with it, Amanda. Reading minds, particularly yours, is not one of my talents.''

''I want to keep working with you on the farm. I want to continue my study of horses and racing. Also, since we are both aware that my ability with the account books is superior to yours, I would like to manage the business ledgers.''

''In other words, you would expect me to allow you to continue much as before, a partner in marriage *and* business?''

She nodded. ''Yes.''

''Agreed. As long as we both understand that I am in command and have the final say in all matters, though

I'm sure you'll wear my ears raw arguing with me at every turn.''

Her answering smile promised just that. ''I would also prefer to keep my own account at the bank, solely under my name.''

This brought a frown to his brow. ''Amanda, regardless of what you have thought of me in the past, I do not intend to be a miserly husband. You will have a household allowance, and any additional bills you might incur for clothing or personal purchases will be paid by me. You will have no need of a separate account. Unless you are already planning to keep a 'paid lover' hidden away someplace.''

''That's more what I would expect of you,'' she countered haughtily. ''No, I simply want some money of my own, to spend as I wish. Other women might not object to using their husbands' funds to purchase their birthday or Christmas presents, but it wouldn't settle right with me. Then there is Betsy, and who knows what other circumstance might arise in the future. I cannot ask you to contribute to the upkeep of my friends when I know you are not overly fond of them.''

''You may have your account. As for Betsy, as long as she is a guest under my roof, I will provide the cost of her care and comfort.''

''Gracious of you, all things considered.''

''Anything else?''

''Not that I can think of.''

Though she still had reservations, her heart was begging her to accept this proposal, with all its inherent hazards. Too long had she denied herself what her heart so desperately craved. Hopefully, Grant would someday come to love her as wholeheartedly as she did him. Of course, he was much too muleheaded to believe a confession of her feelings at this juncture, any more than he seemed to have credited her initial declaration following their first passionate lovemaking. Only time and actions would prove her claim, more definitively than mere words would sway him now.

As much as she might want to rush him toward the truth, Grant would have to arrive at this sublime revelation on his own. Also, he needed to know and believe, deep in his own heart and mind, that love alone had compelled her to marry him, that her longing for respectability had nothing to do with it. Amanda felt that then, and only then, would they truly be happy together, when love and trust were equally shared between them. It was a risk she was willing to take—undoubtedly the biggest gamble of her life.

Grant watched as Amanda contemplated further, obviously thinking over everything they had discussed and unconsciously chewing at her bottom lip in lieu of her usual wad of gum. Finally, with a profound sigh, she said, "Okay. How and when do we accomplish this daring leap into marital bliss?"

"Your enthusiasm overwhelms me," he replied with unfeigned sarcasm. "In answer to your question, as soon as you can get Madame Lalaine to sew up a wedding gown for you. Pay her extra to hurry the job along, and I want the final product to be pristine white, Amanda. Pure, glistening white satin, abounding in lace."

"Grant! For heaven's sake! That's tantamount to throwing mud in the faces of all of Lexington!"

He shrugged, the hint of an arrogant smile curving his lips. "Invitations will be sent to our most important clients, with Senator and Mrs. Whittaker and Art Macy included, of course."

"And Betsy?" Amanda inquired, raising a stubborn chin at him.

Grant didn't bat an eyelash. "Naturally. As soon as I can make arrangements for the church, I will inform you of the date. Put Chalmers in charge of preparing a proper reception."

Now that she'd agreed to this ridiculous alliance, Amanda was starting to have second thoughts. "Oh, God, Grant!" she moaned. "What if no one comes?

We'll both look like bigger fools than ever. Maybe we'd better reconsider.''

"They'll come, if only out of respect for my parents and to satisfy their insatiable curiosity,'' he assured her.

"I don't even know what faith you're affiliated with,'' she protested further, beginning to panic. "Now that I think about it, I really know very little about you. I have no idea where your family hails from, though Annabelle did once mention England. Or what they do for a living. Or what your favorite color is. Or who planted the rose garden at the side of the house. Or where you have your shirts made. Or . . . well, everything!''

"I'm Lutheran, which really isn't such a far cry from Catholicism that you should have any major problem adjusting. For the most part, my family is English, though a few relatives reside in Ireland and Scotland. Quite a strange mix there. Some are farmers, others shopkeepers, with a duchess thrown in, courtesy of my cousin Amelia's wedding into royalty. My favorite color is blue, the exact shade of your eyes, and my mother planted the rose garden. I have a favorite tailor on Mill Street, and the rest of your questions will undoubtedly be answered as the marriage progresses. You already know the most important things.''

"Such as?''

"Such as how to please me in bed. The perfume I prefer to smell on your delicious body. That I like your hair long and loose and tumbling across my pillow. The way I delight in the smoothness of your skin beneath my fingers and the feel of your silken thighs wrapping themselves around me. How crazed with desire I become when you emit those erotic little moans from deep in your throat when I'm making love with you.''

He laughed aloud as color flushed her cheeks. "Getting a bit warm in here for you, sweetheart?'' he teased. "Would you care for a glass of champagne to celebrate our engagement?''

"Save it for the wedding night, you lecherous rake," she retorted sassily, fanning herself with her hand. Her smile matched his as she added, "And kindly conserve your energy between now and then, because I can assure you that you are going to need all you can store in reserve."

Chapter 24

CHAOS reigned at Misty Valley for the next two weeks. Invitations were hastily sent, the farthest by special courier. Chalmers and the chef were in constant consultation over the menu for the wedding feast. Extra household help was hired to polish mounds of silver and china and crystal, and every room in the place soon shone with an added gleam and smelled of beeswax and lemon. Outdoors, a small army of gardeners pruned and trimmed and fussed over the lawn and flowers, while every building in sight was given a fresh coat of paint.

Smiling from ear to ear, Madame Lalaine promised to whip up an absolute confection of a gown, guaranteeing that Amanda would be the envy of every woman who beheld her in it, and every man's dream. The seamstress positively cooed over Amanda's engagement ring, claiming that it was the most unusual she'd ever seen.

Amanda had to agree, but could take no credit for its origin, as it had been all Grant's idea. How he'd managed to get the jeweler to create it so quickly, she could only guess, but within a week of their decision to marry, Grant had slipped it on her finger. Amanda wasn't precisely sure what to think about the ring. Though it was unquestionably lovely, she suspected Grant's peculiar sense of humor had prompted the design.

Recessed into the center of a flat, slightly rectangular bed of mother-of-pearl rested a large heart-shaped ruby. Supporting the stone, and surrounding the mother-of-pearl on all four sides, was a wide rim of irregular gold edging, which flared up from the band itself and had been grooved to resemble individual layers, one atop another. The effect was that of a deck of cards, slightly fanned, the topmost being the ace of hearts.

"It's so unique!" The dressmaker gasped in delight. "And so wonderfully romantic that he should compare you to the highest of all hearts!"

Personally, Amanda wondered if this wasn't Grant's way of making sure she never forgot her lowly beginning as a gambler, something to keep her humble whenever she started to get too high-handed. Still, the ring was so spectacularly beautiful that she'd adored it on sight, and Grant had been so pleased with himself when he'd presented it to her that she hadn't had the heart to question his motives aloud—even when he'd informed her that her gold wedding band, specifically designed to match, was to be encrusted with two small rubies on each side, in the shape of a heart, a diamond, a spade, and a club. Certainly, the rings would be a rare set, and uncommonly well suited to their owner's personality.

In addition to all the other wedding preparations, Grant had placed an announcement of their upcoming nuptials in the local newspapers, and Lexington was abuzz with the news. This, however, proved to be just the start of a very interesting string of events.

Word had it that Annabelle's father had finally gotten wind of his daughter's supposed liaison with the stablehand, and the feathers had hit the wind! All this time he'd naturally assumed that his darling, innocent Annabelle had been bedded and then unjustly abandoned by her one true love, the incorrigible Grant Gardner. Now, much to Mr. Foster's dismay, he discovered more of the truth than he cared to know.

The first thing the man did was to corner his lovely daughter, demanding the truth of the matter. Annabelle, of course, denied everything, but not quite to her father's satisfaction, it seemed. Still suspicious, he then took the young man in question aside for some rather insistent and rough questioning, which produced much more factual, if distasteful, information.

After running the fellow off his property at the point of a gun, so it was reported, Mr. Foster again confronted Annabelle, who promptly turned into a belligerent witch before his disbelieving eyes. In a fit of rage, she confessed that not only had she dallied with Grant and the stableboy, but she had also taken a third man as a lover. Stanford Darcy, by name. Furthermore, the child she now carried had been fathered by either Darcy or the so-recently-dismissed farmhand. She knew not which, though she'd put her money on Darcy, given the choice, especially now that her grand opportunity to trap Grant had failed.

Consequently, Annabelle had been locked in her room and hadn't been seen since, while her father tried to decide what to do with his recalcitrant offspring.

The Foster servants, agog with what they'd seen and heard, couldn't wait to repeat this latest incident, and soon the entire community was aware of what had occurred. The ticket master at the railway station contributed yet another tidbit when he relayed that Foster's former stablehand had taken the first available train to Chattanooga, Tennessee, after purchasing a one-way fare. The lad had been sporting a honey of a black eye at the time.

Soon afterward, Stanford Darcy closed shop, at least temporarily, telling his befuddled secretary to inform anyone who asked that he'd "gone fishing." The question in everyone's curious mind was, "Fishing for what? Or whom? And how long could the wily lawyer remain in hiding from Annabelle and her irate father?"

Upon hearing the news, Amanda was almost as livid as Mr. Foster. ''Why, that low-down, conniving, worthless worm! And to think I trusted him! Well, they'll be serving ice cream in hell before I place my faith in a pair of pleading brown eyes again! That crafty son of a buck!''

''I think the proper term is son of a bitch,'' Grant supplied, he, too, less than thrilled to learn that Annabelle had been spreading her favors so thin, as he'd been totally unaware of it. And with Stanford Darcy, no less!

''I know, but I didn't want to cast stones at his mother's reputation. She might have been a very nice person—with a very nasty son.''

''How nasty was he?'' Grant asked with a frown, wondering if more had transpired between Amanda and the attorney than he knew.

''Not enough to get into my britches, I assure you,'' she retorted huffily. ''Though he did mention such desires a time or two, in a vague sort of roundabout way. The only time he actually let his lips wander toward my chest, Sweet Cheek nearly took his nose off. He was sitting on my lap at the time.''

A wry grin twisted Grant's lips. ''Sweet Cheek, or Darcy? On your lap, I mean.''

She shot him an exasperated look, then couldn't help but smile back. ''The duck, silly. Darcy never got that far.''

''You know, maybe that bird isn't so bad after all,'' Grant conceded.

Amanda giggled. ''Which bird? Sweet Cheek, or Darcy?''

As Amanda walked slowly down the aisle on Chalmers' arm, she was amazed at the number of people crowding the church pews. Grant had been right after all. The cream of Lexington society had turned out, decked in their finest apparel, to witness this wedding—whether through plain old curiosity or merely because in their fickle minds Darcy and Annabelle had now been painted with an even blacker tar brush, making Amanda and Grant appear almost angelic in comparison. Then again, with Grant restored to his former wealth and position, perhaps they thought it expedient to forgive and forget as quickly as possible, and hope the happy bridegroom was willing to do the same. For whatever reason, the church was near to bursting.

Through the gossamer veil that made only a pretense of shielding her glowing face from her audience, Amanda saw Betsy standing to one side of the altar. Madame Lalaine had achieved wonders in creating a gown for Amanda's friend that was somehow both modest and enticing, at the same time fitting Betsy's tiny frame without need of stays or corset that would cause more pain to her newly knitting ribs. In her hands she carried a small nosegay of the palest violets to offset her lavender silk gown, while a garland of the same delicate flowers wreathed her blonde head.

On the opposite side of the altar, beside Frank Hanover, the best man, Grant awaited his bride. He stood tall and dark, and more handsome than ever in his wedding attire, with intense emerald eyes that seemed to impel Amanda toward him by some magical force.

For just a moment his image seemed to waver, Amanda's perception of him distorted as a shaft of sunlight hazed her vision. The gleaming white of his ruffled shirtfront took on a glint of silver; the glimmer of a nearby candle flame cast a mercurial halo over his raven hair. A frond of greenery in the huge bouquet behind him became, for a mere instant, a plume waving above his head. Here, before her bemused eyes, stood her long-awaited knight in all his glorious armor.

As if in a dream, she drifted toward him, with the knowledge that the vows she would take to love and honor this man could never be more sincerely pledged. Her heart overflowing with love for him, she could only pray that someday he would hold the same tender feelings for her, that with time and care, love would grow from his desire for her.

Grant had never seen Amanda look more beautiful

than she did this day. To his eyes, she appeared a dark-haired goddess, gowned from head to toe in flowing white satin and lace. There was a becoming blush to her cheeks, visible even through the gauzy veil. Her eyes shone like twin stars.

His gaze wandered from her face, noting the way the diamond-shaped bodice of her gown molded itself so faithfully to her breasts. Trembling at the base of her throat was the blue topaz pendant he'd given her as a bridal gift, with earbobs to match. In her hands, her bouquet of white lilies quivered slightly atop his mother's Bible.

She was exquisite! Elegance and innocence and seduction rolled into one incredibly alluring woman! As ethereal as a wisp of morning mist, yet as real and captivating as any temptation heretofore devised for man.

Within minutes, the span of a few spoken words, she would be his for all time. To love, to honor, to protect unto death. To have and to hold from this day forth.

And hold her he would, against all those who might try to take her from him. Against even her own fickle female inclinations.

Love her he might not, but his desire for her bordered on obsession, and Grant was discovering that he had a possessive streak, not only for Misty Valley, but also for this beguiling enchantress who had somehow cast her wanton spell over him. And he had the strongest premonition that if he wasn't extremely careful, she would soon entice his heart from him as well.

His hand reached out to clasp hers. Together they knelt, repeating the holy vows that bound them to each other, Amanda's responses emerging soft and trembling, Grant's strong and sure. His touch was warm and steady as he placed the wedding band firmly on her finger, a shining symbol of their unity. Slowly, as if to prolong the moment, Grant lifted the veil from her face, his gaze capturing hers as surely as his lips claimed the kiss to follow. Tenderly, with such gentle passion that it brought glad tears welling in her eyes, his lips caressed hers in wordless praise.

Pulling slightly away from her, Grant studied her glowing face, her huge, shimmering blue eyes, her trembling kiss-blushed mouth. "Smile, princess," he whispered softly, his own lips curving upward. "And prepare to greet your subjects."

The ride home, in the flower-bedecked carriage, was something from a fairy tale, with Grant and Amanda caught in the midst of it. Even then, with Frank and Betsy seated opposite them, beaming with satisfaction, they had little privacy, and would have none for several hours to come.

The reception seemed to go on forever, and Amanda swore she'd never seen so many people gathered together in one place. Extra leaves had been added to the dining table, and still their guests milled about the parlors and gardens, balancing plates and glasses. Gifts not previously received were hastily stacked precariously here and there, to be opened later; while a bevy of servants rushed about replenishing food dishes and wine goblets as fast as was humanly possible.

Champagne flowed endlessly in a small fountain at one end of the dining room. How Chalmers had managed this remarkable feat, Amanda could not guess. Nor could she fail to admire the towering twelve-tiered wedding cake, an awesome display of culinary accomplishment, elaborately decorated with swirls and rosebuds of pink-tinted icing.

With Grant at her side, Amanda mingled with her guests, graciously greeting one and all. As they partook of the bountiful feast, she found little time to satisfy her own hunger, which was probably a blessing in disguise considering the nervous state of her stomach. Yet, amazingly, every time she lifted her champagne goblet to her lips, it was filled to the rim.

Perhaps it was not so surprising after all, she decided, once she caught the devilish twinkle in Grant's dancing green eyes. By the time they had cut the cake,

Amanda was getting giddy—and alarmingly warm! Not long afterward, Grant placed her bridal bouquet carefully in her hands, laughing at the hazy smile she offered him. With a firm hand to steady her steps, he led her halfway up the staircase while a throng gathered below them in cheering anticipation.

Pulling her to a halt, he prompted, "You are supposed to toss your bouquet to the hopeful maidens anxiously awaiting, my love."

"Why?" she asked with a fuzzy frown.

He chuckled. "Because it's tradition, Amanda. Supposedly, the lucky lady to catch your bridal flowers will be the next to marry."

"Oh! Well, that being the case, how can I stand in the way of true love?"

With a saucy wave, she tossed the blossoms into the air, clapping delightedly as they caught in Betsy's garland and tumbled into her arms. "Oh, my!" Amanda exclaimed softly. "Who do you suppose the groom will be?"

"Why don't we find out?" Grant suggested with a grin. Bending, he lifted her skirt above one knee and proceeded to tug at her garter.

"Grant! What do you think you're doing?" she hissed loudly. "My lands! What will everyone think?"

"I'm stealing your garter, sweetheart, to throw down to all the eligible bachelors. It's a common wedding practice."

"Well, leave my stockings, will you please? And for God's sake, stop caressing the back of my knee while you're about it, you devil! It tickles!"

With a laugh, Grant heaved the purloined garter over his shoulder, not even stopping to see who caught it as he gathered his bride into his arms and carried her the remainder of the way up the stairs and into the privacy of the master bedroom. Their guests could continue the celebration without them, looked after by Chalmers and his staff. Grant had much more interesting and intimate activities planned for himself and his beautiful, slightly tipsy wife.

* * *

Had he bothered to turn around, Grant would have been as stunned as the young gentleman into whose hands the garter fell. In dumbfounded shock, Tad Gardner gazed at the garter clutched in his fingers and the retreating figure of his older sibling, his confused mind just beginning to comprehend what he'd witnessed upon walking through the front door and into the crowded entryway. Shaking his head in wonder at the quirks of fate that seemed to rule mortal lives, Tad went in search of Chalmers, eager to learn all that had gone on in his absence—and exactly how the lady gambler had maneuvered his stubborn brother into marriage.

Upstairs, the bride and groom were attempting to rid each other of their clothing, stealing long kisses and hot caresses all the while.

"Hurry, Grant!" Amanda panted as his fingers fumbled with the multitude of tiny, cloth-covered buttons down the back of her gown. She thought to warn him, "Don't tear the dress. Our daughter might want to wear it to her own wedding one day."

"Son," he corrected, smiling at the image of a small replica of himself someday in the near future. It was a humbling thought, and at the same time extremely exalting.

"Your son is going to look a bit odd in my wedding gown, don't you think?" she said, giggling.

"I meant, I want a son," he said, still fighting with the last few buttons. "A farm this size needs boys to help keep it running, someone to take over when I'm too old and feeble."

"Fine, you can have your son, but I want a girl, too. Besides, it will be a long time before you're ready to turn the reins over to anyone else."

After what seemed an eternity, the dress slid to the floor, and Amanda sighed with relief, rubbing her hands across her arms and shoulders. "Thank God! I thought the fabric was going to wear through my skin!"

Grant grinned. "That champagne is really starting to

do the trick, isn't it?'' he teased, pausing to nibble at her nape.

"Yes, you fiend! I was trying to limit myself to half a glass, but the blasted thing never got half empty!''

"Offhand, I'd judge you drank about four glasses worth, all totaled.''

She winced at that. "I hope you know what you've done. I also hope you have a lot of stamina, because I'm going to be wild for you until all that champagne wears off. We'll be lucky if either of us can walk tomorrow!''

"Darlin', I don't care if neither of us leaves this room all weekend,'' he answered, regretting that, because of the horse auction the following weekend and all the preparations still to be done for it, he and Amanda had not been able to plan even a short wedding trip. It would have been wonderful to have her all to himself, with nothing to do but seduce each other for a solid month, but perhaps after the auction they could arrange something.

As she tugged his coat from his broad shoulders and loosened his necktie, he busied himself with the ties to her petticoats. By the time his shirt and shoes joined the growing pile of clothes on the rug, Amanda stood before him clad only in her unlaced camisole, a silky pair of French panties, her sheer white stockings, and her jewelry. Pulling pins from her hair, he wove his fingers through the wavy tresses as they fell in a thick midnight cascade around her shoulders.

On an indrawn breath, Grant held his gaze on the picture before him. "Sometimes I can't believe how beautiful you are,'' he told her, letting his fingers trail to the half-exposed slopes of her breasts, teasing the cloth aside to bare one rose-dimpled crest.

Shivering, her smile resembling that of a cat locked in the creamery, she slid her fingers through the thick mat of dark hair across his chest. Her nails scraped lightly at the brown male nubs hidden there. "I've thought the same thing about you,'' she confessed.

"Did you know that the very first time I saw you, I could scarcely breathe or speak, for staring at you?"

"Well, I was doing my fair share of staring that day, too, as I recall," he admitted with a wry grin. "I still am, I guess. And I like what I see, though I'd like to see more of it right about now." With that, he quickly stripped the rest of her clothes from her, picked her up, and deposited her in the center of the huge bed.

While Grant divested himself of his remaining clothes, Amanda watched, her eyes unashamedly adoring each new inch of flesh he uncovered. The hard work on the farm had endowed him with firm muscles that rippled in a fascinating manner as he moved. There must have been times when Grant had removed his shirt in the sun, for his back and chest and arms were as tanned as his face, while the lower half of him was darkened only by body hair.

When he came to her, she welcomed him with open arms, gathering his hard, warm body close to hers. The contact of their flesh renewed the sensitivity of hers, enhanced to a flash point by the strange effects of the champagne. Wriggling beneath him, she urged him on. "Oh, do hurry, love," she implored. "Before I go up in flames and set the bed afire!"

Grant was more than willing to comply with her demands, knowing that they had plenty of time later to make love as slowly and endlessly as they wished. All night and the whole of the following day, if they wanted. But right now he was as aroused as Amanda. Just the sight of her writhing beneath him, the smell of her perfume combining with the exotic scent of her feminine desire, the titillating brush of her satiny flesh against his, sent his senses spiraling.

It was fast, furious, like the mating of love-hungry wolves. Her enameled nails scored his back; his teeth nipped her throat and shoulders. Their cries of bliss blended in mutual ecstasy, neither caring who heard or speculated on their nuptial activities.

And when it was done, they were still eager for each other, their passions unappeased. Again and again, long into the night, they savored the splendor, languidly loving, taking delight in tormenting one another to the point of insanity and then satisfying the intense longing in the most pleasurable ways possible. The moon was waning, the stars fading against the coming dawn, when, like two battle-weary soldiers, they finally admitted defeat to their satiated bodies.

"You're still painting your toenails," Grant observed on a weary yawn, gathering her head to rest upon his shoulder.

"Yes, but I've changed to a lighter shade, if you'll notice."

"Oh, I noticed soon after you did it. I just didn't say anything. You know, I can't quite discern why, but there's something very sensual about undressing a woman and discovering painted toenails."

Against his chest, he felt her lips curve into a smile. "I know." She laughed.

"Wanton!" Grinning, he administered a slight slap to her bare bottom.

She responded in kind, her nails lightly scraping his buttocks in an erotic caress. "Lecher!"

"Wife," he whispered softly, his lips stroking her damp forehead.

Her answer was to snuggle closer, offering her mouth once again to his.

Chapter 25

IT was later that morning, when Chalmers knocked lightly on the bedroom door, announcing that he'd brought a breakfast tray up for them, that Grant and Amanda were informed of Tad's arrival. With a shout of joyous surprise and only a hint of apology to her, Grant tossed on his clothes and raced downstairs to greet his long-lost brother. Amanda was not far behind him.

They found Tad leisurely enjoying his own late breakfast on the dining room veranda overlooking the rose garden. To their vast amazement, he was wearing a blue uniform with a U.S. Cavalry insignia. To Amanda's further astonishment, Tad rose from his seat to greet her with a warm, brother-to-sister embrace.

"Welcome to the family, Amanda," he told her with what sounded like complete sincerity.

With a baffled frown, she returned the friendly greeting, wondering why Tad should be so genial toward her after all he'd undoubtedly been through since losing his inheritance in that fateful poker game. Still, during their brief acquaintance, he'd never reacted with as much prejudice toward her as his older brother had, though he'd had more cause to do so.

"Where have you been all this time?" Grant demanded gruffly, even as he hugged Tad to him in a brotherly show of affection that went straight to Amanda's heart. "And why haven't you written in all this time? Blast it all, Tad! Just a couple of lines to let me know you were still alive would have been sufficient!"

"Obviously, I've been in the Army," Tad answered, gesturing to his uniform. "As for writing, we've been a bit busy fighting Indians to take much time out for such trivialities, and the mail isn't all that reliable out West, even if you can find a scrap of paper to write on." His face took on a properly apologetic, almost sheepish look as he added hesitantly, "I suppose you heard about Custer and his troops getting massacred this past June."

"Oh, my God! You weren't out there then, were you?" Grant exclaimed, while Amanda fought to breathe at the very thought of the peril her young brother-in-law might have faced.

"Well, actually I was," Tad admitted uneasily. "That's another reason I didn't want to write to you just then. I figured you'd either worry yourself gray or hightail it out there to try and bring me home, and I didn't want you to do either. As you can see, I'm just fine."

"Probably more luck than sense," Grant grumbled, his eyes searching for any sign of injuries Tad might be trying to hide from them.

Tad nodded. "It was that, all right. When General Custer divided his troops, it was pure luck that I ended up in Captain Benteen's company instead of riding with Custer that day. Of course, we saw our share of fighting, more than any of us wanted to; and there was a point when I was sure we were all going to die. But we made it through, held on until General Terry came along with news of Custer, and kissed the planks we stood on when we got back to the Missouri River and boarded the *Far West* for Fort Lincoln."

As he studied his brother's face and listened to his words, Grant sensed a new maturity in Tad. Maybe the Almighty, in His infinite wisdom, knew what He was doing after all. Maybe this experience was what it had taken to make Tad grow up, to learn about responsibilities, though it certainly seemed a heck of a way to have to go about it.

With an effort, Grant swallowed the rebuke so ready to his tongue. Perhaps it was time to give the lad a little respect, to drop the old habit of always correcting and admonishing him. Instead, he asked quietly, "How long are you home for, Tad?"

A twinkle sparked in the younger Gardner's eyes. "Long enough for the newlyweds to wish I'd leave again," he teased. Then he added, "I have about a month while we wait for some of our unit to heal. Then we'll probably head back to fight some more Indians."

"Do you have to return to the West?" Amanda put in. "Can't you ask for an assignment closer to home?"

"To tell the truth, that's one of the things I wanted to talk to Grant about, but I wasn't sure how he'd feel about me after that shock I gave him this spring."

"Tad, we're family. No matter what you've done, you know you can always come to me with any problem," Grant assured him. "Oh, I might rant and rave for a while, but eventually I'll cool down. And there's nothing you could do that would be so terrible that I wouldn't forgive you for it—eventually."

From the corner of his eye, he saw Amanda roll her eyes heavenward in wry amusement. "What?" he barked.

"Oh, nothing," she choked out, trying not to laugh. "It wasn't just that remark about ranting and raving that struck my funny bone. As I recall, you did quite a lot of that when I first arrived here."

Tad grinned. "That must have been when he first found out about me losing half the farm to you, huh?" he surmised. "Boy, that must have been some fit he threw! Makes me sort of wish I'd been here to see it.

And sort of glad I wasn't!'' he added hastily when his brother glared at him.

''You should be glad you weren't here, or I'd have made those Indians look tame to you,'' Grant vowed. ''Now, what is it you wanted to talk to me about? Something to do with transferring to a unit closer to home?''

''Not right next door, but a little nearer and a lot more convenient for traveling home to visit now and then. I want to go to West Point and become an officer. But to do that, I need some mighty good recommendations and maybe a little money to cover part of the academy expenses. Since I haven't proved that much of a scholar up to now, it will help if I can convince them of my sincerity toward this endeavor. Captain Benteen, Major Reno, and General Terry all promised to write letters of recommendation for me, but I really should have a letter of reference from you, too, Grant, since you're my closest relative—concerning my decent character and family background, perhaps expressing your confidence in my abilities. And I thought it wouldn't hurt to see if some of our friends and neighbors can dredge up something good to say about me, while I'm at it.''

''Then you intend to make a career of the Army? Is this truly what you want to do, Tad? Because I'll tell you now that if it isn't, you're always welcome to come back and help me with the farm.''

''No. I love it here, and it will always be home to me, but it's long past time for me to make my own way in the world. I can't do that by leaning on you for the rest of my life. It's really strange, but losing my half of this place was probably the best thing that could have happened to me. It gave me enough of a jolt to knock some sense into me and make me realize what a spoiled brat I was. Besides, I'm not half as good at horse breeding as you are. Your heart and soul are in this business, but to me it was all sort of a grand game, I guess. One designed to put coin in my pockets while I played around and let you do most of the work.''

Grant was tempted to tell Tad that he would sign his rightful half of the property back to him, and that things would be different if Tad decided to stay, but some intuition held the words back. He was glad he'd kept silent when Tad added, "No offense, but I'd rather do it my way, Grant. There's no shame in being a soldier, and I have to admit I feel damned proud of myself these days. I'll feel prouder still if I can make it into West Point—and out again as an officer. I'll feel as if I've accomplished something important on my own. For the first time."

When Tad got his first look at Betsy, his eyes took on a gleam of male interest that made Grant want to bundle his brother off to West Point, or wherever, as fast as he could get him there. Betsy was no better, returning Tad's looks with shy smiles and batting her eyelashes in that coy, feminine way women had practiced since the dawn of time.

When Grant complained to Amanda, she pouted those rosy lips of hers and said, "I think it's sort of sweet."

"Of course you would," Grant responded with a sigh, knowing he would get no support here. "Those are the same feminine tricks you employed on me."

"I did no such thing!"

"Oh, yes, you did," he argued. "Just like you're doing now, pursing those delectable lips at me, making me want to kiss you till you beg for mercy. Not to mention the way you're always making calf eyes at me, and wiggling your fanny around in front of my nose, or making sure your dress is showing just enough breast to make my mouth water."

"It works that well, does it?" She smirked.

"You know damned well what it does to me," he said, pulling her close enough for the proof of his ardor to be felt between them.

It was the middle of the afternoon, and they both had a thousand things to do before the day was over, but Amanda grabbed his hand and pulled him toward the house—and the big bed waiting for them upstairs, "Let's see what we can do to put you out of your misery," she suggested wickedly. "And we'll see who begs for mercy."

At supper, Tad almost laughed himself simple when the half-naked Sweet Cheek hopped onto Amanda's lap, then atop the table, and proceeded to peck at a piece of bread on her plate. Blinking and shaking his head, Tad slid a glance to the opposite end of the long table, where Grant sat glaring at both wife and duckling.

"Now that's what I call a pet!" Tad remarked, just to irritate his brother further, an art he'd long since perfected.

Grant shot him a quelling look. "I'd almost forgotten your penchant for odd creatures, Tad," he replied dryly. "You were the one with the pet copperhead that cost Mother her best cook, as I recall."

"Too bad it couldn't have been Mrs. Divots," Amanda muttered beneath her breath. This brought a hoot of laughter from Tad, who was sitting close enough to hear.

"What was that, Amanda?" Grant inquired suspiciously.

"Nothing, darling. Just grumbling to myself."

"Then grumble a little louder, will you, so we all may hear?"

"This shouting to be heard is ridiculous!" Amanda complained, picking up her plate and moving to a chair halfway between Betsy and Grant. "Is it written in stone or something that a wife must sit half a mile from her husband during dinner?"

"It is customary for the master of the house to sit at the head of the table, and for the mistress to sit at the foot of it, so that none of their guests will be ignored," Grant explained imperiously. "We've entertained enough that you should have realized this, and you've never complained before."

"The table was nearly full on those occasions," she reminded him. "At least then I didn't have to bother

Chalmers, or have someone leave his seat merely to pass the dratted potatoes!''

"She has a point, Grant," Tad inserted.

"Yes. On the end of her tongue."

Thus prompted, Amanda stuck her tongue out at him.

"I'll get you for that, my dear," he warned, his eyes gleaming with promised retribution.

"Before, or after, I get you for directing the word 'mistress' toward me?" she dared.

Tad chuckled. "Oh, this is getting interesting."

"Don't let it upset you," Betsy told him. "They're at each other like a cat and a dog every time you turn around."

Tad winked at her. "More like two cats in a bag, if you ask me."

"Nobody asked you," Grant said. "So kindly shut up and finish your dinner."

All was quiet for a few minutes, though Amanda was working up to a good case of the giggles, and Tad snickered a time or two, until Sweet Cheek began wobbling precariously down the center of the table in search of Amanda. Amanda paid little attention before she heard Betsy's gasp. Looking up, she beheld what everyone else was now staring at in mute fascination. Her beloved pet was weaving and bobbing between the serving dishes as Chalmers rushed to pull the food out of harm's way. The bird, always a little awkward in gait, was even more unsteady than usual, for some reason. Just as he waddled past the creamed corn, he lost his balance entirely and promptly toppled sideways—straight into the middle of it!

"Oh, my stars and garters!" Amanda exclaimed, leaping up to pluck the duckling from his large puddle of vegetables. Sweet Cheek lay limp in her hands, staring up at her with glazed eyes and goo dripping over both of them. Quickly, she wrapped her napkin around him, trying to dry him off.

Amanda was becoming alarmed, especially when she gave him a little shake and Sweet Cheek failed to twitch so much as a pin feather. "Grant, there's something dreadfully wrong with him!'' she cried. "Do something! Quickly! My God! I think he's dying!''

By now the entire table was in an uproar. Chalmers stood as if turned to stone, staring at her with the oddest look on his face. Betsy was choking into her own napkin, and Tad was laughing uproariously and holding his ribs. Grant was grinning like an idiot.

"It's not funny!'' she shrieked. "Do something, damn it!''

"I will, just as soon as I can think of what would apply.'' Grant chortled. "I'd suggest black coffee, but perhaps it's best just to let him sleep it off.''

"Sleep what off? You don't just sleep off a seizure!''

Tad had abandoned his chair and was literally rolling on the floor by now, which came as no surprise to Grant, since Tad had always displayed an outrageous sense of humor. Betsy was holding her ribs, tears streaming down her cheeks. Grant was wearing an arrogant smirk, and if she'd had her hands free, Amanda would have slapped it right off his handsome face.

"The blasted dumb duck has not had a seizure, Amanda. He's skunked to his scrawny little neck on the wine you left at the end of the table. All the while we've been eating, he's been slurping it down as if it were water.''

Amanda's dumbstruck gaze wandered to the duckling still lying slack in her hands, as relaxed and boneless as a jellyfish. "He's . . . he's drunk?'' she asked in disbelief. This brought another wild howl of laughter from under Tad's empty chair and a hilarious giggle from Betsy. Even Chalmers was wearing a silly smile, and Grant's grin had grown from ear to ear.

"Yes, Amanda. Thoroughly and totally sloshed,'' he assured her.

As if to prove him right, Sweet Cheek emitted a belch that would have put the stack on a steamboat to shame, followed by the most delicate little hiccup. This set everyone off again into fresh gales of mirth, including Amanda, who was so relieved to know what was wrong with him that she was nearly giddy with it.

Gently, she handed Sweet Cheek, still wrapped in his napkin nightie, off to Chalmers to be carried off to his tiny bed beneath the stairs. Grant flatly refused to share his marriage bed, or his wife, with the nasty-tempered fowl, and since Grant was a much nicer bed-mate, Amanda agreed.

"Drunk! Well, I'll be switched!" she marveled when she could talk past her laughter.

"That idiot bird is the one who ought to be switched," Grant said, wiping at his watering eyes. "Though you deserve a few good licks yourself. Now that you mention it, it's not such a bad idea," he added, leaning closer and murmuring wickedly into her ear. "Remind me, and maybe we'll try it tonight, once we're alone. The thought of your bare rump beneath my hand is uncommonly stimulating at the moment."

She shot him a wary, half-amused look. "When aren't you uncommonly stimulated?" she whispered back.

He laughed. "Around you? Never."

Tuesday, in the midst of final, hectic preparations for the summer auction, disaster struck. Suddenly, for no immediately apparent reason, several of their most favored foals, as well some of the mares, came up lame at the same time. The foundering horses were among those chosen to be sold in just four days, and Grant was at his wit's end to explain this strange illness that had abruptly afflicted the animals.

Finally Clancy thought to check the bedding in their stalls. There he found, much to everyone's confounded disbelief, walnut shavings mixed in with the sawdust they used to supplement the straw. "Here's yer problem, boss." Clancy nodded grimly. "It'll make 'em founder every time. Walnut has somethin' in it that sort of soaks into the hoof, like water into sand, then goes on to make the poor creature lame. If you don't catch it in time, it can kill 'em sure as a bullet in the brain."

Grant was well aware of the detrimental effects walnut could have on a horse, and he was furious that such an injurious mistake had been made. "Check all the stalls, and change all the bedding, and make damned sure none of it has walnut shavings in it. Meanwhile, I'm going to have a few words with Abel Smith about the latest batch of sawdust we bought from him. The old Shaker must be slipping up, to have made an error like that after all the years we've been dealing with him."

"Me and some 'o the lads'll start soakin' hooves and applyin' plasters," Paddy volunteered. "By Saturday, they'll be right as rain again."

But that wasn't the end of their problems, though the affected horses did improve rapidly once the walnut was removed from the stalls and treatment began. The night before the auction, the gate to the paddock where the selected yearlings were penned was found ajar. Someone, in his haste, had failed to latch the gate properly. Eighteen foals had wandered away before someone noticed, and now they had to be rounded up before they could come to harm.

"How are you going to find them in the dark, Grant?" Amanda asked as her husband and brother-in-law prepared to lead the search.

"It won't be easy, but if we wait until morning, there's no telling how far they might go or what condition they'll be in when we find them. Between coyotes and snakes and holes and ravines, the lot of them could be buzzard bait by sunrise. We've got to find as many as we can tonight."

For hours, with torches to light their way, they scoured the surrounding countryside for the missing horses. They combed every woods, checked every creek and stream and farm for ten miles in each direction. When they finally came dragging back to Misty Valley, sixteen of the runaways found, it was five o'clock the next morning. Three of these had sustained minor injuries, one badly enough to eliminate him from the auction.

In the three hours remaining before bidders would begin to arrive, Amanda pitched in to help the weary men wash and brush and curry the yearlings to their original condition. It had been a long night, and would prove to be an even longer day before the last sale had been made and rest could be sought.

After such a rough beginning, the auction went extremely well, bringing top bids for many of the animals. Throughout the day Amanda and Grant greeted customers and clients as graciously as if they'd slept the past ten hours and couldn't be more refreshed, welcoming their guests like royalty.

Food and drink were offered, arrayed on tables set up under shade trees in the back lawn. Arrangements were made for transporting the horses. Bloodlines were endlessly debated. Not once did Grant allow his weariness to make him cut short a talkative customer or fail to explain, down to the most minute detail, the finest attributes of the horse in question.

Meanwhile, Amanda kept him, and the rest of the staff, fortified with strong black coffee. That, and the inherent excitement of the day, were all that kept Misty Valley's residents on their feet through the long hours.

When the final carriage rolled away, a united sigh of relief rose up. One and all hurried through the remaining chores, some taking time to gulp down a quick bite of supper, while others cared for nothing but a soft place to lay their weary bones.

"Lord, am I glad that's over for another year." Grant groaned, sinking onto the downy mattress without even bothering to remove the coverlet first, or his own clothes. "I could sleep for a month!"

Her eyes at half-mast, Amanda grabbed his foot and tugged his boot off, almost too weak to accomplish the task. When the other boot proved stubborn she yanked at it irritably, landing on her bottom on the rug for her efforts. There she sat, staring at the offending boot, too tired to get up.

"Throw me a pillow." She moaned pitifully, stretching out flat where she'd fallen. "I'm too tired to move."

To her surprise, a pillow came flying down into her

face. "I'd help you up, but I think my legs have fallen off."

"Check your trouser legs. They must be in there someplace."

"I'll check in the morning," he mumbled. "Better yet, *you* can check in the morning."

"Make it afternoon, and you might have a deal." She yawned. "Anyone who wakes me before then is begging for trouble. And don't step on me if you have to get up in the middle of the night to use the water closet."

Chapter 26

By the Monday morning following the auction, all of them had pretty well revived. Grant found Amanda in the study, tallying up the proceeds. "How did we do?" he asked.

She awarded him a smile, the result of her accounting going a long way toward restoring her usual sunny attitude. "Fantastic. We're ahead of last year's sales by about six thousand dollars."

"That's the best news I've had all week." Plopping into his own chair, he propped his feet on the desktop. "I've just returned from the sawmill at the Shaker village, and Abel Smith says he checked the wood shavings himself before the wagons left there. He swears there was no walnut in the batch."

"Then how did it get there?"

Grant shook his head. "I don't know. Any more than I can figure out how the paddock gate got left open the other night."

"That was probably an accident, don't you think?" she asked with a frown. "Grant, we were all running around like our tails were on fire, trying to get ready for the auction. Someone just got careless, that's all.''

"It's carelessness of that sort that can ruin a business in short order. Or cause serious injury to the horses or farmhands. The men know better than to allow their minds to wander to the point of making stupid mistakes like that."

"Well, the auction is over now, and things should get back to normal."

"That brings up something else I wanted to discuss with you. I think, for the time being, at least until I'm certain that no more odd accidents are going to occur, it's best if we postpone our wedding trip a while longer. We will take it. I promise you. Just not now."

"I think you're being overly cautious, Grant," she told him, her smile gentling her words. "But if that's what you want to do, I won't object. Besides, I'd already figured you wouldn't want to go on a trip until Tad's leave is finished. The two of you will see little enough of one another once he's back with the Army."

Grant was touched that she would consider his brother, putting his desires and Tad's before her own. "You're being very understanding, Amanda."

An eyebrow arched over one blue eye. "Does that surprise you?"

"Actually, yes. Not many women would be so amenable to postponing their honeymoon indefinitely."

She laughed softly. "I thought we'd already agreed that I'm not like most women."

Grant was beginning to think he was very, very glad she wasn't.

Amanda was up to her neck in hot water—and a cloud of the most heavenly scented bubbles—when Grant entered the master bedroom to change clothes for dinner.

"Sadie?" Amanda called from the small bathing closet attached to the main room. "Bring one of those toweling sheets in to me, will you please?"

Slipping quietly out of his boots, Grant tiptoed in stocking feet to the connecting doorway. "My, my!" he crooned, giving a low whistle of appreciation for the sight that met his eyes. "What have we here? It looks like my own personal mermaid and back-scrubber."

Amanda's eyes popped open in surprise. Reflexively, she straightened from her lounging position, gracing him with a quick glimpse of suds-slick breasts before slumping beneath her cover of bubbles once more. "Grant Gardner! You're going to give me heart failure one of these days, sneaking up on me like that!" she accused. "Now get out of here before Sadie finds you ogling me and reports your lascivious behavior to all the other servants."

"I have a better idea. Why don't I go lock the door and join you in your bath?"

"Why don't you soak your head in the watering trough?" she called after him as he disappeared momentarily, only to return and begin to undress before her.

"If I'm going to soak my head anywhere, I'd rather do it right here. I bet it beats bobbing for apples all to hell!"

Naked now, he climbed into the tub, slowly lowering himself to face her. As he did, the water level rose precariously, bubbles sloshing over the edge onto the floor. "Grant!" she shrieked, laughing now. "You big ape! You're going to have the entire floor wet, and the ceiling below."

"Probably," he admitted, grinning at her. Leaning back, he raised one hairy leg, thrusting his foot beneath her nose. "Why don't you start here and work your way up, darlin'?" he suggested lazily.

He wasn't sure he trusted that devilish gleam in her eyes as she picked up the washcloth and lathered it with soap. For a moment he thoroughly expected her to toss it into his face, and was mildly surprised, even a little disappointed, when she calmly began to wash his leg. "You do realize, of course," she told him conversationally, as if sharing a bath were an everyday occurrence, "that you are going to emerge from this tub smelling suspiciously of orange blossoms. Now, what will your men think of that, I would be interested to know?"

That thought took him aback a bit. He'd just have to make sure he rinsed the smell off before anyone noticed; because Amanda's hands, washcloth notwithstanding, were doing marvelous things under the suds about now, and far be it from him to stop her.

Before long, he was in blissful agony, and the bubbles were fast evaporating. Only a few still clung to the upper slopes of Amanda's breasts, decorating them with a lacy froth.

With an infuriating smile, she tossed the washcloth at him, the slithery bar of soap following. "Your turn," she intoned mischievously.

Bound to pay her back in spades, he was soon rewarded with those enticing little moans that always betrayed her rising desire. Discarding the washcloth, he let his fingers foray beneath the water, seeking the treasures lurking there. On a sudden whim, he lifted her leg, and before she could guess what he meant to do, he popped her big toe into his mouth and began to suck and lick at it.

Amanda went crazy, thrashing about and shrieking like a demented idiot in the throes of a fit. "Stop . . . that!" she panted. "Oh, my stars!"

He switched to another pearl-pink digit, with much the same result. "Oh! Oh! It tickles unbearably! And it . . . it . . ."

"It what?" he prompted, his teeth nipping.

"It feels so . . . so funny! So . . . tingly and good. All the way up inside me!"

Which was precisely what he'd had in mind. When he'd tormented her sufficiently, by this time fearing she might drown in what little water remained, he pulled her with him out of the tub. Not bothering with a bath sheet, he carried her to the bed and made love with her there until they were both as weak as new-born babes.

"We've missed dinner," she informed him feebly. "What will Tad and Betsy make of that?"

"I really don't care, as long as they aren't indulging in the same sort of games."

Her stomach growled indelicately, echoed almost immediately by his. "We'll wait a while," he told her. "Then, when everyone has gone to bed, we'll sneak down to the kitchen and raid the cupboards."

"What will we do in the meantime?" she asked archly.

"Oh, we'll think of something to pass the time," he assured her.

They did, indeed, but not precisely the way Grant had imagined. Amanda, with a coy smile, somehow talked him into helping her apply fresh polish to her toenails. Of course, one thing naturally led to another, with Grant directing the scenario. Before it was done, Amanda found herself pinned beneath him, her feet thrust into the air on either side and her toes left to dry as they would, as Grant took full advantage of her relative immobility.

Nearly two weeks had passed without incident, and Grant was ready to admit that the two accidents prior to the auction had been just that—freak happenstance. Then, without warning, their troubles returned with a vengeance, and this time Grant was ready to swear it was deliberately done. First, Challenger came up with a lacerated tendon on his left front ankle. Though he wouldn't have to be put down, his racing career was over before it had gotten a good start, and the only thing left was to put him to stud.

His stall was checked and found to be clean of anything that might have cut him. Grant and a couple of his men were carefully combing the paddock where the horse had been pastured, having discovered nothing more dangerous than a stray twig, when Paddy came running, waving his arms and calling for Grant. Out of breath, holding his sides, the young jockey exclaimed excitedly, "Boss! Come quick! Jack went to fetch Fleet Fellow fer me, an' the colt is down in the field, bleedin' like a stuck hog!"

Grant ran, his heart pounding in his throat. He vaulted the fence on a flying leap that sent him tumbling, but he rolled to his feet and kept running, ignoring the burning pain in his chest. When he drew up next to the thrashing horse and the half-dozen men who were trying to keep the animal calm, there was no mistaking the cause of Fleet Fellow's shrill cries. He lay with his hind legs entangled in wire, the strands cutting into his flesh so tightly that the bone was already exposed in several places. There would be no saving this racer, whose bloodlines had promised to make him a sure winner in the next year or two. Even if he didn't contract tetanus and die, he'd be reduced to a pitiful cripple, in pain more often than not. It was not fair to the horse to make him suffer any more than he already was. The only decent thing to do now was to put him out of his misery forever.

Having already deduced this, Sean O'Brian arrived at Grant's side with a loaded rifle. "I'll do it, if you want," the man offered.

"No, I'll see to it myself," Grant answered grimly, knowing it would be like killing a part of himself to shoot this beautiful creature, but also knowing that it had to be done, and that it was his duty.

The single shot that rang out a moment later seemed to echo mournfully to the far corners of Misty Valley. And the awful silence afterward was eerie.

Grant was like a wild, wounded tiger on the rampage. Someone was deliberately sabotaging his livelihood, his beloved horses, and he was going to find out who if he had to search under every rock in ten counties. And when he found the dirty bastard, lynching would be too good for him.

The trouble was, Grant hadn't a clue where to begin looking. There seemed no way to trace the ragged pieces of fence wire that had been found, not only in Challenger's and Fleet Fellow's paddocks, but in several other fields as well. Nor was there any way to tell how the walnut shavings had become mixed in with the bedding, or who had left the pasture gate open.

Anyone from the farm or off it could be responsible for these deeds. Disgruntled employees, offended clients, competing horse breeders, even someone whose horse had run against one of Grant's in a race and lost. The list of suspects was long, once he had time to start compiling names. If he wanted to be thorough and include every possible enemy, especially those he'd made most recently, he would have to include Annabelle, Mr. Foster, Stanford Darcy, and Annabelle's stablehand—though the stablehand was supposedly in Chattanooga now, if gossip was to be believed.

Lacking another course of action, Grant posted sentries around the stables, with standing orders for all the horses to be brought into their stalls each evening. During the day, when the animals were loose in the paddocks, everyone was to keep a sharp lookout for anything unusual. Visitors would be limited to a number that could easily be watched, lest any stray into areas now deemed restricted. Feed, water, bedding, stalls, and pastures were to be regularly examined, and anything of even mild curiosity was to be brought immediately to Grant's attention. Loaded shotguns and rifles were placed in strategic areas, with orders to protect the horses first and ask questions afterward.

Then, with all the impatience of an enraged bull, Grant sat back and awaited what might happen next, and who might be caught in the act.

"I am not going on a picnic with you, Amanda, so put that frivolous nonsense right out of your head," Grant told her. "I am much too busy, and now, with someone trying to ruin the farm, is not the time for such foolishness.''

"What *is* it time for, Grant?" she retaliated. "Moping about and snapping at everyone and everything? Contemplating your problems until you go stark raving mad, dragging everyone else along the same route? Lord, you're so thoroughly engrossed with this thing that you even think about it when we're making love!''

He glared at her. "How would you know what's on my mind, then or at any other time?''

"It's not hard to guess when you're as tense as a watch spring. You woke me up grating your teeth in your sleep last night, and you were clenching your hands into fists even then. Darling, you cannot go on like this. You have to take some time away from your troubles, if only for an hour or two, and let yourself relax. Besides, Tad will be leaving the day after tomorrow, and it would be so nice for all four of us to have just this one pleasant afternoon to spend together before he goes.''

She turned pleading blue eyes up to his. "Put someone else in charge for a few hours and come with us. Please, love?''

When she looked at him that way, her sooty lashes hovering over misty, tip-tilted eyes, Grant was willing to give her almost anything she wanted, though he would never admit such weakness to her. And the way she'd called him "love," as if she truly meant it, made his heart trip over itself.

"All right," he conceded, "but just for a while. I want to be here when something happens.''

"*If* it happens," she corrected. With a smile wreathing her face, she suggested, "You go give your orders for the day, and I'll see about packing the picnic basket and telling Tad and Betsy.'' Already on her way to the house, she stopped, snapping her fingers as a thought came to her. "Grant, where do you keep the fishing poles?''

"Fishing poles?''

"Yeah, you know. Those long things made out of cane, with strings and hooks attached to them."

"I know what they are, Amanda," he informed her dryly. "It just surprised me that you might want them."

"There's no better way to relax than lying in the sun, listening to the lap of the water, and waiting for the fish to bite."

He grinned at her. "Oh, I can think of a couple of better ways."

Batting her lashes at him, she suggested, "First we fish—and if you're very nice to me, I'll even bait your hook for you."

Slowly shaking his head as she dashed off in a flurry of skirts, he admitted softly to himself, "You usually do, minx."

It *was* soothing, lounging about on the riverbank with the sun dappling through the branches overhead and a light breeze ruffling the leaves. It didn't even matter that the fish weren't biting. While the outing didn't make Grant forget his worries altogether, it went a long way toward relieving the tension that had been building inside him for the past four days.

Amanda was delightful, brimming over with effervescent energy. Her eyes sparkled, her laughter was infectious. The first thing she did was to rip off her shoes and stockings and run through the lush grass like a barefoot wood sprite. "Oooh, this feels so good!"

Grant couldn't help but chuckle at her antics. She was like a child set free of all restrictions, gleefully playing hookey from school lessons. "Watch out for snakes!" he called to her.

On a giddy twirl, she landed next to him. "I'll leave the snakes to Tad, if I haven't scared them all off by now."

"Was that what that wild dance was all about?" he asked, grinning.

She nodded, wriggling her enameled toes and sighing. "Partly. Mostly, it was just for fun, though."

They fished, or attempted to. They ate cold fried chicken, and big chunks of cheese and freshly baked bread, and washed it down with wine and peaches so juicy that the nectar ran down their chins. They talked, trading favorite childhood tales, Tad and Grant recalling youthful pranks and Betsy and Amanda telling stories of their river travels.

"When was the last time we did something like this together?" Tad asked his brother.

"Fishing? Lord, Tad, I can't remember."

"Or anything else that didn't have to do with work, or the farm, or horses? You know, Grant, I think you got cheated of your childhood when Dad and Mother died and you had to take over all the responsibilities so young. I guess I didn't really think of it at the time, but while I continued being a boy, you had to assume the mantle of manhood much too soon."

"And you forgot how to play," Amanda added with a sad turn to her mouth.

"Well, now, don't you fret, " Betsy put in mischievously, lightening the mood that was fast becoming too serious. "Amanda is just the gal to remind you how it's done. She might not have had what you'd call a normal upbringin' herself, but that's good in lots of ways. She'll take the stodginess out of you in a hurry."

Grant wasn't certain, but he thought he'd just been insulted in an offhand way. "I know you all think I'm somewhat of a stuffed shirt, but I can be just as unrestrained as the next person."

"Oh, yeah?" Amanda challenged pertly, wrinkling her nose at him.

"Yeah," he retorted, an answering gleam in his eyes.

"Then let's go wading. Take off those clunky old boots of yours, roll your pant legs up to your knees, and wade in the river with me."

"Amanda . . ."

"Or are you too proud to let go of some of your male arrogance?" she teased. "Out here in front of God and everyone?"

Pushing herself to her feet, she gathered the back of her skirt together, pulling the cloth between her legs and looping it through the sash of her dress, fashioning a pair of loose trousers for herself that would keep the fabric from dragging the ground.

Betsy followed suit. Even Tad joined the fun, yanking at his boots. Together, the three started down the gently sloping bank, ignoring Grant, who stared after them.

Amanda had scarcely gotten her feet muddy when Grant grabbed her from behind, making her squeal. "You asked for this, you saucy river witch!" Picking her up, he waded into the water as far as his knees, then promptly dropped her.

She came up sputtering, her dress drenched and her hair dripping. "You rat!" she exclaimed, pushing a soggy strand from her eyes.

Grant was too busy laughing to avoid the hand that snaked out and snagged his ankle. With a gigantic plop, he landed next to her in the river, spraying muddy water over both of them, as well as onto Tad and Betsy, who were avidly watching the horseplay. A hearty game of water tag ensued, with enough splashing and yelling from the four of them to chase every fish in the vicinity into permanent hiding.

They rode home later than Grant had planned, as bedraggled as a band of gypsies. Snuggled next to him in the buggy, shivering in the waning warmth of the setting sun, Amanda sighed contentedly. "I love you, Grant Gardner," she whispered softly, startling him with her sudden confession. "I love you so much it hurts inside."

Beside her, Grant stiffened, struggling with the emotions that rose within him at her unexpected declaration. Doubt, joy, shock—all roiling about in his mind, tingling through every nerve, wrapping around his heart like tentacles. "Don't confuse love with lust, Amanda," he cautioned at last.

"I know the difference, darling," she assured him, her voice as warm and sweet as brandy. "And I know what I feel."

Which was more than he did, at the moment.

Chapter 27

WHEN they returned to the house, Chalmers was waiting for them with a telegram for Tad. It was good news, for a change. His appointment to West Point had been approved, thanks to the letters his superior officers and Grant had sent so hurriedly. Instead of joining his regular unit and heading to the western frontier again, he was to report to the military academy on the fifteenth of October, which gave him almost an extra month to stay at Misty Valley.

Betsy was beside herself with joy. She and the younger Gardner were developing more than a passing interest in each other, much to Grant's disgruntlement. However, there was little he could say, having married a riverboat gambler himself—which was just what Tad told him when Grant first voiced opposition to their growing affection.

"What's that old adage about people in glass houses not throwing stones?" Tad reminded him. "If Amanda is good enough for you, then Betsy is good enough for me. Though in your case, I'd guess it's the other way around. Why the woman agreed to have you is more than I can see."

"It's not quite as simple as you'd like to believe, Tad. I compromised Amanda, to the point where one of my men tried to attack her. In a moment of anger, I let it slip to Stanford Darcy, who was courting her at the time, that I'd bedded her; and after that, what little reputation she'd managed to preserve was lying in ruins. So, you see, our marrying was more a matter of honor than any romantic notions you might be harboring."

"On your part, perhaps. Not on Amanda's. And you can't tell me your sole purpose was to salve a guilty conscience. I know you better than that, dear brother."

"Amanda wanted the respectability my name would give her. She's always wanted to be a lady, and always fell short of the mark. This was her way of attaining that status."

"If you believe that, you're the one who's falling short of the mark—and missing a few brains as well. Are you blind, Grant? Can't you see how the woman adores you? Aside from that, I'm willing to bet Amanda was a lady long before she took our esteemed name. People just didn't want to credit the fact. It didn't measure up with their rigid requirements.

"What is a lady anyway?" he went on. "Is she graceful? Comely? Generous? Isn't Amanda all those? Is a lady faithful? Loving? Where does it stipulate that a lady must be rich, or titled, or have a list of famous relatives dating back to the days of Solomon? Must her talents be restricted to singing and playing the piano and gossiping over the latest fashions? Good grief, Grant! I can't believe you could fail to see what's right before your very eyes! Amanda is a rare treasure, an uncut diamond. Would you trade such a gem for a piece of common glass?"

"So speaks the voice of maturity," Grant commented sardonically, extremely uncomfortable with the turn the conversation had taken. "Or is it experience talking, Tad, from all the wild oats you've sown in your short but eventful years? At any rate, we've strayed from our original topic, which was Betsy, not Amanda."

"Fine. Let's limit our conversation to Betsy and me. Our relationship, and the point to which it progresses, are none of your concern. You may rule Misty Valley, but your domain ends with your land, your horses, your business—and possibly your wife, if she wants to let you believe that. It does not apply to my personal life. So just tuck your nose back into your own affairs and out of mine."

After that, Grant hesitated to offer advice to his brother. Certainly he didn't need any more lectures from a lad still wet behind the ears! And he didn't need to hear him, or anyone else, singing Amanda's praises, either! It was damned irritating! As bothersome as his own mixed emotions these days.

It seemed he did nothing but wander about in a state of constant confusion. Half the time he couldn't even recall what his true motives had been in marrying Amanda, though they'd seemed clear enough before. Had he only wanted Misty Valley back? Had his conscience urged him to propose? Had his desire for her, and his intense possessiveness, driven him to it? Or, somewhere deep down inside himself, hidden far below the surface of his consciousness, was something else lurking? Something suspiciously akin to love?

More and more, as he contemplated these questions, Grant wondered how his life had become such a tangle. The answer was always the same. Amanda.

Again all was quiet for a few days, days of anxious anticipation. When trouble came once more, it took a form no one expected.

Clancy had saddled Lady Mist for Amanda, who wanted to keep up with her riding. Now that she was finally becoming accustomed to it, she almost enjoyed it, was nearly able to relax upon the mare's back. Of course, given the problems they'd encountered recently, she was once again limited to the immediate grounds, but that did not deter her.

Before attempting to mount the little mare, Amanda and Lady Mist went through a now-familiar ritual. First

Amanda fed the horse a small bite of apple. Then, while Lady Mist chomped happily on it, Amanda petted her, stroking her long neck and her velvet nose, until the horse nudged Amanda's shoulder, as if to gently urge her into the saddle.

Everything was fine until Amanda seated herself atop the horse. Then, for no apparent reason, Lady Mist became extremely agitated. She shifted back and forth, twitching and stomping. Unnerved, Amanda tried everything she knew to calm the animal, speaking softly to her, petting her. But when Lady Mist continued to act up, Amanda grew truly alarmed for the first time in weeks and hurriedly dismounted.

Immediately, the horse resumed her gentle demeanor, much to Amanda's confusion. After a few minutes, during which Lady Mist exhibited no more odd behavior, Amanda mounted again. But the minute her bottom settled into the saddle, Lady Mist began to misbehave, this time more violently. Whinnying loudly in protest, the mare sidled up to the nearby fence and tried to scrape Amanda from her back.

With a frightened cry, Amanda climbed down, almost falling in her haste. It was with tearful relief that she saw Grant approaching.

"What seems to be the problem here?" he questioned.

"She won't let me mount her," Amanda wailed, her chin trembling. "More precisely, she'll let me mount, then makes it very clear that she wants me off her back. I don't know what to do about it. Why is she behaving this way all of a sudden?"

With a frown, Grant studied the now-placid mare. "I don't know, honey. She's never acted this way before that I'm aware of. How long has it been since you've ridden her?"

Amanda shrugged. "I don't recall exactly. Two or three weeks, perhaps."

"Well, maybe she's just feeling a little feisty since she hasn't been ridden in a while. Why don't you let me take a little of the vinegar out of her first? Then she should be fine for you to ride.''

''Please do,'' Amanda was quick to offer.

Lady Mist stood quietly until the moment Grant was seated. Then she seemed to go wild. Worse than with Amanda, the horse now bucked, forcefully attempted to dislodge her rider. When Grant tugged at the reins, refusing to give ground, Lady Mist reared. Again and again, until Grant dismounted. ''Damn!'' he said with a shake of his head. ''I simply don't understand this!''

Deciding to take it in stages this time, Grant approached the horse. He stroked her, calming her with gentle words and caresses. Lady Mist nuzzled him, as if they were the best of friends, welcoming his touch. Slowly, carefully, Grant slipped his boot into the stirrup, then eased his entire weight onto it. Still the horse stood quiescent. He swung his other leg across, distributing his weight on both feet, both stirrups. Nothing happened—until he sat down. Again Lady Mist was a creature demented, bucking and fishtailing for all she was worth!

Dismounting a final time, Grant began to check the girth. Finding nothing amiss, he unbuckled it, removing the saddle entirely to check the blanket beneath. ''Sometimes the blanket gets wrinkled,'' he explained over his shoulder to Amanda, who stood watching. ''It can irritate a horse's back, and some animals are more sensitive to this than others. I've never noticed that Lady Mist is particularly so, but there's always a first time.''

The blanket appeared as it should, despite all the ruckus Lady Mist had raised. Perplexed, Grant ran his hand over it, searching for anything that might be pricking the horse—a stiff stalk of straw caught in the weaving, a piece of dirt that might have become lodged in the material. Finding nothing, but knowing the animal must have reacted for a reason, he removed the blanket, with the intent of examining its reverse side.

It was then that he saw the blood on Lady Mist's back, and the deep puncture wounds from which it seeped. ''What the devil?'' With gentle fingers, he probed, finding nothing but the wounds themselves. The blanket had yielded no answers. That left only the saddle. His suspicions growing by the moment, Grant flipped the saddle over. There, imbedded in the underside, were four of the longest, largest, most wicked thorns he'd ever seen!

"Oh, my heavens!" Amanda exclaimed, coming up behind him. "No wonder she behaved so awfully! Why, I can't image the pain we were causing her each time we put our weight on those things!"

"I can," Grant replied, his eyes flaming in anger as he threw the saddle from him and rose to his feet. "And if it had been any other horse, you might have been killed for the agony she went through! As it is, it was *your* horse, the one no one but you rides. And that tells me that someone deliberately meant to harm you, Amanda. Someone with enough spite to want to see you maimed or dead."

If Amanda had been frightened before, she was now filled with terror. "But who? Why?" she asked in a stricken voice, her eyes abnormally huge in her pale face.

"Annabelle?" Grant suggested, as that one name seemed to reverberate furiously through his brain.

"Surely not," Amanda countered. "I know she despises me, but if she'd wanted to hurt me, she could have done so long ago."

"Maybe she wants to hurt us both, now that all her plans have been foiled. Now that you're my wife."

"But the fencing, and the bedding?" Amanda questioned, still reeling with shock. "Could she have managed all that by herself? Could she have known how to go about it?"

"That and more. She's grown up around horses, been in and out of the stables since she could walk."

Grant was striding toward the stable now, a dark, forbidding figure. Amanda hurried after him. "Grant! What are you planning to do?"

"I'm going to ride over to the Foster place and have

a little chat with our neighbor. And, one way or another, I'm going to get some answers.''

"But, Grant, you can't just ride over there, hell-bent on revenge, and accuse her! She might not be guilty of anything more than hating my guts!''

"Maybe so, but there's only one way to be sure, darlin'.''

Without warning, he spun on his heel and gathered her close for a quick, hard kiss. His hand caressing her cheek, he gazed down at her for a long, wordless moment. "You stick close to Tad while I'm gone,'' he told her, his voice gruff with emotion. "I won't be long.''

A short while later, Grant was back, more puzzled than ever. He'd been so certain in his own mind that he'd found their culprit. Now he was totally at a loss again.

Annabelle had not been home. In fact, she wasn't even in Kentucky, or anywhere close, and hadn't been for nearly three weeks. A distraught Mrs. Foster had tearfully announced that Annabelle's father had shipped her South. For all practical purposes, and with the utmost secrecy, he'd bartered their only daughter in marriage to an elderly Alabama planter who had no offspring of his own and was more than willing to claim Annabelle's bastard child as his own seed.

This explained why no one, not even the servants, had seen the girl in some time. It also meant that someone other than Annabelle was responsible for the unexplained "accidents" befalling Misty Valley. They were back where they had begun—completely in the dark.

Life, and work, went on, though not as routinely as before. More guards were posted, both day and night. For the time being, until he had to leave for the academy, Tad was assigned to watch Betsy and Amanda—but most especially Amanda, whenever Grant could not be with her.

While she adored them both and didn't usually mind their company, Amanda quickly began to feel like a fifth wheel around the two young lovers. Additionally, she chafed at the added restrictions placed on her, accustomed as she was to doing as she pleased and ordering her own life. She began inventing excuses to avoid her jailors, spending more hours than usual tagging along at Grant's coattails, since this gave her at least the illusion of freedom and allowed her access to the outdoors and the stables Betsy refused to set her dainty foot inside.

Thus it was that Amanda witnessed a mating between a mare and a stud for the first time, a proceeding to which she had heretofore been barred. Even now Grant hesitated to include her.

"This can get rough, honey, and more embarrassing than I think you know," he warned her. "Maybe you'd better go on up to the house."

"And do what? Bake a batch of cookies? Learn to knit? Take a nap at nine o'clock in the morning? For pity's sake, Grant, I'm a big girl. I've been studying all this in those books of yours, and now I'd like to see it firsthand."

He agreed, reluctantly. "All right, but I want you to stay back, behind the fence at all times. And I don't want to hear one peep out of you the entire while. Now, I'm not foolin' about this, Amanda. You either obey me or march on inside before we get started."

"I'm staying."

It began innocently enough. The mare had been put out in a small paddock by herself. Now, as Amanda watched, two hired hands entered the paddock with ropes, which they attached to either side of the mare's halter. They then led her to the near corner of the paddock, where more helpers waited. Though it seemed odd that they would need two ropes and so many handlers, Amanda remembered her promise and kept her questions to herself.

Almost immediately, a couple of other employees led the stallion through the gate. The male horse was already becoming fractious, anxious to meet his mate. One indiscreet glance at his underside told Amanda that he'd caught the heated mare's scent and was more than eager to do his duty.

The tension rose to a palpable degree as the mare sensed the stallion's presence. To Amanda's amazement, the mare began to preen for him, like a maiden casting "come-hither" signals to her beau, but much more indelicately. She pranced, tossed her mane, whinnied, and flickered her tail to display her slick, swollen genitals to the stud.

The stallion responded with a loud trumpet, his nostrils flared, the muscles of his neck standing out in relief as he tugged at the ropes that prevented him from rushing to her. As it was, he almost pulled the burly men leading him off their feet.

Then, when the horses were within a length of each other, the mare abruptly changed her tune, professing disinterest in the mate being introduced to her. She sidled away from him as best she could, only the halter lines preventing her would-be escape.

But the stallion was having none of this latter-day contrariness. He was close enough now to demonstrate his displeasure by administering a glancing nip at her flank with his huge teeth. She tried to bite back at him, but he was behind her now, and she was effectively cornered within the bounds of the fence and her restrictive tethers.

For a moment the entire scene seemed to freeze in place, though the very air about them seemed to vibrate with a dull rhythm. Amanda, her heart beating rapidly in her chest, held her breath and watched. Her face felt as if it had been set afire, her own loins tightened in expectation of what was to come, and if she'd been offered a king's ransom, she could not have looked away from those two magnificent animals.

Again the mare seemed to change her mind, suddenly as eager to be covered as the stud was to oblige. Before his nose, her tail arched upward, giving him full access to her. With an arrogant toss of his head, the stallion reared. His forelegs came down upon the mare's back, knocking her halfway to her knees. His teeth sought purchase in her sleek coat as he lunged into her.

It was violent, primal, and Amanda now knew why the ropes were employed, the men so attentive. It was to ensure the safety of both animals during this heated uniting. Squeals rang out from the horses as they mated frantically, with a pure, basic instinct that was as spellbinding as it was savagely beautiful.

When at last Amanda could look away, her gaze was drawn to Grant's, as though compelled by some silent command he'd issued. His eyes burned with emerald flames, reaching across the space that separated them to seer her with their fiery glow, and she knew that he was reading the same blatant message in her face that she saw in his. His nostrils flared, and she wondered if he, like the stallion, could smell her pulsing passion.

Her breasts ached for the touch of his hands, his mouth. Her loins felt heavy and hot, throbbing and wet with carnal desire. Incredibly, she could almost feel him between her thighs, pushing, probing, thrusting into her.

Even as her thoughts tormented her, he reached her side. Swiftly, without a word spoken between them, he led her toward the house. Scarcely had the bedroom door closed behind them than they were ripping at each other's clothing. Her shaking fingers clawed at the suddenly stubborn fastenings of his shirt, sending buttons popping off in every direction. Seams tore, ribbons snapped, lace shredded. She tried to rid him of his pants, only to discover his boots were still on, binding the trouser legs halfway down his calves.

Urgency won out. The boots remained as he hobbled to the bed, Amanda held high in his arms. With a shriek, she bounced onto the mattress, Grant landing heavily atop her. His eager mouth clamped hold of her breast, tugging the crest deeply into his mouth, and Amanda thought she would die at the savage surge that vibrated through her. His fingers found her moist womanhood, barely had he touched her when Amanda's world exploded into a thousand shimmering fragments.

Her body was still awash in waves of splendor when he thrust into her. Her silken sheath pulsated about him, drawing him further into ecstasy, suckling at him with wondrous demand, calling him back into her greedy grasp again and again. Deeper. Harder. Faster. Until the madness overtook them both, and they bowed to the fury and the glory of it with glad cries of surrender.

Afterward, wavering between amazement and embarrassment, they assessed the result of their frantic mating. Grant was sporting an assortment of bites and scratches, while he had branded Amanda with several passion marks, some in telling areas. She would be wearing modest gowns with high necklines for many days to come, and unless he wanted to put up with a lot of ribbing from his men, he wouldn't be removing his shirt outside the boundaries of the bedroom any time soon.

Chapter 28

AMANDA wasn't feeling well. It had nothing to do with their zealous lovemaking following the horse breeding. Of that she was certain. Aside from a few fading bruises and ruddy cheeks, the result of Grant's beard scraping her tender face, she'd sustained no injuries—just a lingering glow and a languid satisfaction.

Now, however, a week later, she could scarcely find the energy to make it through the day. At the oddest moments, in the midst of a conversation, she would find herself nodding off. The unusual late-September heat did not help matters. It had been a long, hot summer, and Amanda wished autumn with its cooler temperatures would arrive soon.

In addition to her constant fatigue, which was odd in itself, her breasts were swollen and tender much of the time. Most alarming of all, she'd felt extremely light-headed on a couple of occasions when she'd risen from a chair too quickly.

Amanda hesitated to mention these strange symptoms to Grant, with all else he had to worry about these days. She was glad she'd kept silent when she found herself rushing for the chamber pot early one morning.

Nausea plagued her until lunch, when she suddenly felt ravenous. This newest malady continued for several mornings in a row, always disappearing mysteriously by noon. It was then that Amanda began to suspect she was pregnant, realizing in the process that her last monthly flow had occurred about the same time Grant had proposed to her. She'd had none since their wedding.

Why she was so surprised by this revelation, Amanda did not know. It was bound to happen sooner or later, especially as randy as she and Grant had been. Still and all, the thought of another living person growing inside her gave her pause. Motherhood had not been something she'd contemplated very deeply—until now. Suddenly she had to stop and ask herself what kind of mother she would be. What sort of mother did she want to be? What would it be like to feel the babe grow and move within her? Later, to hold it in her arms, to suckle it at her breast? Her child. Grant's child.

Then there was the fear that, like her own mother, she might die in childbirth. But her mother had been a frail, delicate creature, or so Amanda's father had told her. With determination, Amanda pushed these fears aside, reminding herself that she was strong and healthy, had rarely been sick a day in her life. There was every reason to expect that, with care, she could safely bring this child into the world and love it.

And love it she would, just as she loved the baby's father. The longer she thought about it, the more excited she became. In a few months, she could be singing lullabies to her son or daughter, a small replica of herself or Grant.

Dreamily, she wondered if their child would have green eyes or blue. It would undoubtedly have dark hair, wouldn't it? Perhaps with a tiny cleft in its chin to match Grant's? Would it inherit her yen for chewing gum? Her talent for cards and numbers? Grant's arrogance? His intelligence? Or both its parents' tempers? Whose sense of humor would cast the greater influence?

Once Amanda had adjusted to the idea herself, it was

only by extreme will that she kept the news to herself. Not out of spite, but out of a yearning to first hear Grant declare some sort of genuine emotion toward her, other than desire. Since the day of the picnic she'd told him countless times of her love for him, yet never once had he responded in kind. Too pragmatic to expect any grand declarations of undying love, at least not this soon, she still longed for him to admit to feelings of affection, perhaps admiration—mere fondness would do for a start. And she would dearly adore hearing the word "lady" pass his lips in honest regard for her, just one time before she told him of his impending fatherhood.

After all, what self-respecting wife wanted to think of herself as merely a beautiful decoration in her husband's home? A gracious hostess for his guests? A convenient, warm body in his bed? A human brood mare? If she gained his esteem at all, Amanda would much prefer that it be for herself first and foremost, not for presenting him with a dozen sons and daughters to further inflate his conceit.

So she waited, not even taking Betsy into her confidence for fear her friend would inadvertently blab to Tad, who would then, inevitably, say something to Grant. Besides, she reasoned, there was plenty of time before her condition became evident to one and all. Time, hopefully, for them to resolve the troubles plaguing the farm. Time to savor her secret, to be more certain of Grant's feelings, to pray that love for her would soon take root in his heart.

If Grant wondered why Amanda stopped riding Lady Mist, he attributed it to the fright she'd experienced when they'd found the thorns in the horse's saddle. After a couple of weeks, he confronted her with it.

"You can't let your fears paralyze you, Amanda. You conquered them once before, and you can do it again. After all, you know there was good reason for Lady Mist to behave as she did, and that there is little chance of any recurrence."

"I know that, and I'm not afraid of her . . . not really," she qualified. "It's just this abominable heat that's been exhausting me lately. The last thing I want is to feel more hot and sticky. When the weather cools, I'll ride again." Or maybe not, she thought to herself, for by then her condition might be obvious, and she surely didn't want to risk any harm to the babe.

Even with all their current problems, Grant agreed with Amanda that they should host a small gathering of friends and neighbors while Tad was home. "We should have thought of it before," he told her.

"Before what? Before Betsy?" she asked with an amused shake of her head. "Is that why you're suddenly so intent on this party? In the hope that some other girl will strike Tad's fancy?"

Grant grinned sheepishly and shrugged.

"Well, I hate to burst your bubble, Grant, but I don't think there's much chance of that. Those two have eyes only for each other, and I wouldn't be a bit surprised if he proposed to her before he leaves for West Point."

"God forbid!" It was Grant's worst nightmare. "And I suppose, while he's away at the academy, he would expect us to look after the little twit for him."

"I would assume so," she concurred, her eyes laughing at him. Lord, this man had a stubborn streak a mile wide! It was almost killing him to have to change the superior attitudes he'd held for so long.

Again Chalmers proved his worth by helping to coordinate a barbecue and outdoor dance affair, all on short notice. For the first time in weeks, Amanda found herself wishing for warm, dry weather; so much more convenient than trying to arrange the entire party indoors, since they had invited over a hundred people to this "small" affair.

Though Amanda had met many of their guests at her wedding, she still had trouble trying to match some of the names with the faces. Also, she simply could not recall meeting, or even inviting, half the eligible young ladies who showed up dressed in all their frills and bows and hopeful smiles. She suspected that Grant had gone around behind her back, altering invitations and suggesting that everyone bring nieces and cousins and any visiting virgins.

In the end, it was Grant who sustained the greatest surprise, however, In the midst of the party, as the dancing was about to begin, Tad signaled for everyone's attention. "I would like all of you to meet my fiancée," he announced proudly, holding out his hand to a beaming Betsy. An immediate clamor rose up, with congratulations and questions, and requests to view the sparkling diamond engagement ring now resting on Betsy's finger.

As Chalmers and his aides broke out the champagne, Grant cornered Amanda. "You knew about this, didn't you?" he demanded.

"I did try to prepare you for the probability, if you will recall."

"But you knew before now, and you didn't tell me," he accused.

"Honestly, Grant, until this afternoon, when Betsy showed me her ring, I only suspected it. Tad was supposed to tell you himself—which I guess he just did, along with a hundred other people."

Grant was so put out with her over keeping the news of Tad and Betsy's engagement from him that she couldn't begin to imagine how he would react when she finally got around to telling him about the baby. The thought was so inhibitive that she vowed to put it off as long as possible, just to delay the eventual fireworks.

Grant's disgruntled mood notwithstanding, the party was a success. Amanda reacquainted herself with a few of the wives, and before the evening was over, she had agreed to hostess a few of them in her home the following week. This, if nothing else that transpired that night, pleased Grant. "I'm glad to see that they're beginning to accept you into their ranks, Amanda. It makes things so much more pleasant and convenient."

When his back was turned to her, she poked her tongue out at him, and his holier-than-thou reasoning.

Just wait until he discovered that these *ladies* were not coming to quilt, or to hold a Bible study meeting, or just to sip tea and trade gossip. Not for all the rice in China would Amanda warn him that they were coming to learn poker and play cards!

They all slept late the morning following the party, having seen the last of their guests off in the wee hours. It was Sunday, and even the farmhands had a couple of extra hours to themselves and a lighter schedule that day, though the horses still needed to be fed and watered, and let out to pasture and back in for the night.

It wasn't till almost noon when Grant received an urgent summons to the stables where the mares were housed. Sean O'Brian met him there, as grim as the Reaper himself. "We've got two mares down, an' six more on their way to their knees," he announced tersely. "From the looks of it, I'd say we've got a good case of colic brewin'."

"Any idea what's causing it?" Grant inquired bleakly, knowing that there was a multitude of causes for the malady and rarely a cure, unless the cause could be determined in time and easily remedied.

"Yep," the foreman surprised him by answering. "Come have a look at this, Mr. Gardner."

The man led Grant to a nearby stall, to the feed box, where the animal's hay was placed. Even in summer, when the horses grazed on the lush Kentucky bluegrass, they were given a small amount of hay as a supplement. Not until late fall, when the grass died out, would they begin to grain the animals, allotting them oats and corn and barley to maintain their body temperatures and stamina through the colder months.

"Stick yer hand down in there an' see what you come up with," O'Brian suggested.

From the bottom of the bin, hidden below the hay, Grant pulled out a handful of oats—damp, molding oats! "Oh Christ!" Grant groaned. "It's like feeding them poison!"

"An' this ain't the only one," O'Brian told him,

shaking his head. "Almost every feed box in this barn is the same way."

Without needing to tabulate, Grant knew there were thirty stalls in this barn alone, Thirty prize mares in jeopardy, though only eight of these were currently showing symptoms.

"Have the feed bins in the other barns checked immediately," Grant ordered.

O'Brian nodded. "Already bein' done, boss. So far, this seems to be the only barn they tampered with."

Grant dragged a hand through his hair, weary to the bone with this constant trouble. "Where was the guard when this was happening? How could anyone sneak in here and do all this without anyone knowing?"

"Beggin' yer pardon, sir, but there were a lot o' folks at that party o' yers last night. And it wouldn't have taken much fer one o' them to slip out here unnoticed an' wait till the guard was on the other side o' the barn before sneakin' inside t' do his devil's work."

Grant heaved a sigh. "You're right. Damn it! I knew better than to invite all those people here, but with Tad leaving in a few days . . ." His words trailed into silence.

Before it was finished, they lost ten of the mares. Only by the grace of God, sheer luck, and a lot of work did they manage to save the others. Thankfully, none of the ones that died belonged to clients who had left their mares with Grant to be bred.

This time, though he had nothing upon which to base such suspicions, Grant wondered if Darcy could possibly be behind the numerous mishaps. On second thought, he doubted it, though he wouldn't discount the attorney altogether. Grant didn't believe Darcy was that knowledgeable about horses to have accomplished all this. Oh, maybe the thorns in Lady Mist's saddle, or the gate left open, or the loose fencing wire in the paddocks. But the fouled bedding and the spoiled feed?

Grant didn't think so. This was the work of someone who knew horses, who worked with them. But who? Who? And, for the love of heaven, why? And how was he able to get on and off the property without being noticed? Better yet, when and how would he strike next?

Amanda agreed that when her ladies' group met, she would discreetly question them about Darcy, or anything else they might have heard. Of course, everyone around Lexington knew of Misty Valley's recent troubles via the local grapevine, manned to a great extent by the servants. Now might be a good time to gather a little information of their own.

The following Wednesday, Grant walked into the front parlor and stopped short in his tracks. With open mouth and disbelieving eyes, he took in the sight before him. There, seated at two tables, were a dozen of the most prominent matrons of Lexington society—all playing poker!

It it hadn't been for the stacks of colored chips at each place setting, and for the number of cards each woman held in her hand, he might have been fooled into believing they were playing bridge or piquet. This, and the smug look on Amanda's face, told the truth of the tale.

Pasting a polite smile on his lips and squelching the urge to strangle his wife before all these witnesses, Grant entered the room. "What have we here, ladies? A congregation of would-be gamblers? Are you planning to outfox all of your unsuspecting husbands sometime soon?"

"Oh, what a grand idea!" Mabel Turnbull declared. "How nice of you to suggest it, Grant."

"Yes," another woman concurred. "My, wouldn't that singe Woodrow's socks!"

"Tell me," Grant went on, stopping behind Amanda's chair and laying a hand on her shoulder, exerting just enough pressure to make her aware that he wasn't pleased with this latest mischief of hers. "Whatever happened to whist and pinochle, the latest rage the last I heard?"

Madame Lalaine *tsked* at him. "Oh, much too tame, my boy. Much too tame. Besides, you gentlemen have kept this game to yourselves for entirely too long. It made us curious to know its appeal, and your darling wife and future sister-in-law have been gracious enough to enlighten us.''

"So I see," Grant commented drolly. "Just make sure they don't relieve you of all your pin money and send you home without your horses.''

He was on his way out of the room when another disturbing thought came to him. Turning, he said, "Out of curiosity, I wonder what you ladies are considering next, if anything.''

"Well," Betsy replied, "if we had a roulette table, we could teach them that. I do declare, there's nothin' quite like the sound of a roulette wheel spinnin' around and around. Unless it's the clack of dice. It always makes me think such rich thoughts.''

"Avaricious thoughts, Betsy?" he suggested, his cool green gaze leveling on her.

"Let's be honest, and call a spade a spade here, Grant," she surprised him by answering, seeming unruffled by his animosity. "I know you think I'm a greedy, graspin' money-monger, and I suppose that's within your right. Just as it's my right to consider you a pompous ass—which doesn't make me like you any the less. Strange, isn't it?" she added with a congenial smile as several of the ladies gasped at her outspokenness, while others began to titter and giggle into their hands.

Grant hastened out of the room, deciding retreat was definitely in order, before he let his mouth overload his better sense and offended the lot of them. He should have known better than to tangle single-handedly with fourteen females and all their wagging tongues.

Behind him, he heard the rustle of cards being shuffled and dealt as the games resumed. Mabel Turnbull's voice rang out stridently. "Down and dirty, girls," she declared. "One-eyed jacks wild.''

That night, alone with his wife at last, Grant avowed, "You are the most conniving, wicked wench ever to draw breath! I swear, Amanda! Every time I turn around, you amaze me anew! Whatever were you thinking of, to teach those women to play poker?'' As he railed at her, he began to undress for bed.

''As my father used to say, 'If you can't beat them, join them. Or get them to join you.' That's just what I did, and it worked like a charm. I even learned that Darcy left town this past week, bound for Boston. He's joined up with an established law firm there. So it seems he's not our culprit, either, since he left before the mares' feed was tampered with.''

''I didn't really think he was, but for lack of a better person to blame,'' Grant admitted, yanking his shirt loose and tossing it onto a nearby chair.

Still piqued at her, he settled on the edge of the bed and glowered. ''Does it bother you at all that you and Betsy and the rest of those mean-mouthed women made a complete fool of me today?''

''You made a fool of yourself, my love,'' she told him softly, reaching out to gently grasp his hand. She brought his palm to her lips and placed a tender kiss in the center of it. ''Whether it's cards or life, you have to adhere to certain rules, Grant. You can break some, you can bend some, but there are some you just can't mess with. There is a time to hold and a time to fold, and a smart player knows when to do both. There is also a time to quit while you're ahead of the game. You overplayed your hand, that's all.

''You were outnumbered to start with,'' she went on to explain, maneuvering around behind him, where she proceeded to massage the tension from his neck and shoulders. ''Then you made the mistake of insulting Betsy, deliberately attempting to publicly humiliate her. You fired the first round, sweetheart. You can't blame her for shooting back at you. Because, in case it has escaped your attention, we paupers have just as much pride as you princes, and we really don't care to have our feelings trampled any more than you do.''

By the minute, Grant was becoming more kindly disposed toward the entire female population, and very relaxed. Amanda's fingertips were tracing the ridges of his spine now, her tingling touch magically healing all his hurts, and arousing him at the same time. An involuntary groan escaped his lips as her mouth joined her hands, scattering his back with tiny kisses.

"Do you know what you're doing?" he rasped out.

"I almost always know what I'm doing," she whispered in return. As her arms wound about his waist, her fingers seeking the fastenings of his britches, she added with a husky chuckle, "And before I make a liar of myself, please tell me. Are your boots off this time?"

Chapter 29

CHALLENGER had thrown a shoe, and Amanda and Sweet Cheek were called into service once again to keep the big colt calm while Aaron reshod him. Challenger had recovered nicely from the wound he'd received from the fencing. Fortunately, the wire had not been rusted, and the animal had not contracted tetanus. He would never race against the fastest of his ilk in the Derby or the Preakness, but he could still be ridden and bred, and from him they would get many fine foals.

Now, the shoe replaced, Amanda and the duckling were escorting Challenger back to his stall, where the high-strung thoroughbred could comfortably settle further from his ordeal. Tomorrow he would be let out to pasture again.

It was midmorning, but several stallions were secluded in the barn. Grant was taking even more precautions with the animals these days, having the paddocks and pastures checked daily for debris or harmful objects. He was also allowing only half of the horses out at a time, the better to guard them and gather them when trouble struck again, which he was sure it would when they least expected it.

The barn was dark and cool, a relief from the continuing heat wave, making Amanda wish she could stay there for a while. However, with Tad getting ready to depart for West Point in a few hours, there was too much to do up at the house to allow lingering in the barn. A special luncheon had been planned for just the four of them, a final meal together as a family. It was already past time for her to change into a fresh gown and brush the tangles from her mussed hair, unless she wanted to go to the table smelling of horses.

Spotting Timmy, Amanda waved and called out to the freckled stableboy, the only other person in the barn with her. "Have you finished cleaning Challenger's stall?"

"Yes'm," he assured her with a huge grin and a nod of his head that sent his cowlick bobbing. "I only gots two more to go, and I'm done in this barn. Clancy already checked all the feed bins and the water, like Mr. O'Brian told us," he informed her importantly.

"Good. I'll be sure to tell Grant what a fine job all of you are doing," Amanda responded, smiling. It occurred to her, as the distinctive odor of kerosene wafted past her nose, that someone must have recently refilled the lanterns hanging in various locations throughout the barn. The smell seemed extraordinarily strong this morning, stinging her eyes and nostrils. It was even making the horses edgy, judging from the amount of tromping and neighing they were doing.

She'd almost reached Challenger's stall when the main doors to the barn suddenly slammed shut with a tremendous bang that made both her and Challenger jump in surprise. It wasn't till then, when the barn was cast in even deeper gloom, that Amanda realized that the rear doors had already been closed. Apparently, so were most, if not all, of the stall windows, for it was almost as dark as night in there now.

"Timmy?" she called out hesitantly, suddenly, unreasonably afraid.

"Miss Mandy?" he yelled back, a slight quiver in his young voice.

"Did you close the doors?"

"No, ma'am. The wind must o' done it."

"Is there a storm brewing?"

"Not thet I know of."

Hardly able to see her hand in front of her face, and with Challenger growing more restless by the moment, Amanda felt her way along the stalls, wanting to get Challenger stabled as quickly as possible. "Can you open the doors again, or find a lamp and light it?" she asked the boy.

"Sure, Miss Mandy, but it looks like someone already done that in the mow."

At Timmy's reply, a shiver ran up Amanda's backbone. Fearfully, she raised her gaze to the overhead loft. An eerie glow seemed to hover there. Even as she watched, it flashed brighter, bringing with it a strange whooshing sound. Within seconds, the entire loft was engulfed in bright orange flames!

Amanda's heart leapt into her throat, threatening to strangle her. "Timmy! The barn's on fire!" she screamed, struggling to hold onto Challenger's lead line as the horse began to panic. "Get out! Hurry! Get Grant!"

Her mind was a muddle. Desperately, she tried to calm the thoroughbred, and herself. She had to think! Miraculously, her brain began to function past her rising fear. The horses! She had to get the horses out of the barn! They were whinnying and stomping madly now, as frightened as she was!

Before she could reach the doors, pulling Challenger behind her, Timmy shouted, "Miss Mandy! I can't get the doors to open! They're stuck or something!"

Oh, God! Dear God in heaven! This can't be happening! Amanda's mind screamed out. Abandoning Challenger for the moment, she rushed to the doors Timmy was still struggling to open. Frantically, she tugged at them, heaving her puny weight against them. They wouldn't open!

"The rear doors!" she shouted over the roar of the fire, which now lit the entire length of the barn. But not for long. Thick, acrid smoke was billowing downward even as she and the boy ran for the rear entrance. In her heart Amanda knew they would find these doors tightly barred as well. With their combined strength, they could not budge them.

Tears streamed unchecked down Amanda's cheeks, from the thickening smoke, or terror, or both. One look at Timmy's frightened face only reinforced her own fears. If they could not find some way out, she, her unborn babe, and this innocent child were going to die!

Something soft and smooth brushed against her ankle. Looking down, Amanda beheld Sweet Cheek. The duckling had finally grown his glossy new feathers, which were already covered with soot from the fire and the flaming hay falling from overhead. The poor little duck and the horses would die also, roasted alive, if she didn't think of something quickly.

"The windows!" she cried in sudden inspiration. "Check the stall windows!"

The first three they tried were barred. Finally, she managed to push the fourth open, as if whatever had been holding it shut abruptly gave way. Unfortunately, it was only a half window, not one that opened full-length into the outer paddock, allowing a horse to wander in and out at will.

Choking now, Amanda hefted Timmy up and through the window. "Run!" she barked huskily. "Bring help!"

Hesitating only a moment, Timmy asked fearfully, "What about you, Miss Mandy?"

"I've got to open the stalls to let the horses loose. Have someone get those doors open!"

As he ran off as fast as his wobbly legs would carry him, Amanda took a grateful gulp of the outside air. When she bent, intent on catching Sweet Cheek and tossing him to safety, the perverse duckling dashed away from her into the next stall. "Blasted, dumb duck!" she screeched after him, swiping the tears from her eyes. "You'll fry yet, and it won't be my doing!"

The stallions were thoroughly panicked now, and Amanda not far from it, as she raced from stall to stall like a madwoman, throwing latches and jumping out of the way as the animals charged through in search of freedom from the spreading smoke and fire. Down one side of the aisle she went, dodging flaming piles of straw and hay, careening past an empty stall already ablaze, slapping at her singed skirts and hair, barely able to see or breathe.

At last, as she worked her way down the other side, she found another weakly barred door, this one a double-high entrance opening into the paddock. She started to stumble gratefully through it, only to leap out of the way as the frantic stallions thundered up behind her, intent on gaining their own safety before her.

If she wondered how the horses had sensed their only escape route, she soon had her answer. Behind the final thoroughbred came Sweet Cheek, squawking loudly and flapping his dirty wings, herding the horses before him. With a weak laugh, she scooped him into her arms.

Halfway out the door, she hesitated. Though the barn was a hellish inferno, almost completed ablaze by now, there were still a few stalls she had not checked. From the terrorized animal screams behind her, heard even above the roar and crackle of the fire, she knew that at least three stallions were still trapped inside. Dared she return to release them?

She had only a moment to contemplate her decision before the weakened, burning barn roof collapsed, pulling the connecting walls in upon themselves with a bellow and a shower of flames. The resulting impact sent Amanda flying several feet into the paddock, amidst the milling, fear-crazed stallions, Sweet Cheek still clutched tightly to her. She landed heavily, the air gushing from her aching lungs. For a mere second, stars danced about her head, the world spinning round and round. Then, with a hoarse little whimper, she fainted.

Grant was checking on the mares, those still recovering from their bout of colic, when the first shout of alarm rang out. "Fire!" It was a cry to strike terror into the heart of any horse breeder.

Dashing outside, he cast a hasty glance about him. Flames were shooting from the upper windows of the stallion barn. The entire roof of the huge structure was beginning to blaze, dark smoke broiling skyward. Incredulous as it seemed, apparently no one had noticed it until a moment ago, when it was almost too late to save the stallions, and certainly far too late to spare the barn. They would be fortunate if they could keep the fire from spreading to the surrounding buildings.

On the run, Grant shouted orders to his men, who were already forming a bucket brigade. "Gather a team to douse the stables on either side, and another to turn the rest of the horses into the pastures!"

On the fringes of his mind, a thought nagged at Grant's brain. Why were all the barn doors and windows, other than those in the upper loft, closed? As he drew nearer, he saw several farmhands tugging at the doors, prying at them to no avail. "Boss! The doors are wedged shut!"

"From the inside?" he panted, bending closer to inspect them.

"Don't think so. There's somethin' stuck underneath 'em. Too far and too tight to reach!"

As the man spoke, another fellow sprinted up, breathlessly thrusting an armful of crowbars at his companions. Together, they worked at the doors. From inside the barn they could hear the frightened squeals of the stallions, the roar and crackle of the flames greedily engulfing the dry wood and hay.

"Should we try the outer stall doors?" someone suggested.

Grant shook his head. "The fire is too far out of control, and our chances of finding an entrance not already engulfed are slim. We'd just be wasting valuable time when we need access to the main corridor. It's our only hope of saving as many horses as possible, considering how crazed they are and the amount of smoke."

"What about the rear doors?"

"Blocked," Clancy answered grimly. "Four o' the lads are tryin' t' free them, too."

As they continued to pry at the stubborn doors, Aaron loped up, his dark face wreathed with worry. "Did Miss Amanda make it back to the house all right?" he cried. "She ain't still in there, is she?"

Grant felt his heart stop dead in his chest. For a dreadful moment, he stared at the blacksmith. "Amanda?" he asked stupidly.

Aaron nodded miserably. "She took Challenger back to his stall after she and the duck helped me shoe him."

Not only had Grant's heart ceased to beat, it now plummeted to his boots. Before he could speak, Timmy dashed around the corner of the burning barn, crying and screaming incoherently, his small face streaked with dirt and tears. Finally the boy's garbled words came clear. "Miss Mandy's in there! She's tryin' to let the horses loose!"

Frantically, madly, Grant and the men renewed their efforts to release the doors. Tad joined them now, bringing axes with which to splinter the thick wood. Over the noise of the fire and the relentless pounding, he shouted to Grant, "I didn't see Amanda up at the house!"

"She's in here!" Grant cried back, his voice breaking as he thought of his wife and the terror she must be going through at this moment. Why hadn't she escaped with Timmy? Why was she risking her life to save his stallions, prized though they were? Didn't she realize that he'd rather lose a thousand thoroughbreds than lose her? Didn't she know how important she'd become to him? How dearly he adored her?

On top of this thought came another, just as desperate. If Amanda died in this fire, she would go to her grave never having heard him say that he loved her. Because of his own uncertainty, or mere stubbornness, he had never spoken the words he knew she longed to hear, had scarcely allowed them into his own mind. Here, now, he helplessly wondered if he would ever have the chance to tell her; to hold her in his arms and gaze into her enormous blue eyes as he confessed his love.

Tad caught his attention once more. "Grant!" he hollered, gesturing toward a man standing some distance away. "Isn't that Dell Erkel? Didn't you tell me you fired him?"

Stunned, his brain still reeling with fear for Amanda, Grant stared dumbly for several seconds, trying to comprehend what his brother was saying. With a frown, he gave a short nod. "I did fire him. What the hell is he doing back here?"

It was a sure bet that Erkel hadn't come to help douse the fire. Rather, he was gazing at the blazing barn in rapt fascination, an evil smirk on his flushed face. Grant immediately dismissed Erkel from his mind, concerned only with saving Amanda. But as Tad continued to watch, the man threw back his head and laughed demonically—and Tad would have wagered his appointment to West Point that Erkel was responsible for setting fire to the barn, for trapping Amanda and the horses inside, and for most of the other problems that had plagued Misty Valley through half the summer.

Tad took off at a dead run. Still spellbound with his latest handiwork, Erkel never saw his captor coming, never knew he was being pursued until Tad's wiry young body slammed into his, knocking him to the ground. Immediately, two more men joined in, and Erkel was swiftly subdued, though far from quiet.

"I really done it to ya this time, didn't I?" He cackled fiendishly, his eyes wild with insane glee. "An' not just the horses. I got the bitch, too!" A knockout blow from Tad's fist silenced him at last.

At that exact moment, the barn doors finally gave way, springing open like the lid of a jack-in-the-box. Flames and smoke belched out, snapping viciously at those who would have entered, forcing them backward before its raging fury.

Shielding his face with his arms, Grant forged ahead, intent on entering the blazing barn, his only thought to save his beloved bride, the woman who held his happiness in her hands. Strong arms held him back, though he raged and struggled in their grip. With tears blurring his eyes, he watched in horror as the barn shuddered once, as if shaken by a giant hand, then crumpled into a hellish heap of flaming rubble.

Grant's soul-rending scream blended with those of the trapped horses. "Nooo!" Like a madman, he fought the arms that bound him, until his shocked mind finally stilled his struggles.

His head drooped to his chest, a broken sob quivering through him. He'd lost her, before he'd had the sense to truly appreciate her for the wonderful woman she was. The lady she had always been. The enchantress who'd brought love and laughter into his arid, self-centered life.

Tad was the one who woke Grant from his anguished stupor. Tad, striding up to stand before him, offering Amanda's limp, smoke-covered body into his trembling arms. "I found her in the side paddock with the stallions and that feisty little duck of hers standing guard over her."

Scarcely daring to believe he was being gifted with another chance, just when his life had never looked so bleak, Grant stumbled over his words, his tear-misted eyes never leaving Amanda's soot-streaked face. "Is . . . is she alive?"

"Yes, thank God!" Tad's prayerful exclamation brought a sigh of intense relief from everyone, but most of all from the humbly grateful man who held his wife so close to his heart.

"I don't think she's badly hurt, Grant. Just passed out from all the smoke she breathed in. I've already sent for the doctor—and for the sheriff. Erkel was your culprit all along, and now that he's been caught, things ought to settle down around here."

Like a bedraggled Sleeping Beauty, Amanda stirred slightly in Grant's arms. She gave a husky cough, and her lashes drifted open, her gaze bleary and disoriented as she stared directly into his spellbinding emerald eyes.

As her confusion lifted a bit, she rasped, "The horses?"

"For the love of God, Amanda! Forget the damned horses!" he bellowed, giving her a little shake, only to clutch her ever more tightly to him. "You were almost burned alive in there! I was out of my head, crazy with worry, frantic to reach you! Then, when the roof collapsed, I was sure I'd lost you, and I wanted to die with the grief of it! Don't you ever scare me like that again! I swear my heart would never stand the strain."

"I saved most of them," she told him, not yet grasping the impact of his words.

"I don't care," he declared, carrying her toward the house, reluctant to release her for even that short a distance. "You're the only thing that matters to me, darling. The only thing that makes my life worth living. I love you," he offered softly, the truth of his words gleaming from his eyes. "I love everything about you, from your witch-black hair and your sassy mouth to your impossibly erotic toes."

Her face lit up from within, her smile incredibly white in her blackened face. "Oh, Grant! You can't imagine how happy I am to hear you say it! Now I can tell you about the baby."

His footsteps faltered, and he nearly dropped her before he recovered from the surprise of her announcement. "What baby?"

"The one we're going to have next spring, right about Derby time, I would guess." She laughed up at him, taking impish delight in his astonishment.

His lopsided grin told her how pleased he was with her news. "Lord, lady! You certainly do know how to amaze a man, don't you? Now I know we're going to have the doctor take a look at you when he gets here."

She nodded agreement, then said hesitantly, "Grant, you just called me a lady."

"Are you sure you heard right?" he teased.

"Positive."

"So am I."

* * *

It was the first Saturday of June, 1879, and the stands at Belmont Park Race Track were brimming with excited spectators. Among them, in a front-row owners' box, were Amanda and Grant Gardner and family. Betsy was there, and Tad, who had come down from West Point for the weekend. His upcoming graduation from the academy was to be followed by a long-awaited summer wedding to Betsy at Misty Valley.

Chalmers was also in attendance one more, acting a dual role as chaperon to Betsy and male nanny to young master Daniel Harold Gardner, now an active two-year old. Danny was a beautiful child, with dark hair, an impish smile that lit his blue eyes, and an abundance of energy. At the moment, he was squirming on his father's lap, squealing with glee and trying to see everything at once.

"Paddy!" he piped up loudly. "Want Paddy!"

"Paddy's busy, Danny," Grant answered, bouncing his son on his knee. "Any minute the race will start, and you'll see him ride by on Shady Lady. Just watch now."

The three-year-old filly was Misty Valley's pride and joy. As Amanda had hoped, Shady Lady was one of the finest thoroughbreds the farm had ever bred. With her long, elegant stride, she had easily outdistanced her competitors at this year's Kentucky Derby, and again just two weeks ago at the Preakness. If she won the race today, they would make a grand sweep of the three most important races in the country, earning an elite place in the annuls of racing history, at the very pinnacle of the breeding world.

It was an unheard-of feat, and one Amanda would not have missed for anything—amply proven by her presence here today, nine months pregnant and swollen near to bursting. Grant had tried to dissuade her from making the three-pronged trip so close to her delivery, but Amanda had had none of it. Now, as she rubbed at the deep ache in her back, she wished she'd listened to his advice just this once.

At this point, Madame Lalaine's best efforts to disguise her condition were futile. Amanda looked as if she'd swallowed a prize-winning pumpkin. She had no lap at all and hadn't seen her feet in weeks, her stomach preceding her in an ungainly wobble wherever she went.

But not for much longer, Amanda feared. Her back had been giving her fits since early morning, and now painful twinges were streaking around to her lower stomach with alarming frequency. Unless she was mistaken, she was well into labor already. However, with the main race of the day mere moments away, she was not about to alert Grant just yet. After all, within a quarter of an hour the race would be won or lost. Surely she, and this baby, could wait that long.

As Grant threw a glance her way, she dredged up a serene look for him, smiling through her teeth and valiantly ignoring yet another stomach twinge. "We're going to do it, darlin'," he predicted, patting her hand. "I can feel it."

"I know," she answered a bit breathlessly. "So can I." *Oh, goodness! So can I!*

The horses and jockeys were gathered behind the starting line. Shady Lady had drawn a good position, third from the inside, and Paddy's emerald-green silks gleamed in the sunlight. At the gun, they launched down the track. As one, the cheering crowd rose from their seats.

Amanda, too, made an attempt to stand, but no sooner had she found her feet than a warm gush of water streamed down her legs, soaking her stockings and slippers, and puddling around her. "Oh, no! Not now!" she wailed, her cry going unheard in the commotion of the race. Clutching the rail before her, she eased back into her chair as a stronger pain claimed her breath, nearly doubling her over. Through a daze, Amanda heard the shouts of the spectators, caught just a glimpse of green a couple of minutes later as Paddy and Shady Lady galloped for the finish line a full length ahead of the other horses.

The triumphant grin on Grant's face told her they'd won, as he tossed Danny into the air with a whoop and caught the child close to him in a huge hug. Then he turned to her, still smiling widely. "Well, Mrs. Gardner, do you think you can waddle down to the winner's circle to collect your prize and congratulate your favorite jockey and filly?"

Ruefully, she shook her head. "Not this time, Grant. I hate to disappoint you, but I think you're going to have to pass those honors to Tad. Your second child seems to be in an awful rush to make its arrival."

Grant's smile melted, his face taking on a ghastly gray hue. "You're in labor?" he asked huskily. "Now?" He was only vaguely aware of Betsy lifting Danny from his grasp.

Amanda nodded, gesturing lamely at the puddle at her feet. "Here and now," she confirmed.

Quickly regaining his usual imperious composure, he bellowed, "Damn it, Amanda! I told you this trip would be too much for you!" The tenderness with which he lifted her from her chair into his strong arms belied his stern words. "I suppose last time I was just lucky that Danny arrived two weeks prior to the Derby," he muttered to himself.

As he shouldered his way through the milling crowd, Chalmers forging a path for them, Grant continued to rail at her. "When are you going to start listening to me, you stubborn twit? How close together are the pains? So help me God, lady, if you have this baby before we get back to the hotel and locate a doctor, I'll wring your blasted neck!"

"For heaven's sake, Grant!" she panted past a receding pain. "As many foals as you have helped deliver, you can surely manage to aid the birth of one small child. I don't know why you're going into such a panic over it."

"This is my child we're discussing, not a dratted horse!" he retorted. "Why do you think I had Doc Lowell practically camped on our doorstep when you were due for Danny? Lord, Amanda, if anything were to go wrong—if anything were to happen to you, I'd lose my mind!"

He hugged her tightly to him, releasing her only long enough to hand her gently into the carriage Chalmers had confiscated, and hastily gathering her back into his embrace as soon as he found his own seat. Another wave of pain caught her in its grip, clawing its way through her, tearing a whimper from her throat. "Hold on, sweetheart," he crooned softly now, stroking a straying lock of inky hair from her forehead. "We'll be there soon. Just hold tightly to me darlin'. I'll take care of you."

By the time they reached their hotel, his fingers were numb from the strength of her grip on them. They charged through the lobby, Grant shouting orders to the hotel staff on his way to the elevator. "Get a doctor! Or at least a midwife! Gather fresh towels and sheets! Don't just stand there gaping! Move! Now!" They scurried to do his bidding, just as Amanda knew they would. She would have laughed, if it wouldn't hurt so much.

"Your timing stinks, love," he told her as he settled her on the bed.

"Mine?" she gasped out. "You're the one who behaves like a randy stallion every summer, like one of your thoroughbred studs in a frenzy of lust! If you could manage to keep your britches buttoned, and your amorous attentions to yourself until fall—or winter . . . Oooh!" A long minute later, through a sheen of tears, she said, "Dang, that hurts! You don't know what I'd give to trade places with you right now!"

He chuckled. "Not on a bet, sugar. And I haven't noticed you holding me at a distance along about August and September," he added pointedly.

"Oh, go soak your head!" When he stepped back from the bed, she grasped hastily at his sleeve. "Don't you dare leave me now, Grant Gardner! You were around for the fun of making this child; you can damn well stay for the labor of it!"

"I was just going to get a damp cloth, honey. And a fresh nightdress for you," he assured her.

Between spasms, he undressed her, and directed the maids when they arrived with fresh linens for the bed.

Through her gathering haze, his was the only voice she heard, his the only touch that soothed. Foggily, as the urge to bear down overtook her, she realized that the doctor had not yet come. As she labored to push forth their child into the world, Grant stood ready to receive it into his strong, capable hands.

First, a matted mop of black hair appeared, quickly followed by a tiny red face scrunched into a frown; shoulders, back, little flailing arms and hands; small, wrinkled buttocks. Last, the legs and feet, until a daughter lay in Grant's outstretched palms, wriggling and wet and miraculously whole, and wonderful to behold. On her own, obviously as headstrong as both of her parents, their baby began to cry loudly, clearly upset at being thrust from the warm nest of her mother's body.

"It's a girl," he whispered, gazing in awe at the miniature life before him. Reverently, as he gently toweled her dry, his eyes cataloged ten tiny fingers and toes, perfectly formed nails, a bow-shaped mouth that was a replica of Amanda's, and ridiculously long lashes which shielded eyes that even now promised to be as green as his own. "She has a stubborn look to her chin, Mandy. And your long legs." Grant's voice trembled with emotion.

Tenderly, he placed the baby in Amanda's eager arms. "She's adorable!" Amanda sighed, both weary and elated. "We make such beautiful babies, Grant. Is it because I love you so?"

"Or because I love you just as much, if not more," he answered with a kiss to Amanda's damp brow.

They had agreed, if this child was a girl, to call her Miranda, which was the closest they could come to a combination of both of their names, since Danny was christened after their fathers. But now, through a veil of joyful tears that matched Amanda's, Grant reached out to touch the downy cap of hair and murmured softly, "Misty. Our precious Misty."

So their daughter was dubbed from that moment on. And it was little wonder that Misty's birth outweighed their other significant triumph of the day, the winning of the prestigious Belmont Stakes.

However, in the years that followed, especially whenever Grant started feeling full of himself, Amanda never failed to remind him that Shady Lady, the little thoroughbred filly he'd named for her, had far outshone her rivals. As had Amanda. Shady or not, they were both dynamic forces with which to reckon, and most definitely ladies of the highest caliber.

Long did they reign supreme.

Avon Romances—
the best in exceptional authors and unforgettable novels!